Space Station X

Space Station X

A.Z. Rozkillis

Space Wizard Science Fantasy
Raleigh, NC
www.spacewizardsciencefantasy.com

Cover art by MoorBooks
Editing by Courtney Brooks
Book Layout © 2015 BookDesignTemplates.com

Space Station X/A.Z Rozkillis.— 1st ed.
ISBN 978-1-960247-23-0

For Nancy

CONTENTS

Chapter One

It wasn't that Jax was in *love* with her Space Station. It was more she felt connected with it on a deeply personal, emotional level.

"Malfunction detected, Level 1."

Jax opened her eyes to the dim amber glow of her quarters. The hum of the Station core was a steady rhythm of background noise. The alert sounded again—robotic, emotionless—indicating the message on the console screen.

"Malfunction detected, Level 1."

She groaned as she rolled herself out of the nest of blankets in her bunk, stretched to unkink the knots that had formed while she slept, and made her way to the backlit control panel readout. The display indicated a blown fuse on the Station's outer ring. It was only routine maintenance; the whole point of a fuse was to have them blow if there was ever any surge of power, instead of having the rest of the system fail. Jax figured she had time. The communication panel crackled again, this time with a lively voice.

"Jax, did you get that notification?"

Maybe she didn't have time. Jax rolled her eyes to no one in particular, except maybe the cluttered surfaces of her berthing, and the various tools scattered about. She wasn't planning to respond, but the comms sparked with another call.

"Jax, do you copy?"

Jax thumb punched the reply button, maybe more aggressively than she intended, but it still felt satisfying.

"I got it, Saunders. No, I don't need your help," she growled, followed by flipping the comms panel to "off." Of course Saunders was monitoring all of Jax's maintenance alerts, like she was *looking* for an excuse to use that comm. But the alert had been logged, and Jax had a job to do.

She wrestled a flame-retardant coverall from where it was puddled on the floor from the day before. It didn't matter if it was covered in grease—it was black. It didn't matter if it wasn't clean—who was she ever planning on encountering that she needed to impress? Jax ran her fingers through her hair, which would have to pass for an attempt to tidy herself and hauled her work belt around her waist. She gave a single passing glance at the rest of her quarters. Littering the small space were: station schematics strewn about; knickknacks of varying size and shape which she had been tinkering with over the years; and a lengthy, strangling, creeping green vine emanating from a singular hydroponics module adorned with a scribbled nametag that read "Ralph." Jax thumbed the door latch open.

"Didn't even get time for coffee," she grumbled as she shuffled out the door. It slid in place behind her.

The Station flooring of Level 5—where Jax's berthing was located—sloped upward, away from her in each direction. It was far more noticeable and pronounced here than on the outer rings. Jax scanned to her left and right as if watching for traffic, but of course she would be alone up here. In reality, she was considering the most efficient route. To her left there was the route to the Common Access shaft, the main stairwell that served as part of the Station structural support to its center core. The stairwell allowed all Station residents access to other levels, as long as they were granted access. Really, anyone on Station could access Level 1: Docking freely, which is where Jax needed to head. Level 2: Supply, and Level 3: Medical were more controlled in entry and exit. And, of course, there was the infamous, all-access, Level 4: Berthing.

It was this last level Jax contemplated how to avoid. Level 4 was more commonly referred to as the "Meat Market," at least by Jax, though she had heard some residents use the moniker on occasion. What else could you expect from a bunch of lonely deep space transients, stuck on a space station as they awaited their connecting transport to their next destination? The age range, general lack of fuck-all to do, and non-committal nature of the place put nearly every person who stepped foot aboard the Station "on the menu." It usually made Jax's skin crawl when a new transport would drop off a fresh batch. People were marooned here for anywhere from a week to three months, but they would run the resources dry in a few days, then scrabble at whoever was next to show up. Then as far as Jax had cared to observe, everyone would swap partners one to the left, and start all over again.

Well, at least one person wasn't on the menu. Jax shifted to her right and headed down the corridor in the opposite direction of the Common Access shaft. She passed wall panels of digital readouts, the doors to the navigation computer, and various other components of Station control. Around the bend of the endless curving ring housed the smaller of two machine shops with Jax's private stash of tools, as well as the defunct Station biofiltration room. The sterile, metallic walls of those other spaces called to Jax as preferable destinations for her day cycle, but duty called first. She savored the final moments of solitude before needing to fling herself into the possibility of interaction with other people.

This time in the day cycle there would absolutely be Station residents using Common Access to travel from the Market to the first level and back—in some pathetic cycle of hoping it would bring excitement to their day—finding it just as stark as their unwelcoming temporary quarters, then backtracking with absurdly high hopes the return journey would bring the thrill they sought. Jax was grateful that Level 5, which housed Station Power and Life Support in addition to her quarters, was entirely off limits from Station residents. The trick was finding the most efficient route to this foreboding fuse malfunction, while also conveniently avoiding Level 4.

"Dammit Saunders, this could have waited. I could have just dealt with this on off hours when everyone is sleeping. Or does this power your jukebox?" Jax allowed herself to grumble, with only Station's walls as confidant.

Luckily, no one knew Station as well as Jax did, as she had long since mapped out every possible back access and shortcut through Station's internal structure. That's what happened when someone self-isolated on a space station for ten years, especially one so far from Earth they blessedly never had to see that shining, blue shithole ever again. Jax was content in her posting, and as far as she was concerned, humanity had said "good riddance."

At a gap along the wall, between a room housing the major Station computer processors, and a series of designated diagnostic readout displays, Jax popped open a metal panel, whose rivets had been stealthily replaced by hidden hinges. This route took her down a conduit shaft, following the power lines that ran from the center support struts of the Station core to feed power to the outboard rotational engines. Sure, it was not the smartest idea to scamper up and down massive coils of electrical wire, which carried thousands of volts to the magnetoelectric plasma engines that supplied Station's steady rotation and subsequent artificial gravity. But there were few entities that Jax considered herself intimately familiar with in the universe, and these systems ranked number one on her list. She poetically figured if today was the day they decided to fry her ass like bad eggs, then it was as fitting an end to her as any.

"She died doing what she loved: scurrying along a space station electrical conduit in a desperate attempt to avoid the batting lashes of a beguiling, horny graduate student." Scribble that on her toe-tag before shoving her corpse from the airlock.

At Level 2: Supply, Jax had to squeeze out of the conduit shaft to cross the hallway to the maintenance access well. She briefly glanced down the arcing corridor, past the sealed storage bays. A spike of alarm shot through her spine. Just at the horizon of the corridor, where the sloping floor rose up beyond the curve of the ceiling, Jax swore she saw a glancing shadow, the outline of a figure. She froze. Supply was only accessible if anyone had a reason on record to be there. Jax made a habit of avoiding doing anything that wasn't her job, but she was at least vaguely aware Station manifests dictated there currently shouldn't be anyone on this level. At least, she hoped no one was here. There were so many places to hide.

Jax realized she had been standing statue-still, like a prey animal waiting for a predator to glance over her. Her brain spun on a single wheel trying to land on a more intentional action. She toyed with the idea of tracking down whomever might be illegitimately traipsing through her Station. No, *that* was a job for Security. Saunders was supposed to still be in her office, where she would have gotten the fuse alert.

Jax blinked and refocused her line of sight down the corridor. The glancing shadow was gone, and Jax shook her head to clear her thoughts. Today's cycle was not the day to engage in cardio, chasing blasted transients through the bowels of her Station. Jax put the shadow out of her mind and crossed the hall, shouldering through the side hatch that led to the maintenance access well.

This was just another hidden Station void, but roomier, and without the imminent threat of electrocution. Simply a series of ladder rungs for her to work her way down. It was easier as Jax descended to the Station's outer rings where gravity was more pronounced. The passage was situated closer to the Station exterior and, since it was also an intended access route, it had the occasional window. This didn't make much of a difference out here. The Station did not orbit any major star or planet. There were no breathtaking nebulas, or spirals of cosmic creation. It was dark. What light was visible came from distant stars, so far away from Station and Earth that none of the constellations made sense anymore.

Jax still took a moment to look outward at the endless expanse of deep space. Nothing loomed beyond the Station walls but the endless suck of eternity. There were no approaching craft needing to pick up the exterior marker lights, or the glow of the outboard rotational engines to see them. This infernal place really served as nothing more than a distant outpost to break up the monotony of deep space travel. Sometimes Jax wished it could be even deeper in space than it already was.

Jax was situated between a supply lift shaft and Level 1 functional docking rooms. In her moment of contemplating the infinity of deep space, her ears pricked. A faint, rhythmic sound—far too organic to be part of normal Station operations—bled through the nearest wall to her. She leaned in and heard the tell-tale grunting and moaning associated with two wayward Station residents getting far too familiar with each other, in her damned maintenance closet. What was with them today, hiding everywhere they shouldn't be? Jax hammered on the wall with her fist and bellowed through the thin interior metal.

"For fuck's sake, if I catch you screwing in there, I will make you clean up the mess with your own faces!" she shouted at the snug access shaft around her. She couldn't be entirely sure they had heard her, but she also took grim satisfaction at the idea that hearing a wrathful disembodied voice mid-coital tryst would certainly ruin the mood. But seriously, she was Engineering, not a janitor. She was sick of travelers finding new and aggravating places to fuck in her Station. What in hell was so hard about keeping it in their pants for a few weeks while they waited on a damn ride? Try a decade of self-loathing in deep space. Jax was doing just fine.

The sex noises had dissipated, meaning either Jax's scare tactics had worked (great), they had just changed location (not great), or they had finished (gross). Either way, Jax didn't want to exert the energy seeking them out, so she decided to go with the first option, and carried on down to Level 1.

The maintenance access shaft deposited Jax roughly half a degree from the supposed fuse of doom she needed to fix. Mercifully, no one appeared to be meandering the visible arc length of Level 1 she could see, not even the carnal culprits she had just discouraged from soiling her storage locker. Jax allowed a self-satisfied sigh of relief.

Level 1 had the best windows on all of the Station save for maybe staff quarters. Each window was alternated by a docking port airlock. A younger version of Jax might have taken another moment to appreciate the lack of interesting view arcing beyond the thick glass, the beauty of their isolation, and the spine-tingling realization that if anything were to happen to them out here, they were so far away from even the most remote glimmer of humanity their screams would have long since faded into the cosmos before any form of rescue might reach them. But current Jax just wanted to fix this problem and get the hell back to her bunk, and a date with a packet of dehydrated espresso. It was not like anything interesting happened out here anyway.

This particular fuse—the most excitement Jax might very well have in ten day-cycles—was located in a wall panel. Jax considered this to be the best of possible options, as it was a quick, discrete fix, allowing her to pop the panel open, pull the fuse, drop a new one, seal the panel, and skulk back to her Level 5 hideout in record time.

"Seriously Saunders, this is *not* as critical as you thought," Jax mumbled.

"Oh good, you made it."

Jax nearly jumped through the panel opening into the merciless void of space. At least she had the self-control to not scream.

Jillian Saunders, the Security Officer and only other permanent Station resident, had a grand habit of sneaking up on Jax when Jax absolutely did not want it. And Jax never wanted it, ever. Of course, having only been on Station for the last six months (or was it eight? Jax hadn't really been counting) meant Saunders didn't have quite the same Station knowledge Jax possessed. But she did have access to all the closed-circuit security camera footage, and she was on the same Station alert system notifying Jax when something was in dire need of fixing, like life-threatening fuses. Coupled with a trigger-happy use of Station Comms, this usually allowed Saunders to track down Jax's position rather quickly.

Jax had made an effort to increase her scurrying, so she might stay one step ahead of the youthful Security Officer. At least, she assumed youthful. Saunders was probably only a few years younger than Jax, but Station life and Earth life tended to screw with one's ability to display the correct age on their face. Saunders had a face that was aggravatingly charismatic. It was smooth and clear, devoid of any line or mark that might betray a number of trips around a distant sun. Typically, a deep space denizen's age could most reliably be seen in their eyes, and Saunders' sparkled with a glinting green wit that said she was only just getting started with a long day of messing with Jax. Her constant expression of welcoming charm was one Jax had started to associate with a devious nature. As it stood, Saunders clearly got a kick out of whatever little contest she maintained between them. And no matter how ageless deep space kept Jax's appearance, the other woman was going to take years off Jax's life with how often she managed to pop up unannounced.

Saunders fixed Jax with a friendly, gamely smile, as if this little endeavor was the highlight of her day. Jax glared at Saunders and returned to shoving her forearms, head, shoulders, and whatever else she could cram into the tight panel space that housed the offending fuse.

"I assure you, Saunders, this does not need a security detail. What are you *doing* here?" Jax could hear the shift and rustle accompanying the Security Officer resting her weight on her hip, looping her thumbs into her belt, and squaring her shoulders in her blue security jacket. Jax could hear it, and see it in her head, which only soured her mood more.

"I'm just trying to keep up my familiarity with station operations. I wanted to know what types of station faults require more attention than others. I figured I could learn from you, our resident technical expert, since you do *such* a good job of keeping this place running." Saunders' voice had a lyrical quality to it that acted like a natural calming agent. Jax usually had to fight the innate urge to give in to the soothing sound. It was probably why she had been drinking so much more coffee lately. In this case, she chose to use the Station walls as a protective shield and ignore the casually dropped compliment about her being a "technical expert."

"Or at the very least I could always watch your six for you," came an unprompted reply to Jax's frosty silence. A frosty silence that broke with that comment.

"I absolutely do *not* need you watching my ass, either!" Jax barked into Station's meteoroid-resistant, composite outer armor.

"Just offering!" Saunders chuckled, much to Jax's dismay. "You also could have told me over the comms this was nothing important, but you turned your comms off, didn't you?" rang the chipper voice of the Security Officer.

Jax swore under her breath. She doubted simply telling Saunders this wasn't an issue would have prevented Saunders showing up at all. The Security Officer seemed awfully fond of seeking out Jax's company, which put Jax on edge.

This deep into her beloved Station's wall panel, Jax's face was pressed firmly to the nearly six inches of impenetrable outer hull, separating her from the devastation of deep space vacuum. Her "technical expertise" meant Jax didn't need a light to find what she was looking for. Her deft fingers knew every fuse, circuit, bolt and rivet on this Station by careful touch. Jax launched herself another inch deeper into the cramped space to reach, her ear pressed almost painfully to the unyielding metal in an effort both to reach her quarry, and maybe block out anything the Security Officer might say that would require Jax to respond. A faint scratching sound permeated through the inches-thick metal, from the *outside* of the Station.

Jax flinched where she lay, three-quarters of her body hanging out into the corridor, guarded by someone Jax did not particularly want to encourage to stare at her bottom half. In her tightly contained wall panel, Jax turned her head slightly, as if looking at the colorless and shapeless swatch of Station armor might help her better understand. Nothing could be *outside* the Station. There was *nothing* out there. Saunders must have noticed her change because, regrettably, the other woman felt the need to check up on her.

"Jax? Are you okay in there?"

Jax released a string of soft expletives to the surrounding circuitry for the momentary crack in her demeanor and shook her head. Lack of caffeine meant her brain was coming up with all sorts of fun fantasies today. She surged forward again, leveraging her hips to thrust herself further toward her target and farther from her unwelcome company.

"I'm fine Saunders. You can go now," Jax called, letting her voice bounce off the confining space. She doubted Saunders could even hear her, but maybe whatever was scratching would get the hint and buzz off from her imagination.

Having successfully cornered the offending fuse (not like it was hard, the damn thing had popped wide open), Jax emerged victorious from the panel to rummage in her tools for replacement hardware. Saunders shifted her weight in the silence of Jax ignoring her, having clearly not gotten Jax's invitation to depart, and apparently decided it was best to fill the dead air with more updates.

"The last transport, from three days ago, topped off our residents at fifty-five. Well within our two hundred limit capacity."

Jax had never known Station to be anywhere *near* capacity.

"It's an interstellar research group, studying deep space gravity wells, waiting one month-cycle for their sponsor to get their next route mapped and sent along. Nice group, most of them fresh off their PhDs."

Jax tensed. *Another* research group? Of course, that was the typical demographic to find themselves out here. The Station was always lousy with a few of those teams, all waiting for some connecting transfer ride to a deep space posting. Jax was sure none of them would even register her presence, but she made a mental note to stay even more aloof and avoidant of The Market. Best she avoid the risk of anything too...*familiar.*

"I set them up on the back forty degrees of Level 4." (Good to know, the better to hide from them). "A few of them were planning to prep a welcome dinner to get to know the other station residents while they wait, if you wanted to join us." Why did Saunders' voice sound strangely hopeful?

"I'm not particularly interested," Jax emphasized to the new fuse she had dug out of her bag. She scrutinized the small markings on the fuse, making sure it was the right capacity. Now was not the time to tell Saunders how insignificant this problem was, only to proceed to blow the side of the Station open with a bad fuse match.

Having confirmed the correct fuse, Jax dove head, shoulders, and whatever else fit, back into the side panel to replace it. The static air between her and the Security Officer could have sparked a Station fire, but Jax was comfortable in it. Her sharp remarks were mostly a screening tactic. She was glad someone cared about the people on Station, so she didn't have to. Saunders seemed to have a knack for it, but she also seemed to think Jax could be persuaded to take interest.

"I just figured you wanted to know, in case it affected any of your work is all." The bounce had gone out of the Security Officer's voice, now taking on a more strained and leading edge. It was still distressingly pleasant to hear, but clearly not fueled by the upper hand. Saunders had to be grasping at conversation by this point. Why did she have to *do* that? Why did she have to seek out reasons to talk to Jax? Station posts were lonely in description; she should have realized that when she took the job. Jax had put up with Saunders seeking conversation for the last eight (or was it ten?) months.

Having replaced the fuse, Jax pulled herself from the panel and closed the space up again. Saunders was still standing there, which commanded Jax's attention as she rose from her position on the Station floor, tools resecured around her waist. Jax set her jaw, preparing to look the Security Officer full in the face.

"Keeping track of the people on this Station is your job, not mine. You keep them under control, and I keep the Station from falling to pieces. That's the job description."

These stations had long since become so routine in their operation that such staffing was all they really needed. One for people, one for parts. That reminded Jax, she had information to put the Security Officer off her game.

"Speaking of which, your Station records indicate no one should have Level 2 access, but there's people sneaking around up there," Jax offered casually. And she was right, it did put Saunders on pause. The shorter woman narrowed her fair, but defined eyebrows in confusion.

"My manifests are right. No one should be on Level 2..." Saunders countered. Jax just shrugged. She wanted as little to do with it as possible.

The Security Officer's expression of confusion lingered as she ran her hand through her dirty-blond hair. It was long enough to maybe be tied back now, but it had been shorter when she arrived (how long HAD Saunders been on Station?). There weren't really options when it came to getting a haircut out here.

With Jax now standing, Saunders' eyeline dropped several inches, to land more even with Jax's jawline. Jax enjoyed the new vantage point, and the distance it afforded her from the Security Officer.

"Nice new cut you got there on your chin. Maybe I can patch that up for you up on Three?" Saunders replied, distracted once again from leaving Jax for more pressing matters. Maybe Jax didn't like this new vantage point after all. She grunted and scuffed at the scabbed-over scrape she had likely sustained missing a step in one of her more crowded escape routes. She was nimble, but not always graceful. And she didn't need Saunders touching her face.

"It's fine—I'm *fine* Saunders. Worry about your own people," Jax growled.

Finally, Saunders looked like her favorite game had come to a close, which gave Jax a sense of relief.

"All right Jax. Is the malfunction resolved?" Saunders said it with a sigh, breaking her eye contact as she spoke and seeking somewhere to look at on the far wall.

"Good as new. Shouldn't interrupt your groove," Jax said flatly.

"Right. Well, thanks for keeping things running." Saunders had finally turned back down the corridor to the Common Access entry point, either to go investigate Level 2 for herself, or perhaps just to return to her quarters on Level 1.

Jax stood there an extra minute watching the silhouette of the Security Officer retreat. It wasn't that she detested the Officer; no that really wasn't it at all. It was the constant feeling of familiarity she always left in her wake that had Jax first feeling lost, then feeling bitter in its dissipation. Saunders' silhouette hadn't quite passed out of the curve of the sloping Station floor before Jax slipped back into the maintenance shaft and out of the threat of further human interaction.

As Jax ascended the maintenance ladder, another quiet sound pricked her ears. This time it wasn't fornicating residents. At least, it didn't *sound* like it. It was a scuffle. A scuttle. A clicking sound? And it was coming from within Station walls. A decade on a space station made one finely tuned to the ever-present series of hums and deep bone-throbbing bass noise, emanating from the pressurization, plumbing, powering, heat expansion and contraction that made a station run. But this was new, and just outside the threshold of hearing in the noisy shaft. There it came again, now somewhere off to her other side: a skittering. Jax paused on a rung, waiting.

She didn't hear it again. Maybe it really was Station residents engaged in another go at each other. Or worse, maybe it was contraband cargo escaping that Jax would inevitably have to mention to Saunders. She grumbled to herself and started back up to Level 5.

Chapter Two

Jax's quarters on Level 5 were nestled between the main Station core access shaft and the primary control room for life support. This was by design, as it was assumed those were the two most critical locations the Mechanical Engineer would need to access on tight notice. This had the added benefit that, unless something went wrong on another level, Jax could spend the majority of her time holed up in her own secure post, doing the more important tasks of her job without having to venture down to the lower rings.

When Jax wasn't maintaining the steady operation of Station's mechanical systems, she was hiding in her bunk, pouring over Station schematics. Or she might instead wile away her rare free time tinkering with bits of hardware and mechanisms, in some ceaseless effort to make them better, or create something worse altogether. Or she could thoroughly entertain herself by musing over Ralph's tangles and whether she should attempt to use the tenacious plant's clippings to restart the biofilter room. It was a glorious solitude, surrounded by things Jax knew, understood, and could exact a secure amount of control over. For the most part. Ralph didn't particularly take orders from anyone, Jax included. But the Station gave her a purpose, and a generally pleasing distraction from anything else in life.

The Security Officer's quarters on Level 1, were placed there by design as well. Someone on Station should be readily available at the Station's largest access point. Unfortunately, the current Station Security Officer did not seem content to stay on her own level. Nor did Saunders particularly take orders from anyone either, unless it was Station Management, and even then, Jax had a suspicion that the Security Officer was wary of the bureaucracy. Jax had to admit, grudgingly, that it was probably more effective for a Security Officer to be familiar with the residents on Station, and the rules that governed them. But why did she always have to drag Jax into it?

"Jax, are you there?" the comms crackled. Jax swore.

"Feck." It came out wrong around the flashlight between her teeth, that Jax was using to peer into some abomination of reverse engineering. She hadn't quite figured out what it would be yet, but the potential of kludging together some new widget usually kept her energized enough to feel rebellious. Jax threw caution to the winds and did not reply to the call.

"Station Engineering, this is Station Security, over." Fuck, that was an official call, and Jax couldn't ignore it. She spat out the flashlight and blindly reached behind her to jab the comms panel.

"*What?*" She didn't feel like elaborating to play to Saunders' little communication script, though she *should* have responded with a much more standardized "This is Engineering, go ahead." Instead, she kept her thumb on the comms panel an extra few seconds, blocking Saunders from replying on her end until the channel was clear.

"We have a bunk issue on Level 4. I need your assistance."

Jax placed her engaging bundle of wires, servos and loose screws down on the desk with a finality. Of all the places she didn't want to have to venture, this was a call to the Market itself. The hairs on the back of her neck bristled at the thought. Or maybe she just needed another go with the clippers. Maybe it was time to shave it all off again; a form of self-flagellation for an unforeseen slight Jax figured she had made, most likely her own existence.

Jax found herself blissfully attempting to ignore the Security Officer's support request by contemplating an aggressive, self-administered haircut. The hair was currently cascading over to one side in a scraggly black waterfall, nearly shoulder length, the sides having recently been shaved within the last few weeks.

"Engineering, do you copy?" Dammit, that pulled Jax back from considering if bald was in vogue again this far from any real social structure.

"Engineering copies," Jax resignedly replied to avoid having to carry any conversation. She also knew if she didn't haul down to the Market soon, the Station Security Officer would exercise her privilege of post and appear on Jax's precious Level 5 to drag Jax down to Level 4 herself. At least Jax was dressed this time.

The Common Access shaft was going to have to be her route. Sure, Jax had squirreled away a few emergency access points that could get her to Berthing without having to take the shaft, but it's not like she wanted any of the residents to see her popping out of walls. Heaven forbid it give them new ideas about places to hide. She laboriously dragged her tool belt from where she had deposited it on the floor the previous day cycle and lugged herself out of her quarters and away from whatever engrossing tinker project she would much rather be working on.

The main stairwell shaft was the roomiest course of travel through the Station by far. And that was particularly absurd because nothing on the Station was roomy. Common Access was an unremarkably tight zigzag of corrugated and perforated metal stairs that formed the various switchbacks between each Station level landing. It had stark, dented metal railings, and the same efficient and sterile looking UV/LED lighting to guide the way. If it wasn't also the harbinger of far too many forced social interactions, Jax would have loved it like any other section of her beloved Station. Jax pretended the sinking feeling in her gut as she descended the clanking steps was due to the slight increase in gravity as she traversed to a larger radius, and not her dread at engaging with *people.*

Outside the main access point to the Market, there stood a small knot of residents. They looked like they could be some of the research group who had recently arrived, not that Jax paid close attention. She made a concerted effort to not make eye contact, though she still managed a quick scan of the scene. This group hadn't started looking bored yet, so Jax estimated they had only been on Station a few days.

Jax hoped her ears wouldn't noticeably perk up if she caught them talking about some obscure research regarding deep space metrics for measuring gravity. She hated that some small part of her still yearned for that life. But those years were behind her, and she doubted any of them would want anything to do with her snooping around their research, her being nothing more than a simple space station Mechanical Engineer. After all, *they* were post-docs. She usually managed to tune groups like this out these days, to avoid their attention and disruption to the bubble she had enveloped herself in.

Instead, her ears picked up an entirely different conversation.

"Did you feel that last night?"

"Yeah, that was wild!"

"Do you think there's something more we can do?"

"I asked her if we can use the first level, I want to see if we can feel it again!"

Jax's face pinched in disgust. So much for noble academics. These transients were already indulging in other passing opportunities.

Thankfully no one spoke to Jax as she skirted around where the residents hung off the railings, talking about who knows what filth, and passed through the open-frame, wedge-shaped fire doors to the level. She figured she had been successful enough in her avoidance, but Jax couldn't shake the feeling of their eyes on her. She was a New Face after all, and the more she hid from people, the more interesting she became when she emerged from whatever rock she stored herself under.

This would also be why Jax hated Level 4. She could feel the stares as she stalked down the center of the corridor seeking wherever Saunders had stationed herself. Of course, she could have asked over the comms, but that would mean making *conversation.* As it was, she knew she was drawing attention to herself, passing several small groups of residents.

The Market was a dull series of alternating doors and wall panels, with the occasional porthole showing nothing in particular. The doors were the same, slightly trapezoidal shape as the one to Jax's own berthing, or the entrance to the level from Common Access, so they fit with the arc of each Station level. Knots of leisurely residents who Jax had no interest in committing to memory were gathered in groups of varying sizes, leaning in open door frames, lounging across common area couches, or leaving the common lavatory and workspaces. It felt like a crappy collegiate dormitory in space, complete with someone's sock hanging from a door latch, indicating the occupants were busy. Gross. Jax trudged onward along the bare metal floor panels.

"Hey, Engineering!"

It was some favorably cute-looking, pint-sized redhead, who looked like she fell somewhere between the studious nature of the research teams and the gung-ho boredom of the soldiers who occasionally used the Station as a waypoint while awaiting drop orders. Great.

Jax liked to think of herself as a Station wraith, a mythical bog creature, one who was more cryptid than reality. But it was a depressing fact she knew she could draw appreciative attention from any red-blooded human. It's what had gotten her in trouble in the first place. And then again. And again. And out here it really didn't matter what human took interest in who; everyone typically made themselves fair game when they were this stranded out in space. The isolation also made them bold.

But Jax wasn't fair game, and she had learned her lesson. The redhead tailed her for a bit down the corridor, waiting for a response. Jax obliged with a glassy stare aimed to slide ever so slightly over the top of the woman's head, before passing her in silence on her way to whatever this problem might be. It was almost a disgruntled relief when the tidy figure of the Security Officer edged into view, and the resident gave up her pursuit.

Saunders was leaning against the wall outside a berthing door, some thirty degrees down the corridor. This time she did have her hair tied back, at least on the top. The shorter hair on her neck seemed to have escaped this plan and instead created a pale fringe against the copper undertone of Saunders' neck. She appeared to be engaged in some amicable conversation with a couple residents who Jax couldn't recall seeing before, not that it was out of the ordinary. It wasn't like Jax cared particularly, but their conversation did seem casual enough.

Saunders usually maintained a decent level of interaction with those who passed through the Station, though Jax never saw her take too much interest in the residents. That was something Jax was quietly hopeful about: that Saunders was perhaps equally as work focused as she was, and not seduced by bored deep space denizens. Saunders turned her head as Jax sauntered up.

"Oh, *there* you are," she said, almost cheerfully. Then, horrifically, she turned to the residents and *introduced* Jax to them. "Rose, Collins, this is Jax, our Station Mechanical Engineer. She keeps us spinning. If something doesn't work on the station, best to still come find me, since Jax only talks to machines. But she does *such* a good job at it. Jax, Rose and Collins are part of that research team I was telling you about. They specialize in...gravitational theory and deep space phenomena, am I getting this right?" Saunders looked over at them as if to check, avoiding Jax's heavy glaring.

The Security Officer rarely missed a chance to saddle Jax with an awkward exchange. The residents, having nodded encouragingly at Saunders in her recount of their work, had looked eagerly to Jax as well, like Jax would take some sort of interest in them. Jax refused. Once upon a time, she had worked her own theory tying the concept of artificial gravity wells to electromagnetic field manipulation, but then she had fucked off to be a reclusive space station mechanic. It was a perfectly reasonable career choice. Who else would "keep them spinning"?

Jax's complete and total failure to even acknowledge the pair of residents made for uncomfortable silence, punctuated by what Jax hoped was a heated glare at Saunders, as if to say, "You brought me here for *what* exactly?" After a few moments, the small group of residents bid Saunders goodbye and wandered off. Saunders turned her full attention to Jax.

"Real bedside manner you have there."

"I want nothing to do with their bedside. I'm guessing they're off to get 'busy,' or have they not even been here long enough?" Jax mused over the Security Officer's shoulder.

"*They* are actually siblings. They run the lab. Not everyone on this station is as obsessed with sex as you are, Jax."

"I literally caught two fucking in my auxiliary maintenance locker yesterday. I'm going to run out of bleach before the next resupply shipment!" Jax countered.

"Well, at least the only people allowed on deep space transit are all of legal age." Saunders shrugged dismissively, giving a half smirk in reply. Jax fumed.

"And I am *not* obsessed with sex!" Jax growled.

"Pity," Saunders remarked, her face a visage of innocence, her eyes a glinting green.

Jax felt her face flush and knew she would regret whatever followed if she didn't refocus herself on her loyal servitude to her precious Station.

"If that's all you brought me here for, you shouldn't have bothered. I had to wander all over, looking for you," Jax replied, holding her tone as even and devoid of emotion as possible. She refused to give Saunders the satisfaction.

"If you bothered to wear your comms when moving about station, I could have told you where we were located," Saunders countered. There was some small exasperation in her voice. While it was better than the horrendous teasing from only a moment earlier. Jax bristled at the idea that Saunders could be annoyed at *her*.

"Oops," Jax responded, sarcastically. It's not like she had taken her time or anything.

Saunders proceeded unfazed.

"Did Corine ask you about her hardware repairs?"

"Who?" Jax asked, genuinely confused. Why would Saunders ever expect her to know the name of someone on this Station?

"The woman who walked up with you? She was asking me about the availability of machinery for hardware repairs on some of her equipment, and I told her to ask you when you stopped by?" Saunders raised an eyebrow. Jax felt her face go blank. "She was walking up with you...did you even notice her?"

"Uh, no, did...not...notice her. Is *that* why you brought me here?" Jax coughed, avoiding the eye contact, and instead aiming for a disinterested study of the far wall, as she scanned her peripheral vision for the resident who might have had an actual need for a mechanic. Not that Jax would have willingly let anyone use her shop equipment. But the main repair station on Level 1 was open source. Everyone should know that, even if Jax had horded the best tools up on Five for herself.

Saunders exhaled in what gallingly sounded like frustration, but when Jax hazarded a glance, the other woman had set her expression to businesslike before proceeding.

"Resident stated that the O2 vent stopped working last night. Said there is no longer any airflow," Saunders reported, now sounding very much like a Security Officer, despite the welcoming curve of her face, and the disarming nature of her features. She had stood up from her perch against the wall and angled herself in a way that indicated she intended for Jax to follow her into the berthing. Jax didn't move; she made an effort to revive her aggravation, despite the appreciation that the conversation had turned to strictly work.

"So you brought me *here?* I could have done this from a better access point, these types of fixes almost always require back access," Jax complained.

"And I could have told you that if you answered your damn comms," Saunders replied, this time letting her usually positive demeanor crack. Touché. Jax didn't really have a way out of that one. Having pushed her fingers a little too close to the fire, she accepted the burn. Jax instead narrowed her eyes and jutted her chin out to say, "lead on." Saunders led the way into the room.

The quarters on the Station were not some five-star hotel, not in the slightest. Jax would have ventured there were nicer prison cells out there. But this was not supposed to be a vacation getaway; it was a layover, a waypoint, a passing memory of unpleasant time wasted in effort to reach something far better. A cramped extension off the Station level side, most berthings were no wider than two arms-widths and housed up to four residents at once. Living space was confined to stacked bunks and a smaller personal latrine. Larger spaces were available for leisure on the level in the form of common areas. At low-capacity, Saunders seemed content to let them all spread out as much as possible. As such, residents usually had entire berthing areas to themselves, unless they chose otherwise. If Jax had it her way, she would corral them all in as few rooms as possible to cut back on the inevitable cleanup and mess. But Saunders' job was "people," so Jax relented.

This room seemed to be occupied by at least one person, and quite possibly whatever additional partners they entertained. Graciously, the occupants had fucked-off elsewhere (or maybe not so graciously? They better not be back in her auxiliary maintenance closet), and the room was empty save for her and Saunders.

"Got the report this afternoon around lunchtime. I guess he thought it might solve itself, but he said it's been a day cycle or so by now..." Saunders rattled off as she led Jax to a halt just inside the berthing door, forcing Jax to peer over her head to the mess within.

Saunders wasn't really short. Jax figured it would probably be inaccurate to use that type of description, especially since anyone standing next to Jax usually *looked* short. But Saunders was undoubtedly *efficiently* shaped. Her shoulders looked even and sturdy in her trim security jacket. That jacket was standard issue, but it fit perfectly snug around arms and a torso that were more proportional than they had any right to be. Her hips were perfectly balanced with the heft of someone who could set her weight and dodge a problem in an instant. Saunders' hands—not as rough looking as Jax's, but still betraying a young lifetime of being used for work—always looked like they were ready to act, and usually were placed tentatively on the edge of her security belt. Where Jax was all lengthy angles, Saunders looked like a sleek, fit, brawler, ready to burst into action.

"Jax."

Jax snapped her attention back to Saunders' face, despite her best interests, as Saunders had turned around to address her.

"Are you going to actually inspect the air vent or are you just going to stare at me until I do it?" Saunders pressed. Jax scowled.

"It's not like I could get to it with you in the way," she grumbled as she edged past the officer, making sure to avoid any physical contact if at all possible.

The vent in question was set into the wall above the top bunk. Jax gamely climbed up the ladder to the thankfully unused top bunk to get a better look. It didn't take a Mechanical Engineer to be able to identify that there was a lack of airflow coming from the vent.

Jax pulled a multitool from her pocket and pulled the screws out of the vent so the grating could come off. There was nothing she could see from the angle she was sitting at. She resigned to instead snake her arm up to the shoulder in and around the curve, both directions, to see if there was some obstruction. Even with her lengthy reach, she found none.

"Well?" called Saunders from below.

"Yep, it's a vent all right," reported Jax, importantly, feeling the sharp edges of the vent dig into the side of her head as she felt around.

"And?"

Jax glared over her shoulder down at the Security Officer.

"And there's no O2 flow, just like someone gainfully pointed out. It's not like I can really do anything about it from here. These vents are too small." Jax extricated her arm, and replaced the vent grating, screwing it in place and pocketing the multitool. She climbed back down the ladder to plant her feet on the same floor level as Saunders, who had been once again intently watching Jax scramble and worm her way through dull tasks. For some reason, the berthing was starting to feel even more cramped. Jax tightened her shoulders up, nearly brushing her chin with the collar of her coveralls.

"I'm also not convinced it wasn't some pair of hormone-fueled strangers who figured it was a good idea to go fuck in an air vent and kick something out of place, since that's literally happened before. Or maybe, they are stashing food in there again. That was a fun one last time," Jax concluded, avoiding looking at Saunders directly, and instead gazing slightly over her shoulder at the surrounding mess.

Maybe it really was the food thing. It looked like someone hadn't returned their dishes to the galley in a few days. The residents were on the hook for cleaning up their mess before they moved on, or they were fined and limited in what stations they could utilize in the future. From what Jax could see of her face, Saunders looked like her job had already exhausted her for the day.

"You know if you bothered to actually get to know them, you might not think every single person on this station has the singular goal of screwing their way through the day, or screwing you out of yours. This is Kivan's room. He's a long-haul transport pilot, just waiting on his next transfer. He happens to prefer reading, and chess, if you cared to ever find out."

Jax faltered, as she caught sight of various playing cards and game pieces strewn about. She did miss the challenge of a decent card game or board match, but the idea of needing other people to interact with was less than desirable.

"It's not that I don't want to bother to get to know them. It's that I don't want them to bother to get to know me," Jax responded.

"Good point, and they are probably better for it. Can you fix it?" Saunders asked.

"Of course I can fix it, I'm just not doing it here. And no, I don't need your help," Jax spat, before the Security Officer could even think of the idea.

Saunders always seemed bent on the concept of helping Jax, like she envisioned herself aptly handing over a wrench while Jax sweated away cranking on some engrossing mechanical calamity that required an extra set of capable hands to address. Not that Jax had considered this prospect or anything. The Security Officer's hands seemed perfectly capable, Jax just preferred to avoid such scenarios as fervently as possible.

Jax also avoided telling Saunders where on the Station she would fix vents from. Let her take the time to wander back to her quarters, comb the CC footage, then meander back to wherever she might pinpoint Jax to be. By that point Jax could have slipped through a back access, fixed the problem, and be blissfully back to her tinkering on Level 5.

"Wasn't even going to bother offering," said Saunders, as she exited the room, leaving Jax to stand there amongst the discarded underwear, maybe wishing Saunders had at *least* offered.

* * *

For the record, Jax only intended to access the air vents from Medical. It was one level down, but contained the main vent branch for O2 supply. This was done because in the event of a medical emergency, it was preferable that the medical bays have the strongest O2 flow. It meant peeling a ceiling panel back and climbing up a vent shaft, but it was nothing really new for Jax.

She made a detour by her quarters to pick up the tools she knew she needed, hydrate the single living thing she willingly interacted with on a regular basis, and chug the remainder of her morning coffee. Then Jax indulged in her Station knowledge to take a route wholly avoiding the Market, and Saunders, altogether.

Jax reappeared on Level 3 from a small side access she had built-in within the first three years on Station. The Station was built efficiently, without a lot of space left to waste, but that depended on how you defined "space." Jax found plenty of overlooked shortcuts that were perfectly serviceable if you were willing to accept a potential unpleasant death. This one, in particular, passed the heating and cooling lines, resulting in a risk of severe burn by either temperature extreme, but she had long since covered them with spare Station insulation, which made it an effective shortcut from her quarters to Medical in short notice.

Level 3 was also empty, as it should be. All residents had access to Medical, but accessing the level required logging their location and entry time, which could then be scrutinized. This was done for safety and record keeping. Station supplies, especially precious medical supplies, were only delivered on rare occasions with the semiannual supply drop-off. As a result, it was excessively emphasized to every temporary resident that while Medical was there for their use in their time of need, that it was not there for their abuse. This was standard on pretty much all stations. As there had been no recent medical emergency, there was no reason for anyone to be there.

Jax located the ceiling panel covering the vent system access. It was up against the wall, atop a ladder recessed into the Station's structure. She climbed up and undid the panel latch to pull it aside. The opening was large enough to hoist herself up and into the void above. She pulled the panel closed behind her. If anyone did wind up in Medical, they would have no idea she was there.

The dim light from the level below shone up through various cracks. Cracks weren't a problem here, where she was wedged between two levels of the Station. Each ring that housed a level used the outer circumference of the ring as a floor, and the inner circumference as a ceiling. Electrical, environmental, plumbing, and life support systems were routed up and along each and sandwiched between the rings. The walls needed to be impenetrable from space debris and failure, as they were the barrier between the living conditions on Station and the unforgiving void of space.

A less-experienced mechanic might have brought out a light, but Jax didn't bother. The creeping light sources from below were enough.

She rolled to the side to see a main access port for the primary vent shaft. This vent section was larger than the ones in the berthings. At about eighteen inches wide, twelve inches tall, it was an opening she could easily wedge her shoulders into. The branch leading to the blocked vent was off to the left. Jax pulled the access port open and proceeded to crawl inside. It wasn't graceful to say the least, taking a fair amount of grunting and scuffling, earning her a nick to the right ear tip against the vent lip. Was that another skittering sound?

Jax froze. It was hard to tell over her own metallic scuffle in the vent. But she swore it was just outside the range of her hearing again. She waited, frozen, arm and shoulders now half deep in an air vent.

This was a fantastic place for some contraband livestock, probably mad with panic at its unlawful space adventure, and hungry from neglect, to find her half hanging out of a confined space. Maybe she needed that flashlight after all.

After some blissfully silent moments, she extracted herself from the vent and pulled out her light to scan the immediate area around her. Nothing. Exhaling in a frustrated snort, she returned to her task.

Wedged down into the vent, light shining ahead of her, she was able to see the vent branch that wasn't working. The airflow seemed just fine where she was accessing from, so the problem could only be isolated to the small branch off to the berthing in question. She peered around the right angle to see if there was anything of note but could not make anything out.

Cursing her resigned responsibility of having to play janitor and plumber to a populace of ungrateful Station transients, Jax pulled her router snake from her side pouch and unwound it. The metal snake clanked predictably against the vent as it worked its way around the bend to whatever blockage was preventing airflow. After what felt like a cramped three minutes of winding, the snake impacted the blockage and Jax hit the latch release, snagging whatever it might be. She wriggled her way out of the vent and back into the ceiling void so she could sit up easier and wind in the snake.

The metal snake withdrew from the vent, as slowly as it had been unwound. It was clearly dragging with it whatever it had encountered as there was an added resistance to its pull. As the end emerged from the vent it appeared to be dragging fabric in its wake.

"Damned transients! Just stuff your underwear wherever you want, why don't you?" Jax complained. She closed the access port and rolled back over to the ceiling access panel. She pulled it open and climbed down, dragging her tools, and the vent clog with her.

Back in the cold sterile light of Medical, the ceiling panel securely back in place, Jax held up what she had found in the vent.

"Fuck."

It was fabric all right. Some garment, once upon a time. And it was entirely caked with obscene amounts of dried blood.

Chapter Three

A far more functional adult would have immediately gone to security after finding discarded, shredded, blood-soaked clothing in an air vent. A moderately functional space station mechanic would have, at a minimum, returned to the berthing to verify the airflow had been returned.

Jax stubbornly refused to be either of those people, choosing instead to stalk back to her bunk on Level 5. She convinced herself it was so she could get a better perspective on things before she proceeded with Station protocol, but really, she didn't want to burst in on Saunders in a moment of grasping need for the Security Officer's valued expertise.

Back in her quarters, a workspace swept clear of littered schematics, crunchy dried leaves, loose bolts, and washers, Jax spread out the gruesome fabric under a bright overhead lamp. This gory find was clearly someone's shirt at one point, which did bring a small wave of relief that it wasn't undergarments. But that meant someone had used a shredded shirt to stop a not-insignificant amount of bleeding. Jax avoided the Station's populous, but she still got notifications when a med bay was used. Someone doing this much bleeding should have alerted her to a resident using Medical, which would have meant more than just finding discarded clothing.

Jax stepped back and leaned against the recessed desk space next to her bunk, crunching a schematic under her hips, and picked absently at some of Ralph's older, crustier leaves. She needed to give the plant a good pruning—it had started snaking the full perimeter of her berthing seeking whatever light source its measly photosynthesis could use. This shirt, worryingly, seemed to have blood *around* the shredded fabric, indicating perhaps the shredding had caused the bleeding in the first place. This left some unpleasant conclusions for her to consider. The foremost issue was that whatever had occurred had been kept quiet.

Perhaps some grave injury had occurred, and the Station residents had covered it up. Crime wasn't really a thing on stations. They were prohibitively far from any of the possible conflict zones. Anyone else flying this deep into space would have a passport and a recorded reason for passage. Doing something unsavory out here essentially meant the end of your space-faring life as you knew it; passage revoked, settlement permits nullified, job contracts cancelled, that kind of mess.

Of course, human differences still lead to disagreements and conflict. There were no projectile weapons allowed in space, due to their nasty tendencies to blow holes in the side of space stations, but blades still existed, as did threatening blunt objects. Station Security was outfitted with an assortment of close contact defensive weapons, mainly a nightstick, and a taser for *really* bad instances. Jax shuddered at the idea of some Station transient stalking around, shredding shirts and the people inside them, and wondered how Saunders might react to such a concept. Would she argue with Jax that it would be impossible? That her precious residents couldn't be so vicious? The Station Security Officer certainly cared for her people, but Jax wasn't sure if that care was enough to ignore potential murderous monsters.

Speaking of monsters, maybe it wasn't a Station resident at all. A faint memory of scuttling drifted back through Jax's mind. Holy hell. Jax hoped there wasn't some swarm of contraband creatures out there shredding and eating Station residents. She didn't like these people, but she didn't want to see them become dinner either.

There were, as of yet, zero encounters with intelligent life out there that didn't originate from Earth. What life was found on further planets was not capable of traveling interstellar on its own. Trade laws meant you couldn't just up and take a herd, a pack, a pod, a swarm of whatever creature from planet A to planet B. There had been a stack of paperwork a mile high, Jax was certain, just to install the failed biofiltration lab around the bend, with living (and soon to be dying) plant life. But Jax had heard the rare story of unscrupulous transport companies fudging the lines on their manifests and catching even their transport pilots off guard. The only way Jax could be certain the Station was clear of an unfortunate infestation would be through doing a Station manifest check. This meant, once again, relying on Saunders.

It wasn't that Jax was so intent on avoiding the Security Officer she would fail in performing the basic duties of her work. It was just Jax preferred to think there was rarely ever a need to muddy the water between their two separate duties to this Station. Jax typically figured there were few things she could not handle on her own, and nearly a decade on Station had managed to prove her right. It also meant she was far overdue to encounter a situation where coordinating with her only coworker was inevitable. Deep space murderous shenanigans were probably the clearest incident possible.

This late in the day cycle, Jax figured there was only one place she could find the Security Officer. There existed a small galley, for better or worse, on each level of the Station. Berthing had several, to accommodate the residents, but the other levels had small, designated food areas. Jax had her own down the hall, which thankfully aided in her ability to avoid others. The ones on Levels 2 and 3 were usually left sparse and in a state of disuse. The one on Docking was where Saunders typically ate her meals, when not convening with residents on Four. Jax untangled herself from one of Ralph's creepers, packed up the shredded, bloody shirt and took a lesser-used route through the far side of the Station down to Level 1.

As predicted, Saunders was in the galley. She had already eaten, and was sitting at the table with a tablet, no doubt reading some important and informative news article, or Station status. In an effort to not seem beholden to anyone, Saunders in particular, Jax swept into the room with a façade of bravado, as if it was not entirely uncharacteristic for her to appear in her coworker's previously isolated galley.

Saunders looked up with a start as Jax stomped over to the coffee machine. Food be damned, she would rather have caffeine.

"Jax."

Saunders said the Mechanical Engineer's name as if it would confirm she really had entered the room and was not, in fact, a hallucination.

"What is this mess?" Jax said peering into the coffeepot at whatever dregs had surely been stewing there since the start of the day's cycle. She gave it an appraising sniff, pulled out the filter and dumped the already brewed, stale coffee back over the cold grounds. She flipped the switch and let a twice brewed cup of absolutely vile black sludge drip into a spare mug.

"Much better," she said, taking a sip from a now steaming cup of what smelled like engine degreaser. Whatever shock had come over the Station Security Officer at Jax's sudden appearance faded, and whatever initial question she had for Jax was rephrased.

"Why are you *like* this?" Saunders exhaled in a huff Jax just knew had puffed her floppy bangs out of her green eyes.

"A general disdain for human existence, my own included," said Jax, sipping the liquid that burned for more reasons than the temperature, and avoiding confirming her suspicion about the bangs. "Don't worry, I ask myself that question all the time."

"I suppose you drink it black like your soul. For fuck's sake Jax, you could have just made a fresh pot. There's grounds in the cabinet." Saunders sounded exasperated, but Jax thought she caught a trace of laughter beneath the admonishment.

"I like it bitter," Jax quipped. She let her presence fill the room for a bit as she mulled over the lip of her coffee mug, staring at the far wall of the small galley. Saunders seemed to let this go on for a moment longer than Jax had expected, before finally speaking up again.

"So, are you here for a reason, or...?" the Security Officer asked, her voice trailing off as if she really could not be sure.

Acting like the question was snapping her from a daydream, Jax perked up, placing her coffee on the counter beside her.

"Yep, checked your vent leak. Found the problem," she said.

"And did you update it in the station logs?" Saunders replied, already pulling up the log through her tablet interface.

"Not yet," Jax coughed on her abominable beverage. She never bothered updating logs.

Saunders put down her useless tablet and leaned back in her chair to look at Jax.

Jax let herself avoid eye contact for a moment longer before shoring herself up and staring down the Security Officer dead in the face. She was putting a fair amount of effort into keeping her complexion from flushing. It did not help that whenever she did resort to eye contact with Saunders, the Security Officer's mouth quirked ever so slightly in a way that was entirely distracting.

"And....?"

Jax suspected that Saunders' expression was exactly that of someone who, under any normal working environment, would have found this conversation to be routine: just the Station Mechanical Engineer providing a systems update. But instead, having been forced to work with Jax, Saunders probably was wondering why the hell Jax was bothering to tell her a damn thing at all.

Jax also knew she couldn't stall the conversation much longer without things getting weird, and maintaining this much eye contact with Saunders was gnawing at her gut like the battery acid coffee she consumed. She broke away to dig down into her utility pack and pull out the dreaded shirt, which she then unceremoniously tossed onto the table. It was a good thing Saunders had finished eating.

"What the fuck?"

At least, in the moment, Saunders could react appropriately. The Security Officer had forcibly flinched away from the bloody projectile and managed to catch herself with a sturdy grip on a nearby countertop to keep from tipping over off her seat. A single crease formed between now-furrowed, sandy eyebrows.

"Ah, yeah, I had a similar reaction," said Jax, returning to her coffee. Saunders was now nudging the shirt carnage off her discarded tablet with a look of disgust. She pinched the corners of it to unwrap it gingerly.

"You pulled this from the vent?"

"That's where the blockage was. I wasn't planning to go diving anywhere else today," Jax responded. Saunders ignored the sarcasm. In her defense, Jax was sure shredded bloody mystery shirts were not the best time for deflecting, but she really only had one setting when things got rough. "I haven't gotten any med bay notifications. Have you?"

"I have not. And you get all the same notifications I get; you know that." Saunders had managed to spread the shredded fabric out and was now examining the clearly ominous ripped holes. "And this is fresh. Like in the last day or so."

"Right, well, this means there's someone wandering around with considerably less blood than before, who has yet to notify us. Or worse yet, that someone isn't walking around at all anymore, and we have yet to find out who. You're the keeper of Station records for who is residing here. Has anyone gone missing?" This was probably going to be the longest conversation the two of them had engaged in this past year (had it been a year?). Saunders looked up.

"No one is missing that I know of. I'm more concerned with what caused the damage in the first place. An injured resident is one matter, but a risk to the rest is a greater issue. Did you search the med bay level?" Saunders replied.

"No, I didn't search the level. I'm not Security," Jax responded. She tried making it a sharp remark, but her voice faltered ever so slightly. What *she* had done was gotten the fuck out of there.

"Well, I don't know this station as well as you do, and you seem to think there are a lot of places for residents to get up to no good," Saunders replied calmly. She had fixed Jax with her stare again. Her eyes were a little too green sometimes, which usually made Jax's ears feel hot.

"Get up to sex games 'no good,' not shredding and bloodletting 'no good,'" replied Jax, her voice a slightly higher pitch than she preferred.

"All right, I think it's probably best if we backtrack our steps through Medical to make sure we didn't miss anyone," stated the Security Officer, returning her gaze to the rumpled mess in front of her.

"Whoa, whoa, what is this 'we' business? I just said I'm not Station Security," Jax protested.

"And I said I don't know the station as well as you do. If neither of us caught wind of some grievously wounded station resident until now, there is a real chance they are stuck somewhere only you might know how to find. I need you to walk me through this," Saunders replied, like it made the most sense in the world. And, begrudgingly, it did, though Jax was not thrilled about the idea of showing Saunders all her Station secrets.

"Fine," Jax said, defenses worn down. This was *really* going to be a long night.

Saunders insisted they stop by her quarters for her defensive weapons. Jax staunchly waited in the hallway. Saunders emerged with her security belt fastened around her hips, nightstick, flashlight and taser secured to the sides. Jax felt a bit empty-handed in just her utility belt. She supposed in a pinch her multitool could pitifully scratch some crazed space assailant. She contented herself with a jab at Saunders to ease the tension.

"You gonna be any use with those? I always took you for being too friendly with the locals to be someone who resorts to force," Jax said.

"I seemed effective enough at force while serving in the military for a contract," responded Saunders. Damn, Jax should have seen that one coming. "But thank you for saying you think I'm friendly." Fuck, Jax should have bit off her tongue instead.

"Are *you* going to tie back that mane of yours?" Saunders inquired. Jax glared. The thought had crossed her mind, but now that Saunders had mentioned it, she would refuse. Really, it was time to shear it all off, and let the cycle of growth begin anew. First, a shorn skull, then regularly shaved sides until it got too long to control. It was Jax's way of measuring time out here: cycles of hair.

Saunders must have interpreted the look of resistance on Jax's face because she amended her question.

"It just seems a bit wilder than that slick mohawk you had going on when I first got here."

Shit. How long *had* Saunders been here, noticing Jax's choices in haircut? Jax seemed to be rooted to the spot and barely realized Saunders had started off toward Common Access to Level 3. She snapped out of it and bolted after the Security Officer, hoping her falter seemed intentional, and not at all awkward.

This was absolutely the longest Jax would have found herself in the presence of the Security Officer, despite the months, however many, they had been working on the same Station. Most of that avoidance had been Jax's purposeful doing. As they picked their way up the Common Access shaft Jax felt a prickle of sweat on her back, indicating her general discomfort at the situation. She contented herself with pulling off the sleeves of her coveralls and tying them around her waist, leaving her in just a grey undershirt.

At this time in the day cycle, there would be no residents around. They paused on the landing outside the doors. Saunders glanced over at Jax as she fidgeted with her clothing, and within her own skin.

"You good to go?"

"Are you giving me an option?" Jax replied, trying to avoid sounding hopeful.

"No, not really, Engineering," Saunders replied mildly.

"Well, I'd rather get sucked through a gateway to hell than deal with this right now, but here we are," Jax grumbled.

Saunders rolled her eyes and swiped her access key to initiate an official staff access of the level. The doors rolled into the wall, opening to let them inside. Saunders marched forward, and Jax grudgingly followed in her wake. Once the level's doors had closed behind them, Saunders turned and disabled them, preventing anyone else from entering or exiting through Common Access. Any medical emergencies would just have to wait.

They made their way down the corridor. The Medical lights were as harsh and blue tinted as ever, washing everything in a flat light that screamed "hospital."

"Wait here," Jax said, reclaiming some confidence in the feeling of giving Saunders an order.

She had a recessed access panel to a maintenance locker here. It was mostly where she accessed electrical circuitry if it failed, but it was roomy enough for a person. She squared her shoulders to fight off the creeps of hunting for a bloody victim or criminal in a sterile, abandoned, space station med-bay, and threw the panel open with a little more force than she intended.

It was empty. Jax cleared her throat, and secured the panel again, making a pointed effort to ignore the side glance she felt from Saunders. So much for regained confidence. Luckily enough, Saunders seemed to share Jax's apprehension, and refrained from commenting on how jumpy Jax seemed. They continued onward.

"So, is there a reason you have so many shortcuts rigged up around here?" Saunders asked. She had her tablet out again as they walked and was tapping away at the screen. Jax could hardly understand why that was necessary, unless Saunders planned to digitally inventory every container they searched through. And if that was the case, why did they need to talk? Jax had intended to keep her trapped zipped for the duration of this short stint of cooperation. But Saunders seemed to hate silence.

"Makes for efficient travel and keeps me away from people. I figured that was straight forward enough," Jax replied reluctantly. But she could practically hear Saunders roll her eyes in response, which afforded her some small satisfaction. They continued down the corridor, sweeping each med-bay as they went.

"Have you ever encountered something like this before?" Saunders asked, after they had swept yet another bank of med-bays. Jax gave an exaggerated shrug as she addressed one of her back-access routes. No one was inside, dead, dying, or otherwise.

"Someone stole kitchen cutlery once. But they were just hoping to stock their transport with it. Besides, that was Security's job. I left it to them." No, she had not encountered much violence on this Station in her tenure. It was gloriously boring, which would be why she liked it so much. Stations with more action had larger staff to run them. Things weren't supposed to get this weird out here.

"Sometimes, it is hard to believe how much you refuse to get involved," Saunders replied, as she opened a medical storage locker, and tabulated the contents on her screen, still recording a quantity zero bloody bodies.

"Had a guy who showed up and thought he knew more about dual current electrical routing than I did. Caught him trying to remap the stator sequence. I cared about *that*," Jax replied. Saunders finished her inventory and turned from the entirely unoccupied medical storage locker, closing it behind her.

"And how did that go?"

"Well, that time Station Security had to intervene because I offered to let him re-wire the outboard rotationals from the exterior, without a pressure suit," Jax replied, checking under the surgical table of a nearby med-bay. Saunders had paused in her search to look at Jax.

"Got caught kicking him out an airlock," Jax simplified. Then she followed up with, "Kidding. But that did take a month to correct after he got escorted off Station." Saunders proceeded with her sweep, probably relieved she wasn't working with a homicidal maniac.

"This is nerve wracking. I just saw everyone at that dinner the other night. I'm concerned that might have been the last time I saw one of them," Saunders lamented, after they had cleared a few more degrees in silence. Jax exhaled aggressively, both from the built-up tension of checking every dark corner she passed, and the thought of Saunders spending time in the Market.

"I'm sure you aren't the only person who would feel that way," she said, as if that might be a comforting thought. She then decided it wasn't and went for something more distracting.

"You sure spend far more time on Level 4 than any other Security Officer I've known," Jax mused, offhandedly, before realizing she had said it aloud. The uneasy nature of their work was keeping Jax from better regulating what slipped through her filter. Saunders was across the hall checking a room, but she still heard.

"I mean, it was in the job description," Saunders replied.

"Family dinners and crunching weights in the gym with residents is in the job description?" Jax meant to say this as a jab, but it sounded more like curiosity than she had intended.

"Well, being 'friendly and courteous to all temporary residents'—how do you know I use the gym on Level 4?" Saunders paused.

Jax was turning from a spare supply locker and froze, unable to respond in a way that wouldn't make her want to go investigate the outboard rotationals without a pressure suit.

"I don't— there isn't a gym anywhere else on this Station," Jax said, still not moving.

That response was *not* better. She glanced up at Saunders standing with her back to a dark room, as lightless as the void of space outside the Station walls. In that instant, she could see some bloody Station specter bursting from behind her to spare them the awkward nature of this moment.

If only that would really happen. Instead, in a greater swell of horror, Saunders looked down at her arm, flexed, looked back up at Jax and *winked.* Jax glared at her with enough power it might fuel the Station on its own and turned to hastily climb up a wall ladder. It was suddenly very crucial that Jax check the ceiling space and hide the unsightly flush suddenly covering her face. Confronting space critters or bloody residents seemed preferable in that instant.

"Can we just focus on making sure whoever is donating blood to my Station isn't also wrecking my Station in the process?" she asked, aggressively, from the open void of the ceiling panel.

Jax busied herself with a sweep of the space near the vents, hoping some trail of blood would keep them from revisiting that previous line of conversation. Though, finding blood in the ceiling void would probably just encourage Saunders to crawl up there too, which made Jax grit her teeth.

The thing was, to any outsider, it should certainly seem Jax harbored an excess of distaste for the Security Officer. But to anyone who was also Jax, that was not the case. Jax *did* like Saunders. A lot. That was clearly a *problem*. Jax had a type, and she had pegged Saunders as fitting the mold almost immediately upon Saunders' arrival to the Station. Saunders *was* friendly; she took genuine interest in the lives of the Station residents, the Station, and Jax herself. She had this infectious positivity that threatened every foundation of Jax's term of penitence in isolation out here in the endless void.

The ventilation along the edges of the ceiling void was clear of carnage. Jax shifted to scanning the underside of the plumbing and sewage pipes that hugged the top of the cramped space.

Jax wished she could be casual about Saunders. She wished she could relent. But years of mistakes had taught her that she would latch on to anyone who showed her the slightest interest, which would inevitably just make things *so* much worse when they ended. Her solution had instead been to cultivate this vat of disdain she lived in. Then along came this ray of light, stuffed in a short, muscular, care-free package, and that ate right through Jax's desire to stay firmly separated and shrouded in darkness.

Having cleared the plumbing of any wrongdoing in their predicament, Jax rolled over to the opposite side of the narrow space to make sure there were no incriminating horrors to be found near the primary electrical conduits. The conduits appeared to be as innocent as the plumbing.

If Jax knew anything about herself, it was that the only way to survive a working environment with the Security Officer would be to make as much of an effort as possible to be aloof and insufferable until Saunders' contract was up. Therefore Jax, the cryptid bog-creature of Level 5, had made every possible effort to save her own hide from an excess of embarrassing human emotions, and their subsequent fallout, by avoiding Saunders at all costs.

Yet here they were, shifting room to room on Level 3, hoping a crazed Station resident didn't burst forth from a squirrel hole Jax had forgotten to close, brandishing any manner of sharp shirt-and-skin-shredding tools. This was a threat Jax should very much hope to find herself focused on, but she instead had to wrestle with the idea that she was more on edge from the extended contact with the Security Officer. The longer she spent in Saunders' presence, the more it became clear Jax should keep her distance.

Jax shouldered through a segment of ceiling, full of insulation and conduit to see what might lurk on the other side. The curtain of unkempt hair tangled in her face like a spider web, and Jax felt a moment of regret over stubbornly refusing to tie it back. She tossed it aside and used her light to scan a void seeming to have less spill over from the corridor lights below. Nothing popped out at her, but another faint skittering sound scratched at the edge of her hearing. She whirled around to look behind her, aware she was hanging between two sections of ceiling. Jax swore a thankful curse she hadn't reacted by calling out the Security Officer's name. Who knew how that might screw with her plans to keep them separated.

A scan of the space behind her revealed nothing crawling from the darkness. Jax gave a long and steady exhale to try to calm her nerves. She turned to continue her ungainly low crawl through the conduit and ducting. The beam of her flashlight flickered over the cramped space ahead of her and briefly flashed over a pair of tactical boots. Jax went still.

Her flashlight beam had already rolled past onto another dark corner of the ceiling void and Jax swallowed hard. She knew she needed to draw the beam back over what she had just seen, but willed herself to think that if she just kept rolling, it would be as if nothing had been there at all. She hoped against all odds it had just been a trick of the light. Gritting her teeth, Jax forced her hand to drag the pale light beam back from where it rested to the dark corner. With an overwhelming sense of dread it landed, again, on a pair of tactical boots.

Jax couldn't move. For a moment, that felt like an eternity, she indulged in the opportunity to study what she was looking at. The boots were grey. They were similar in style to the ones Saunders wore, but more like the ones that were standard issue for the space marines passing through the Station. They were peeking out from behind a boxy HVAC vent, situated in such a way they looked to be attached to someone laying prone, just out of sight.

Jax's throat felt dry. Somewhere below her waited her only coworker, probably growing impatient with Jax's dawdling in a ceiling void. Suddenly the notion of Saunders' company seemed incredibly welcoming.

"Jax? Jax, where did you go?"

As if right on cue, Saunders' voice rose up through the gaps in the ceiling like the dim beams of light Jax usually relied on for visibility. Jax had been shoring herself up to inspect a possible dead body in an air vent, but the sound of Saunders' voice elicited motion from the formerly still pair of boots. Whoever they were attached to started to move.

"Wait!" Jax managed to get out of her mouth.

As if spurred by her presence in the void, the boots, and whatever legs they were attached to, slipped from sight around the corner of the HVAC vent. Jax found her body reacting faster than her head would process and she surged forward. A shout from Saunders below her followed, as Jax burst around the corner of the HVAC, tiny light in hand.

The ceiling void was a cramped space. The Station's efficient construction limited available room for maintenance purposes only. Jax was practiced in maneuvering through the bundles of wire and venting, avoiding the pipes that were too hot or too cold, and the dust that escaped the air filters. It was tedious work, as ease of motion was not considered in the design. As Jax hoisted herself around the corner of the HVAC box her blood turned to ice. The rapidly receding pair of boots *scuttled* away from her behind another barrier. There was no way any normal human could move that fast in such a confined space, especially not on all fours.

Jax felt panic squeeze her square in the chest.

"Nope. NOPE! *Nope!*" She announced and pushed herself feet first toward the nearest exit panel.

The echo of the ceiling panel clattering to the floor resounded off the stoic and sterile med-bay walls. Jax didn't even take the time to relish the alarm Saunders registered as she dropped herself ungracefully to the corridor flooring and pushed herself away, staring up intensely, at the void above her.

"Jax, what happened?" Saunders was already next to her, following Jax's gaze toward the dim void she had just materialized from. Jax panted shallowly on the floor before finding the ability to speak.

"I, uh, I think they're up there," she squeaked, not even bothering to try to maintain any semblance of self-assuredness.

What snapped Jax out of her moment of intense terror was the image of Saunders not waiting for any further instructions before bolting for the nearest ladder up to the ceiling void. Jax registered what was happening at a slightly slower speed than she preferred and lunged after Saunders.

"Wait, what the fuck are you *doing?*" Jax hissed.

Saunders, already three ladder rungs up the wall toward the void, looked down at Jax, who could not for the life of her remember when she had ever put her hand on Saunders' boot. A flash of glancing emerald down to where Jax's fingertips still lingered on absolutely immaculate boot laces, and an arched, sandy-colored eyebrow, told Jax Saunders was equally caught off guard by the contact. Jax removed her hand as if it were burned, and looked back up at the other woman frozen on a ladder.

"Jax, we are here to rescue someone who is injured, and you said you found them. What else would I be doing?" Saunders asked, incredulous. Jax stared mutely back at her. Saunders shook her head and continued up the ladder.

"WAIT!"

Saunders stopped and turned around again, looking impatient.

"Okay, they..." Jax gulped, looking around for anything that could provide the confidence boost she felt she was sorely lacking. Saunders looked like she was ready to leave Jax behind again. "They, sort of...I dunno, ran away?" Jax finished feebly, locking eyes on Saunders' intense green stare. Saunders narrowed her brow in confusion.

"So, they aren't injured?" she asked slowly.

"I...I don't know, but they moved. Fast. Like, freaky fast." Jax was starting to feel stupid. She felt her face flush with embarrassment. Saunders seemed to study her from her perch. "Just, it might not be our victim up there..." Jax offered, hopelessly.

Saunders apparently understood. She pulled her taser from her belt and hoisted her torso up through the void. Jax shrank back from the wall ladder.

"Are you coming?" Saunders called from where she was still hanging out of the opening.

"Fuck no! You kidding me?" Jax barked.

Saunders' face appeared again under the edge of the panel.

"Jax, I need your help in here. I don't know what I'm looking for."

Jax looked nervously up and down the sloping corridor, then took a step forward, thrusting a thumb at her own chest.

"'*Engineering,*' remember?" she hissed.

"Yep, and these are your systems up here. What, Jax, are you going to just leave me to fend for myself over here?" Saunders called back down. Jax was climbing the ladder before she could think of another response. She contented herself to grumble about it the whole way up.

Being crouched and crammed in the ceiling void with Saunders was exactly as uncomfortable as Jax had imagined. Only now they were looking for someone with inhuman speed scurrying around in a space that had taken Jax nearly ten years to learn how to awkwardly flop through.

"Where were they?" Saunders asked, taser pulled out and pointed.

They were crawling, so Saunders could not simultaneously support a flashlight. Jax realized too late she had left hers down in the corridor. Saunders rolled her eyes and handed Jax hers from her hip. Jax snagged it, glowering, and flipped it on. She trained the small, sharp beam over toward the corner of the HVAC box she had seen the person crawl away from.

Saunders hoisted herself around the box and into the small opening behind it.

"What? Jax come on, bring the light." Her voice sounded muffled. The cramped space seemed tighter than Jax could remember.

Jax wanted nothing more than to be doing literally anything else in that moment, but she complied, and squeezed around the corner as well, now regrettably shoulder to shoulder with the Security Officer.

"You said they were over here?" Saunders asked.

Jax was putting an insurmountable quantity of energy into ignoring the nearly full, side-long press of the woman squeezed next to her, and the familiar, dreaded, feeling it brewed somewhere around her midsection. She only barely registered the question and had to shake her head to clear it enough for an answer.

"They were over there," Jax replied training the light in the direction she had seen the boots crawl away in. Saunders low-crawled forward, straining to fit through the tight space. Jax felt it was much more important to stay behind and operate the flashlight. Saunders only managed a few feet of motion before she stopped.

"This is a dead end," she called. Jax strained to see around Saunders' legs, trying desperately to keep her line of sight on all things space station and no things Security Officer.

"Okay, yeah, that makes sense, this butts up against the Station firewall. There's no way through to the next series of voids." Jax replied, now getting a less terror-filled lay of her Station's more intimate zones.

"So how could they have gone over this way?" Saunders asked, turning herself slightly in the cramped space.

"I—" Jax suddenly felt her face flush hot. The more she thought about it, the less she could be certain she had seen anything at all.

Saunders had managed to turn around and crawl back. Jax extricated herself from the cramped location and sat back in the roomier section of the void. Saunders joined her.

"Could they have gone over that way?" Saunders asked nodding toward the section of venting and conduit Jax had shouldered through.

Jax looked over her shoulder. No, she had been through there only a moment ago. They would have seen someone cross over the ceiling hatch from the flooring.

"There's no way they could have gotten over the hatch without us seeing them," Jax replied. She brushed her tangle of hair away from her face again. She really should have tied it back. "And, this is the only accessible void in this ninety degrees. There are firewalls at each end, and no way to get to the next void from here." Jax was aware the more she talked the more insane this sounded.

"Okay," Saunders said evenly. Jax turned to look at her in the dim light, swallowing hard in the process. Saunders had fixed her with a steady stare, then moved to lower herself back down through the hatch opening. Jax watched her descend for a beat before realizing she was being left behind in a possibly inhabited ceiling void, and she, too, bolted for the ladder. Saunders' presence suddenly was sorely missed.

Back in the sharp lighting of Level 3, Jax had to squint to let her eyesight adjust. She retrieved the discarded ceiling access panel and apprehensively laid it against the wall, deciding she would re-install it at a later date, with maybe less threats scurrying around. Saunders was still quiet and contemplating.

"I'm not fucking with you, I thought I saw someone," Jax huffed defensively, rubbing at a new scrape on the heel of her palm that she must have acquired in her desperate attempts to escape ceiling void specters.

"I think it's been a long search. There wasn't any blood up there, was there? Other than your own?" Saunders pressed, glancing at the motion of Jax's hands. Jax shook her head, mutely, and jammed her hands in her coverall pockets lest Saunders find an excuse to bandage her up.

"Maybe we need to check the CC footage," Saunders mused, instead of offering to patch Jax's minor injuries.

Jax hunched her shoulders, hoping to regain some of her stoic demeanor. She knew she was failing miserably.

"Let's, just...finish this level." Saunders seemed hesitant. Jax wanted to maintain her bravado, but she felt slight relief that at least the Security Officer was not teasing her for the moment of panic. Saunders had already walked off down the corridor and Jax followed.

They continued through the rest of Level 3 in near silence, their search proving fruitless. Medical was as spotless and unused as the Station's records would say it was.

"You're sure of how many residents are on Station?" Jax asked, as they had wound full loop and returned to the Common Access entry. Her eerie encounter and the silence of the remaining search had thoroughly unsettled her. Jax wanted so very much to reassume her bristly nature and reposition Saunders at arm's length, but she begrudgingly admitted she was relieved to have the Security Officer's presence. Even if it meant dragging her up every ladder to quickly scan every subsequent ceiling void. Of course, Jax was also massively pissed off about this sudden yearning for company, but she was still feeling a little on edge.

"I suppose we need to check the manifests to be sure," said Saunders, as she exited to the stairwell. She paused, looking up at the route that would lead them to Level 4. Jax waited, unsure what to say next.

"I feel like I should go wake everyone up and do a roll call, but I don't want to incite a panic," Saunders sighed.

Jax looked longingly up the stairs to her quarters on Level 5. She could return to her tinkering project, and maybe find a better way to route Ralph around her berthing rack. Saunders turned to head down the steps to the Security office, and Jax felt her body step toward her safe haven two levels up. The searing image of human legs crawling far too rapidly away from her flashed through her mind and made her pause. Jax was a force of one; she had not needed backup in years, and was not planning on changing that any time soon. But for the first time in a decade, the idea of stalking back to her room *alone* filled Jax with a strange sense of impending dread.

"Are you coming?" Saunders called from behind her. Jax refused to admit the relief she felt in turning to follow Saunders back down the steps to Security.

Chapter Four

In the security office, a place Jax rarely chose to find herself, Saunders scanned the CC footage from the past few hours. Jax leaned nervously against the opposite wall, her brow furrowed as the CC footage flitted past. She hated watching herself on screen as it was a constant reminder of her every minute action. And here, she got to simultaneously watch for creepy specters and her abysmal interactions with Saunders. The shorn hairs on the back of her neck were prickling with anxiety.

"It's unfortunate they don't have it in the ceiling voids too," Saunders mumbled as she shifted through the camera angles.

"Why the hell would they put cameras in the ceiling voids?" Jax snipped, unable to filter her reply amid her growing dread in scanning the videos. Cameras in the ceiling voids would be handy right about now. They could show that Jax really did see someone inhuman crouching above their heads. It could also provide a ceaseless source of amusement for anyone wanting to watch Jax gracelessly flounder between levels as she fixed plumbing and pulled gore from the air vents. Maybe Jax was relieved there weren't cameras in the ceiling voids.

Saunders had glanced over to Jax at her outburst, but simply shifted her weight and continued her scan.

"I'd also say it's unfortunate there aren't more employees on a Station like this. It would be useful for dealing with this kind of mess."

Jax shrugged her shoulders uncomfortably. "Pssh, like they would waste anyone else on a Station this remote." She then shut her trap because she wasn't sure if that was an offensive thing to say to someone. Or if Saunders' comment was a dig at Jax, due to her desire for someone better to partner with.

The silence mounted, along with a pending doom as the cameras flitted across screen. There were Jax and Saunders scanning the med bays. Then there were shots of them checking each dark corner of the arc where Jax held her stashes of maintenance equipment. Jax grimaced at the poorly angled shot of her fleeing the void, before pitifully following Saunders back up into the darkness. But there was nothing. Saunders pulled herself from the video footage and switched to mulling over the Medical access records on her tablet again. The CC footage continued to loop behind her.

"Doesn't look like anyone has been in there since that resident broke an arm hauling in cargo," she said. Had Saunders been on Station *that* long? Jax also resigned herself to the fact that she clearly didn't bother to keep track of time. Either way, she knew that had been ages ago.

"What about the footage?" Jax asked, betraying far too much interest than she preferred.

Saunders waved her hand dismissively behind her.

"That's going to take hours to comb through, but I'll set it to review mode, see if it catches anything. If it does, it'll kick a notification over to my interface tab here," she indicated the tablet in her hands. "But they shouldn't be in there unless they swiped access. And you checked your back access routes..."

Jax let her trail off. The footage was inconclusive. The manifests were useless. The adrenaline of her little excursion had worn off, leaving her feeling generally deflated. But there had been skittering. It had been there, playing at the edge of her hearing. Jax internally debated whether she should bring up the prospect of deep space stow-aways. She already had the sneaking suspicion Saunders thought she was imagining things.

"Can you check the supply manifests?" Jax asked, attempting to sound casual. She shifted to a nearby chair. Saunders glanced up and over at her, looking like she intended to ask a question, but Jax had refrained from asking with any form of sourness to her voice. Saunders typed in the database to bring up the report.

"Were you thinking anything in particular?" she asked, scanning the readout.

Jax had piled herself into the chair now, her back slumped, work boot heels on the seat edge, knees in the air. It was the kind of position someone might have, once upon a time, told her was "unladylike," which Jax couldn't have cared less about. She had never been good at "lady like." She looked past her legs, over to Saunders and faltered. What was she supposed to say? "Got any skittering space bugs in there?"

"Well, only residents with anything in storage have access to Supply. I know you said your manifests are up to date, but I told you I thought I saw someone there the other day. What were the last few stored shipments that weren't slated for Station use?" Jax asked instead. She figured the Station stores weren't going to be the problem, which would eliminate a solid quantity of deliveries.

Usually long-haul transporters would arrive, park their load in a docking bay, and either await transfer pilots to haul it away again, or on rarer occurrences, unload to long term stores until the next transport arrived to pick them up. It meant some supply stores were temporary, and held in-bay for, at maximum, a couple of months at a time.

"We pulled a load of replacement parts slated to leave in four weeks for the next system over. Did the inspection on them. It was all hardware, no criminals," Saunders replied. "Everything else was station supplies from four months ago." She looked up at Jax.

That was nothing to go on, and Jax didn't feel like theorizing that the Station stores had erupted in ravenous, cosmic, arachnids. Saunders' face flushed with a deep look of exhaustion that Jax felt she could relate to in her soul.

"I suppose if we don't figure this out by tomorrow, I'll have to put a notification in to Station Management," Saunders sighed, rubbing her forehead as if to banish a headache. Her hair had long since given up on being contained by whatever single tie she had used to keep it out of her eyes. Now, similar to Jax's mess of long, dark scruff, it was curtaining over her face in soft, pale, choppy chunks. She made half an attempt to brush the dark blond strands behind her ears. Jax made an aggravated effort to relocate her line of focus and rolled her head back on her shoulders to look at the dimming overhead lights. The late day-cycle Station programming was desperately trying to lull them to sleep.

"That'll be a waste of time. They won't give a shit until you have at least one and a half bodies," Jax grumbled. Saunders glanced up.

"Yeah, even I know that, and I haven't been here that long. Deep space municipality bullshit means they'll ask a million questions and then check in on *both* our jobs. If they actually cared, they would give me more than a taser. But this is uncontested territory, so I'll just make do with sticks and stones."

"Yeah, and this far out here, you see anyone coming a month in advance. It's not like they snuck up on us. Besides, *what* the fuck would anyone want with my Station?" Jax asked this question more to herself.

"*Your* station?" Saunders quirked an eyebrow.

Jax shrugged in response and slouched her feet off the chair to get up. Saunders powered off the screen readout of the records, stashed her tablet in its holster on her belt, and also rose to her feet.

"Well," Jax said. The intensity of their earlier search had dissipated, her embarrassment spread thin across the stifling fear that at any moment they would fight some cosmic horror, or that she might continue to say stupid shit. There were no answers for them tonight, and they had spent far too much time in each other's company. Jax had exhausted herself of adrenaline, both from the search for dead bodies, and the strain of holding her own against Saunders. She very much intended to leave and make her way back to her quarters.

Suddenly, Saunders' face lit up with energy both alarming and foreign to Jax in her exhaustion.

"We need to think about this differently! I don't want to get Station Management involved any more than you want to. Maybe we should brainstorm some ideas!" With that, Saunders yanked open a drawer under the main comms console and rummaged about, emerging with a sketch tablet and stylus. Jax stood dumbstruck as the shorter blond turned and made a beeline for the office door.

"Jax, come on, we can make better coffee in the galley!" and with that, Saunders disappeared from the room.

Distant alarm bells rang in Jax's head. Thus far, she had found herself following the Security Officer throughout every nook and cranny of her Station without the slightest resistance, despite her every instinct telling her to quit while she was ahead. Now she was being invited to coffee in the Level 1 galley. Absolutely not. They could talk in the morning through truncated comms panel calls, placed across the safety of 5 levels of space station. Jax would slip out of this office and drag herself back up to her cramped quarters and Ralph's strangling leaves. Their search had been inconclusive, the videos were useless, and Jax had had enough.

She stepped into the corridor and looked after Saunders. The Security Officer's feet had not quite disappeared with the arc of the level, since Docking had a much larger radius. Jax hefted her shoulders and adjusted her tool belt. Then she turned her feet away from the direction Saunders had walked. Let the Security Officer take her time figuring out where Jax had disappeared to. Jax could be in her bunk and under the covers, hiding from all things skittery and unnerving by the time Saunders put in a call to comms.

Jax let herself trudge onward toward the far side of the Station, where the employee access shaft could take her directly home without any added effort. Behind her, the CC footage scanned for anomalies Jax was certain it would never find. And somewhere, eighty, ninety, or more degrees Saunders sat, once again, in a galley, without any idea where Jax could be.

Jax let herself muse over the agony of the evening. It was a rough start, filled with demeaning janitorial work, only for it to have veered hard left into uncharted territory. The harshest part of the ordeal had not been the terrors or the mystery, but the revelatory ease with which Jax found herself working alongside Saunders. And Jax hated that she might have liked it. She needed to stay vigilant, or she might end up just screwing herself out of the good thing she had going here on this distant junk heap.

At some point, far enough away from the Security Office, Jax felt her pace slow. She heaved a sigh to alleviate the tension she had felt growing in her shoulders. Something at the window portholes to her left caught her eye.

There was nothing. There would always be nothing. Jax hadn't even bothered with the local star maps because it was nothing but a void out there; inky black and desolate. But now it seemed to call to her. Jax had once spent a romantic evening, early in her tenure and alone with her keep, gazing admirably out into the abyss, appreciative of the security it offered her in its seclusion. That enamored feeling had faded to something comfortable and familiar. But now, it was as if her feet were moving with a mind of their own, as Jax felt some gentle nudge in her soul, guiding her toward the windows and back out into the endless dark.

That pull had Jax nearly flush to the window now. Normally the interior lights were angled to avoid simply recasting reflections of the inside of the Station. The windows needed to function as actual windows, showing approaching transports. But it was late in the cycle, and no approach notifications had gone off, so the soft interior lighting and weak pinpricks of starlight made it easy to simply just refocus her vision on her own reflection. But Jax was practiced at letting her eyes relax and letting her brain filter out the near-frame images reflected around her, so she could zone out into the black depths beyond. Jax felt herself seeking that solace she had found ages ago in this isolation.

With her forehead now pressed to the glass, Jax instead felt a jolt. Then she heard a shout. In the corner of her unfocused vision, she saw the reflected image of Saunders running up the corridor toward her. Jax flinched and bolted back from the window to look at the approaching Security Officer. But the corridor was empty. Jax shook her head, trying to recover from the almost hypnotic feeling that the endless cosmos could have on anyone who gazed on them too long. She pressed the heels of her palms to her eyes to rub them clear of any hazy daydream and scanned each direction of the arcing corridor. As her senses cleared, Jax could only feel like she had imagined the whole thing, and even as she came back to grips with her surroundings, she could hardly recall it happening in the first place.

"Alright, this has been way too long of a night," Jax lamented to the empty corridor. She jogged away from the porthole and around the curve toward the back access stairwell.

Instead, Jax rounded the curve and came face to face with the entrance to Saunders' galley. This stopped Jax dead in her tracks again. She looked over her shoulder at her previous path, then back again at where it had led her. Somehow, she had been so absorbed in her own thoughts that her stupid boots had carried her past the back stairwell and right back around to the place she had been trying to avoid. Hazards of living on a giant wheel.

"Jax, are you coming?" called Saunders from within.

Damn Jax's treasonous feet for making enough noise to wake the Station, while keeping her from her escape. Jax's ability to sneak had dissolved entirely by this late hour.

Resigned to a fate she had desperately tried to avoid, Jax heaved her shoulders in a massive shrug, and finally entered the galley.

"Took you long enough. Did you get lost?" Saunders said, not looking up from her perch.

Saunders had dumped her stationery unceremoniously on the galley counter. The shredded bloody fabric still lay in a stinking display on the main table. Jax peered cautiously at it as she skirted around Saunders and hefted her form up to sit on the counter. Saunders had clearly been scratching away on the sketch surface.

"I needed to take a walk. To, uh, clear my head," Jax mumbled. She eyed the coffee machine she had defiled earlier. Saunders glanced up at her, nodded, then returned to her scribbling. "Uh, what, exactly, are you doing? I thought you wanted to work on this shirt issue," Jax asked, nudging the edge of the table with her work boot, to indicate the awful mass that lay across it.

"Sometimes I do better when I can sketch out my thought process in real time, and the small tablet screens just don't cut it," Saunders replied, as if she sensed Jax's apprehension and confusion. "Why don't you get some coffee started—on second thought, here," Saunders thrust the stylus at Jax's chest. Jax fumbled the small tool as Saunders looked her squarely in the eye.

"*I'll* make the coffee," Saunders concluded.

Jax slid off the counter and skirted past Saunders who had made her way over to the coffee machine. The sketch pad glowed dimly on the other side of the counter and Jax attempted to scrutinize Saunders' writing. The Security Officer offered to narrate as she worked.

"So, we checked Level 3. Found nothing conclusive, but you *think* you saw someone in a ceiling void. And, when we went back to check, there was no one there."

Jax grunted as she looked at the notes laid out in front of her. There had been too much "thinking she saw something" happening lately, and it was not a comfortable feeling. Saunders continued behind her.

"Video review is going to take a while, but manifests prove inconclusive. We still need to poll the residents and check Level 4. We should try to be discreet about that, or else they'll get nervous. Level 2 should be sealed, and no one has card access currently, unless you think there's some back access they might have found—"

"Well, what do we even know about the guy who had bloody rags in his air vent? Have you talked to him yet?" Jax interrupted and glanced up. Saunders had paused, coffee grounds still in her hands and not in the coffee machine where Jax needed them to be.

"No, I haven't talked to him yet, as we prioritized doing a sweep of Level 3, then decided to not wake the residents..." she trailed off, as if she was hoping Jax would catch up to the conversation. Jax squeezed her eyes shut. Right, this had all happened this night, and only just this night.

"Usually, I'd say we should sleep on it and reconvene tomorrow, but I'm irked. I can't tell if the residents are in potential danger, or if this is just some mess blown out of proportion. This whole thing is particularly concerning, and I'm not sure who else I would be able to talk about it with. I would appreciate your input. Hence, I figured I'd entice you with a better cup of coffee?"

Jax was momentarily stunned. She wanted to tell Saunders to please *not* attempt to be enticing, but her objection got lost somewhere in the back of her brain. This allowed Saunders to follow up with:

"Also, you haven't been quite as insufferable as usual, so I figured I'd capitalize on it."

Jax had tried to leave, she really had, but that had failed. And by now, Jax figured she needed coffee to successfully make it back to Level 5 anyway, so she heaved a sigh, and pushed any thoughts of escaping this business out of her mind.

"I suppose I can continue providing minimally insufferable input," she grumbled. She returned to the sketch pad in front of her as Saunders resumed her task with the caffeine generation.

Even trying to play nice, Jax felt useless. Saunders had mapped out their whole evening with bullet points as efficient as her boot laces. Saunders was pushing a clean mug into Jax's hand before Jax could do anything but firmly place the stylus down on the countertop.

"Since Kiv brought this to my attention, I doubt it's him," Saunders continued.

"Who?" Jax replied, confused.

"The resident whose air flow was blocked by bloody evidence of foul play?" Saunders added, her voice sounding tired.

Jax huffed into the coffee and took a scalding gulp. It begrudgingly tasted much better than her usual sludge, not that Jax felt like admitting it.

"I just don't see why he would split someone open, hide the evidence in an air vent, and then *tell* me about it," Saunders continued, nodding over her shoulder at the shirt.

"Or maybe that was *exactly* his plan," Jax mumbled, chasing a thought that bloomed in her coffee mug then sank back down to drown in the dregs. "Murder his roommate, then throw you off the trail..." no, that sounded stupid, even to Jax. She sighed. There had been too many gruesome details to this evening that had started with a perfectly enjoyable tinkering with her gadgetry, that patiently waited on her above. Jax resigned herself to present a peace offering.

"Look, I can do a check of Level 2 tomorrow. I told you I thought I saw someone up there the other day, even if your records say otherwise," Jax said hurriedly before Saunders could protest. "Besides, I saw a notification a light fixture had gone out, so I need to get in there for replacements. I can run a sweep and see if anything adds to this mystery." Saunders seemed to perk up at this collaborative statement leaking out of Jax's mouth, and Jax instantly felt regret.

"I can accompany you if you like, since you think you saw someone—"

"No!" Jax heard herself say, more forcefully than intended. Saunders looked a little taken aback. "Just, fixing lights doesn't require security," she stated rapidly.

"Well, of course not, but this is more of a security matter than a mechanical one, don't you think?" Saunders countered. She nursed an indulgent sip of her own drink, fixing Jax with a green stare over the lip of the mug.

"I'll be fine. You need to check on your residents. I can fend for myself," Jax replied insistently. It would be best not to prolong this.

Fortunately, Saunders seemed to accept this answer, as she smiled a determined smile and reached past Jax for the stylus again. Jax dodged out of the way and back to her spot on the counter as Saunders returned to sketching out her plan.

"All right then, I'll do a review of the facilities and residents on Level 4. I'll talk to Kivan, and his partner, and ask about other air vent issues," Saunders stated, as she finally returned the stylus squarely on the counter surface to signal she was done. "We can meet up after your repairs and see if that gives us any more answers to this mess. I suppose there isn't much else we can do about it tonight." Her response faltered at the end, as if she too was ready to put this out of her mind.

"Right, well, I suppose that means it's best I get out of here," Jax replied, hoping Saunders caught on to her desperation to be free of this engagement. Instead, Saunders looked up at Jax with that same intense green stare, and that smile that tugged at the corners of her mouth. It was not helping.

"Thanks for working on this with me, Jax," the Security Officer replied softly. It rooted Jax to the spot where she sat, opposite her exit from the galley.

Jax had felt so desperate to maintain her air of aloof disinterest in anything pertaining to the Station Security Officer, but this had, in fact, been an amicably fine experience. Maybe she had walked the level full circle for a reason. Maybe it *was* time she start being minimally insufferable on a more regular basis. Maybe Jax had been alone out here long enough.

"What made you take this job, Saunders?" The question left Jax's lips before she could stop it.

The Security Officer blinked. She seemed equally taken off-guard by Jax's lack of venom. She dropped her gaze for a moment before shrugging.

"I finished my contract and needed a job. I wanted to find something I could contribute to," she responded. That was a perfectly boring answer.

"Why? I would assume staying on contract would not only fill your need for a job but also a contribution," Jax responded, brow furrowed in genuine confusion.

Saunders had now leaned against the galley table, skirting the contents as she rocked her head from side to side, in the manner of someone juggling a decision or answer. Jax, meanwhile, mentally kicked herself. She knew there were several reasons, some of them deeply personal, that someone might not renew a contract.

"I guess you could say my service was not what I expected. I figured it would be exactly that: a job and a contribution. And then I spent five years stuck on a rock mopping floors. It's a crapshoot. Sometimes you're out there providing security detail to a new planet, really making a difference, and sometimes you are forgotten in a rear detail. I didn't think it was necessary to keep that up." She finished with a sense of resignation.

"So you came here? Like this is any better than mopping floors," Jax scoffed into her empty mug that she now clutched for comfort more than anything. Saunders laughed. An actual sincere laugh. Jax felt scandalized until she realized Saunders wasn't laughing *at* her.

"Here, on station, I feel like I get to occasionally help people, and interact with them as they pass through. I figured I could have a more lasting impact." As Saunders said this, the mirth faded a bit from her voice, and she turned her face toward the shredded cloth on the table, turning black with the exposure to UV LEDs and central air flow.

Before Jax could press onward, however, Saunders snapped out of it. She fixed Jax again with her intense green stare.

"I will say this much, I was not expecting it to be quite as lonely as it's turned out."

This statement came with its own snap of unexpected animosity. Jax felt a lump of guilt form in her chest.

Of course it was lonely here. That was why Jax chose to stay indefinitely. Though, she was sure her own shitty attitude had made this posting far more remote than any original job description had made it out to be. She let the awkward silence drop around them. The minutes ticked by. Jax figured she really should leave.

"Jax, can I ask you something?" The animosity was gone. The voice was soft again.

Jax shifted her gaze quickly to Saunders' eyes and just as quickly looked away again, toward the door.

"Depends," she said, eyes chasing her exit.

"What's your name? Like, your real name? 'Jax' can't be all it is," Saunders asked. This weird new socializing had made her *bold*.

"That *is* all it is," Jax responded, a little more aggressively than she had intended. But she had been doing so well at being nice, at least by her standards. Maybe Saunders really did deserve an amicable coworker.

"I stopped using any other names ages ago," Jax relented to disclose. "Right around when I left Earth. I didn't want to take that part with me. I picked up some odd jobs on Mars and was pretty good at whatever I tried. Someone called me a 'jack-of-all-trades' and then the nickname 'Jax' stuck. I didn't see a reason to go by anything else."

In fact, Jax had also never seen a reason to ever tell anyone this ever before. She had kept her mouth shut for over a decade. Her journey to Mars had only been the beginning; the start of an endless spiral out and away from whatever self-induced carnage she created in her wake.

"You seem to have an unnaturally high level of distaste for your own home planet. This whole 'general disdain for human existence,' it's not endearing," Saunders said. It wasn't an accusatory tone, but Jax still felt called out. She opened her mouth to complain but was cut off.

"Jax, did you *really* see something up in the ceiling panel?" Saunders asked, inquisitively. Her head was cocked to the side, as she considered Jax sitting across from her. Jax squirmed. Had she seen something? Had she seen shadows on Supply, or reflections of Saunders chasing after her on the far side of Docking? It was all madness, and Jax hated feeling like she couldn't trust her instincts. Besides, the idea of gaining an unsavory reputation as someone who saw and heard things did not sit well with her either. Jax didn't need anyone calling her mental capacity into question. She *needed* this job. It gave her purpose.

"I think I was just...tired. Been a long day, probably a trick of the light." Jax fidgeted and weighed the impact of making her seem temporarily inept versus permanently inept. She figured she could roll with a brief setback.

"Ah, well I wouldn't want to keep you too long then, if you would rather get some sleep," Saunders offered, genially, now smiling, ever so slightly.

"I...I should go," Jax trailed off, realizing her line of sight had paused a bit longer than necessary on that small smile curling the Security Officers lips. Jax swallowed, harder than intended.

Saunders broke the intense gaze of her sharp green eyes and nodded, looking over the close quarters of the galley, their notes, and the shredded rags on the table where hours earlier she had been eating in peace. Jax fidgeted uneasily in her seat, shifting her weight, finding the motivation to right herself and leave. She watched the stylus Saunders had been writing with slowly roll off the counter toward the exit and the windows beyond, as if it was leading Jax to her true goal. Jax stared absentmindedly as it dropped to the flooring with a light clink. Her gaze shifted after it, as her thoughts sought her excuse for an exit.

"You know, Jax," Saunders piped up, snapping Jax from her stupor where she sat, "as weird as this night's been, it's been nice having a coworker for a change." She turned back to Jax with a wink, and a spreading grin. Jax felt her face flush and the heat of it propelled her from her perch on the counter.

"Right, well, long night. Like I said. Should probably sleep," she mumbled. From the corner of her eye, she saw Saunders right herself from her lean against the table. A shock of wet-sand colored hair extricated itself from behind her ear to hang in front of her sharp stare. She now watched Jax far more intently than she had before.

Before Saunders could invite Jax into any other mysteries for the evening, Jax strode out of the galley and into the corridor. She angled herself directly toward common access, figuring her best route this late would be direct, even if she did find a wayward resident still adjusting to the Station day cycles.

"Jax," came Saunders voice from behind her.

Jax paused, took a deep breath, and set her shoulders before summoning every ounce of self-respect she could gather and glancing back at her only colleague in multiple parsecs.

The Security Officer had followed her out into the corridor.

"Don't be a stranger," Saunders piped up to fill the moment of silence between them.

Jax lifted her chin in acknowledgement, then turned on her heel and strode into Common Access.

Jax was several steps up, in the more aggressive gravity of Level 1, before a thought struck her. That stylus. It had been stationary on the table. Then it had rolled off. Things didn't roll on Station. Either they were bolted down, or someone pushed them. But because gravity was simulated by the outboard rotationals spinning the concentric rings of the Station, the force vector on all items was always down toward the flooring. Something had pulled that stylus off the counter toward the galley exit. There was no gravity in that direction.

Jax stood, puzzled, in the stairwell. Gravity used to be her specialty, so she knew this was a weird occurrence. A creak of the stairwell scaffolding shook her loose and she spun, half expecting to see Saunders had followed her. Again, there was no one. Jax felt haunted and shivered where she stood.

"I'm losing it," she growled. "I must have kicked the counter while I sat on it. Too much shit going on..."

Jax had repairs to see to. She had promised Saunders that much, nothing more. She didn't have a need for this to be anything more than her duty to the Station. Jax resumed her climb to Level 5.

Chapter Five

Jax woke up pressed against the void of space. When she finally gained enough consciousness to peel herself off the window bordering her bunk, she realized she had overslept. The late evening and unnerving proximity to Saunders had left Jax in a fitful sleep, rolling from side to side all night. It was hardly a surprise for her to open her eyes only to see the endless expanse yawning out beneath her, but still, it was not the most welcoming way to join the waking reality. That's what she got for moving her bunk against the far wall.

It had not really been Jax's intention to ignore her promise to the Security Officer. She really did intend to follow through on her plan with Saunders. But Jax had a crick in her neck and her lower back felt stiff from all the crawling around she had done the night before. By the time she managed to drag her ass out of her quarters, Jax found a much more pressing need for more coffee and to clean and reinspect the main air filters located on Level 5. She figured she might as well eliminate any other blockage issues at the source while she was at it. She could then work her way down to her duty on Level 2, just as they had planned, but maybe at a less conspicuous time in the day cycle.

No air filter routine maintenance was complete without a visit to the defunct biofiltration lab. Jax usually stopped by once a day-cycle to reconsider the value of expanding the space. Station Management had determined, at some point well past her initial contract conclusion, that anyone this deep in space might benefit from the added company of unassuming plant life. Jax knew it was also a cheap oxygenation hack, which appealed to the bureaucratic types. They had carved out one of her machine labs, moved the off-brand printers to another storage nook and built up a minimally funded bio-lab with various benign greenery. Jax had assumed some of it would at least be functional, like a potato, but that would have made too much sense.

Predictably, the whole operation had failed, as Jax was a mechanic, not a gardener. But upon accepting the daunting task of stripping the rows of failed hydroponics from the walls, Jax had found a single stubborn sprout refusing to join the rest of the wilted trash destined for airlock disposal. Jax had never considered herself having a green thumb, but Ralph was insistent about staying alive.

Recently though, its leaves had been dropping more frequently, and they crunched underfoot. Jax had even noticed some deterioration patterns on the leaves that looked abnormal for Ralph's usual continued growth. In fact, it almost looked like the work of pests, which was an impossibility on a Station such as this. It probably meant Jax's luck was running out with the foliage, and the thought irked her. She was loath to admit she enjoyed the company of a weed, but Jax typically spent her spare time waffling between wanting her print shop back and wanting to give Ralph the life it deserved. That probably meant revamping the biofiltration lab to help Ralph get over whatever was bugging it.

Therefore, Jax found plenty to keep herself conveniently occupied away from the hazards of the rings below.

Several hours later, covered in the scent of oxygen scrubbers and hydroponic gel, Jax meandered into the control room for Power and Life support, nursing yet another cup of coffee, stewed from the morning dregs. She twirled one of Ralph's recent clippings in her fingertips as she pondered the strange holes that had been plaguing its leaves recently. She slumped at the main console with her feet on the counter and reclined as she studied the damaged greenery. It wasn't until then she recalled her poorly executed commitment to teamwork with her singular coworker.

"All right, well I'm not going to go inspect that level *now*," Jax snorted into the coffee mug. She convinced herself it was because her back still hurt, and the day was late. It was not at all because the concept of boldly poking around Level 2 looking for ghosts and horrors *alone* was just far too spine tingling. It wasn't that she was creeped out, Jax just did not have the energy to run a full inspection of the whole Supply Level. At least...not *alone.* Not now. Now it was time for a shower, and—

"Dammit, you're going to blow another fuse!" Jax cursed under her breath, slamming the damaged leaf to the console surface and hulking forward to glare at the computer readout panel displaying a constant schematic image of the Station. The power line was spiking down on Level 1. Jax zeroed in on the screen layout to conclude the only cause would be Saunders blasting that infernal music machine again. Why couldn't she use those magnetic ear clips everyone was carting around years ago? The ones that meant no one else had to be subjected to the strangest niche interests in ancient rock music? Although, admittedly, Jax was not current on what popular consumer tech was in use these days. She hadn't paid attention since her exodus from civilization, and if it wasn't something she was tinkering with, she regularly ignored whatever the residents hauled on board with them.

Either way, Saunders was about to blow yet another fuse down in the Security Office. And Jax did not want to get hauled out of bed at some stupid hour to by a chipper and strangely flirtatious blond begging her to come patch her errors. And wasn't Saunders supposed to be polling the residents to address their brewing mystery? What was she *doing* down there?

Jax dropped her coffee mug on the counter near the navigation control panel and tilted her head back to release the aggravation. She let her mane of hair hang back from her face for a brief moment before snapping her head back forward, drawing a curtain of scraggle in front her eyes. Apparently, she was leaving Five after all. At least when she was done admonishing Saunders for her poor taste in music Jax could convince the Security Officer it probably *was* more of a security matter to review Level 2 with her than Jax had previously suggested.

Jax swung by her quarters first, to grab her tool belt, but when she got there, she considered changing her coveralls for something less grungy. Not that she had much, nor that she *cared* what Saunders thought about her choice in fashion, but she should at *least* make an effort to not wear the same article of clothing for three cycles in a row.

Feeling slightly more fit to tell unruly Security Officers to quit taxing the Station's auxiliary power grids, Jax squared her shoulders and slogged her way down to Level 1 through the more open and accessible employee axis strut on the opposite side of the Station from Common Access. Her trip was free of any phantom or shadow she could have imagined, which left Jax feeling relieved and emboldened in her march around the outermost ring toward the anticipated heavy thundering beats that would be emanating from the other side of the Station.

For this late in the afternoon, Level 1 was strangely clear of residents on any typical pilgrimage. Usually there would have been a few still wandering the bland, metal-walled corridor looking for any possible semblance of entertainment before finding someone to knock boots with in an airlock.

Come to think of it, Jax should probably check the airlocks while she was down here. But she had a mission to see to first. Jax was hardly within twenty degrees of Security when she was assaulted by the obnoxious synthetic power chords radiating outward.

Wincing against the audible deluge, Jax strode confidently up to the Security door before her nerves promptly failed her. Or perhaps it was that the door was open, and Jax stumbled upon the image of one pristine tactical boot propped up on a stool, while Saunders' hips moved in an entirely distracting manner to a beat Jax could hardly decipher. Inside the office, Saunders was far too preoccupied with giving a stellar performance of air guitar with her nightstick, otherwise Jax surely would have been noticed as she stood dumbstruck in the door frame. The mop of dark, sandy hair mercifully obscured Saunders' vision and gave Jax her route to escape, as soon as she found functionality in her limbs again.

Jax dodged away from the door frame and nearly slammed her back into the wall just outside the Security Office. She would have worried the sound might alert the officer inside, but the music was far too loud for that.

It was another moment or two before Jax realized she still had not moved. What the fuck was she waiting for? Either she was here to tell Saunders off for illegitimate use of sound equipment in the void of deep space, or she should stalk off to haunt Level 2 herself. But still Jax clung to the wall paneling outside the Security Office.

The tune switched to something with *far* too much energy for anything that had been popular in the last several centuries. Jax glowered, but also bit her bottom lip in frustration. Last night had gone...unexpectedly, to say the least, in spite of the weird, gory finds she had endured. She had spent the evening in the company of Saunders and lived to tell about it. Maybe Jax had finally outgrown her stupidity. Maybe she could be an amicable coworker to someone without making a mess of things. Maybe they could team up again and tackle this issue, together.

The racket was cut short, followed by a curse from inside the office.

"Shit! Not again..."

Jax's attention snapped back to the office door, her ears pricked for any clue as to the next moment's surprise. There were a few muffled noises and thuds, then an audible sigh.

"Well this isn't going to fix itself any time soon..."

Jax winced. Some computer readout somewhere was telling her empty post, five rings up, that another fuse had blown.

"Well, she's not reading her alerts up on Five. Probably off fixing something somewhere else—Oh! Excellent, Aviry is working on leg day!" There were some light scuffling sounds, and Jax almost missed her exit.

"Shit," Jax hissed to herself, turned tail, and sprinted up the corridor to the nearest airlock panel. She ducked behind it just as she saw Saunders' boots leave the office and enter her quarters. The Security Officer emerged moments later, carrying a gym bag and headed for Common Access. She'd be up on Level 4 pumping weights with some of the military guys soon enough. Figured, if she was a vet.

"Fuck," Jax slid down the airlock wall, her knees bent up to her chin level. Why had that felt like a close call? She had gone down there to hassle Saunders about her tunes, and instead she had bolted like some skittish critter. *One night* of amicable partnership and Jax was acting like an idiot. There were *real problems* on this Station to deal with. Jax needed to buck-the-fuck-up.

And why was she even here? Saunders could learn a thing or two from the silence of her blown boom box. It's not like Jax had actually reconsidered her need for company while she planned to inspect Level 2...

There wasn't a point to sticking around now, unless Jax wanted to wait until Saunders was done in the gym, and back, sweaty from a workout. Jax uncurled from the wall. But, hold that thought. She had traversed the Station rings to warn Saunders of an impending blown fuse, and here she was, ready to fix said blown fuse.

Better yet, Jax had an inkling why that dumb juke-box kept going on the fritz. She only needed a few modifications at the main Level 1 breaker box and she could avoid this scenario ever happening again. Saunders could rock out to her heart's content, and Jax could swing by to gloat at how she had outsmarted the most obsolete of on-Station tech. Maybe then Jax wouldn't need to ask for company, Saunders would just insist on joining her, and Jax could pretend to be upset about it again. Almost normal, right?

The Station's Level 1 main breaker box was back about a ninety-degree arc away from Common Access and Security, set into the main bank of airlocks. It was located near the cargo airlock opposite the single freight lift shaft, designed to haul storage cargo from Level 1 to Level 2. And since Jax had sagely equipped herself with her best tools and spiffy clean work clothes, she was ready to tackle this nuisance.

The electrical breaker line running to Saunders' office and quarters was routed along the base panel near the outer hull of the Station. It had several break-out locations and enable plugs, but the real problem was that it was drawing too much power from the main box. Jax cracked open the panel and perused the wires.

Replacing the fuse was, once again a no-brainer, and far more efficient without Saunders staring at her backside. But outsmarting the wiring was a challenge Jax thrived on. It was especially energizing to think of her conversation she might entertain afterward.

"Oh, I suppose you might be wondering why your blasted boom-box hasn't been frying the Station lately? No worries, I just fortified the Level 1 electrical schematic. You know, so I don't have to be bothered fixing it all the time. You're welcome!" Jax mumbled to herself.

Or, she could be nice about it. That's what normal humans did, right?

"Hey, I uh, figured you would appreciate that I fixed your electrical wiring so your music doesn't shut off..." Jax tried. Nah. She would just fix it and never say a damned thing about it ever again. That was more her style.

A few splices and re-routes later and Saunders would be head-banging to mummified oldies for the rest of her contract on Station.

Jax patched the panel back in place, huffing with exertion in the cramped corner near the largest airlock. Then Jax jerked back from the airlock door and scrambled away on her hands and feet like a crab.

Something had definitely scratched at the airlock door.

Without any lights indicating it was in use, and no suspicious sex noises to accompany it, Jax was certain there was no way anyone or any*thing* could be on that side of the door. She regarded the smooth metal panel bisecting the livable environment of the Station with the last vestibule of safety before the void.

Cautiously, she inched forward again, switching from her crab walk to a crawl so she could place her ear against the metal.

A scraping sound ground against the opposite side of the door, like sharp nails gouging through steel. Jax shoved herself away and stared up at the thick glass inlaid in the door, expecting something to be staring back at her. But it was as dark as an unused airlock.

A beat or two and Jax regained her composure. This jittery feeling was stupid. Her Station was her fortress, and her home. She refused to be bested by her imagination and adventurous choices in coffee consumption. She hoisted herself to her feet and regarded the airlock door. Whatever she had heard would be just below the lip of the window. All Jax had to do was flip the light panel on and peer inside.

The few feet between the toes of Jax's boots and the wall that held that light panel seemed like a yawning stretch of space-time continuum. The inside of the airlock was so dark. Jax could easily just return to her quarters and live with her waning smug satisfaction at doing an anonymous good deed for her singular fellow employee.

But then she would be bested by a scratchy sound. Jax huffed out a breath, took a long stride to the wall, and jabbed at the light panel. The inside of the airlock glowed, almost blinding with the LED flush, and Jax squinted before craning her head down to look toward the corner of concern.

There was nothing there.

Jax stepped back, her brow scrunched in confusion. This whole mess of a couple days was really annoying her. Most likely, the recent batch of transients had a few practical jokers in their mix. Maybe it was a thumb-size audio file repeater, playing creepy sounds, stuck to the door they entered when they docked on Station. They were probably snickering at the creeped-out rube who kept their bunk airflow running enough to dissipate the stench of their nightly couplings. All this would clear up once they took off in however many weeks Saunders had mentioned.

Jax growled in distaste at the thought and jabbed at the airlock light to turn it off again. The airlock interior was plunged back into inky blackness, so dark that the interior Station light was suddenly reflected in the glass of the window. A glancing motion in Jax's peripheral made her jolt and she whipped her head around to make sure Saunders had not caught her being weird or anything. Instead, she saw the glance of a shadow, like the indication of someone just beyond the curve of the Station flooring. Like up on Supply the other day.

"Hey!" Jax barked, hoisting her tool belt around her waist and jogging after her target. The shadow didn't react, but it did fade, as if a trick of the light. Jax grumbled and marched after it, just to be sure. She arrived at the section of flooring she swore had been where the person stood, but it was empty.

A flash where she had come from caught her eye and Jax sprinted after it, now letting the full force of her annoyance take center stage.

"I swear, I'm gonna bolt you to the plumbing if I catch you!" she roared.

Back up the arcing Station flooring she found herself between the lift shaft and the cargo airlock again. These jerks were getting a decent laugh at her by this point. There would probably be a video uploaded to some forum on the crappy bandwidth by the end of their stay. It made Jax livid.

A notable thud sounded behind her and Jax whirled around. Her attention snapped to the doors of the lift shaft opposite the largest airlock. The lift should be here on Level 1, awaiting the next supply load, but Jax had stashed it on Level 2 so she could make some modifications. The lift doors should be closed, sealed, but of course Jax always had a way around these systems. Not wanting to lose an opportunity to march some shitty transient prankster straight up to Saunders' door with a note stating, "Exhibit A: shitty transient," Jax jabbed her elbow at the override and the doors cracked apart. She shouldered her way through to squint in the gloom of the lift shaft interior.

It was empty. What the fuck. Jax made one last pass just to be sure she wasn't missing an opportunity to parade some loser around as an example why residents should be confined to their rooms, then angled herself to leave. As she swung her head around, she caught a glimpse of a figure, standing stark still and far too close to her, just to her right, inside the lift.

Despite her desire to maintain the composure of a pissed off mechanic finding people where they didn't belong, Jax screamed and bolted from the lift shaft. Her feet carried her the full ninety degrees back to Security before she could reorient herself. She was irrationally certain there was someone hot in pursuit. Forgetting entirely that Saunders had vacated the office for the Level 4 gym, Jax pounded on the Security Office door.

Somewhere between her relentless assault on the Security Office out of sheer panic, and Jax's level headedness returning, the neighboring door to the Security Officer Quarters slid open. Jax froze, her fist mid-pound and glanced, panicky, down at Saunders who was simply dressed and still holding a towel to dry off her hair from a shower. It must have taken Jax longer than she thought to fix the wiring.

"Jax? What the hell are you doing?" Saunders asked, her face a mix of confusion and concern. Jax glanced at her fist hovering against the door frame, then back at Saunders, before remembering her encounter.

"I think there's someone in the lift shaft!" Jax blurted out.

Predictably, Saunders went from quizzical to action mode. She tossed the towel back into her room and grabbed her flashlight from her belt hanging on the nearby hook. Jax could only step back and out of the way as the shorter woman marched past her.

Jax trailed Saunders back around the curve with hesitation. The open lift doors loomed ahead, like a dark cavern waiting to consume them. Saunders flicked on her flashlight and inched closer to peek inside.

"Did you see who they were?" she asked.

"I wouldn't know who they were even if I did get a good look," Jax quipped.

"Right, right, you just do machines," Saunders replied offhandedly, and she cast her beam into the open lift doors.

"I don't *just* do machines," Jax grumbled under her breath. Saunders didn't reply.

"And you just left these doors open?" she asked.

"No, I opened them, and saw someone..." Why did this sound familiar? Jax swallowed her words and bit her tongue. This was stacking up to be an entire repeat of the night before. It was probably some asshole fucking with them the night before too.

It was therefore not a surprise when Saunders pulled her head back out from the lift shaft and glanced at Jax. "Well, there's no one in there now. You shouldn't leave these open, it's dangerous. We have enough to worry about."

"I didn't leave them open, I..." Jax trailed off and glared at the doors instead. She was getting tired of this game. She stepped forward and shouldered the door closed, sealing it with the control panel. No one but her and Saunders should be able to open it. When she stepped back, Saunders was standing far more casually than Jax felt was acceptable for this tense moment.

"Well, I'm glad you at least came to get me. I'll remind everyone to stay out of the lift shaft, as it poses a safety hazard. If I didn't know better, I'd say we're starting to shape up into a decent team out here," Saunders stated, amicably.

Jax scoffed.

"I just don't want them in my way," she replied. She wanted to add "bleeding everywhere, scaring the shit out of me," but she figured against it. Instead, finding herself back in Saunders' presence, she felt strangely more at ease about it all.

Saunders leaned casually against the—now closed—lift doors. The corner of her mouth quirked up in response.

"I know, I know, 'people are my responsibility' and all. Did you check up on Level 2 like we planned?" she shot back. Jax felt her face flush.

"No, I had some, uh, really important repairs up on Five to take care of," she offered, meekly, suddenly entirely unable to think of a way to mention that she might want company up there. Instead, she countered with, "Did you talk to the residents like *you* planned?"

Saunders actually looked apologetic, which caught Jax off guard.

"Ah, no, I was reviewing the manifests and video data this morning, then ran a scan of recent reports, so I could be sure of who is supposed to be here. I thought I could talk to the Terrestrial Surface Force team about what they might have noticed, but Aviry wasn't in the gym when I checked..." Jax's face had gone blank.

Saunders snorted and hoisted herself back up to standing. She stretched her arms over her head in a manner Jax assumed mitigated any cramps from hefting absurd amounts of weights in the gym upstairs. Saunders held the stretch a moment longer than seemed necessary before turning on her heel and heading back toward her quarters.

Sensing a receding moment, Jax's feet followed after her. What was this new intent she was exhibiting? Her entire modus operandi had been diligently avoiding Saunders to keep from falling into Jax's usual traps. That was how she kept falling from grace: giving in and latching on until it was too late. But here she was, following Saunders back around the bend, away from the jump scares stalking her.

"I would argue you're a long way from 'really important repairs on Level 5' right now," Saunders stated to the curving station corridor ahead of her. She didn't bother looking back to see if Jax was trailing her.

"Just checking on some wiring alerts..." Jax attempted, in self-defense.

"Ah, more important than lighting and trespassing, bloody residents on Two?" Saunders trailed. Jax could hear the smirk in her voice. Being called out made Jax's neck flush. She compensated by rubbing where her mane of hair itched against the only bare skin visible under her coveralls.

"I mean, if you wanted to meet up again about last night, all you had to do was ask," Saunders declared, rounding on Jax. They were back outside her quarters, and Saunders leaned gently against her doorframe.

Jax fidgeted on her feet. She could do this. She could ease off and be amicable. She was a big girl, who had spent years out here ruminating on her failures. Surely, she had learned a thing or two; grown as a person in that time.

The door to Saunders' quarters rolled aside and the Security Officer inclined her head toward the interior, shoulder still leaning on the frame, arms crossed over her chest. Jax tried to avoid staring.

"Or you can just come hang out. It has *got* to be lonely up there on Five." There was a sharp glint in Saunders' eye, like she had made the final move in a chess match. Jax felt her mind go blank at the insinuation. Just last night she was desperate to escape this company and now she was arguing with herself about why it really might not be such a bad idea. Not that Jax wanted to admit that Level 5 had its drawbacks.

"Of *course* its lonely, why do you think I *like* it up there?" Jax heard herself snap. Saunders' eyebrows raised minutely.

"Well, sorry for the assumption. I suppose it is quite fitting of your character," she replied, dryly.

Jax growled, then surprised herself by boldly striding past Saunders and into the Security Officer quarters.

"Maybe you don't know enough about my character," Jax countered, standing square in the entry way and peering over her shoulder at the shorter woman who followed her inside.

Saunders didn't look put off in the least by Jax's entrance, and she let her smile widen as she allowed the door to slide closed behind her.

"Maybe you should tell me more about it then," she replied.

Chapter Six

Where Jax's quarters were a dimly lit nest of mechanical knick-knacks and cluttered tools, Saunders' quarters were the polar opposite. Jax had long since labeled the Security Officer in her head as having far too sunny a disposition to hold the Station role and had used this as an attempt to maintain a level of contempt for her. The state of her quarters only managed to reinforce this supposed character trait, but the contempt was getting hard to muster anymore.

To be clear, Jax had, at no point ever, intended to find herself inside the quarters of the Security Officer for any reason less than this place being the sole source of space station failure. And even then, Jax figured she would just choose to "go down with the ship." But now she found herself standing in a brightly lit, clean and cozy-looking berthing.

"I mean, take a seat Jax, you take up more room standing there like that," Saunders said.

Jax looked at the available seating. Why were there throw pillows? On a space station? She unclipped her tool bet, and let it drop to the floor with a satisfying *thunk* before she tossed the throw pillow off the nearest chair and dropped herself in the seat like a bag of hammers. Saunders seemed unfazed by this brash effort at redecorating. Jax glowered in return, from her new and improved, pillow-less chair as the Security Officer drifted through the room, tossing the damp towel she had been using into a practical looking hamper and re-stashing her flashlight in its holster.

Jax felt a sharp stab of panic at realizing she had been letting her eyes follow the efficiently shaped form of her coworker, and she chose to instead busy herself with scanning the walls. Saunders had pinned up several glossy plastic posters of Earth: sweeping views of nature, animals, all things Jax had willingly left behind.

"Why do you have all these?" Jax indicated to the posters. She was looking at one showing a vibrant sunset over mountains. Saunders paused in her meanderings about her quarters and followed Jax's line of sight.

"I suppose I just like reminders of home. Don't you?" she replied.

"No, I don't need any reminders of that place," Jax responded. She had long since forgiven Ralph of its more terrestrial origins, but otherwise avoided any visuals representations of that planet, or any planet for that matter. But Jax let her vision linger on the poster for a minute more before returning her attention to Saunders. The Security Officer had gotten her minute space in order and had positioned herself into the only other available seat. It made Jax wonder why both her room and this room had two seats at all. It's not like Jax had ever expected company. Had Saunders?

"Right, well, it's nice having you around more…" Saunders trailed off with an air of anticipation. Jax glanced up to make excruciating eye contact and had the sudden urge to re-evaluate her intentions of being here. Right, she probably wouldn't mind having a second set of eyes, and hands, on a search of Level 2, if only she could muster the courage to ask, while still maintaining a shroud of curmudgeonly independence. Once this whole mystery was solved, Jax fully intended to resume cohabitation at arms-length. Unless something else came up. Nothing ever came up.

"You said, 'don't be a stranger,'" Jax quipped, feeling satisfied with her ability to sound aloof.

"Oh, certainly not a 'stranger,' maybe just 'strange,'" Saunders stated, her eyes reflecting the mischievous smirk accompanying that statement.

"Fuck-it, I'll see you later," Jax growled and made a grab for her tools. Even if having backup was enticing, she wasn't in the mood to spend a whole evening getting teased.

"Oh, come on, Jax, you can stick around. I appreciate the company!" Saunders protested.

Jax glared at her but slouched back into her resting place.

"Hey, we barely even got to chat last night. You got to pry into why I took this job, but you never told me; why did *you* take this post?" Saunders asked. She had fixed Jax with a stare that pinned her to the seat.

Jax felt a sinking regret at not taking her exit when she had the chance. This wasn't going in the direction she had intended, and the last thing Jax needed was for her to lose sight of their trajectory. Besides, that little twitch of the corners of Saunders mouth, the one that said she was enjoying this moment, made it really hard for Jax to look away.

"That's not an easy question to answer," Jax responded, her voice faltering from being put on the spot.

"Oh, come on, you asked me, it's only fair!" Saunders protested.

"Ask me something else," Jax countered, her words a little more pleading than she intended.

Saunders cracked a grin. Instead of changing the subject, she narrowed her eyes in a fleeting moment of calculation that should have been another warning to Jax and popped up to peruse a side locker at the base of her bed. She pulled out a bottle of clearly contraband alcohol. Unessential flammable things were prohibited in space. Alcohol was flammable, and Jax was impressed.

Saunders returned to the seat opposite Jax and dropped the bottle and two glasses down between them.

"The thing is, the more you dodge the question, the more I want to know," she said, with a sly grin. Saunders pulled the cap off the bottle and held it out. "Don't leave me hanging, Jax. Here, I guarantee this will help," she said, matter-of-factly.

Jax fixed her with a stare of her own. What good would it be to admonish Station Security for breaking...security protocol? Besides, if Jax was so stressed lately she was seeing and hearing things, maybe a drink was exactly what she needed. She jutted her chin out in a short nod and sat up as Saunders poured out two glasses.

"Cheers," Saunders said, handing the glass back to Jax.

Jax took it and peered inside. It had been years since she had anything like this.

"This is probably a terrible idea," she mumbled under her breath.

"Well then, we can suffer through it together," Saunders replied, taking a long sip.

The Security Officer reclined comfortably in her seat. Jax finally allowed herself a more formal appraisal of who's quarters she was in. Clearly fresh from the showers, Saunders had attired herself in her simple, standard tank top, and her tactically fitted, standard-issued, grey security pants. Saunders propped one bare foot up on the table between them, and Jax realized either she had not put boots back on in her haste to assist Jax's panic, or she had removed them while Jax had been staking claim to the chair. Saunders draped a toned arm across her raised knee. Only at that sight did Jax realize how much she had been staring.

Saunders, seemingly pleased with the attention, lifted her glass in a toast and rephrased her question.

"All right, Engineering. What's the story?"

"Fine," said Jax. She also leaned forward on her knees, closing the gap between them further, as if they were conspiring. But really this was just Jax testing herself. All these years of penance. Maybe she could finally relax and seek out some form of fellowship out here. She focused on the glass she gripped in front of her with her grubby claws, and not the Security Officer's lack of sleeves. Then Jax took a long draw of the liquid and coughed as it burned her throat. It had been so long since she had drunk anything alcoholic, it immediately hit her head with a wash of fuzzy feelings. She hoped this would not end in regret, but she was here, and so, she would play along.

"I came here to escape."

Jax let her eyebrows narrow and a smirk flit across her face. The statement should have come with a sense of foreboding, warning the Station Security Officer that Jax was not a box to be opened. Instead, Saunders snorted into her drink.

"Am I to expect such dramatics for the rest of the night?" she coughed. Jax scowled.

"You asked, don't act disappointed when it comes back to bite you in the ass," Jax countered.

"Counting on it," Saunders laughed. "But, fat lot of help escaping out here if it all ends in whatever creepy, bloody mystery we are currently dealing with." Her arms rippled as she stretched in her seat and took another drink. Jax's mood darkened, especially as she continued to fail to ignore Saunders' more toned assets. So she grit her teeth and leaned back in her seat. Clearly Level 2 inspections would have to wait.

"I made a lot of terrible mistakes when I was younger. Mistakes that left me no options but to run. Have you ever felt like there's nothing left for you in the whole universe but to get as far away as possible?" Jax swallowed hard to cover a lump in her throat. She didn't particularly *like* talking about this.

Saunders sobered up quicker than Jax anticipated. Her face washed sympathetic, and she leaned forward, elbows back on her own knees to consider the glass in her hands. Her fine, shaggy hair fell back across her eyes in a damp, drying curtain.

"Okay yes, I know exactly what that feels like," she said, softly, and her green eyes glanced back up at Jax. It caught Jax by surprise and she felt a funny drop in her gut. She shook her head and looked away.

"So what were you escaping from?" Saunders pressed. Jax could hear the earnest curiosity in her voice, and she covered her nerves with a gulp of her drink.

"I was a pretty promising research assistant once," Jax admitted, into the bottom of her own glass. She shot a glance back over at Saunders, who was now listening with rapt attention, and not a trace of mockery. It sent a pang through Jax's chest, since she had known such attentiveness in her past lives, and knew it rarely led to better outcomes.

"I figured there was more to you than just a mechanic," Saunders replied.

"I mean, I am just a mechanic," Jax protested, "and I was only ever a student. I never got the chance to be more."

"Are you about to tell me that you crossed paths with some illegal science experiment that exiled you to the outer fringes of known deep space?" Saunders asked, letting her voice gain a friendlier tone than the engaging sympathy of her earlier remarks.

Shit, that *did* sound like a really good story. Jax let her eyes lock onto Saunders' green ones as she mulled over how to respond. Across from her, the Security Officer brushed her hair from her eyes and rested the smooth curve of her jaw in her cupped hand as she stared back, imploringly. Why did she have to have such *attractive* ears? Why did Jax have to be so predictably distracted by them?

"No," Jax said, hesitantly, pausing for effect, and also to figure out what the hell she could say next. How could she pour the true, crushing reality of her exile into the minute space between her and the singular object of her ill-placed affections without breaking down every constructed form of protection she had ever built in pursuit of her salvation? Because the truth was, Jax had gotten her heart broken. She had loved the research work she had once done. And it was more than just her place in the world of academia that she had lost.

"'Nuthin' illegal. But it still got me in worlds of trouble." Which was true.

"You already told me you dropped everything you knew and took off for Mars, took up odd jobs and whatever could get you by," Saunders supplied. They had been on the precipice of this very conversation the night before, and Jax had managed to escape. Why had she willingly come back? Some weight drew her forward, like the gravitational pull of an invisible neutron star, beckoning her fingertips toward the bottle. Jax she poured herself another drink.

"I'm not sure what other details of my story are relevant," Jax shrugged, taking another gulp. The burning had subsided.

Saunders let out an exasperated sigh that caught Jax off guard. The officer smirked, rolled her eyes and blew the traitorous shock of hair out of her face again. She reached forward and snatched the bottle from where Jax still held it. Jax felt a jolt as the cool metal of the container left her fingers.

"I'm trying to *connect* with you here Jax," Saunders huffed, as she also poured a refill. "We're both out here, on the municipality's least frequented waypoint station, where we only get data dumps and comms every forty-eight hours, and management inspections once every two years. We know transports are arriving two weeks out. The biggest change I've noticed in a full year of working here, aside from the bloody mystery we have currently, is you hammering on my door all of a sudden. But you lead off with 'I escaped' and then want to leave it at that?" she scoffed. "There's more to this story, I know it."

A fuzzy warm feeling swam up in the back of Jax's mind. Contrary to her every moment of self-loathing, Jax suddenly wanted to laugh at her own absurdity, and wallow in her own gallows humor surrounding her misfortune. She had a drink in her hand, and some amicable company, and this all felt a lot more enjoyable than whatever sad and pitiful fall from grace Jax would have originally narrated.

"I had my research *stolen* from me," Jax offered, indulgently tipping her glass forward in a toast of sorts. Saunders had looked like she was going to continue her tirade, but she paused, faltered, and the corner of her lips curled slightly.

"All right, *that's* more like it. Backstabbing academics! No wonder you are such an abominable mess toward the research teams that land on station!" she inferred. Which was also probably true. Jax despised the evident success of those groups, as well as their ability to flaunt that success while fucking the weeks away waiting for an opportunity to go off and be yet more successful. But she wasn't about to say that to Saunders' face.

"Could you please imagine that I am more complex than that?" Jax hissed, knowing full-well that was probably as complex as she could be. Saunders adopted an expression of mock surprise.

"Oh no Jax, there is nothing complex about you!" she chuckled. "So, who stole your research then?"

That was too much information. Jax wasn't ready to give that detail up. Not here. Not yet. She was nursing an angle of vengeance and revenge. She was trying to spin this story to make herself the martyr she needed to feel she was. If she went down that particular rabbit hole path of her tail, then this whole story crumbled at the foundation. And it was a part of the story Jax so desperately wanted to forget herself.

"Doesn't matter," Jax mumbled. Saunders raised a skeptical eyebrow.

"Doesn't *matter?* Jax, I'm asking you your life story, you tell me you are a disgraced and exiled academic hiding out here and then you tell me it doesn't *matter?*"

"No, I just mean.... You wouldn't understand..." Jax stumbled. But the room got frostier with that statement.

"Try me," Saunders barked, and she looked challengingly at Jax, who felt herself shrink in her seat. "I'm a jarhead, but I'm not an idiot," the Security Officer snapped.

And *this* would be why Jax preferred to hide on Five. She couldn't even have a conversation without just stumbling into being a mess. And now she needed to fabricate an exit from the discomfort of this moment.

"I...I don't mean that you're an idiot—"

"You just think you're smarter than everyone here?" Saunders offered.

"No!" Okay maybe sometimes, Jax thought, tangentially. She squirmed a bit and looked flittingly at the door. When she looked back, Saunders' face had softened again.

"Okay, sorry, so it's a tender subject," Saunders sighed. "So what *can* you tell me?"

Jax couldn't bring herself to talk about it. She had loved her research dearly, ached for what she had lost, and clung to her post as Station Mechanical Engineer because it was the closest she would ever get to her first love. But losing her work wasn't all that had made her run.

"I did try to fight it. I thought I could pick up with a different research team, start over. It was never about the degree, or the prestige. It was about the science. And that was taken from me."

"Can you at least tell me about the science?" Saunders offered.

Even with the discomfort of the previous exchange, Jax smirked before she could stop herself. This part of the story was still enjoyable.

"I was going to build the next big thing in deep space propulsion," Jax admitted clandestinely. She relished the satisfaction she felt from seeing Saunders' eyebrows rise, visibly impressed. Oh, it was such a familiar feeling, impressing girls with her hard work. Too bad she always did a shit job of maintaining that impression. Jax took a long drink to help remind herself that was part of her problem.

"And what does that entail?" Saunders sounded genuinely intrigued, and Jax felt a brief spike of gratitude.

"Ah, well, it's got to do with generating gravitational singularities from magnetic fields...if you take a high powered solenoid..." Jax had scrunched up her face, trying to recall some distant abstract of her thesis, but Saunders coughed across from her.

"Okay, maybe I don't understand *that*," Saunders interjected. Then she laughed. Jax wasn't sure what type of reaction she needed to have now. Did Saunders want her to agree with her? Or defend her?

"Uh I can maybe try to break it down—"

"No, it's okay. I mean, it certainly *sounds* attractive," Saunders mumbled, as she took a sip of her own drink. She then seemed to realize what she had said and raised her eyebrows to hide the brief look of embarrassment Jax didn't miss crossing her face.

"Okay well in layman's terms, I was working on a project that would essentially make, like, a black hole, so space craft fall forward rather than push forward. But it was just a project, and then I crossed paths with the wrong type of people..."

"Sorry," Saunders interrupted again, "Who exactly are the 'wrong type of people' in the research world? Terrorists??" She looked scandalized. Jax was treading carefully now.

"No, just...rivals. I...took a bad gamble, put my trust in the wrong places, and before I knew it, I had no other options but to *run*," Jax admitted forlornly.

"But *why* Jax?" Saunders pressed.

Jax didn't want to say why. So she went with the next closest thing.

"They took my work, and I had *nothing* else to do. Nowhere to go with my career. I needed to, I dunno, get away; carve out something different for myself where my mistakes couldn't follow me. And back on Earth, someone gets to build the next best thing in how to cross the galaxy. I get to hide on the fringes of it, keeping this place 'spinning' with tech that is centuries older than anything I ever dreamed of working on."

"Well, that certainly explains your torrid love affair with the Station's engines, that's for sure," Saunders quipped, and stretched again in her seat.

"It's the closest I feel to my true calling, surrounding myself with the needs and wants of this deep space abomination," Jax replied, glancing dramatically around the confined quarters and the heaving rings of Station beyond.

Saunders had closed her eyes, listening, but was now rocking her head side to side, nodding along, loosening up her neck as Jax went. It made it hard to focus on what details Jax needed to keep under wraps.

"I can certainly understand wanting to feel connected to a true calling, but I didn't realize that deep space engine design was so cutthroat. Why couldn't you have stayed on Mars?" she asked, cracking an eye to survey Jax.

"Because my mistakes follow me, apparently," Jax shrugged. Saunders regarded her now, both eyes open, eyebrows knit together in confusion. Jax made a point of not looking in the other woman's direction.

"Your mistakes of crossing the wrong people? They followed you here?"

"No.... I mean I just kept making more mistakes..."

"You kept crossing the wrong people?"

Saunders *had* been playing obtuse now. Jax sighed, exasperated.

"No, I just, kept...trusting people, and letting my guard down. It just pushed me further and further away." Jax stated, hoping it would be enough.

"Then I guess this *was* how far you needed to run to hide from those mistakes?" Saunders asked, gently. Jax heaved another sigh and glanced back toward the table. Saunders was already holding the bottle out to her.

"Yeah, this seemed to be it. I tried a few deep space transports, a few hopper worlds, but this is the only place I have been able to really find the protection I need," Jax admitted, pouring more of the clear and rancid smelling liquid into her glass. Despite the burn of the alcohol, Jax caught a hint of something more pleasing, and realized it was probably whatever soap Saunders had used. The thought mixed strangely with the added liquor in her system.

"Odd then, that this place suddenly might be less welcoming," Saunders mused pensively.

"What?" Jax stumbled, being pulled from sorting how she felt about the allure of Saunders' soap.

"Just that there is definitely something weird going on here. You said so yourself last night, that you haven't encountered anything like this: injured residents, secrecy, violence..."

"Honestly," Jax started, knowing full well she wasn't going to be completely honest, "I have a feeling it's just some of your residents pulling pranks on me. I know they have it out for me!"

At this, Saunders gave out a long and gratuitous groan as she hoisted herself up from her seat. Jax, surprised at the sudden motion, leaned back and away in her chair, to keep an eye on the trajectory of the energetic blond in her company.

"Here we go again, Jax. It's you and the damned residents. If this place is the best protection you can get across the whole universe, why are you still so pissed off at them all the time? They're just passing through, why can't you just let them be?" She side-stepped around her chair and stared out the trapezoidal window in her berthing to the endless night beyond.

"I *do* leave them be, they just keep getting in my way!" Jax protested. But Saunders wasn't listening, not as far as Jax could tell.

"I won't discount that maybe there is a simple explanation for all this mystery, Jax, but I can't deny that it's freaking me out," Saunders admitted. Jax didn't think she was a simple mystery. "I filed a message to Station Management. I know they won't get it for a couple day cycles, but I at least needed to follow protocol."

Oh, right. The *real* mystery. Jax instantly felt herself get grumpy.

"What the fuck, Saunders. I can handle whatever this tin can throws at me. It's my responsibility, I don't need Station Management's support. They're useless anyway."

Saunders tilted her head back over her shoulder to regard Jax from the porthole. A pale blue, almost ultraviolet light flickered, barely comprehensible across her face, and Jax couldn't tell if it came from inside the Station or outside. Must be inside. There was nothing out here but the endlessly arcing pin pricks of stars too far away to count. Saunders gave an impatient sigh.

"Don't worry Jax, you have at least a month to fix your precious station before Management can do a damned thing about it. Besides," she turned her face back to the window, "this is supposedly a 'people problem,' which is *my* responsibility." She said this almost forlornly, and Jax thought, for a fleeting moment, that if she was a better teammate, she could have helped Saunders realize she didn't need the help of some distant bureaucrat. But then Jax caught a glimpse of the shape of Saunders neckline, starting at a point just behind her left ear and trailing down to a muscular shoulder, and all thoughts about how she could improve the situation vanished.

Well fuck. Jax was drunk. What the hell did she think she was doing here?

It was uncomfortably silent for several minutes. Jax felt the wave of fuzzy drunkenness swim around her. She didn't have a response handy to stave off Saunders' reasoning for contacting management. At least Saunders was right. They wouldn't even be getting a response for days, or even weeks. And even then, what would they have to report? The pranksters were gone? The Station continued to spin? It's not like Management expected anything less.

"Well, Jax, I'm sorry for the heartache your past life brought you. And whatever else brought you here," Saunders intruded on Jax's thoughts. Jax snapped her attention back to the window. Saunders had her back to it now and her arms spread out on the ledge as she regarded Jax, curled over herself in the chair.

"Pshh, what do you know about heartache," Jax quipped, drunkenly, before she realized it was a shitty thing to say. The green flair that sparked in Saunders' eyes confirmed Jax might have crossed a line.

"Plenty, you ass," the Security Officer replied, deadpan.

Jax had already shot herself in the foot and had spent half the evening trying to not eye up the other woman in her presence, so she figured she might as well press onward.

"None from up on Level 4?"

Saunders leveled Jax with a stare that pinned her to her seat. Her hair had dried enough now to look soft and fluffy where it fell in her eyes again.

"Jax, no one has *passed through* this Station that has even remotely caught my attention. But I don't linger on the details of who is matched with who up there. You do." At this, Saunders gave Jax an appraising look, starting at Jax's grungy, unlaced work boots, dragging up her wiry slouched frame, and boring into Jax's own eyes with her searing green stare.

It was unmistakably a look of intent, and Jax realized she probably should be leaving. There were no Stations further away than this. Saunders broke the stare and turned back to the window. Jax shook the drunken buzz that was now fueled by some other source of adrenaline and rose to her feet. The door was right behind her, but the window was closer. And Jax's feet were not agreeing with her.

"Look, I don't trust people anymore. No one has given me a reason to trust them in the ten years since I left all that behind me. And I trust myself even less," Jax reasoned, almost pleadingly, as she stepped up to the window alongside Saunders. The contraband bottle and two glasses sat empty behind them.

"That's bleak," Saunders replied, and turned her head to face Jax. The faint, strange, ultraviolet hue returned, but Jax was already associating it with the contrast it made across Saunders' soft features.

"Bleak? It's my whole existence. I'll let you know when someone proves to me otherwise," Jax mumbled, her words suddenly jumbled together. "It's safer for me not to let anyone else near me."

"Well, I'll be honest, that sucks," Saunders stated simply.

Jax winced. She leaned against the window, considering what her next response would be, feeling more and more like she didn't care how much closer she got to Saunders in this moment. But Saunders suddenly bounded away, leaving Jax propped strangely against the berthing wall at an awkward angle, musing to no one in particular. Jax pursed her lips in annoyance, both at herself and the other woman.

"Right, well I guess I can't change your ability to trust anyone. Backstabbing academic elites and getting chased out of your own solar system are pretty brutal. But at least I can rely on you doing your damnedest to keep this place running!" Saunders called out, as she started rummaging in another locker.

Jax dipped her head and attempted to leisurely turn so her back was at a more comfortable resting posture against the lumpy outer wall. She eyed the short blond from across the small distance of the berthing, suspicious of what Saunders might produce next. How many bottles of swill did she have stashed away in here?

"Just figured you deserved a fair warning. I'm a mess," Jax admitted, smugly. Drunkenly.

"Right. A mess. Well, not that I haven't been enjoying this revelatory experience, but let's lighten things up then, why don't we?" Saunders announced, with a mischievous air to her voice, snapping Jax's attention from her reverie.

Saunders popped up from her spot holding an incredibly battered and ancient music player. It was the kind that stored and played music data files, as opposed to whatever digital archive might exist on a tablet or within the computer system. Jax winced. Of *course,* the inherent nemesis of every fuse on Level 1 was older than the Station itself.

"This thing was acting up earlier, but I think I managed to get it humming again," Saunders replied, assessing the power connection. "Humming" was one way to describe the cacophony that tiny ancient sound demon could emanate.

Jax must have been making a face, because Saunders let out a clear and hearty chuckle, and cocked her head to the side, regarding where Jax leaned against the window.

"You know, trust issues aside, you don't have to stay pissed at the universe for every waking moment of your life," she laughed.

"I'm not pissed at the universe. The universe wouldn't care. I'm just getting a good look at my Station electrical system's public enemy number one. Why do you even *have* that thing?" Jax countered.

"Because everyone needs *something* to keep themselves sane out here," Saunders replied. And Jax couldn't fault her for that.

Saunders clunked the battered machine down on the table and nearly tripped over the wiring as she maneuvered to the more open part of the room. Jax's arm instinctually twitched in an attempt to catch the other woman, but Saunders caught herself and bent over the display readout to see what tunes were queued up.

"Ah, yeah, this one is a good one!" she grinned at Jax and hit play with a wink.

It only took three chords and Jax was groaning.

"Saunders, this song is so *old!* Why are you obsessed with music from five centuries ago?" Jax moaned.

"You *really* don't keep good track of the times out here, do you?" said Saunders, already cranking her arms to another invisible guitar solo. "This is a cover. And besides, how do you know I'm 'obsessed' with it?"

Jax smirked. She could answer that question without incriminating herself in how much she managed to pay attention to the Security Officer's affairs.

"Because it pounds an Earth reminiscent headache into my brain whenever I'm within a level and a half of the Security Office," Jax growled over the drum solo. "And I just told you I have no fond memories of Earth!" But this was a new experience, being able to openly appreciate how much Saunders was enjoying her awful playlist, as opposed to covertly watching from the door frame, or from the gap in the ceiling panels while she was fixing conduit over the gym on Level 4...

"Your loss then," Saunders shrugged over her shoulder. She was bouncing around with more than enough energy for the both of them. She seemed to enjoy having an audience. She finished her solo act and suddenly turned to Jax in full force, closing the distance between them.

Jax played stubborn, letting some internal argument wage within herself. This was her precipice; her final stand of defiance. She had come here, chasing some ghost of a longing desire to give into needing human interaction, at the behest of needing to prove she was no longer the trash heap she had been in her youth. She should be able to dance with a cute coworker and not suffer the consequences beyond that.

Not that Jax would give in willingly. She forced herself to be hauled, physically, from where she leaned. It conveniently required Saunders to wrap her hands around her arm. This might all be okay. Maybe Saunders was right, and Jax could lay off the disdain. Maybe only a little.

Of course it happened the next song that revved up was one Jax actually knew and liked. A mix of lowered inhibitions, poured over the most successful human interaction Jax had sustained in years, meant her body moved before she could stop it.

Jax was gangly, but that didn't mean she was uncoordinated. Ungraceful, sure, but she had a few decent dance moves stored in some dusty corner of her brain, saved only for days off after college exams, or drunken evenings on a trash-heap of a deep space waypoint Station halfway between nothing and less-than nothing with a coworker she could only *sorta* remember she was supposed to keep her distance from. By this point though, Jax wasn't so sure she needed to keep her limbs under control, and the drunk feeling gave her the confidence to bust a move without being self-conscious. Besides, the more Jax dusted off her decade old rhythm, the more Saunders seemed encouraged to dance closer.

The chairs got kicked out of the way and the table was shifted to the side as they stomped around to some band that had been dead for maybe a couple centuries, until Jax doubled over wheezing from the cardio workout. Saunders kept dancing, pausing only to nudge Jax's shoulder to say, "come on keep going."

"Sorry, I don't work out regularly like you do. If it's not lifting power coils, I'm not lifting it," Jax replied, panting, not even aware of what she was saying anymore. Her head was swimming from the exertion and the alcohol.

"I'm just thrilled you've noticed."

Saunders relaxed her energetic display and clicked the music over to something that was less up-tempo. Jax stood up, and found Saunders used the opportunity of Jax's shoulders being lower than hers to wrap her arms around Jax's neck.

Jax leaned back against Saunders' arms in a fruitless attempt at distance, standing at her full height above the Security Officer. But it was almost comical now. What else had she expected after a night like this? It was a final fleeting moment, where Jax could only distantly remember whatever had brought her here. Only vaguely could she recall all her reasons for isolating herself; for keeping her distance. All those reasons made *such* good sense. But the alcohol was making things warm and fuzzy, and Saunders was fixing her with that stare again, the one that accompanied the slight curl to the edges of her mouth, so Jax didn't back away. Her hands had somehow found themselves bracing at Saunders' hips and failing in the matter. They were apparently swaying to the beat now like it was some grade-school dance.

"You know, it's been hard on this Station," Saunders said, looking up at Jax through sandy brown lashes, her eyes heavy lidded, her hips closing the gap between them with each sway to the music.

Jax kept her mouth shut. She was dangerously close to saying something dumb, so she would wait for Saunders to say something just as stupid. Instead, Saunders' fingers seemed to gently twine their way into the longer hair at the base of Jax's neck.

"I was hoping for at least the camaraderie I had while in the service. Especially when I saw you for the first time. I've had a hard time adjusting to the idea that was not going to be the case. I actually considered short touring to get back to some normalcy," Saunders admitted.

Jax could understand that. This Station, while her salvation, sucked for anyone who wasn't trying desperately to pretend that life was the worst option of several outcomes. Saunders' face was close enough now for Jax to make out the small details: the round shape to her jawline, her upturned nose, the adorable little jut of her chin, the relaxed arch of her eyebrows, the smooth invitation of her flushed cheeks. She smelled warm and soft, and equally intoxicating as the drinks they had shared earlier. Jax felt herself slipping. Her grip on the precipice was failing.

"There's some weird shit out here, Jax," Saunders stated matter-of-factly, as she tossed her hair out her eyes again. "But you can be pretty cool when you aren't trying to piss everyone off. It might not be so bad after all, having to figure this all out, with you on station," she mused, now letting the soft curves of her chest make contact with Jax's own. Her whole body felt excruciatingly warm where it pressed against Jax. Warm enough to ignite so many distant memories. Jax managed to stay mute, but her body was saying more than she had ever intended.

"Listen, I know you have this whole thing where you pretend to not care, and act like nothing around you affects you. You've made it clear, you just don't like people, or trust them. But, I suppose it's worth it to say I'm here, taking a genuine interest in you; that I appreciate your company," Saunders concluded.

Their hips were now pressed together, and Saunders' hand had dropped to Jax's jawline, along with her gaze. Jax felt a lump in her throat, a heat in her chest, and a blaze spreading between them. She also felt her hands softening on Saunders' waistline, her fingers fiddling with the band of grey tactical pants, and the soft strip of skin beneath them. The spinning buzz from the drinks had successfully eaten into her resolve.

This insufferably cute, fit, sunny-side-up, little ex-soldier was too damn close, and making herself tantalizingly closer. Jax only faintly now remembered her pledge to keep her distance, but Saunders was suddenly saying all the right things, and Jax could smell her sweat and feel the warmth radiating off her from the dancing she had been doing. And now Jax wanted to ignore any of the past year or so of desperately trying to put as much space between her and Saunders as was physically possible on a remote space station. Here she was, opening her damn mouth.

"This is wildly unprofessional," Jax murmured. *Such* a romantic. But Saunders was closer than her willpower had strength for.

Before Jax knew it, they were kissing, and the fuzzy blur of whatever contraband alcohol they had consumed was running in circles around them, mixing with the aching familiarity of human contact they were both desperate to feel. Saunders' lips were soft and eager, and her hands were exactly as capable as Jax had imagined they might be.

Her objections forgotten, the last barrier now far beyond reach, Jax let herself fall. In the end, the bed was right there, and the moment was too definitive to turn down. So Jax relented and gave in to all her old mistakes all over again.

Chapter Seven

Jax woke up with a headache that could only have been brought on by the excruciating process of the first alcohol she had consumed in years leaving her system. It could also have stemmed from the dawning realization she was not in her own room, not in her own bed, and the naked arm of the Station Security Officer was thrown possessively low across her hips. It was a headache that told her she had absolutely fucked up her calm and comfortable Station status quo and that was clearly not all she had fucked. And all because she dared to think she, and anyone else out there, could possibly have been anything other than exactly what she had known them to be.

Jax was *not* better than her past self. She was probably worse. And she needed to get out.

She spent the next several minutes strategizing her escape when a less elegant one presented itself. A mid-level alarm blared in the quarters, the same alarm Jax would have heard if she had spent the night in her own damn bunk and not between the legs of her only colleague.

"WARNING! Outboard rotational engine failure, two-hundred and fifty degrees," the alarm message flashed on the console screen near the Security officer's door.

That was not an insignificant problem. Whatever possible nightmares had plagued them the past few nights were incomparable to the dangers associated with the Station failing. The alarm also woke up Saunders, who blearily swept her hair back from her face to look around the room, thus freeing Jax from her grasp. She seemed to take a moment to absorb that Jax was still there, presently naked in her bed. But Saunders' reaction was less panicked and more "situation status" assessing. Jax used this opportunity to bolt.

"I uh, I need to go get that," she mumbled, over a tongue that seemed damaged from alcohol and overuse. She scrambled for the clothes she could find, failed to locate a sock, and settled for a bare foot in her work boot. Saunders sat up in bed.

"If you give me a minute, I can go with you. This one sounds important," she said groggily.

"No!" Jax was a little too forceful in her reply, but panic was blooming in her chest, and she needed to get out of there. Saunders seemed to wake up at the response.

"Jax, it's okay—"

"No. Nope. Not okay. No, this is the engine system that keeps gravity running, 'keeps us spinning,' so definitely something I need to go work on. Right now. Alone."

She was shrugging her coveralls over her shoulders and edging toward the door, tripping over a displaced chair. Saunders shifted in her bunk, the blankets falling, and forcing Jax to look anywhere but the figure in the room with her.

"Okay," Saunders said evenly.

Jax was looking pointedly at the wall for her tool belt, or whatever else she had brought with her to this infernal place. She assumed Saunders was scrutinizing her with the heavy judgement and knowledge that Jax was about to do exactly what she had disclosed as her pattern of behavior: running from her mistakes. The door latch couldn't open fast enough, then Jax was standing alone in the hallway. Nevermind spooky, creepy shit, devious resident pranks, and whatever failures the Station might currently face; it was all incomparable to the massive amount of regret Jax was suddenly shouldering.

She only had one option really, and that was to go fix the damn outboard rotational engine. And of course, Jax was without the right tools. She had, quite stupidly, not thought to bring her engine fixing A-game with her on her apparent mission to bed the Security Officer. She set off at a jog down the corridor. At least the two-hundred-and-fifty-degree engine was at the opposite end of the arc, putting some distance between herself and the security quarters. Though at this point, a universe might not be enough distance.

The outboard rotational engines were placed every ten degrees along the Station exterior perimeter. That meant there were thirty-six in total, set up on alternating series of dual redundant strings. At any one time, a single string was in use, firing eighteen engines, at every other location. If one string failed, the second string would turn over and keep the Station spinning as a backup.

The engines were low-thrust producing, magnetoelectric-plasma driven, old technology, but reliable and easily maintainable. The Station really did not require any external work. Fuel was stored in segments between major and minor airlocks around the perimeter of Level 1, with regular access ports, and flow restrictor valves accessible from the Station interior. Each engine was installed on a support structure surrounded by its own airlock. If one failed, the Station Mechanical Engineer needed to only pop the correct floor hatch, pull the engine into its airlock, open the back access, and perform repairs as needed. Once done, the Engineer would close the floor hatch and lower the engine to the Station ring exterior.

The Station Mechanical Engineer was currently cursing excessively under her breath for her overwhelming lack of judgment.

Jax reached the two-hundred-and-fifty-degree engine and tapped furiously at the control panel to start the process of drawing the engine in from its location on the external circumference. As she waited for the airlock indicator to turn green, she mused over the millions of shortcomings she had revealed and the absolute trash heap she had gotten herself into.

"Absolute fucking idiot," she swore to herself. "You had one job here, and you *liked it*. And then you had to go and make a fucking mess of things. You didn't learn your lesson with the first time you screwed around out here and this time it's your goddamn *coworker*. You can't just watch this one leave in three weeks. What the *fuck* were you thinking? It took you years. *Years* to get to this level of life comfort. All you needed to do was stay the fuck away from stupid mistakes and you would have been fine."

The airlock turned green, and Jax hauled the floor panel up and away, taking a certain satisfaction in the strain of the physical labor. The exertion was her penitence. The call of Station duty was her only escape route. She dropped into the engine well to look over the damage.

There was not any clear issue with the engine. This was good on the one hand, because an impact or damage from space debris would mean a complete part replacement, which they had precious few of. But on the other hand, it meant troubleshooting the engine, which was a more arduous process.

Jax hopped up from the engine well and over to a maintenance hatch. She might have been without her primary tools, but enough years on this Station had taught her to stash essentials on every level where she might need them. She pulled a multimeter and a standard wrench set from the panel and returned to the engine well.

The name of the game now was hunting for where the engine's power might be getting diverted. It was a long, tedious process requiring checking and rechecking electrical continuity. On any other day, Jax would have hated it, but today she was exhaustingly grateful. Dammit, she needed a shower.

Working through the endless copper coils that powered the engine's electromagnets, Jax had time to ruminate on her choices. She was livid at herself, of course, for slipping up and falling back to old habits. It had been stupid of her to think she could ever be someone who just casually hung out with anyone she was remotely interested in. True to her character, she was a clingy, worthless mess, who was only good at setting fire to her surroundings.

But the thing was, she was also mad at Saunders.

Sure, Jax had given in, but Saunders had charmed her with her laugh, and plied a tale from Jax with cheap swill that made it so easy to just slip into terrible old habits. Then Saunders had been so fucking *welcoming* and *understanding* and, what the fuck was she doing with that damned contraband alcohol?!

But, even in the fog of a hangover, Jax knew every misstep leading to their ending last night. She let herself get drawn down to Level 1, after her successful escape the night before, then in her moment of being spooked by *nothing*, she had been *weak*. She had run right into Saunders' trap, and Saunders had taken her in smiling. Then, Jax had shown Saunders even an ounce of vulnerability and Saunders had used it like an invitation.

For the life of her, Jax couldn't think of a single reason why Saunders would have any particular interest in her. Hadn't Jax made the most valiant effort in showing Saunders just how much Jax was a bad idea? And, oh fuck, those *dance* moves. Jax felt her face burn with shame at the memory surfacing through her hungover fog. What other *atrocious,* uninhibited moves had she sprung on Saunders? Well, besides the obvious of course, though Jax was sure she had made a fool of herself in *that* regard as well.

This was why Jax couldn't trust anyone. She had let her guard down and entrusted Saunders with just the slightest variant of her story. Jax had left out the heartache and the real source of betrayal that fueled her exodus, and even *that* wasn't enough to tell Saunders to stay away. And it hurt. Because if Saunders had been serious. If Saunders had wanted to prove that she was different from every other person who had hurt Jax along the way, then why did she have to lead them into bed together? Why couldn't she have let them get there at a more natural pace? They had hardly spoken to each other in over a year, and in three nights, they had said to hell with boundaries, and gone straight to knocking boots. If Saunders had cared. If she had really, truly, been listening, then she would have noticed that what Jax needed was time.

But instead, Jax had been seduced. Again. And Jax only knew one way to deal with that anguish. Run.

There were only so many options available to her now. Running back to Saunders was not one of them. In fact, so far from it, it wasn't even worth considering. That left the remaining options. First, that she would immediately request a transfer off Station. She could easily find herself on that research transport leaving in three weeks.

It was such a tempting thought that after all these years of Station dwelling, Saunders would awake one morning to the knowledge that she had been the power to drive Jax from her home. And Jax would be gone. Saunders would have no way of knowing where she went and be left with the knowledge that she had been the catalyst of a new Jax exodus.

Or, alternatively, Jax could double down, and become as aggravatingly horrendous as she could possibly muster, really laying the vitriol on thick. She had spent the year trying to avoid this by keeping Saunders at arm's reach. Maybe she just hadn't been trying hard enough. And this was *her* home after all, why *should* Jax leave? Instead, she could make such a hostile work environment that she hastened Saunders' motivation to short-term her Station contract. Essentially, Jax would drive Saunders clear of the Space Station by being a complete, and utterly unforgivable, ass.

Neither of these options stuck well with Jax. She loved her role here, and the comfort she felt in it. This Station *was* home. But she also knew she just no longer had the energy to be so excruciatingly terrible anymore.

Besides, she *liked* Saunders. That was the worst part. And she couldn't deny that some small part of her had really wanted last night to happen, and maybe, happen again. Perhaps some distantly forgotten part of her brain had thought that, given the time she needed, things might have developed further between them. And it had been nice, for one, brief instance, that Jax felt she had someone to call on when things started getting *truly* weird.

It was such a pipe dream though. No one ever stuck around, or wanted any more than to use her, after they got what they were after. Jax didn't think she could fathom the inevitable rejection and pain of seeing Saunders move on to something far, far better than her.

A slow and steaming bitterness rolled over her. She needed to seek further isolation, before the Station residents started their daily roaming cycle. She needed to solve this engine issue and get back to her closed off level.

The engine was playing coy in a way that made Jax's fury bubble over. She found herself kicking the side wall of the airlock, wanting desperately to knock the life back into the engine, but knowing it was far too delicate for such abuse.

As the emotional magnitude of her stupid, careless choices from the night before began to eclipse her ability to function at her one and only job, Jax found herself huddled against the back wall of the engine well, knees pulled to her chest, eyes stinging with tears.

She was supposed to have grown in her solitude, developed better self-control, secured her ability to resist these types of mistakes. After all was said and done, Jax hadn't even been able to survive a single day of working in close proximity to Saunders, before she was felled in the hunt.

Jax lost the fight against the wave of anger and resentment, and let herself cry, hidden and shaking in the engine well, too overcome with her own failure to think clearly.

* * *

Jax gave herself twenty minutes to wallow in her misery before she tightened up her resolve, squared her shoulders and went back to the engine coils. One more pass over the main coil showed a slight short, diverting current back into the engine body and not fully though the coils. That would weaken the magnetic field. A quick patch.

Jax returned from the maintenance locker with the repairs. Another twenty minutes later and the engine seemed operational again. Jax felt satisfied with the fix, and she was back at the control panel lowering the engine back out into service.

She was about to leave when she saw another red engine alert pop up on the maintenance screen. A second engine, same string. These engines were robust enough that it was unlikely two would fail in succession like this. Jax stared at the engine failure location for a minute longer than necessary.

This might not have been a small short after all. That wouldn't really account for the engine failure. Two engines failed in succession on a single string meant the system redundancy was at risk, and it also meant the problem might be more centralized. That meant the problem wasn't in the engines themselves, but the core.

A strange light backlit the panel for her, causing her to turn around. The Station windows had a sudden odd glow to them. Jax stepped over to the glass.

Station windows were several inches thick and used sparingly. Each point was a potential weakness, having to be regularly inspected. The thickness of the glass distorted the starlight from the other side, though in reality there was nothing much to see usually. The flash happened again, like it was just outside her vision. Jax swore under her breath, her previous emotional stress being replaced with other concerns.

"That better not be an arc at the core," she whispered. An arc near the core would cause all kinds of electrical issues. And this Station was not exactly young. She needed to spend the time at its heart, focusing on what might be ailing it, while ignoring what might be afflicting her own.

Jax returned to the maintenance panel and cancelled the second engine failure notification. It would send out alerts, both to her, and to Saunders, if ignored. Then she would need to talk to Saunders to explain why she was ignoring an engine failure, and Jax *was not* ready for any conversations with Saunders right now. Better to just cancel the alert, and any other pending, so she could take the time to look at this in peace.

Jax sealed up her maintenance access panel, secured the screen, and did one last sweep of the area. The prospect of disappearing into the Station core for some indeterminate amount of time seemed like the best compromise to her ever-straining heartstrings.

She heard the quiet shuffle and low vocal intonations of the first Station residents making their way down on pass number one of their daily, boredom-driven pilgrimage. Or perhaps they were bound to plant more jump scares to creep Jax out and force her hand at even worse mistakes. Either way, that was her cue. She found one of her quick access routes back up to the top levels and slipped inside.

As she started her climb upward, she swore she once again heard another skittering sound. Her self-absorbed, internalized loathing meant she really didn't care.

Chapter Eight

The Station core was the main power hub of the whole structure and operated on self-reciprocating design concepts. If the Station was a wheel, the core was the axis on which it turned; gyroscopically stabilized to counter resist the Station rotation. It used a nuclear reactor source to provide jump-start power to the Station's outboard rotational engines, but as the Station exterior rings rotated, the core's counter rotation efforts acted as a massive stator, converting that rotational energy back into stored energy to eventually be sent back to the engines. It was not a perfect machine, but it was damn efficient.

There also wasn't any gravity in the core. Jax was grateful for this, especially after an unplanned and unfortunate night in the more punishing gravity of Level 1. No wonder Saunders was in such good shape—no, Jax did *not* need reminders about that. She needed to focus on her Station's needs.

The only way she could run full diagnostics on a possible failing engine string was from the core itself. Jax could pull Station reports from any terminal, but the core served as the central hub of every connection, which made it the only place she could track each engine on its respective string and isolate a potential failure.

She had to access the core through the narrow Station support strut, up on Level 5. There were four of them but only one was made for human access. The other three were designed for electrical routing, and Jax had drawn the line at turning those particular routes into anything other than their intended purpose.

Jax stormed down the short stretch from her tool storage to the main core access strut, brandishing a current reader, a portable diagnostic machine, and her primary tool belt. Three steps from the port frame, she walked through what felt like a tangle of sticky webbing. She stopped dead in her tracks and sputtered, waving her hands in her face. A skittery echo seemed to patter down the wall behind her sending a jolt down Jax's spine.

Jax flipped her hair out of the way and spun around. There was nothing there, of course, but it had effectively pulled her from her moment of self-loathing. Her face clear, Jax scanned the walls and floor of her isolated Level 5. The corridor was clear. No ethereal spiderwebs could be found. She really needed to cut her hair again sometime soon.

This was stupid. Jax had spent so much of her life stubbornly loving this distant outpost. In one night, she had gone from feeling comfortable in her home, to jumping at every small noise and shift in lighting, then jumping into bed with the first person who had talked to her extensively in a decade. Jax needed to get a fucking grip. She resumed her mission toward the Station core, but felt a tap on her left shoulder. She stopped and spun. Nothing. Another tap, now down by her right leg. Jax looked down at the leg of her coveralls spilling over the untied laces of her work boot.

Jax stood motionless in the corridor, waiting. A sudden feeling like several gigantic spindly legs scuttling up her back threw her into a flail. She yelped and spun several times on the spot, attempting to shake off whatever was on her back. She tossed her hands over her head, in some desperate form of self-protection, and slammed her back hard into the nearest wall. She braced herself for the impending crunch of whatever assailant was busy spinning a web from her backside, but nothing came. Instead, Jax managed to briefly knock the wind from herself, and she squeezed her eyes shut while she regained her focus. A faint skitter snapped them open again, and she looked, panicked, from either end of the empty corridor to the other.

"This is some grade-A bullshit. I have *got* to lay off the coffee, *and* the women," Jax bellowed to the empty surroundings. "None of this would be happening if I had just gotten a normal night's sleep!" She forced the bravado to buoy her spirits.

Jax shook off the itchy feeling and dove at the access strut ladder. Better to get to a place she knew she was safe than waste any more time where her imagination, and worse yet, her feelings, could catch up with her. She hit zero gravity about halfway up and floated into the Station core access.

"All right Lady. Are you going to tell me where it hurts?"

Jax, of course, never expected the Station to answer; she wasn't crazy. After all, it *was* just a machine, with flat-toned, pre-programmed alerts and notifications. It's not like it had intelligence. But Jax would have gone mad years ago if she never spoke to *anyone*. She found that at least engaging with the Station kept her dialogue skills from getting too rusty. And in her opinion, while the Station might not be imbibed with an artificial intelligence, it still had *personality*. She did, however, keep their little chats to the safety of Level 5. She didn't need anyone thinking she had finally lost it out here on the edge of the universe.

"Just, don't take it personal I left you alone for the night. I wasn't...expecting that...either." Jax might have said that line to herself, and not the steadily spinning, deep space monolith surrounding her. She reached out to touch the core wall. "You know I could never leave you, don't worry about that. I'm sorry I let the assholes living down there mess with you." The words of affection were her own little joke.

The central core diagnostic lab was triple the width of Jax's shoulders, but roughly thirty feet in length. It was made of deep-space-grade titanium alloys, overlayed in several locations with reinforced composites. The cylindrical length housed multiple points of access to various vital Station systems. Bolted and hinged panels hid swaths of wiring and network connections. Breakout panels with connector ports and digital screen readouts allowed Jax rapid access to diagnostic tests. Gently blinking and alternating indicator lights gave the constant impression the Station was thinking, processing, and pondering on the minor happenings within her rings. Long, slithery coils of power conduits ran from one end to the other, connecting to the interior via heavy, ungainly metal clamps. A throbbing, almost subconscious hum filled the confined space, emanating from the massive bulk of the Station rings rotating around the center stator hub. The control systems on the lower levels were merely ports into a fraction of the Station's capabilities. The numerous automated and synchronized systems allowing such a behemoth to survive on the tender love and care of one singular Jax, all functioned fluidly and efficiently because of the powerhouse that was the core. This was the beating heart of her Station.

A pressure suit was tacked to the wall near the entrance, which should be worn regularly when running core operations. Jax only ever suited up in it if she planned to play with the wiring or drop the core down to vacuum. The suit made for a tight turn around, but without it she could comfortably drift up and back as need be. It let her get a bit more up close and personal with the core, which she preferred. It felt better that way.

"Two engines, ma'am. Why are you dropping two engines? You planning something?" Jax whispered to the multitude of access and electrical panels surrounding her. She pulled back a wall covering, exposing the breakout box behind it she could use for checking electrical continuity.

This was a welcome escape for Jax. She could stay here, easily for hours—days even; her absurd haircut tied back and out of her face, an assortment of snacks to keep her from starving, and a communications panel she could turn off permanently. The hum of the behemoth rotating about her was a comfort that could drive away every irrational feeling she had been battling thus far this morning.

"Basic diagnostics babe. You won't feel a thing." Jax pulled out her current reader and plugged it in to start reading out electrical coil potential between connections. "Just, whatever you need. As long as I can just stay up here with you and she can't come find me."

Her intent was to thoroughly pull all Station diagnostics, run a full restart sequence on the redundant engine string, and hide out as long as was necessary for Saunders to forget they had ever fallen into bed together. Then Jax planned to continue hiding for however long it took for her to forget her serious lapse in judgement. She estimated at least a week, though she figured it would take more than a month.

In reality Jax only lasted about three hours before she remembered that snacks, work, weightlessness, and self-depreciating hatred aside, she still needed a toilet like a normal human. Jax was mid-diagnostic pull on the left string ninety-degree engines she knew would take a longer period of time to run, so she reigned herself in and drifted back down to the gravity of Level 5 to relieve herself. Dammit if she had really forgotten the affect alcohol had on her. The Station spinning didn't help either, as she had been fighting off the urge to hurl all day.

Jax cautiously poked her head from the access strut to examine her route to relief. The corridor was, as should be expected, still free of strange ghostly spider webs, and abnormally sized web spinners. Jax willed herself to relax in the Station she called home, rid her overactive imagination of absurd fanciful thoughts, and allowed herself to exit the strut.

Jax was just about to re-enter the core access strut, however, when Saunders walked up. This time the whole back of Jax's neck pricked with heat, rather than the ethereal tap of imaginary spiders. This was *not* part of the escape plan. Saunders looked like she was trying to present a peace offering to an eldritch terror.

"Jax, wait," she said, as Jax had taken one look and made a beeline for the access port to the core access strut. Jax froze, one foot on a ladder rung, arms already reaching up a level. She let her shoulders sink in resignation.

"I have work to do," Jax offered, somewhat pitifully. She hoped it was enough for Saunders to give up. It wasn't.

"I know, and I'm not trying to get in the way of that, just…" Saunders had trailed off. Jax did not want to turn around to look at her. She instead pulled her hands off the rung of the access ladder and leaned back against the back wall of the strut. She had maybe ten minutes before the diagnostic readout got spoiled by being over exposed. She wished it was less time.

"You just left so quickly this morning. I felt like I needed to check on you. To make sure everything was okay?" Saunders sounded like she didn't think she believed what she was saying either. Typical.

"Yeah, I'm fine. Perfectly fine. You don't need to worry about me," Jax found herself saying, all the more aggressively for the fact she had been stewing on this exchange in her head for the better part of the afternoon.

"But I do worry—"

"Don't. Why bother? I mean, it was whatever happened. Casual or however you planed it—"

"What? I didn't—"

"You clearly had *some* sort of plan. You got out of me what you needed, and here we are." Jax cut Saunders off. She knew if she let her talk it would all just go tumbling downhill.

"Jax, that's not fair—"

"You don't want to know what I think is fair. I have a whole Station to keep running. You might need to focus on the people, but it would be a real shit job if there's no Station for people to even be on the next morning. It was a distraction, that's it, and now I have a whole string of failing engines I need to solve before we hit a wall, so maybe it's a distraction I don't need right now." Jax was feeling a bit unhinged.

There was a very real, very sad sounding voice at the back of her head that kept saying she didn't want to hurt Saunders, that maybe Saunders really *did* care about her. Maybe Jax could let her in. But no, there was a much louder voice saying it was by far better to draw first blood and scorch the ground around her.

Jax had been saying all this to the ladder rungs of the core access strut. She finally allowed herself a glance at Saunders, who was standing in the middle of the corridor—Jax's corridor; her own personal Level 5. Saunders wasn't crying. She had a heated, tight look on her face implying she was ready to defend herself, but she didn't even try.

"Well, did you at least finally do the sweep of Level 2 like we planned? I finished reviewing the CC footage. And I wanted to tell you I polled the group on Level 4. No one seems to be missing, but they do have some widespread issues with their ventilation systems."

Jax sneered in self-defense. "What, didn't feel like telling me about this last night? Had better ideas?"

"I *told* you last night I hadn't gotten to it yet. And *I* seem to remember *you* being the one hammering on *my* door last night—" Saunders made the first attempt at protest, but Jax didn't want to let her get started.

"If you haven't noticed, I have a hell of a lot more pressing matters than figuring out who the hell in your group of degenerates is a raging, blood-thirsty psychopath. I'm a trained Station mechanic, not a goddamn janitor. Your residents are probably just fucking around with each other. And they're fucking with me. Let them live in their own stench for a minute. Maybe they will learn." Jax was breathing hard and starting to see red.

"I think you need to lay off the residents for a moment here. Okay, so you're upset about last night—"

"I think what I *need* is for you to leave me the hell alone for a change," Jax seethed.

"You know, I get it. You only understand how to run. Go ahead and be a victim, Jax." Saunders was drawing herself up to a full height. No matter how much shorter she was than Jax, Jax felt small in this moment. "I'll just assume this is a rejection then," she finished. She turned to go. Jax slumped her shoulders as she looked at the rungs again. She thought Saunders had left, but she was standing with her hand on the level's exit latch.

"Just maybe—if you ever think about it, Jax—maybe it's less about people treating you like shit because they are shitty people, and more about you being a shitty person yourself."

That hurt. Jax narrowed her eyes in threat mode. She didn't bother looking at Saunders again.

"If you ever do decide you need help, let me know. I'll be willing to give it."

"The only help I need from you is for you to do your own damn job and keep it from getting in the way of mine," Jax spat at the ladder in front of her.

That nailed it shut. Saunders didn't say anything else as she turned the door latch and exited the level. Jax glared at the ascent in front of her an extra minute before launching herself back up to the core.

"What does she think she's getting at?" Jax said hotly to the humming core around her, as soon as she floated free of the access strut. She felt the hot prick of tears in her eyes again, which only soiled her mood further.

"It's like she plotted out that whole mess. I thought she was *nice.* I thought she was friendly. Hell, if she'd just been, I dunno, just...it was nice feeling like I could have someone else to talk to around here. Other than you, and that damned plant." Jax jammed a loose panel back in place where it had popped open. "That's what I get for slipping even a little." She watched the diagnostic screen read-out tick by for a minute or two, letting herself drift from the walls in the lack of gravity.

"All right, *fine,* so I maybe went down there without a good reason to. Just...I like her. *Liked* her. And I knew it was a bad idea, I *knew it,* and couldn't do anything to stop it. It's like I never grew at all out here. It's all fun and games and then it always turns out like this, with someone breaking your heart and asking to stay friends. And just, *I can't lose you too, Station! Not now!"*

"Diagnostics Complete" flashed on the screen. It was punctuated by a beep indicating her scan was done.

The engine diagnostics were stupidly inconclusive. They all seemed fine. She couldn't even detect the issue she had cancelled out on the second failure down on Level 1 that morning.

"Oh, come on. Not you too! Why does everyone want to fuck with me all of a sudden? What, are you jealous?" Jax slammed a fist against a metal panel, and it made her hand hurt satisfactorily.

She used a handhold to pivot and braced her back against a smooth part of the core wall, wedging herself with her feet across the diameter and squeezing in near a small console readout.

"You know you mean everything to me. I'm here to take care of you."

Jax ran a full reboot on outboard rotational engine string 2, just in case. When that was done, she warmed up the engines and swapped primary rotation to string 2. She followed up with a full reboot on string 1, just as an added layer of caution.

"Just hoping to give you a clean bill of health, love. I'm pissed as hell at them all, but we can't go letting them all get sucked into deep space or anything," Jax mumbled to her keep, surrounding her. It was an unprecedented workload, since the Station only needed such a systems check once every several years, but she wanted to be sure. At the very least, electrical continuity seemed accurate across the board.

Jax's long term hideout in the core turned out to be a brief excursion. She did a last pass over the full systems central circuit board and made her way back to the access hatch.

"Nothing else, okay babe? I'll stay away from hot Security Officers, and you keep us alive. Deal?" The Station, of course, abstained from answering for both of them.

Jax pulled herself from the Core into the Access Strut, sulked back down to her own quarters, coffee, and a shower she sorely needed. There were no spiders, and Saunders was nowhere to be seen.

Chapter Nine

A full-scale alarm sounded loud enough to launch Jax from her bunk. She hit her head on the corner of her chair and swore colorfully enough to curl the corners of the schematic pages littering the surrounding surfaces.

Holding one hand to her head, she slammed against the side maintenance readout screen and jammed her elbow at the comms panel to make sure it was off. She missed, smashing her elbow on a sharp corner, swore some more, then managed to hit the switch. Now was not the time for her to field questions from Saunders.

It was a full outboard rotational engine string failure. An active cascade, in current process. It meant one engine would fail and tip the next on the string. If it reached the end of the line, it could tip the second string, and the whole dual redundancy would be useless. The Station would be stuck on its auxiliary rotational power at declining gravity until core stator friction inevitably pulled the Station to a halt, and the power systems would shut down. Without the momentum of the already spinning Station, it might lead to not being able to restart the rotation sequence. It would mean chaos.

At this point there was only one solution: Jax needed to disrupt the cascade, flip the breaker switch keeping the failures from reaching the second string, then hoof it back to central core to hit restart before the engine strings went into permanent shutdown. A problem of *that* magnitude would require a long and lengthy process of hauling support repair technicians out to the Station and might even call her credibility under scrutiny. Not a headache Jax wanted. There was not a lot of time.

Boots barely on, bleeding from a busted eyebrow, hair not even remotely under control, tool belt still swinging from her arm as she pulled her coveralls on, Jax had to hit the Common Access Shaft fast. There was no time to try to avoid flirtatious Station residents, as there was no doubt they had also heard the massive alarms ringing throughout the

Station for high-level alerts like this. Everyone knew something was wrong.

Jax was hitting her top land speed manageable in work boots, but her traction was crap. That was because the gravity percentage had already dropped. She could feel the reduced weight even as she hit the first level in an ungraceful sprawl from the central access main door. Several clearly alarmed residents backed against the wall as she sprinted down the corridor, trying to outrun a cascade that was already thirty degrees ahead of her.

The sloping curve of the Station was only an optical illusion; it wasn't actually an uphill jog, but psychologically it was like sprinting up a mountain. Jax never really ran, ever, not even if she needed to. Her shortcuts almost always allowed her to get where she needed to be in time, and this fading gravity was sucking her energy dry, with more effort going into keeping her feet in contact with the ground. It felt like running into a strong headwind.

She gained on the endless curve before her then had to dodge a knot of residents who had apparently been using Level 1 for some halfway executed research experiment.

"Get the fuck out of my way!" Jax screamed, as she hurdled some fancy looking equipment. What the hell did they think they were doing taking over a Level 1 corridor like that? If this were any other point in her life she would have insisted Station Security deal with them, but she didn't even have time to think of that, and it most certainly was *not* an option.

The engine maintenance panels on the wall were flashing red as she passed, indicating the failed locations. Each red panel alternated with a subdued green indicating the cascade had not yet flipped to the redundant side, but she was running out of Station circumference, the degree marks on the wall ticking past as she ran.

Jax rounded the curve and sprinted full tilt past the last red light before she realized she had gone an engine too far. She turned to sprint back, baseball sliding into the flooring at the base of the engine access panel and wrenched it off its screws.

There wasn't time for multitools. Jax shoved an arm shoulder deep into the panel and reached for the breaker switch. She saw the engine just ahead of her cascade into failure. She winced and yanked. The switch flipped. She opened her eyes to stare with bated breath at the engine access maintenance readout on the screen above her. She counted the seconds in her head, one by one. The light stayed green. She exhaled.

"Stay," she whispered.

It wasn't over yet. She had flipped the breaker to halt the cascade, but not swapped the engine string over to the redundant side, in case the cascade started on that end too. The sudden drop in outboard rotational power dropped the gravity percentage another ten points. It was now hovering at around the seventy percent mark and would be even worse with each level up in the Station.

This type of failure was unprecedented. There were backups and systems in place to prevent this. Jax should have never needed to enact this type of scenario, otherwise why would she be alone out here as the sole caretaker of this behemoth? She wracked her brains for what her initial training had told her about this as even a *remote* possibility. Jax needed to get *back* to the Station core to perform a full restart before the engines kicked over to the redundant string, and the cascade continued. That meant a sprint back up to Level 5, this time in far less gravity. Her clock was ticking. She scrambled up from where she lay prone and realized once again, her fastest route would be Common Access.

Somewhere between Supply and Medical, the bulk of Station residents had poured into the Common Access stairwell, complaining loudly about the sudden drop in gravity. Jax was sure some had suffered impact from dislodged baggage and containers. In fact, she heard some of the complaints as she shoved through.

"Hey, what gives? Emerson just got hit in the head with the waste bin."

"Engineering, are you going to explain what's going on?"

It was too late to change routes to escape the throng of concerned transients. Jax had to shoulder through, not bothering to respond, which had never been a problem before. This time seemed different, however. They were irate. There was a growing sound of panic in their voices. Seriously, had they never experienced an ounce of unexpected gravity drop? But the crowd seemed to close in more tightly the harder she tried to push through them. It seemed like every resident was right there in the stairwell at once. How many were on Station? Fifty-five? That couldn't be right.

Jax wasn't quite sure what direction the first blow came from, but she sure as hell felt it. It knocked her across the side of the head and launched her though the tight crowd to the far wall of the stairwell. The throng of residents seemed to give easily for having been so tightly packed. She staggered, holding her head where she had been hit and propped herself up against the railing. The crowd appeared to part around one single resident.

Jax hadn't bothered to really get to know who was there and for how long, but she did recognize this guy as being someone fairly new to Station. Maybe in the past week?

The resident was wearing a crazed expression Jax felt was uncalled for in the current environment, imminent Station collapse not-withstanding. But more to the point, he was winding up for round two on Jax's head. Jax managed to dodge, but the crowd was squeezing in again. Way more than fifty-five residents. Jax would bitch at Saunders about it if she survived. And if she ever spoke to Saunders again.

The resident geared up his fists for another blow, and Jax was by no means, even remotely, a fighter. She was a pacifist to her core. Oh she was shrouded in a piss-poor-attitude exterior, sure, but Jax was never one to go looking for a fight, and usually turned and ran from confrontation. But there just had to be something about Jax's face that seemed to be asking for trouble, in one form or another. If it wasn't someone looking to saddle Jax with the emotional baggage of heartbreak, it was someone who assumed Jax wanted something else broken instead. Maybe it was the angle of her chin, or how pointed her nose was, or one too many healed over slashes and gashes across her face from crawling around the heating and cooling systems, but Jax was certain her mere appearance just provoked some people. Not that she had ever tried testing or confirming these theories. And Jax had never had to throw a punch in her life; was not even sure if she could without making a fool of herself. If any occasional asshole was ever around looking for a fight, Jax was usually just nowhere to be found.

Yet here she was, ducking a hail of blows from a resident who clearly had read far too much into the lore around "Jax the Station Mechanical Engineer." She made do with lowering a shoulder into a nearby knot of residents, not caring who got shoved down the steps, and forcing herself out of the way of the hammering fists of this crazed nutcase. His momentum carried him forward and sheer luck left Jax's legs sticking out far enough to trip him. His head hit the wall hard enough for her to hear it, and she capitalized on the moment to make sure he was out cold.

She gave a single furtive glance, turned to continue her sprint through the crowd before another resident could get handsy, and nearly knocked Saunders off her feet. The Security Officer was descending from Level 4.

"Where the fuck have you been?" Jax bellowed.

Saunders was looking past her with concern for the slumped figure of the Station resident. Jax needed to get to the core: the clock was ticking.

"I told you I needed you to do one thing and one thing only. Do your damn job and stay the hell out of my way as I do mine!" Jax spat and shoved past Saunders to continue up the route. She only briefly glanced over the railing a level up to see Saunders kneeling down to check the pulse of the fallen resident. Then Jax slipped through the door at Level 5.

The hazard lights in Level 5 were flashing red. It made the whole place look like the walls were bleeding, the center core seeming like the pulsing aortic valves of a human heart. The low gravity here was worse. Jax needed to get up the core access strut, but now she was having an even harder time maneuvering the walkways.

She was aware the timer for her to restart the outboard engine string was ticking low, but she was having a hard time focusing. That resident must have hit her head harder than she thought. There was a gnawing, clattering feeling just outside her range of vision, like the spidery twitch of too many legs spindling out behind her. She shook her head and dove at the core access ladder. The low gravity allowed her to half float enough to grab a rung. From there out she relied on arm strength to pull her up to the core.

As she ascended, she had a vague, gripping panic that a dark void was following behind her, though really it should have been the red, throbbing hazard lights spilling into the strut from below. She willed herself not to look over her shoulder and shook the sharp throb of pain from her head where the resident had struck her. She reached the core entrance, and flung herself inside, like a child escaping the prying hands of a phantom from under their bed. Nothing pursued her from the access strut.

"What the hell is going *on* with you?" Jax shouted at the tight walls around her. She shifted her attention to the core status, as if some horrendous change might manifest for her to contest in glorious mechanical engineering warfare.

There were no changes to the core. It was as weightless and still as ever, with only a single flashing warning light to notify her of what was happening below. Jax shoved herself down to the manual override switch to start the reboot process.

"I literally did this. Yesterday!" she hissed.

Had she screwed up the sequence and started the cascade? Her head felt like it was full of buzzing, and she had a hard time focusing. No, Jax knew this Station like her own hands, and she was a patent expert in this particular engine system. More than any other mechanic. Just a decade ago she had been poised to help a research team on the next breakthrough in Station engine string functionality that would have made Stations like this one nearly obsolete. If only she hadn't gone and fucked it up. There was a lot of that going around lately.

Jax took a few deep breaths and worked to clear her head.

"Okay, once more, with feeling. Please do not murder us all before I get my next cup of coffee," Jax exhaled.

She would not make the same mistake twice, not with her Station. Confident in her sequence of actions, Jax started the reboot cycle and restarted the primary engine string. She knew the Station would rotate just long enough for her to bring the system back online and reboot the redundant string. Gravity should only drop a few more percentage points. The light in front of her flashed red for a moment longer then swapped to steady green. The system was rebooting. Jax closed her eyes in relief.

"You are going to take years off my life. Have I not given you enough already?" she asked the emotionless Station, as it slowly regained its spinning momentum.

Chapter Ten

Something was going wrong on the Station. Jax lay in her bunk, surrounded by her cruddy tinkering inventions, and Ralph's stringy vines with newly holey leaves, and stared at the ceiling, with the gyroscopically stationary core beyond it.

The gravity from the failed thruster string reboot had returned at a steady enough pace the Station had been able to return to normal functionality in short succession. Jax had not bothered to venture back down from Level 5 to verify anything. She ran diagnostics from her hub in life support and core control and plotted a way to seal off the Common Access entrance and avoid the rest of the Station all together. She could tinker together some mini remote robot...things...to haul a spare screwdriver, fuse or two, down to the rings below her, and carry out all her duties remotely from here on out. The idea was appealing both for the isolation, and for the opportunity to attempt some mini robots again from whatever scrap components she had not already disemboweled up on Level 5. She might actually be successful this time instead of just breaking something.

This whole plan seemed great until she realized several lights had blown out on Level 2.

Her dreams of locking herself in on Level 5 to weather whatever failures the Station might succumb to would need to wait. No one was ever on Supply. No one *needed* those lights. But Jax still had a job out here, and with no nifty yet-to-be-kludged robots to remotely help her, it was not like she could just let her Station fall into disarray. She could no longer avoid her commitment to inspecting Level 2. And by now, it was definitely something she would be doing alone.

The concept of hauling herself out of bed felt dauting. Her years of calm and engrossing solitude had been thoroughly disrupted these past several days. Instead of simple repairs and isolation, it had been a constant high-octane-driven ride of dizzying peak after dizzying peak, and the crashes in between were starting to stack up to their own headache.

Jax's head swam with intruding thoughts as she chugged, bullet point by bullet point, through a list of possible causes for the Station failures.

In parallel, Jax scraped through her own raw and shredded feelings about her encounters with Saunders. She lingered in her quarters, indulging in the opportunity to assess her life choices from the security of her own bunk.

It was a later start to the day cycle that saw Jax finally lugging a ladder down the corridor of Supply, pulling a service cart full of replacement UV/LED light tubes. She had originally gone down to replace the two flagged on her maintenance panel as having burnt out, but once she got down there, she found at least three more. The lights were heavy, and she didn't feel like making multiple trips to get the replacements, even if they were stored on this very level.

This was Jax's third trip up the ladder to achingly lift her arms overhead and work the blown tube clear of its casing in the lamp. It was straining, cramped work, repetitive and exhausting, not to mention done in poor lighting by design. To add to Jax's growing resentment, this was at least the second time she had been in the act of changing a light only to see another fizz out further around the curve of the Station. She was going to have to return to the light storage locker and get more soon.

There was another nagging issue keeping Jax on edge: she kept hearing things. First it was a quick hush, something just outside the scope of her hearing, then, there, it sounded like the click of a door latch. A footstep? The hairs on her arms and neck prickled.

A decade in space made a person mostly immune to the head games coming from Station life. Many new residents would complain of things feeling off, but Jax knew the Station better than its makers, and she had long since overcome any feelings of apprehension about the place. That was, until these past few days.

It did not help Jax was still aware she and Saunders had never solved the mystery of the not-missing, grievously injured Station resident. Similarly, they had not deciphered what might cause such a grievous injury. No, she and Saunders had discarded that irrelevant problem for other activities. Perhaps the Security Officer had made headway on that issue, in the days since they last spoke, but Jax significantly doubted she would be getting that update after their last encounter. Jax couldn't be sure whether she wanted it at all.

Jax jumped. There it was again. Clearer now. Footsteps. Quiet, and rapid, just around the curve of the Station. She already had more than one encounter with someone, or some*thing* that had inexplicably rapid footsteps.

"Who's there?" she called and readied a scathing threat; something to do with ejecting their socks out with the trash so they would be barefoot until their transport arrived. But the threat died in her throat. Then Jax felt stupid. No one on Station should have access to this level right now. It required key card access. Saunders had told her that long-term contained just the one payload. Jax wanted to doubt a single cargo in long term stores was worth someone scurrying around for. Maybe, at most, the damn key locks were busted, and these were those same shitty residents screwing with her again. Just another thing on a long list of things just absolutely going to shit on this can.

The jittery feeling stayed with Jax as she worked her way down, now finding herself at the apex of the Station ring: the furthest distance from the Common Access entry.

This had to be the busiest Jax had ever been in her time on Station. How could it be just days after a mid-level engine failure, an entire level's lighting system decided to give up the ghost? Was she really that shit at her job to overlook this many problems? She prided herself on having maybe found something she was good at for a change, but like everything else in her life, along with these lights, Jax had blown it.

She climbed back down the ladder to pick up a tool she had left on the cart and looked back over her shoulder the way she had come from. She thought she had heard footsteps again, but instead, saw at least four lights behind her were out. Two of them were ones she had *just* replaced. How the hell was *that* happening? What were the odds that not only were all the Level 2 ceiling lights aging out at once, but those she had in back storage as replacements were also at the end of their rope? Jax cursed under her breath. She might not even have enough replacement lights at this rate. No, this wasn't ageing hardware. It couldn't be.

Power surge. That would do it. Something in the Station's electrical system had shorted out and was diverting power to Level 2. Too much power and the lights couldn't take it. It would fry each and every one of them one by one. She should have known; it really did seem too bright on this level.

Well shit, that was a different fix all together. It wouldn't be worthwhile to keep chasing each light. The power surge would just fry the next one she installed, and she would piss away her entire back stock of replacements in a fun whack-a-mole game of high voltage nonsense.

Jax stood, hands on hips, utility light still stuck between her teeth, brow furrowed. She would need to abandon this task and head back to Power and Life Support, to cut power to the level and find the electrical short. She sighed as she mentally prepared to switch tasks and turned around.

A distant snapping sound caught her attention, and she looked to her left, only to hear it again from the right. Again, on alternating sides, in rapid succession, Jax realized in overwhelming horror it was each and every ceiling light snapping out of existence as the excess of electricity fried the circuitry.

Snap! Snap! Snap! Darkness was closing in on her from each direction. She felt her whole body flinch as the light directly above her head, one she had *just* finished wrestling with, winked out with a blue tinged fizz. She was thrown into an oppressive darkness, with the small shine of her utility light illuminating barely anything more than a few inches from her face. There were not even emergency lights, the absence of which clearly indicated a power surge. The dark of space was enveloping and deep, and not even the sparse windows down the corridor provided relief. It seemed as if the stars had gone out with the rest of the lights.

Then, deep within the corridors of the Station, a low, creaking, straining of metal could be heard, like the pressure of deep ocean on the hull of a submarine. It echoed down the halls as if chasing the dying lights. This was a sound Jax had never heard before. No force in existence could cause such a structural moan of lament in the bones of her Station. Jax even thought the Station shifted, ever so slightly underfoot, as if moving with the ache it vocalized. Beside her, the cart full of lights rolled ever so slightly toward the corridor wall, as if being drawn toward the sounds. It was all entirely impossible. It *had* to be Jax's overactive imagination. But as she was struck dumb by what in hell that sound could mean, Jax heard another, more familiar, if equally unsettling sound.

Those were absolutely footsteps. This time it wasn't even the teasingly quiet ones she couldn't quite tell were real. These were clear, crisp, concise footsteps, and they were steadily approaching her.

Jax suddenly wished she had an entirely different array of tools with her. Feeling completely vulnerable, she reached back for the ladder behind her, in a pitiful attempt to ground herself to something.

A blinding light flashed like a spotlight on Jax, who swore and tripped backward over the ladder, backpedaling until she made contact with the wall. She lay there, frozen in fear, bracing herself from falling over entirely and taking the cart of LED tubes with her. The light seemed to study her, blinding her in the process, and causing the encircling darkness to creep in from all sides. Then the light flicked rapidly to the floor, and off her face, reflecting off the floor panels and back up again to show Saunders standing there.

"Jax, what the fuck are you doing here?" she asked. Jax took a minute to pant spastic shallow breaths, her back pressed so flat to the wall, she hoped it might let her phase through it. She blinked as the glowing edges of her vision cleared from the blinding she had just endured. She looked from her ladder to the cart full of replacement lights, then back at Saunders.

"Fixing the damn lights. I said they were burning out," Jax stuttered out. She was still on the verge of screaming.

"That seems to be going well for you," Saunders replied, nonchalantly, flicking her security flashlight up to the dark ceiling and back again.

Whatever panicky scream Jax had stifled was being redirected into something else. She didn't like this vantage point, huddled low on the wall, looking up at the boots of the Security Officer.

"What the ever-living hell do you think you are doing sneaking around in the dark like this!" Jax had turned her rising scream into a full-blown retort.

"I'm 'doing my damn job,'" Saunders responded, and Jax could hear the quotation marks in her voice as Saunders threw her own lines back at her. The Security Officer was still scrutinizing Jax, rooted to the wall, and Jax could barely make out her features in the void that surrounded them. "You told me to do it, since you were 'just the Station Mechanic,' so here I am. Of course, this whole business would be easier if we could actually work as a team, in the very least to maintain station functionality," Saunders said.

Saunders had shifted her weight in the gloom and pale reflective glow of her light and laced her thumb through her security belt. She looked like she was gearing up to pitch in on Jax's workload, but Jax had far too much adrenaline pumping to be thinking rationally anymore. It was dark, it was creepy, and she was on edge.

"We are not a team," Jax hissed. "Teammates don't fuck each other." Though that was hypocritical, given Jax's history.

"Wow," Saunders replied.

"I still don't need, or *want,* your help," Jax responded, through gritted teeth. Saunders looked annoyed.

"I think an argument could be made that you do. You have *got* to accept some people want to be someone you can rely on," Saunders replied, letting her head fall to the side as if the conversation was exhausting her. That only made Jax crankier.

"What on Earth and every other planet makes you think you are someone I should rely on?" Jax said, then immediately regretted it. Maybe she had wanted to rely on Saunders. Maybe she just didn't like being taken advantage of time and time again.

Saunders shifted her weight back over her center and threw her arms up, first running the fingers of her empty hand through her lengthening hair to join her other behind her head before dropping them back down at her sides aggressively. It was a motion exuding frustration. It caused a jarring strobe effect as the flashlight swung wide and glinted off the multitude of metallic surfaces inside the dark Station corridor.

"Never in my life have I met someone who was ever this pissed about having sex with me. Sorry for thinking you were an adult!" Saunders exclaimed. She fixed Jax with a sharp glare, a more ominous glint than green in the dim light from the flashlight trained just below Jax's chest. Jax glared back at her and scrambled to her feet.

"You sure do know the exact wrong things to say, don't you," Jax replied, grabbing at tools that didn't need to be collected, and throwing them on the cart where they didn't need to be. She was certainly winning in this game of projection, because everything coming out of her own mouth needed to be censored.

"I cannot possibly fathom what, in all of the damn universe, hurt you so badly back on Earth that made you such an insufferable jerk. You think getting your research stolen gives you a pass to be this awful? Get over yourself, Jax. If I knew it was going to be this much of a shit show I wouldn't have bothered," came Saunders' response.

Jax just didn't want to hear any of this. Not right now, probably not ever. It would be perfectly fine if Saunders just shut the hell up and stopped appearing in Jax's fortress of solitude on the regular.

"Well maybe you should run with that idea and stop bothering me now," she shot back, folding up her ladder.

Saunders looked at her in the side glow of her flashlight, then turned sharply, to walk away back down the corridor to the exit.

"Enjoy the dark then. Shame on me for taking an interest in you." But Jax couldn't be sure she heard it. Jax couldn't be sure what she was hearing any more.

Saunders' footsteps retreated down the hall, echoing softly and growing quieter with every step, but also sounding like more steps than possible, like each step created exponentially more. With her retreat, the darkness around Jax filled the void, sweeping over her and the small utility light she now mournfully realized was probably not nearly effective enough.

Jax grudgingly admitted that despite the scare, she had felt fractionally safer with Saunders present. She grappled with the idea that if she wasn't so terrified of whatever whirlwind of mistakes she might have kicked up, Saunders was exactly the person she might have wanted to keep her company alone in the dark, on an abandoned level of a failing space station located an oppressive distance from anywhere even remotely more human. She hated it. And she hated the creeping fond memory of how good it had felt, for one night, to feel like she could be close to this person. But that was exactly who Jax was. Someone who clung to stupid choices, and only dug herself deeper. Her self-loathing seemed to eclipse the shitty light in her hand.

Jax kicked at the cart piled full of spare lights and figured it was probably best to leave it there until later. It wasn't like it was going to walk off or anything. She was about to turn to follow the dissipated echo of Saunders' footsteps when she heard the unmistakable buzz of a light turning on. She turned slowly to her left and saw, just beyond the curve of the Station corridor, opposite the route Saunders had retreated, a faint light spilling over.

"What?" Jax squinted.

It had to be a ceiling light, based on the color and angle. But the thing about a power surge is the extra electricity would fry the lights. In fact, the last several she had replaced before they all went out had been physically cracked and burst, with scorch marks from the added voltage. She had heard them snapping and popping as the whole level had been dropped into darkness. A burst light can't suddenly just turn back on again. Even the LED tubes she was replacing still couldn't magically come back to life after a surge like that.

Maybe it wasn't a surge, but then, had all her lights made a death pact agreement on the same creepy day? She needed a closer look.

Jax walked down the corridor toward the single light. The darkness behind her felt tight, and encroaching. She repeatedly glanced over her shoulder into an unforgiving void. The skittery sound was back again, though she still couldn't tell if it was real, or in her head. She felt like she couldn't tell if her interactions with Saunders were real or in her head either. Had they even slept together? Was she just inventing reasons to be terrible to her? Were there really fifty-five residents on Station? Or were there fifty-six? The light ahead seemed to be further away than she had expected. Or was it moving?

But it wasn't moving; Jax did eventually catch up to it. A single ceiling light, impossibly illuminated again, glowing too brightly as the extra electricity surged through it, no doubt about to face a fate much like the one its fellows had experienced. Jax looked up at the light, wondering how it had managed to turn back on in the first place.

Then she looked down. Haloed cleanly in the sharp cone of light emanating from the singular, over-achieving LED tube, and encircled efficiently in its own crimson backsplash of fresh blood, was a single human eyeball, its nerves trailing like a vicious tentacle.

The ceiling light went out in a blue tinged fizzle, and the entire hallway was plunged into total darkness. From all sides the skittering returned, far too loud and far too close to be imaginary. This time Jax really did scream.

Chapter Eleven

Somewhere around the mid-section of Level 3, the maintenance access panel shot off its hinges with enough force to clatter across the floor, scraping the metal and smashing into the far wall. Jax threw herself through the opening into the cold light of the med-bay, landing hard on her shoulder and twisting her body violently to face the dark void of her recent escape route.

"Not a prank. NOT a prank!" she panted, her face dripping sweat and covered in the grunge of climbing up a dark and cramped escape route. A new gash trickled weakly from a cut through her left eyebrow, but she didn't even bother to swipe at it.

Her utility light was gone, lost in the scramble to escape whatever was down on Level 2. Jax waited, frozen on the floor, primed to bolt should anything follow her out of the darkened maintenance route.

"This can't be real. It can't. But that was real. What the *fuck?*" Jax mumbled. She filled the yawning silence with her own disbelief while she anxiously watched the darkness from which she had emerged.

Nothing followed her, and after an added moment to catch her breath, she grabbed the busted panel and crammed it in place over the opening. As she tried to get it to clip back into its abused hinges, she noticed a wedged piece of trash blocking it from reattaching. Jax cautiously reached her fingers forward, wary of anything that might emerge from the shadows of her escape route, and snatched the scrap from where it prevented the panel from clicking in place.

She would need to rivet it back to be sure. In fact, she would need to do far more than simply rivet a panel back in place: Jax needed to lock off Supply all together. Cut full power to the level to stop the power surge, seal each quick access route she had squirreled away, and cut all card access. She pocketed the trash and backpedaled away from the panel.

Killing the level's power supply would send it into Life Support Shutdown Mode. It meant anything stalking that level would be short on light, low on heat, and all together lacking in oxygen. And whatever had almost gotten her back there on Level 2 needed to be locked off fast. The rising panic in her gut threatened to become vomit.

There were maintenance control boxes on each level for locking down a Station section *if* there was an emergency. Of course, locking off a whole level and dropping its life support systems would require a full level sweep and lockdown checklist to make sure no one was left stranded, but with skittering shadows full of severed body parts, Jax wasn't taking chances.

She swiped her key on the control box touch pad panel and accessed the level shutdown procedures. It would require a backdoor Jax shouldn't know, but having spent this long hacking every single loophole and hidden corner of this Station, Jax knew how to bypass the controls. Let them cite her for it. They could hand her the citation along with a handshake as she perched atop a pile of freeze-dried, dead, eyeball-eating space insects.

The level lockdown procedure went into effect, she heard the vent systems shift over as valves closed, and electricity was re-routed. This process would effectively cut full power from the core and leave the level close to dead. The doors would seal and the whole place would become a grave. She needed to run the med-bay loop to close up her own side access points too. It would be pointless to lock down a level just to have horrors escape through some route she had unintentionally left open. She pulled a spare rivet gun from her auxiliary maintenance closet, still free of blood thirsty criminals, and headed down the corridor.

Her shoulder felt strained from where she had burst through the panel earlier, so she had to handle the heavy riveter with her weak side, and riveting each access route shut took far longer than she liked. She kept expecting to hear a panel clatter open ahead of her, unleashing a chitinous swarm of nightmarish abominations.

But Jax made it the full loop back to the common access point, without anything unspeakable bursting from a dark corner. For whatever reason, Medical had maintained some strange semblance of normalcy. The lights weren't even threatening to burst, which told Jax the surge really must be isolated to Level 2.

She stashed the rivet gun and looked up and back along the corridor one last time before taking a passage directly connected to Level 5 without connecting to Level 2; one of two she had left unsecured.

Jax re-emerged on Level 5 and immediately sprinted to the Life Support control room. She wanted to verify her override had worked, and confirm power was cut from the level. She still would need to find the short causing the surge, but she needed to be sure the level was secure.

The flashing alert in the control room told her the Station had at least registered the shutdown. The screen told her oxygen levels were dropping on Supply and temperatures were already starting to equalize with the outside. Anything on that level was going to be dead soon.

A rising, panic-filled, syrupy horror washed over Jax, spreading first from her gut, up her back and radiating from her ears. It caught the breath in her chest and doubled her over.

Locking off a level required all of Station staff approval, even if there were only two of them, along with sweeps and double checks to confirm the level was clear for lockdown. It was a whole process that needed to be logged in the system so it could not be bypass-hacked. This was all for a reason. No one should be able to just lock off humans on a doomed space station level to slowly die in a vacuum of artificial deep space.

And Jax's overwhelming sense of horror told her that in her animalistic panic, she had not verified Saunders had left Level 2 before she had locked it off. For all she knew, she had just condemned the Security Officer to death.

Jax slammed a pause on the shutdown sequence from the main console and replayed the series of events in her head.

How long had Saunders been gone before Jax had turned to inspect the light? They had been located at the Station apex from Common Access. Was that long enough for Saunders to walk the length of the whole supply level? Supply was a longer level than level 5, as it was closer to the outer circumference. Saunders could have taken the staff access stairwell, but it had been in the opposite direction she had departed in, and Saunders seemed to always stick to Common Access.

Jax jumped over to the comms panel she had turned off in recent days. Her thumb hovered over the "on" switch. She didn't really want to call out pitifully to the void, in a precious hope Saunders might respond, confused at her suddenly relieved and uncharacteristically emotional voice. But this was life and death. Jax could suck it up for a hot minute to make sure she hadn't just killed someone.

Yet, still, she hesitated.

A swimming paranoia she had never felt before filled her, overwhelmed her, hissed in her ears like a high pitch ringing and filled her head with fleeting fears. Was Saunders even there on Level 2? Had she ever been? Of course she had; she was real! Why wouldn't Saunders be real?

Wait, *was* Saunders real? The doubt smothered Jax, putting a wrapping, cinching feeling in her chest. When was the last time a real person had wanted anything to do with Jax? Maybe Jax just imagined it all? Had Jax also imagined a swarm of skittering legs and a severed eyeball? Was she just that jumpy? Jax pulled her hand away from the comms box and ran it frantically through her tangled mess of hair, pausing to put pressure on her temples to quell the rising hysterics.

No, she was sure Saunders was real. But maybe that was the problem. Maybe Saunders was *too* real. But if she was real, was she alive?

She jammed her hands in her coverall pockets to keep them under control, and away from the comms panel, but she emerged with the trash she had pulled from the access route down below. She unfurled it to see that it was more fabric. Only this time it was some dark green shred of something or other, different than the blue of Security Officer jackets, or the black of Mechanical Engineering coveralls. At least it was not the dark red of soaked blood. But Jax didn't own anything made of this fabric.

"They *are* using my access routes," she hissed. And crumpled the scrap in her fist. And if they were using her access routes then of course there could be people on Level 2 when they weren't supposed to be. People who she might have just trapped...

Jax spun on the spot trying to sort through her panic, then reached back to the comms box. There was a whisper of a skitter. She froze. Her thoughts spun again, the anxiety spiking.

There were even worse questions. W*hy* had Saunders been there? What direction had her footsteps come from originally? Maybe Saunders was working with them? Showing them Jax's secret passages? Maybe Saunders had come from the direction in which Jax had found the eye. Maybe Saunders *was* the bloodthirsty maniac. She had feigned such surprise Jax was seeing and hearing things, maybe it was her way of throwing Jax off the trail. Maybe she was out to get them all.

Or, again, maybe Saunders just wasn't even real. That would certainly explain her aggressive interest in Jax: nothing but a manifestation of Jax's own desperate loneliness, as she fought off a brigade of aggressive transients infiltrating her Station and killing each other. And whatever had attacked her down on Two...that hadn't even been *human*, which was impossible. This was all impossible.

For a second, or maybe a third time, Jax pulled her hand from the comms button and squeezed her eyes shut. There was too much happening at once. No way could *that* many impossible things have occurred on Level 2. But she was wary. Her distrust in the Station, in the residents, in Saunders, and herself was reaching an overwhelming level.

Jax couldn't be sure of much, save for one thing always keeping her grounded. She needed to save the Station.

Saunders might need to wait. Even if she was on Level 2, she knew where the emergency oxygen masks were stored. Hell, she could show her cohorts down there where to get them. The sequence was paused. Jax needed to isolate the power surge and make sure the Station was secure and not at risk of taking any more lives. Then she would deal with the fallout that was Saunders.

"No."

Jax shook her head. Too many weird feelings and thoughts were swimming around in her mind. This was madness. This was just Saunders. Just call her and check. How hard could that be?

Her hand extended toward the comms box again and the Level 5 lighting dipped, throwing her into near darkness, before swelling back to normal levels.

"Shit!" Jax swore, abandoning the comms box and throwing herself into the corridor. This surge might be actively killing the Station with every passing minute. Jax needed to get into the core.

In any given period of time on the Station: an Earth year, a Hair Cycle, one-hundred-thousand rotations, Jax usually had to venture into the core only once or twice. This week, her Station's most intimate center of operations seemed to be the place she found herself the most. Jax made her way back into the Station's core to seek the source of the electrical short.

"I thought we made a deal, babe," Jax shouted when she got past the halfway mark of the access strut and floated, hauling herself along by the rungs of the ladder. "I'd stay away from Saunders, and you wouldn't kill all of us. Well, have I got news for you!" Jax hoisted herself into the core and over to the pressure suit in its stored location. This much surging power meant it was smarter to suit up for the work ahead.

Jax wriggled into the suit clipped to the wall. She latched the helmet seal and released the suit clamps to allow her to float. In the narrow core it meant she could only move up and down, and she could only see directly in front of her. It required a full body lean to see anything that might be over her head. Typically, it meant Jax would have to blindly rise or fall, unable to see what might lie directly below or above her. It was claustrophobic. But it was also grounded and had an air supply.

"First, you give me engine failures. Now, you are power surging. And can you *please* tell me what the *fuck* is scuttling around your darkest corners? I do *not* have the time for fighting infestations on top of this." Jax ripped off the cover to the main circuitry for the stator connectors. She would have to check coil by coil to see where the voltage was routing itself.

Jax worked from each power coil down to each wire juncture. She started at stored energy sources, and moved through each strut connection, starting with the one routing power to Level 2. No other levels seemed to be experiencing power surges, which decreased the likelihood of this originating from a center location, but she needed to be sure.

"This can't be right. Station, don't *you dare* give me cascading failure after catastrophic failure then play coy with me. Or are you going to make me split you open and dig around in there?" Jax shouted at the machinery surrounding her. Her surface checks weren't going to cut it. Jax would have to check the stators themselves.

The whole Station operated on a concept of electromagnetics. From the outer engines to the stator core, everything operated on the concept of using electricity to create magnetic fields, then capturing induced magnetic fields to use the energy elsewhere. The core itself was several stacked sections of massive copper coils wrapped around the center spoke she now floated in, and gyroscopically stabilized to counter rotate against the Station. The stator was segmented to provide power to each level, capable of having each section be isolated from the others. The access strut was really a fork branched out to bracket either end of the core axis. The other fork prongs were used for conduit routing, resulting in eight fork prongs, one of which being the main access route for Jax. The stator coils were stacked between each set of fork prongs, encircling the center, and secured with panels.

These side panels could be removed to expose the core center magnet coils. It also meant depressurizing the core, and therefore merited wearing the pressure suit, as little now stood between Jax, the magnet coils, and the vacuum of space. She could work without venting, but the pressure differential was a hazard. Luckily Jax was already dressed.

"All right, bitch; hold your breath," Jax hissed. She hit the pressurize button on her suit and vented the core. She used the handholds to push her body down to the stator access panel and opened the latch. Jax would have to block off the stator to check for a problem. Near the first stator panel were its primary supply and return switches allowing her to isolate the coil and protect her from electric shock.

"Black before Red, or you'll be dead," she said, her breath fogging the helmet visor. She flipped the switches, cutting power to and from the stator. She pulled open the panel.

It was a good thing the suit was grounded. A flashing arc of current sprang out from the panel and nearly fried Jax in her suit. The arc was coming from a burst coil in the stator. Was this the eerie light she had seen outside the Station windows? Jax colored the silence with a litany of profanity, some of which she had invented herself. She closed the panel, dragged herself back to one of the other control switches, and isolated the coils on either side of Level 2's. The levels would run on draining stator power for the next few minutes while she isolated the short.

"Fuck, what's with the shit attitude?" she roared at the Station around her. Once she caught her breath, she maneuvered herself down to take a look at the damage.

Now live voltage was effectively removed from at least two levels, she could get a closer look at the mess in the core. Had her Station been suffering from a fatal heart condition she wasn't even aware of?

"What the fuck could do this to you? You're not that old, girl, I checked your heart just last year," Jax whispered.

The wires were burnt to a crisp in one section and one wire had crossed over several others. This meant electricity was skipping one coil and conducting through another. Instead of storing up the energy and releasing it evenly to all the outboard rotational engines, the stator coil was instead looping the stored power back over to all of Level 2.

So the outboard engines were running on their own limited stored power, which was certain to run out soon. That would explain a cascading failure. She should have isolated the neighboring coils before cracking the bitch open. Stupid.

The Station took this moment to finally respond to her with a groan and scream enveloping her in a wave of panic. The magnitude of the noise echoing through the core sounded like the Station might even separate into two halves of one disk, floating dead in space, leaking a blood made up of the very lives held within it, through broken levels and an interior laid bare to the ceaseless and infinite vacuum of space. Jax felt the core shake around her, in a manner she had never felt before. The violent shudders reverberated up and down the core, angrily, then slowed, like ripples in water. Jax braced herself against the core walls as the vibrations dissipated.

"Please girl, do *not* break up on me right now," she pleaded. There was no rescue plan. They had the ability to lock off levels from damage, but there were no lifeboats. Even then, they would be lost to deep space—a nearly unfathomable distance from any salvation. The Station quieted.

Jax needed to fix the arc first. Everything else needed to wait.

The stators, now isolated, were nothing more than cold lumps of copper coils, each wire nearly an inch in diameter. Jax pulled the wire causing the arc to free from the tangle, then looked at the damage closer. Very few things could cause damage like this. One was fire, which she had been pretty certain had not occurred. She would have noticed if her Station was on fire. The next would have been an impact of sorts, but that would have been accompanied by several other, possibly larger problems. Another could be bad manufacturing, or a discarded tool. But Jax had not been in this panel for years, and all her tools were accounted for. Considering the Station was probably close to a hundred years old, it had proven studier than a bad lemon off the factory floor.

"This doesn't make sense. Your core doesn't just up and break on you like this, not when I've been sweating my ass off for you for so long," Jax spoke to her surroundings, bracing herself in the suit, against the walls. She assessed the damage to the single stator.

Only tertiary causes remained as options, and these skirted the edge of plausibility. A large electromagnetic field spike might have been powerful enough to fry the stator coils. But that would likely have been caused by something else happening on the Station first. It's not like EMF spikes just came out of deep space, especially if you were nowhere near a star or black hole.

"I can't fix this, love," Jax said, resigned. It meant a much larger repair than just one Mechanical Engineer could manage. It meant Jax wasn't good enough. Her heart broke with the realization. It nearly brought back the tears from days before, which was less than ideal in the weightless pressure suit. What she could do, in the meantime, was cross-strap the busted stator to Level 2, which was already out of commission, and route the power from one of the other coils back down to the outboard engines and life support systems. Those were highest priority. It was a cheap fix, but all Jax had to offer.

"Looks like that one delivery of hardware in short-term supply stores is going to be stuck there far longer than a few weeks. Hope everyone stocked up on the snacks they like, because food is gonna get real boring for a bit." Jax was relieved they had emergency stores for vitals on other levels such as Medical and Berthing. They wouldn't starve with Level 2 locked off, but they would need to call for backup repairs if they wanted to maintain functionality.

Jax didn't like that she only had such sparse options to fix this problem. But she was notably limited. She rerouted the power off the bad stator, further condemning Supply, and patched the panel back in place.

The repair done, she willed herself back up to the isolation switches and paused before flipping them.

"Be nice," she said, and flipped the supply and return back on. No Station killing electrical surges. "Good girl. Just give me some time. Please." She repressurized the core, and pried herself out of the suit, which now sported some fetching new scorch marks.

Jax gave one more look around the core, then returned to Power and Life Support.

From her post down in the control room, Jax reassessed the Station status across all levels. Level 2 was sealed and locked off; still paused mid-shutdown sequence. She could not identify any other power surges coursing through her system. The Station should be electrically sound until help arrived.

But it wasn't just electrical issues plaguing them. There was also this new and particularly concerning issue of the Station experiencing very real structural stress. Jax didn't even know where to start with the structural issues, or what could be causing them. Maybe the arc had reversed current and caused some of the engines to counter each other, putting torsion on the main support struts? Her reset the other day would have corrected that, but the impact might be more treacherous. Counter thrusting engines could do more than cause structural damage; it might throw them off position in space.

The Station operated on an autonomous positioning system. The star trackers could identify the key points of light, billions of miles away, telling the Station where to stay in a three-dimensional void, when there were no recognizable features to otherwise navigate off of. Jax was not personally well versed in guidance, navigation and control, but her perch on Level 5 afforded her the ability to review the Station positioning system. Over the years she had gotten more familiar with it.

She pulled up the navigation pane on her screen. That couldn't be right. The interstellar coordinates seemed off. The star trackers were working, but they seemed to be struggling to pick up the stars. She might have to recalibrate them later, when everything else was done going to shit.

Stars winked out of existence all the time, having died millennia earlier only to have the last moments of their life slowly dawn on anyone watching so many lightyears away. But to have that many stars die at once was...weird. Jax might need to relent and call for backup sooner than later. It would take weeks for anyone to arrive. She hoped the Station would still be here when they did.

Back in her berthing, sitting on the edge of her bunk, Jax admitted to herself with a sense of sudden dread, that her delay, and her rush to save the Station, had potentially doomed her fellow Station employee. Had she condemned Saunders to a potentially unpleasant fate of suffocation, freezing, and consumption by the pinching maws of deep space insectoids? Or had she locked her off with whatever crazed maniac was running around shredding people? Jax swallowed whatever complex feeling rose from the concept, raised a heavy hand to the comms box and flipped it on. She at least had to make sure. Her finger lingered over the call button. The comms box crackled to life.

"FOR FUCKS SAKE, ENGINEERING. DO YOU COPY? I NEED YOUR HELP ON LEVEL 4!"

Chapter Twelve

Jax lapsed in judgement and jammed the call button, hard.

"Saunders!" she cried. There was relief. Then concern. "What is it?"

"It's easier if you just come down here!" called the Security Officer. That was weird. Saunders always wanted to tell Jax too many things. Why was she suddenly being aloof, especially amidst such panic? Jax's relief was replaced by her growing feeling of suspicion.

Saunders had gotten off Level 2 pretty handily then. Maybe she was better versed in the Station than Jax had anticipated. Maybe Saunders knew what Jax had encountered in the dark of Level 2. Maybe this was part of some diabolical plan. Anxiety spiked and Jax hesitated to answer. The comms box crackled again.

"Engineering, this is critical!" came Saunders' voice. It sounded like Saunders, but more forceful. There was a slight edge Jax had never perceived before.

"Copy that; on my way," Jax said, far more calmly than she felt.

She stood up, fretfully looking about her quarters. Too often this week-cycle, she had found herself at the bad end of a nasty surprise, being woefully unprepared. But what the hell could she do to prepare for what was happening on Station right now?

Jax scanned the small room, the schematics stacked haphazardly everywhere, the trinkets she tinkered with, the tools she had stored against the far walls. She couldn't show up armed to the teeth. What would that say to the Station residents? Would that tip off Saunders that Jax was catching on?

Then her eyes landed on it, obscured slightly by some of Ralph's more prominent leaves. Perfect, just a day fixing the pipes. Jax emerged from her quarters to venture down to Level 4, her hands wrapped firmly around the mid-section of a perfectly normal, entirely discrete, thirty-six inch, cold-rolled steel, adjustable spud wrench.

Common Access was pretty much all she could use at this point. She had little trust in some of her other routes, and they would be harder to maneuver with her being so inconspicuously armed as she was. This time there were no residents in the stairwell, sticking out a little leg to capture the attention of whoever was shopping for such luxury. It was weird; this same stairwell had been packed with a mob of distraught residents just a day cycle ago. Jax pushed through the Market doors to find the mob had just shifted to a different location.

Saunders had her back to Jax, her feet braced in a defensive stance, left hand out in a universal sign of "back off." Her right hand reached behind her for her nightstick. Had the residents caught Saunders in a violent act? Was Jax being called to muster behind the wrong side of a fight?

"Everyone, calm down!" Saunders was shouting. It was clear they had been backing her up to the level entrance, as the comms box Saunders had used to call Jax on was several degrees up the Station corridor, hidden behind the shoulders of irate residents.

"Can one of you please explain what's going on around here?" shouted a woman, who looked like she was part of the stationed military squad, waiting for their drop orders. She wasn't in a uniform, but her t-shirt looked official. It also was the same color as the shirt covered in blood down in Saunders' quarters.

That the soldier had addressed them both tipped Saunders off Jax had walked up behind her. So much for any element of surprise. Saunders actually looked relieved as Jax walked up.

"What *is* going on?" Jax asked. She was entirely certain not a damn one of the residents had ever heard her speak normally, was even more certain they all expected her to have the deep, gravelly voice of a gargoyle. Saunders had backed up so her shoulders were even with Jax's.

"Our residents have some…er…uh, complaints," Saunders stuttered.

She had paused, ever so briefly, as she saw Jax's weapon of choice. She looked back up at Jax, flashed a "what the fuck?" look that was gone too quick to be really noticed, then back toward the crowd. Jax figured since she had started talking, she might as well continue. It seemed easiest to address the soldier who had spoken up first.

"Well?" Jax was really not used to actually talking to people. She figured fewer words were best.

"There's someone here that shouldn't be," the soldier responded. Jax's felt the hair on her neck bristle.

"We keep station logs. Everyone was accounted for yesterday," Saunders replied, sounding almost indignant. The soldier wasn't having it.

"I hear footsteps. Someone is stalking us. I saw something on this level. I tried tracking them down, but they were a few steps ahead. I went the full circuit and they were gone by the time I got to Common Access," she added. This chick looked like she could bend Jax in half, so Jax wasn't about to argue with her. Saunders, on the other hand, looked almost offended, which, again, weird.

"And I keep hearing scratching sounds," piped up another resident. This was a nerdy looking guy with long hair and an unkempt beard. Jax faintly recalled him as someone on a research team, deep field posting.

"Yeah, I heard that too!" Several other voices piped up. None of this was helping Jax feel better about things. Her Station. Her poor, faithful Station. What was befalling it? It was her salvation and her source of peace and safety. And now it was crumbling to dust beneath her.

"Show them, Kivan!" someone said. Another resident. This time Jax didn't know what might have brought him here, but apparently his name was Kivan. Wait, *that* Kivan? From the infamous "first bloody shirt"? He came forward, holding a crumpled ball of fabric. Jax realized it was supposed to be white, but instead it was a dark, nearly black shade of burnt, stale blood.

"I found this wedged behind a panel. And the worst part is, I haven't seen Paul, my long-haul teammate, since last night. Something's wrong here. Where did this blood come from? Where is my teammate?"

Jax had a sinking feeling. What was it about this one guy and his ability to find bloody clothes all over his room? She recalled Saunders' dismissal of him as a suspect and it only reinforced her distrust in the Security Officer. Jax appraised Kivan with a look she hoped said, "You might be more involved than you think." But she was also concerned "Paul" might have gotten stuck on Level 2. It would be a poor show of integrity if she were to accuse a resident of murder only to find she, herself, had murdered his buddy, in a hail of confusion surrounding darkness, terror and too many skittering legs.

"Do you have a delivery load in short term storage right now?" she asked, praying to the cosmos that the answer would be "no." If it was a "yes," she was more than ready to think Kivan and his cohort were far more knowledgeable about skittering, severed body parts and bloody clothes than they let on. She was also far less ready to hear she might have killed someone in her panic.

"No, we're waiting on a drop off due in a month," Kivan responded. Relief. But also, more mystery. Jax still didn't feel like trusting anyone's word.

"Okay. So just to let everyone know, we have had a serious mechanical failure on Level 2. Supply has been locked off. We will have to go in and check to see if...Paul...is down there. But in the meantime, we need you to stick to your own quarters. Please limit your time maneuvering around the Station," Jax said.

It was the most she had said to any Station resident in a decade. Saunders was looking at her like she had just become a whole different coworker—one who not only functioned in small company, but also had a fuck-ton of pertinent information critical to be shared with, bare minimum, the Station Security Officer.

Never mind that last part. The Station's residents seemed perfectly willing to listen to the timely Station Mechanical Engineer who was clearly on her way to do some Very Important Plumbing work.

"Station Security and I assure you we are taking your concerns seriously and are diligently working the problem." Jax sealed this delivery with a forced smile. Based on the reactions of the residents, and a flinch she felt more than saw from Saunders, her smile was just as un-nerving as she felt it was, so she hastily wiped it off her face.

The residents had stopped advancing. Some at the back were disappearing into their rooms. Jax turned pointedly to Saunders and gave her a look that she hoped said "It's apparently important that we leave now, just don't think I want to be leaving with you." Saunders at least got part of the message because she backed away from the remaining knot of residents and turned in tandem with Jax toward the exit.

Once out the door into the abandoned stairwell Saunders turned on Jax.

"Care to explain *exactly* what you were talking about in there?" she hissed, sandy eyebrows narrowed, and a jawline that had once been incredibly soft and smooth now looking jagged and taut. Jax tightened her grip on the wrench.

"Not here," Jax replied, also under her breath. She gave a quick glance at the Berthing level doors, which had slid shut behind them. Saunders glanced over as well, then back at Jax with a quizzical look that said, "then where?" Jax narrowed her brow in distaste and stomped down the stairs one level, stopping just outside Medical. Saunders followed at a pace behind, seemingly wary of Jax. Finally, at least one level from earshot, Jax turned around.

"After you...left...Level 2, I had some...issues," Jax began. It was an entirely useless statement, but Jax didn't want to tip off Saunders in case she turned out to be the culprit standing in front of her, a whopping four inches shorter. "I had to perform an emergency shutoff of the level to secure it," she finished.

"Without doing an official sweep? Without informing *the Security Officer*? You secured an entire level without *the Security Officer?*" Saunders exclaimed. Her stare was intense, her green eyes boring into Jax, burning her face.

"More like I overrode the system and shut off the entire level from life support to stop a massive electrical surge," Jax amended. Saunders' face flushed red. She looked like she might shout, which, if Jax was being honest with herself, seemed like an overdue response. Saunders instead opted for closing her eyes and exhaling.

"Jax, this is bad—really bad. First, we have residents complaining about being stalked, I have you throwing bloody clothes everywhere, then you cut off entire levels from life support without following proper protocol! How do you *think* this is going to pan out?" she pressed. Jax noticed Saunders was still in her defensive stance. Something clicked in her head.

"You think this is *me?*" Jax hissed.

"You're making a pretty damn good case for yourself," Saunders shot back. "You're the one with secret access holes all over this place. You creep in and out like a ghost half the time. It's sketchy as hell, and unsettling. I bet you think it's a great trick, but right now it's definitely casting you in a spotlight." Jax could see how that might add up. But she knew there was an alibi.

"Well, what have you seen on the CC footage?" Jax replied defiantly. This time it was Saunders who looked guilty. Aha! Jax cockily lifted her wrench to rest on her shoulder, then realized how that might look and dropped her arm again. Saunders had narrowed her eyes and turned her face slightly, though her stare remained on Jax.

"I haven't had a chance...to check the CC footage," she said, hesitantly.

"Ha, well something tells me we need to do that," Jax replied, triumphantly.

She turned to go down to Docking. If Saunders couldn't be bothered to check the CC footage, what was she even doing on Station? "I suppose I can once again do your job for you," Jax added. Saunders had started to follow her down the steps.

"Jax, you do realize if you shut off Level 2 without a protocol sweep, you might have killed a station resident?" Saunders asked.

Jax stopped.

She turned and glared at Saunders.

Saunders glared back.

This relationship was not salvageable. They turned and continued down the stairwell to the Security Office on Level 1.

Chapter Thirteen

Once again, Jax found herself back in Station Security. Setting foot in there once in her tenure would have been too many times, but it was a week for setting records. She didn't wait for Saunders to take over the reins, instead opting to bull smash her way through bringing up the CC footage herself. She knew the systems well enough to at least open a saved video file.

Jax started with what she figured would be a dead knockout: the footage from Level 2 when Jax was fixing the lights. She hoped the CC footage hadn't also degraded in the power surge, but the camera network was on a different circuit than the lighting. It was possible this might be the smoking gun she needed. Nevertheless, she struggled to find the right timestamp. Had this really only been mid-morning? What time was it now? She needed coffee. She didn't think sleep would be an option for a while.

"Help yourself, why don't you," Saunders snipped from behind Jax.

"I *am*," Jax replied through gritted teeth.

"Of course. I'm 'terrible at my job' but you are skilled in not only failed deep space research, but security footage and unfortunate plumbing incidents," Saunders sneered.

Jax whipped her face to the side to offer a thoughtless retort, but Saunders was giving her self-defense wrench a side eye. It was now leaning against the security desk. Jax begrudgingly admitted maybe Saunders had good reason. In all her years on the Station, Jax had only ever needed to use this wrench once, and that *was* for an unfortunate plumbing incident. Though in Jax's opinion, all plumbing incidents were unfortunate plumbing incidents. Maybe her choice of weapon was not as inconspicuous as she thought it was. The video filled the screen and Jax pressed play.

"Just watch this," she ordered.

Each level had a series of wide-angle cameras placed at set degree intervals along the corridor. They were positioned in such a way an observer could pan through each camera to track a single individual moving down the hall. Briefly the target would be on the peripheral, then pass directly under the camera, before moving to the far peripheral to appear on the next camera. Video files could be accessed remotely at various Station locations and personal devices operated by staff, if such devices were, in fact, operational. But Security was the central hub for the servers controlling the footage. It wasn't state-of-the-art, but, then again, what else could be expected on an aging tin can that was nothing more than an interstellar bus station.

Jax could use the arrow controls to toggle between varying cameras or seek a single person and hit track mode to track their route around the ring. She opted for toggling, and started with the camera that caught her work path, starting at one busted light and moving to the next. It showed her very clearly working her way down the corridor. She paused on the camera showing her watching the lights drop out one by one, encroaching on her location until she was plunged in darkness. Then a light from the far side of the video interfered with the camera's transition. It was Saunders walking up. Jax noted Saunders came from the same direction she left in, the direction opposite where Jax had found the eye. The video caught their argument, and Jax felt no need to watch it. Saunders apparently didn't either.

"What are we watching *this* for?" the Security Officer asked, not masking her aggravation. Jax leaned back against the desk, arms crossing her chest.

"Just figured I needed to clear my name is all," Jax said.

"This isn't clearing up anything. I was there for this," Saunders huffed. She looked from the footage over Jax's shoulder to fix Jax with a decidedly cold stare, hands braced on her hips condescendingly.

"This is some bullshit, Engineering," she said. Jax narrowed her eyes. "And what the hell do you think you're doing with that wrench? Your paranoia has reached an incomprehensible level of stupidity. If you're going to stalk the halls with a murder wrench, then I need to route some calls to get you pulled off station," Saunders threatened.

"It is *not* a murder wrench, it's a spud—"

"And I'm over this attitude. Here I thought we were turning a corner. I wanted us to have a better working relationship—"

"Apparently that's not all you wanted."

"—Well excuse me for being human and craving some connection! And here you are, the new source of my misery. For all I know you've been haunting this station long enough!"

"Haunting? This is my home! This Station is my whole life, my whole existence! Why would I sabotage it now?"

"Some people might find it absurd you have more feelings for a fucking space station than for your fellow human beings," Saunders spat, hoisting her belt and flinging her hand at Jax in exasperation.

Jax didn't want to hear it anymore. She turned back to the footage on screen. Sure, Saunders had come from the other direction, but the level was a loop after all. Maybe, if she could peg the camera angle to catch Saunders in a murderous rage, she could feel justified for her Tool Of Unusual Size. Saunders kept the onslaught going over her shoulder.

"Maybe you shouldn't be left to your own devices out here. I was told station contracts were supposed to be five years, tops. That's probably for a good reason. Any longer and you risk turning into a stubborn, insufferable, dreg of the human race, with worse taste than the coffee swill you choose to suck down."

"My coffee is *not* swill—" Jax was in the process of defending herself when something caught her eye on screen.

Saunders was winding up with a response but Jax cut her off. "Will you shut up for one damn minute? Look at this!"

Jax had been fiddling with the arrow keys around the whole arc of cameras on Supply. First, she had tagged Saunders' route using the "seeker" function to trace the officer in the dark footage, around the bend through her exit, then back again to her entrance from Common Access (so she didn't come from the opposite direction of the level). The level was effectively abandoned, as it should be. Then, panning from one camera to another, Jax could see even more busted lights along the level she had not yet seen on her maintenance readout. Finally, she had edged up on the camera right where the bloody eyeball had been found.

But there wasn't an eyeball.

Instead, there was a Station resident. She was wandering, in an aimless small figure eight, head bowed, and feet shuffling. It was hard to get a good look at her face. The whole image sent chills down Jax's spine. This person had been just out of sight the entire time she had been working. Just around the curve of the Station, and just out of reach. Jax recalled the echo of footsteps, how they had multiplied, faded in and out, and seemed to come from every direction. Then she was filled with the sinking horror that there *had* been someone on Level 2 the whole time. And she had probably killed them. She pulled the green fabric scrap from her pocket again and looked down at it forlornly.

Saunders moved up to stand next to Jax at the security desk. Her eyes were fixed on the screen. Jax glanced up again and watched the resident grow more fitful. She was smacking her head with the palm of one hand, clawing at her face with the other. She turned her body in such a way her blood-soaked shirt became visible.

She looked to be having a panic attack. She broke into a violent thrashing stance, waving her arms about as if fighting off invisible assailants, before throwing her back at the wall and pulling her knees to her chest. She seemed to be looking off screen at something, which appeared to drive her despair deeper.

Jax was rooted to her spot. She still couldn't see the resident's face, and whether she was already partially blinded. Then the lights went out.

The Station cameras were equipped with a dark mode feature that could adjust to low light, but sudden switches in brightness resulted in a lag of a few seconds. There was a delay before the night mode could switch on and capture the scene again. It had only been a moment, perhaps a two second drop in feed, but then the resident was gone. In her place was the lonesome dismembered eyeball, looking like some abominable unworldly slug in the green tinged night camera.

Jax felt sick.

"What? What *is* that?" Saunders asked, over her shoulder. Jax couldn't find the words, so she toggled the camera to zoom in as best it could on the pre-recorded feed. "Is that? Fuck."

Saunders was already leaving the office, seemingly beyond caring about their current argument, possibly to go clean up the evidence.

"Don't you dare leave!" Jax barked, managing to find her voice. Saunders wheeled back around looking like she was fully ready to unleash a well overdue tirade. But Jax just indicated the still rolling CC footage.

The feed reset its zoom and continued in dark mode for another minute. The video time stamp indicated it would have been right when Jax was being, once again, confronted with her poor decisions by Saunders not twenty degrees away down the corridor, captured on a different camera.

Then, just like Jax had expected, the light somehow came back on. Jax felt like she was in a shower of cold sludge as she saw herself appear on camera, first squinting at the light, then noticing the prize on the floor. Then the lights went out again. Now Jax had something new to watch for. What had come after her in the darkness?

Instead of finding an answer, Jax watched herself flail in ungainly panic. She looked like she was fighting off a swarm of bees. But there was nothing on the camera. She felt confusion, and a throbbing in her head. The caricature of her on screen seemed to gain resolve and bolted for the access hatch she had stashed in a wall panel: her escape. She could see her feet pulling into the wall and the panel sliding shut behind her. And that was it. The cameras were still, the eye the only item out of place.

Jax didn't know what to say. She had removed her hands completely off the controls. Saunders no longer looked like she was on the warpath up to Level 2, and she had maneuvered back besides Jax. She reached down and toggled a few arrows to see if the resident had wound up elsewhere, but it appeared the surge had degraded a decent number of the camera angles. There was a real chance the resident had remained locked on Two, subject to whatever horrible fate she had faced. Saunders clicked off the video and returned to the main file footage. She slumped against the desk and hung her head.

"Okay, I can admit, that doesn't make my case against you more secure," she said. Jax decided to not feel embarrassed about her reaction on screen.

"But *why* didn't you come tell me about this Jax?" She turned her head to look at the Mechanical Engineer. "What, did you think it wasn't necessary? There are irate residents, gouged out eyeballs, and attacks on a secure level. And then you're locking down the whole mess and possibly killing someone in the process and you what, went back to your hideout up on Five?"

"I thought it was you!" Jax spat out. She figured at this point, might as well play her cards. "You were the one who snuck up on me in the dark. You were there already; I didn't know what direction you came from. For all I knew you were coming from violently blinding a resident, I don't know!" Jax was shouting now, though she wished she wasn't. Saunders was now definitely not leaving and had turned her whole body to face her. She looked affronted. But Jax had already started her diatribe.

"The residents have been absolutely out of control lately, and that's *your* job—"

"Oh, sure, let's keep talking about how terrible I am at my job!" Saunders roared back. Jax felt her face getting red.

"You're letting them set up lab equipment?? On Level 1? That's a trip hazard!"

"There's *nothing* happening on this shitty station that could possibly prevent them from using some space—"

"Do NOT call it a shitty Station—"

"They just wanted to take gravitational readings, they said they picked up some signals—"

"And what makes them, or you, think that *this* Station is somewhere they can do their stupid research?"

"I thought you might be *interested* in it!"

They were really squared off at each other now. It was like a whole week-cycle's worth of pressure was erupting, and Jax could practically feel the steam boiling between them. Saunders had pulled herself up to her full height, and even though she was shorter, it was still formidable.

"Why would I care about their fucking science experiments, I have a Station to keep 'spinning!'" Jax retorted.

"I'm just trying to keep the fucking peace around here, and you're hell bent on being the exception to that!" Saunders snapped, her eyes glinting.

Jax continued, energized by her indignation. "Yeah, well *I'm* the one finding blood and spare body parts strewn about in the dark. So much for 'keeping the peace,' I have no idea what *your* hand has been in all this!"

"Maybe if you hadn't been such a colossal twat for the past few days, you would know *exactly* what my hands had been up to," Saunders countered. Damn, she had that response queued up fast. Jax felt her ears burn, as well as her gut. She scowled. Saunders' expression shifted to one of exhaustion and she stepped back from their screaming match.

"Jax, why would I spend a whole year on this Station just to suddenly go rogue and mutilate our residents?" Saunders asked, sounding sincerely offended. "Besides, you are the one who might have actually fucking lost it with isolation sickness. You've been out here long enough. And you are just enough of a shifty asshole who has voluntarily been marooned on a space station for a decade. Who knows what you are capable of!"

"I think this clearly shows I am NOT the one slicing and dicing here," Jax retorted, jabbing a finger at the screen.

"I think it clearly shows you are struggling with *something*," Saunders responded evenly, the lines in her face smoothing out, making her look bemused. Jax flushed hot in the face, this time not fueled by memories of Saunders' hands.

"Look," Saunders continued. She shouldered past Jax and pulled up a second video string, not degraded, showing her pacing on Level 1, looking distinctly frustrated by something. She paused for a moment before stepping into her Security Office, only to emerge with a flashlight, heading for Supply. On another screen she could be seen swiping access and entering the level to find it already dark. Her flashlight could be seen clicking on as the Common Access door closed behind her.

"I went to see if you needed help, not blind anyone. I get maintenance briefings too, you know. I figured you needed someone to lighten your workload." Was that a fucking pun? On a space station full of murderous invisible monsters?

"You've made it clear, in no uncertain terms, that you do not, under any circumstances, need my help. Fine. I accept that," Saunders continued. "I can accept I'm just not someone you feel you can trust. And that's fine. But Jax, you cannot expect to go on existing like this without letting someone—anyone—step in and help you. You'll drown out here alone."

Jax didn't want to let her have the final word, but she was exhausted. The next day cycle had started hours ago. She had replaced lights, and fought the darkness, seen and heard things she couldn't understand, nearly been fried by a busted Station core and now all this. Jax just wanted to sleep. But she couldn't, not with this mess happening.

"Look, something really fucking *wrong* is happening here," she said. Jax didn't know how to end her statement, but then the entire Station lurched violently, accompanied by the aching groan of straining structural supports. The room dropped into a flashing red light and an alarm blared. The screens with the CC footage wiped clear and replaced the videos with large warning notices.

"WARNING! MULTIPLE STATION FAILURES DETECTED. STATION LOCKDOWN STARTED!"

Chapter Fourteen

Jax had thoroughly lost count of how many emergencies this had been. In fact, she was surprised she could muster the appropriate response of grabbing her wrench and bursting from the security office. Once in the corridor, however, she found herself dazed. The flashing lights were nearly unrecognizable, and Jax couldn't isolate what exactly might be going wrong.

Something snagged at her shoulder and Jax swallowed a shout. She wheeled around to find that Saunders had tailed her into the corridor and was now gripping a fistful of her coveralls. Jax would have assumed the Security Officer was apprehending her, but instead Saunders was looking plaintively out of the nearest portholes.

"Jax! Jax there's something out there!" Saunders spat in a harsh whisper.

Jax felt loath to let her eyes get drawn to the windows right now, but even out of the corner of her sight she saw an unnatural movement reflected in the glass. She flitted her sight toward the portholes and the darkness beyond, but all she could make out was the reflected flashing lights of their pending emergency.

"Theres nothing out *there*!" she growled and shrugged her shoulder hard enough to break it from Saunders' grasp. "Theres *never* anything out there, but there sure as *fuck* is something wrong in *here!*" Jax snarled as she backed away from the windows and further along the corridor, seeking a panel readout to tell her what might possibly be going wrong now.

But the nearby panels were dark.

Exhaustion radiating from her core, Jax started off toward her back route, away from Common Access. She needed to get back to Power and Life Support. Saunders followed her.

"I don't need you to shadow me! This is a *mechanical* fix. You need to be with the residents," Jax barked.

"Bull*shit*—" Saunders started to object.

A figure burst from a side panel access route into the corridor. It was a Station resident, possibly even the one who had attacked Jax in the Common Access shaft while she had been fighting a gravity dearth. Except now his face was covered in blood running from deep gouges across his eyes. It looked like he had been trying to scrape something off himself. And he was screaming.

"I have to kill them! I have to *kill* them!" He was waving his arms around wildly, like the poor resident they had observed on screen, who was also most likely sporting some facial damage. And also, most likely dead. This new resident, very much alive, seemed to be warding something off with his flailing.

"Fuck, he's hallucinating," Saunders said quietly next to Jax. Jax didn't take the time to let that make sense. She was busy backing away.

"I need to kill them before they take *over!*" bellowed the resident.

Saunders, Jax was horrified to see, was edging *toward* the resident, her hands up, to try to calm him. She watched as Saunders' right hand reached for the taser. The Station alarms blared in Jax's ears, and the red warning lights flashed. She was distantly aware the Station was experiencing a massive failure that might kill them all.

Saunders had gotten a step too close to the resident. He lashed out and grabbed the placating hand she had led with. For all of Saunders' fitness and experience, she was still a short, female Security Officer against a massive hulk of a Station resident. He twisted and managed to grab her taser arm, flinging her to the side.

Saunders made a sound that started as a growl and ended in a whimper. Her forearm was locked in a vice grip, her other hand uselessly trying to unlatch the bloody, gnarled fingers threatening to snap her arm in two. Jax briefly considered her options and went with hefting her wrench and sprinting toward the pair as the resident bellowed again, this time some incomprehensible nonsense.

Jax got three steps closer to the fray when a new sound joined the mix. Amid the alarm blaring, Saunders shouting, the resident spewing violent nonsense, the red warning lights flashing, there rose a voluminous, chittering. A massive army of skittering legs, swarming from every far corner of her mind. The wrestling pair also heard it. The Station resident stopped flailing for a half moment. Saunders looked around her, her free hand still desperately trying to pry the man's hand off her.

Jax saw the movement again, out of the corner of her eye. She snapped her attention back to the portholes, daring the horrors of beyond to find their way inside, but instead she saw the reflection of the corridor. She saw what looked like many, pinching, twitching legs, scuttling toward them. Jax flinched away to see the corridor was still empty, but the sound only got louder.

Then, from what seemed like every vent, every side panel, every corner of the Station, a swarm erupted. The floors and ceiling were littered black with a roiling, throbbing mass of insects. They were massive, footlong, terrible things, with snapping pinchers and an absurd number of spindly, segmented legs. Their sleek armored bodies rolled over one another as they converged on the raving resident.

The resident, for his part, had gone mind-meltingly mad. He shredded his vocal cords as he desperately returned to waving his arms about, fighting off the onslaught of arachnid-centipede-things. Except this time, he also used Saunders to swat them away, flinging her back and forth as he refused to let go of her arm. Saunders was screaming through gritted teeth, and Jax was desperately trying to avoid getting swarmed.

The only option was to pick the unhinged resident and Saunders over the many legged horrors behind her. At the same time, the first wave of insectoids dropped from the wall and ceiling onto the resident's head. He responded by yanking Saunders to the side. Jax saw a bug creature land on her and heard her scream. Now Jax was also on the resident trying to pry his grip free of Saunders, but a different bug abomination started up her leg. Jax screamed and jabbed at it with her wrench, only to catch a flailing sledgehammer of a fist to the chest, knocking her back. The bugs started crawling up the resident's legs, in a massive swarm that would take Saunders with it.

"Fuck that," said Jax, supposedly to herself. She wrapped her hands tightly around her wrench and swung. The clunky end contacted the resident's head with a sickening sound. There was no crunch, no feeling of knocking a block of wood, just a feeling of a three-foot wrench sinking into the head of a massive, screaming, homicidal behemoth. The resident released Saunders' arm and fell heavily to the ground. The swarm of space insectoids enveloped him like ants on a dead frog. His body twitched spastically under the skittering legs.

Jax had retreated with her wrench and Saunders limped over to join her.

"Let's get *out* of here!" Saunders shouted.

Jax, not breaking her eyes away from the ravenous swarm, curtly nodded once and shoved Saunders toward a side access route. The panel sealed behind them, and Jax pressed her back to the ladder rungs behind her, wrench bared across her chest like a call to arms. Saunders had her nightstick drawn; her only source of protection since her taser had been dropped and smashed in the fight. She was panting and sweating, but her arm seemed fine.

"It doesn't look like they're following us," Jax said. Saunders nodded. Jax still didn't move. In some distant corner of her mind there was a dying space station she needed to fix, but that didn't seem important right now.

"I killed him," she said flatly. She tightened her grip on the wrench. Something was rising in her throat, and she had to swallow hard.

"He attacked us," Saunders said, gently, though she was still breathing hard. She looked at Jax with concern.

"There's so much going on out there I can't be sure *what* was happening," Jax said. The painful lump in her throat swelled. "If I really did kill him, and the woman on Level 2, and the missing long-hauler, I'm done. I have nothing left.

Career over, life over, just...over." Jax felt her voice faltering. She was staring at the access panel hatch and through, to the multitudinous horde of ungodly horrors awaiting them. She was staring through the horde and the outer wall of the Station, deep into the endless void of space.

Saunders stepped in front of her line of vision. Her face was set, her lip bleeding, and her eyes sharp.

"I saw it too. He was taking me down with him. I'm still Station Security, I have a say in this. And I say, we need to worry about this later. The station is failing,"

Jax refocused on the woman in front of her. She took in the tousled, dark, sandy hair sticking to a sweaty forehead, a smooth sloping line of brow that studied her, and the grim line set in traitorously soft lips.

Saunders continued.

"This is why I wanted us to stick together. There is some legitimate shit going down out there and it's beyond both of our pay grades to deal with it alone," she finished.

Jax, for once, did not feel like she needed to argue.

An alarm blared through the layers of Station to reach them in their hideout. Things were still falling apart out there.

"I need to get to Level 5," Jax whispered hoarsely. Saunders nodded.

Jax jammed her wrench in her tool belt loop and started up the ladder. Saunders followed quietly in her wake. This route went straight to Power and Life Support, with only a small vent grate of an exit on Medical. It didn't stop at Berthing, but still had to pass the level, routing somewhere between two resident's quarters.

As they ascended to the Station's inner ring, Jax became oppressed by a new and terrifying realization. The residents were screaming. It was wordless misery and wails of tortured anguish. Whatever mass of creatures had befallen the crazed resident on Level 1, clearly had come to Level 4 too.

Saunders faltered on the landing below the ladder ascent past Level 4.

"I should be in there, helping them," she said forlornly. There was an intense, almost animalistic look of urgency in her green eyes. Jax noticed Saunders' pulse was visibly increasing, just below her jaw line. The Security Officer's adrenaline was spiking beyond what a climb through the bowels of the Station might induce.

A loud thud resonated through the metal surrounding them. Jax winced at the sounds she was hearing. She could imagine bodies were being thrown against the Station walls.

Saunders flinched and made a rapid motion toward what might be a direct route to her people. Jax nearly missed her chance to stop her. Saunders couldn't leave now. Whatever was happening, it was horrible, but none could compare to the endless void that would be the lifeless Station if they couldn't stop the failure.

Jax dropped a wrung and shot her lanky arm out to grab Saunders by her jacket epaulet. The Security Officer snapped out of her flight and shot a confused and pained glance up at Jax.

"We need to save the Station first. That's the protocol," Jax said gently. She had to reach far back in her life to recall such tenderness, but it was clear Saunders needed the news to be delivered as carefully as possible. So Jax swallowed hard, set aside the past several days-worth of disdain for the shorter woman, and attempted to make her voice as disarming as possible.

Saunders faltered. Her face turned to Jax and their eyes met, apprehensively. Jax could see some internal struggle manifesting behind the green glistening in the dim light of the maintenance ladder. Though Saunders' jaw was taut, those were tears Jax could see. It dawned on Jax that Saunders took her commitment to the Station populace almost as seriously as Jax took her commitment to the Station.

Saunders broke their eye contact and looked back down the access route, then up at the walls bleeding with the distress of the other people on Station. She clenched her jaw, throwing the usual soft curve of it into a sharper bulge of muscle, nodded and grabbed the rung next to Jax, who let go of the officer and returned to her own grip. They made their way up to Level 5: Power and Life Support.

Chapter Fifteen

Once they reached Level 5, Jax felt calmer. Even her back-access routes required her own codes to enter, and the level would be entirely locked off to anyone that wasn't her or Saunders. It meant they could seal out the hell brewing in the levels below.

Jax made a beeline for the Life Support control room, suddenly unable to remain quiet.

"I've been running core diagnostics all week. Every time I go in there it's something else I didn't see coming, and I can't fix. I had to lock off Level 2 because there was a massive power surge from a busted stator, after having to reset every engine string—"

Jax was walking through the last few days out loud while pulling up diagnostic screens. For once, she didn't want to have to retreat to the core. She was out of ideas, and things just kept getting worse.

"Cool, so let's just assume I don't know a damn thing about anything you just said. But if it makes you feel better to talk about it, I'm all ears," Saunders replied from near the room's entrance. She was leaning apprehensively against the windows looking out onto the corridor. Jax had almost forgotten she was talking to another human, and not herself, or the Station.

"I'm just saying, it's too much. I've never experienced a Station failure cascade like this. It's like the whole Station *wants* to die and take us with it." Jax had hit peak frustration. She hammered both her fists on the console desk, then shook the monitor before sinking into the control seat.

"What do you *need? How can I fix you?*" she pleaded with the cold machinery that was keeping them alive.

"Do you...often...talk to the station like it's going to respond to you?" Saunders hazarded as she moved into the room. Jax looked up in alarm from where she had been imploring a solution to appear in front of her.

"What? No! I mean, it's not like I expect an answer." Though, that would be a lie in this case; Jax very much was pleading for an answer. "Who else would I talk to regularly though?" she blurted out, not thinking.

"I dunno. People. Me. Just a thought."

Jax responded with a frenzied hammering on the keyboard again. She was reaching a breaking point. She could go back into the core, run another reboot sweep, check every coil, restart every system. Who knew where they were in the failure sequence. The Station would hit a lockdown mode soon, then they would be a dead battery—lifeless in deep space. Ten years wasn't enough for her to know how to save them.

"Okay, can we just...pause for a second here?" Saunders was saying, this time from over Jax's right shoulder. Jax, her face in her hands, her far too long hawk of hair falling over her fingers, shook her head. The outlook seemed bleak. Pause what? Waste more time? Pause.

"Wait—" Jax popped her head up and looked at Saunders. Saunders, for her part, looked like she had been about to reach for the monitor, glancing down to where Jax was sitting.

Jax turned back to the monitors and grabbed the keyboard. She keyed through the database, pulling up a back program she had prepped in probably the first year on Station. It was built off an already-existing sequence, but Jax had streamlined it.

"The Station is in a cascading failure because there is a 'power problem.'" She was trying to simplify things, so Saunders wouldn't get lost in translation. She kept typing away. She needed to alter part of her code. "'Power' comes from the core and goes to every level. It gives us light, heat, air, then it powers the engines that give us simulated gravity." She glanced at Saunders who was looking at the monitor. Saunders didn't react, but Jax needed to keep going.

"So, we have been experiencing 'power' failure after 'power' failure. First the engines weren't getting enough…'power,' then the lights were getting too much…'power.'" Jax was having to mentally slow herself down to keep this pace. Saunders had finally turned from the screen to look at Jax typing away.

"Why do you keep saying 'power' like that?" she asked.

Jax huffed. "Would you rather I say alternating current and direct voltage differential?"

Saunders gave a soft, weak smirk.

"Fair point, go on."

"Sorry, just this what I used to study when I was still a researcher. I know this stuff like the back of my hand, but… I'm trying to explain this," Jax huffed, trying to keep her frustration down.

"And I appreciate that Jax," Saunders replied, softly. Jax felt her ears flush hot, and she stumbled onward.

"Right, so the whole Station has a reactor for its jump start, but its own rotation tends to keep things charged and running." Saunders' face went blank again. Jax stopped typing and looked at Saunders squarely. She held up her hands to mimic her words as she spoke, making a fist with her right hand and circling it with her left. "The Station is a wheel. The center of the wheel," Jax shook her fist for emphasis, "is a battery. The battery spins the wheel, and the battery gets charged as the wheel spins?" Saunders' face sparked a bit of understanding, and she lifted her chin, signaling Jax to continue.

"Right. So, I can lock off the battery. It will cut power from the whole Station," Jax continued, returning to her search through Station computer archives.

"I might not be a technical person, and this might be your hidden expertise shining through, but 'cutting the power' just tells me the whole Station would be dead. How does that help us?" Saunders replied.

"Right now, I have an impending threat that will kill the Station no matter what, and I can't isolate it. If I let it go, the Station is a dead disk in space. But we also have another, serious fucking problem going on here, which we need to work on. And, you are right, we probably shouldn't split our resources in this."

"Hell of a way to say, 'I need your help, Saunders' but I can see how that's hard for you," said Saunders, dryly.

"Not *now,*" hissed Jax. She was re-loading her script to the Power and Life Support system. "I prepped this years ago, based off Station maintenance programs. It's designed for far, *far* more stable conditions, such as having the Station *not* full of murderous, raving, lunatic residents, but desperate times call for desperate measures," she finished.

"And what is this plan exactly?" Saunders pressed.

"I kill the connection to the power source. The power will stay put—it's a reactor after all—but it won't be powering the rest of the Station. That cuts off whatever power surge or arc or whatever might be happening. There's still stored juice in the stator, and I halted whatever arc was draining the engines' applied voltage, so the Station will keep turning on built up and stored power, but that will run out eventually. It's not a perfect machine, its efficiency is less than 100% more like 70%. Okay, you don't care about the numbers." Saunders' face had gone blank again.

"Essentially it means the Station can keep going on stored power for, maybe six hours? Before systems shut down, gravity drops, and we go 'dead disk.'"

"Wait, wait, maybe I still don't understand how this place really functions, and I know, it's not my job, but how does gravity just 'shut off'?" Saunders had shoved her hands out in front of her as if to put on the metaphorical brakes. Her smooth forehead creased again, in what Jax was starting to understand meant a headache's worth of trying to understand the mess surrounding them. Jax heaved a sigh. They were running out of time.

"It doesn't shut off...that's just a phrase. But like I was saying, it's not a perfect system. The outboard rotationals, the engines, they provide the constant force to keep us turning. But if they turn off, the friction in the system will break down our rotation fast enough and we'll feel a sudden drop in gravity. Then it's really hard to get us turning again.

Especially with all our power drained. I can maybe get one possible jump start out of our system, but the rotationals aren't designed to provide that kind of force often." Jax hoped this all made sense coming from her. She had experience, in her past, trying to explain things to those who knew less than her, but her skills were rusty, and the threats were mounting.

"And why would we want to risk this?" Saunders asked, seeming to at least grasp the idea that they were under siege. Her face had gone soft again with what could be resignation.

"It gives us six hours to try to figure out where the real problem is without additional failures stacking up against us. We can go level by level to look for the issue. We can also take this time to figure out what the fuck is happening to the people on Station." Jax figured she should try to avoid adding to Saunders' current headache.

And that last comment seemed to resonate better with Saunders. She really did *care* about these people. Jax figured it was nice someone did. Why did Saunders have to be so...*good*?

"Okay, that puts us on a tight turn around. There are five levels, so it gives us about an hour on each level with little time to spare. I suppose it's better than nothing," Saunders said.

Jax hesitated with her finger on the execute key. Would that be enough time? It would have to work. She needed the space to breathe without worrying about another surge or dropped wire sending her sprinting back to the core. She pulled her finger from the button.

"Okay, so I need to get back to the core before the six hours are up. No matter where we are and what we are doing, I need to drop it and run back. If we haven't found the problem at that point, it might just restart the whole mess, but the alternative is better than dying in a frozen space frisbee," Jax stated. She was essentially telling Saunders that either she, too, would need to drop whatever they were doing, or submit to them splitting up. And for some reason,

Jax was suddenly not very keen on them separating. Saunders nodded.

"Do you need me to do anything?" she said.

"Yes, actually." Jax got up from the chair to make room and pointed to the "execute" key. "I need to go climb the access strut to the core. This script will execute a shutdown procedure, but I need to physically isolate the, er, 'battery,' from the stator motor. I can start the script and then go, but it's going to save us time if you stay here and start it while I hit the ladder."

Saunders gave Jax an uncomfortable look. It finally dawned on Jax how sincerely Saunders did not want them to split up either. Whatever chaos was happening below, it had clearly spooked them both. But an hour was not enough to sweep a whole level for whatever was killing the Station and its residents. Every minute counted.

"Okay. Fine. On one condition," Saunders stated, firmly, despite the audible waiver to her voice—a reflection of the stress bearing down on them both.

"Yes?" Jax hazarded in reply.

Saunders seemed to relent, and she slid into the seat Jax had vacated, looking at the monitor in front of her.

"I'm writing a report to Station Management," she said, hauling a command prompt port window up on the screen.

"What?! Why?" Jax protested, her voice rising panicky in her throat. Saunders snapped her head around to look up at her, eyebrows cinched in near annoyance.

"Because that's protocol Jax, even if they don't get it for a week, at least there's a record of something going wrong!"

Jax shot her hand down on the keypad to stop Saunders' fingers from typing. She pulled back on the force at the last moment. It was not her intention to hurt Saunders, much less her fingers, she just wanted the other woman to hold off on this absurdity. The fingers in question stilled under her hand.

"I can *handle* this, Saunders! I don't need them sniffing around out here!" Her Station was going to hell, the last thing Jax needed was bureaucracy tossed in with it. "I never file reports. The Station always just logs my repairs just fine!"

"I know you don't file your reports. I file them for you," Saunders interjected, firmly, yet gently, nudging Jax's hand aside so she could access the prompt window again. Jax let her hand be moved, caught off guard by the admission.

"*Saunders!*" Jax hissed. They were running out of time. Saunders was ignoring her as she typed. Fine. Jax exhaled loudly and aggravatingly.

"Okay, can we at least take care of this reset, then log the report? That way we can include any details from the core?"

Saunders stopped typing. She glanced up at Jax, then sighed and looked back at the other screen.

"What do I need to do?" she asked. Jax, relieved, pointed to the script.

"When I call from core access, hit the execute key."

"I'm supposed to hear you from core access?" Saunders looked up incredulously.

Jax indicated an attached communicator on her hip. And jabbed the green "on" button on the wall panel near the consol.

"I promise I won't turn you off this time," she replied.

"Good to hear you're willing to turn me on now," Saunders mumbled, in a comment so at odds with their moment of functionality Jax faltered.

"Ten...ten minutes..." Jax managed to stammer. Saunders looked back up at her, clearly nervous. Jax swallowed and continued. "I need to get up the access strut, in the suit, and down to the master switch," Jax stated.

Saunders nodded, her face set in determination.

Jax pulled her sleeves on and zipped up her flame-retardant coveralls. She walked to the door leading to the Level 5 corridor, leaving her wrench and tool belt behind. She wanted to travel light. Saunders got up and followed her. The door opened and Jax stepped out into the hallway.

Level 5 had a much more pronounced curve than the other levels, as it was the smallest diameter ring. It often felt like being in the bottom of a bowl. Jax started toward the access strut and looked over her shoulder at Saunders, who stood with her head and shoulder craned into the hall, watching her retreat.

"Ten minutes," Jax repeated. She didn't know why she felt compelled to be reassuring at this point in her life. She turned toward the core access strut just in time to see a massive skittering swarm of the horrifying bugs ooze out of the vents and access panels.

Jax screamed and fell backward, scrambling over her own feet to avoid the onslaught of pinching legs and mandibles. From the far curve of the Station level came thundering footsteps. Impossibly, the violent resident from Level 1 rounded the curve, very much *still* alive, though he shouldn't be. He also shouldn't be on this level, especially not with half his head caved in and the skin from part of his face chewed off by the hungry swarm that had welcomed him into the fold. He bellowed some inhuman noise and set a single, dead, eye on Jax, who was suddenly unable to find her own two feet.

"JAX, GET BACK IN HERE!" came Saunders' bellowing voice from over her shoulder.

In a moment of physical spark, Jax twisted her body, slipped on the floor, smashed a kneecap, gained traction, and scrambled for the still open door to Life Support. Saunders had stepped fully into the hallway with a fire extinguisher which she now aimed over Jax's low shoulders to hurl white, gaseous cover fire, giving Jax time to throw herself back into the Life Support room. Saunders ducked in after her, a cloudy white fog in her wake and Jax slammed the emergency closure switch. The door sealed shut, locking them both inside.

Jax lay on the floor panting, catching her breath, then rolled to the side to clutch her bruised knee. Saunders had remained with her shoulder to the door jamb, the extinguisher at her hip, prepared to fire again. Jax was pretty sure all that did was give their assailants a shroud of white fog to hide in, but she didn't think it was a good time to share such an opinion.

"That's impossible! There's no way he could be up here," Jax gasped, still catching her breath. Her knee also hurt like a bitch. "I can maybe understand the bugs, but not him. He was very much dead when we left Level 1."

Jax pushed herself up and away from the door frame until her back hit the Life Support console. She looked up at the interior windows leading to the corridor. They were coated in the creatures, their bodies hazy in the misty remnants of the fire extinguisher fog. Through what gaps they could see in the spiky exoskeletons, it was clear the crazed resident was right outside the room, waiting for them. They were trapped.

Saunders backed away from the windows. She sat back on the floor next to Jax. The red warning light, indicating the Station was still in active failure, flashed steadily around them. Jax closed her eyes to calm her breathing. She was out of ideas for good. Instead, she focused on just getting her bearing of her immediate surroundings: the hard edge to the console, the cold metal floor panels, the warmth of Saunders now sitting near her in their pitiful hideout. Next to her, Saunders inhaled sharply. Jax snapped her eyes open.

The hallway was empty. Not a bug in sight, nor a murderous zombie resident.

"What?" said Jax.

"They were just there," Saunders said, shakily. "Then I blinked, and they were gone."

Jax hoisted herself to her feet, wincing as her knee took weight, but it didn't seem broken. She hobbled over to the windows and peered out. Nothing. She put her hand on the door latch and looked down at Saunders. Saunders looked as if she was contemplating being sick to her stomach, but she nodded. Jax hit the switch and stuck her head out the open door. Nothing. Not even blood from the resident, or litter from the horde. The level was clear, clean, and quiet. Jax drew her head back in the room.

"They were there. I saw them," Saunders was saying from the floor. "And you saw them! Of course you did. It's not like I'm hallucinating."

Jax gingerly stepped back over to the spare control seat and sat back down again. Saunders was still on the floor. A thought had sprung to mind and Jax needed to mull it over. It couldn't be possible. And it couldn't be real. It was bordering on science fiction at this point, and she had been someone reasonable for far too long to start getting fanciful now, but why not.

"What if it is a hallucination?" Jax said. Saunders looked up from the floor.

"What?"

"Stay with me on this, okay?" Jax rushed. They were so very short on time here. "This whole Station, the battery, the engines, the core, it all runs on electrical magnets. Electromagnetics. It's what happens when you run current through a copper wire, it sends out magnetic fields. The Station is shielded to keep the residents safe, but the Station is getting old. What if—just, what if—there's a leak in the shielding and the EMF is getting through?"

"Jax...what the fuck are you talking about?" Saunders groaned, flopping her face into her hands. She peered up at Jax from under her shaggy hair and through her fingers.

Jax squeezed her eyes shut, so tight it was painful, trying desperately to find a better way to explain.

"Its...hokey science really. They used to use it in theme park haunted houses long ago. It's been suggested electromagnetic fields, or EMF, can make people feel...paranoid, on edge, sorta spooked. Its why whenever you see copper pipes in an old, supposedly haunted house, you say 'Check your plumbing first.' Rumor has it that really sensitive people can experience hallucinations, like shadows and stuff at the edge of their vision."

"I would argue this is far more than shadows at the edge of our vision," Saunders stated.

"Yeah, I know. But this is not just some crap haunted house with bad plumbing. Maybe the hokey science was real, and maybe the massive burst of EMF leak from a Station core reactor, coursing through miles of copper wiring running throughout the whole length of the Station could kick the EMF field so high that it really does turn into full scale hallucinations."

At this, Jax turned rapidly in her seat to face the monitors, and dropped the executable script from view, in preference of calling up CC footage. She always had the same access as Saunders, she just refused to do something that wasn't her job, unless it meant proving a point. She snagged the CC footage from Level 1 and cycled through it.

"There!" she pointed to the screen, as Saunders got back to her feet.

It was the corridor arc right where Jax and Saunders had first encountered the resident and the swarm. It was blissfully clear, save for Jax and Saunders acting out a grizzly fight for their lives against nothing in particular. They looked insane. In fact, anyone on this Station might look insane fighting off bug hallucinations.

"The CC footage doesn't pick up the hallucinations," Saunders said carefully. She pulled herself up to sit on the console desk and put her face in her hands. Jax paused the video to lean back in her seat. Saunders looked like she was brewing a particularly aggressive headache.

"Jax, that just seems like such a stretch," she groaned after a minute. Jax narrowed her brow and jutted her arms out in presentation to the now blank CC footage screen.

"But that proves we are seeing things!" Jax protested. Saunders tilted her head to the side and jutted her chin out. She eyed Jax from under a furrowed brow.

"I mean the electromagnetics. That *sounds* like junk science. It could just as easily be something in the air vents. Remember, all the residents started complaining about the air vents," Saunders offered.

Jax jutted her own chin out to regard the Security Officer. Somewhere behind her another flashing light emphasized that the Station was still in an active failure, and they needed to arrest any further descent into destruction.

"I personally fix those air filtration systems, even ran a sanitization routine on them just a few days ago. And they are designed to run on analog. They are literally the last system to go. I don't buy that."

"Yeah, well you've been a shifty fucking asshole with a piss-poor attitude all week, Maybe I'm going to be slow to just believe everything you say," Saunders snapped.

Jax felt like she had been slapped. She opened her mouth to argue, but another alarm went off, and she swallowed her reply. They glared silently at each other before Jax finally could bring herself to answer.

"Okay, fine. Maybe there's more than one possible cause. I'll grant you that. But it doesn't explain everything, though," Jax conceded, through gritted teeth. "It doesn't explain how you and I keep seeing the same thing. You *are* seeing the same things I'm seeing right?"

"Horrifying nightmare bugs and a massive meat monster, yeah," Saunders replied. Accurate descriptions.

"I don't know if an air vent leak from hell or an EMF is powerful enough to make us see that *same* thing. So I suppose that kills the hallucinations theory," Jax stated. She felt defeated. She had really hoped it was all in her head, and not in everyone else's too.

"Shared dream theory," Saunders said. Now Jax was confused. She looked up at the Security Officer sitting next to her.

"What?"

"Have you ever woken up to find out you shared a dream with the person next to you?" Saunders asked.

Jax gave her a look that said *do I look like the kind of person to wake up next to anyone regularly?*

"Okay, fair point," Saunders stated before continuing. "There's still a lot of speculation on it, but it was theorized that, in cases where two people in close proximity had similar dreams, that it might be more than just shared external stimuli. That is, they weren't dreaming the same thing because they had just experienced the same thing and their brains were processing it similarly. There were a whole bunch of tests on it a couple decades ago, but the military had invested into it since their soldiers kept having the same dreams when stuck bunking together.

"Essentially, the idea was that one person would kick off a dream sequence, and their body would react, emitting various pheromones and subtle signals that would be picked up by anyone near enough or tuned in enough to them. It would trigger a similar response and dream in that person too." Saunders finished her theory. Jax mulled it over.

"That still doesn't really account for such a vivid hallucination," Jax grumbled. "I mean, what, I think space bugs, squirt some chemicals from my brain and now you also see my space bugs? That's a bit extreme."

"It sounds like magnetics causing hallucinations is extreme too. And you are right, it's unlikely some simple problem with the air vent would cause all this. Seems to me there's some next level shit going on here."

"Okay but can they hurt you? I mean, he had a real grip on your arm down there. A hallucination can't *do* that," Jax replied.

"Yeah, but my arm is fine. He should have broken it. I think our brains just fill in the pieces where we need it. I didn't even have a bruise when we made it into the hatch. And nothing followed us, remember?" Saunders had a point.

"I still don't want to risk falling victim to something that doesn't actually exist. Can we use your tablet camera interface to track us and see what's real and what's not?" Jax offered, wracking her brain for solutions.

Saunders went for her belt, but paused.

"What?" Jax trailed off, cautiously.

"Looks like that also got left down in Security," Saunders replied, apologetically. Jax grunted in resignation. "Well, we can use yours, can't we?" Saunders pressed, as if it was an obvious solution.

Jax shifted nervously in her seat and swallowed hard, as she glanced at anything but the pointed stare of the other woman.

"Can't," Jax mumbled, mostly to the worn-out patch she was intently observing on the elbow of her coveralls.

"You were issued one too, right? How else do you read maintenance reports?" Saunders pressed.

Jax figured a quicker answer would be better than explaining that she never bothered to read useless reports.

"Because I took it apart. Like seven years ago," she admitted.

"What? Why?" Thankfully Saunders didn't press further about the stupid reports.

"Because I figured I could make it work better for something else..." Jax trailed off.

"Of course you did, you fucking gremlin," Saunders sighed, sounding entirely exhausted.

"Hey this place works!" Jax objected, indicating the failing rings of behemoth Station surrounding them.

"But not your management issued systems tablet," Saunders countered. And there wasn't any argument for Jax to provide. Instead, she hazarded a glance back at the Security Officer, who was not looking at Jax, but instead scanning the room around them. Jax took the opportunity to recenter the mission at hand.

"We still would have a problem though."

Saunders turned her face back over to Jax, who rose from her seat, changing her line of sight from being below Saunders to even with hers. "Even if we did have something to access the CC footage while mobile, it won't change the fact that while the hallucinations don't show up, whatever happened to that woman on Level 2 did. That was real."

"We are going to have to go back down there and check," Saunders said gravely. Jax hung her head. Saunders was right. They also needed to check the level for the shielding problem.

"I'll override the lock-down. The environment should equalize. We can do that first and give it an extra minute before we cut power from the core. I know we are already working against the clock, but we'll need a small boost of power to that level to at least make it habitable for us. It should be okay to enter by the time we finish with Levels Four and Three. I have a portable gaussmeter we can bring.

It reads out localized magnetic field levels. I know for certain that we have a power source problem, whether it's to blame for the things we are seeing or not. Gaussmeter might tip us off to where the shielding is weakest."

"And if it's not the EMF?" Saunders asked, looking a bit green in the face. Jax furrowed her brow, straining with the effort to think harder than she felt possible given how little sleep she had managed in recent memory.

"I was tinkering with an oxygen level indicator I cobbled together from a few spare parts. I have no idea what you think is in the air vents, but I guess we can use that to check the air as we go."

"Don't you have oxygen masks in your quarters? I know I and the residents do," Saunders hazarded.

"Okay, yeah. We can wear those too, but they have a limited range. They'll only be good for a couple hours," Jax replied.

Saunders gave Jax a look that seemed to say there weren't very many other options.

"Fine. I'll grab them from my quarters with the gaussmeter and the oxygen indicator," Jax exhaled. They paused, hanging on a moment of stability before they threw themselves face first into the void. Jax fidgeted and glanced at Saunders, who had also seemed to be avoiding her eye contact.

"What?" Jax asked, sensing there was more.

"Jax, I swear I saw something...outside the station," Saunders admitted, looking hesitant to even bring it up. Jax felt herself defaulting to an eyeroll but managed to hold off.

"Saunders, there's *nothing* out there. We're the only Station in three parsecs, and it takes at *least* a month to get here. We talked about this," Jax was still getting exasperated. The tension and the terror surrounding them left a permanent prickle in her spine, and she couldn't be sure what *anyone* was seeing anymore. She chewed on her lip in hesitation. "*What* exactly, did you think you saw?"

Now Saunders looked apprehensive.

"Nothing, just, movement, in the portholes."

Jax felt her stomach clinch at a similar memory. And a scratching at the airlocks...

"I couldn't make it out. I— maybe I couldn't tell if it was inside, or outside." Saunders sighed in frustration. Jax squirmed uncomfortably. Problems inside, those were within her control. Usually. But, problems outside, those were almost beyond comprehension.

"Didn't we just determine we're hallucinating?" Jax offered, tentatively.

Saunders looked reluctantly back at Jax, who felt a bit of relief at the lack of portholes in Power and Life Support. She was not ready to stare out into the void of space only to see it staring back at her.

"Fine," Saunders relented. She turned away from Jax, who had a different, equally troubling thought.

"Right. So, also, uh, maybe we hold off on that report until we *really* know what we are dealing with?" Jax mumbled. She didn't feel like writing anything containing the words "space zombie" or "cosmic insectoid". She braced for an argument.

"Yeah, that's fair," came the reply.

Jax snapped her eyes up to meet Saunders, who looked back with a grim expression. All right, maybe they could set their past aside and be on the same team.

It was not easy setting foot back in the corridor. Jax knew the odds of a real threat were higher coming from a dying Station than a swarm of hungry deep space critters, but it still gave her goosebumps.

They unlocked Level 2, letting its environment stabilize with the rest of the Station, and Jax reloaded the executable file. Climbing the ladder to the core was excruciatingly claustrophobic, especially combined with the itching fear that a swarm of teeth and legs might appear from each end at any time.

Saunders remained in the Life Support room to run the script. She seemed even less thrilled about splitting up, and Jax couldn't blame her this time. But they had already spent a spare half-hour wrapping their heads around the whole predicament, so time was precious.

Back in life support, fifteen agonizing minutes later, the Station main reactor now cut off from the Station itself, Jax entered the Life Support door with a bundle of hodge-podge meters, indicators and emergency oxygen masks. Saunders wore a strained, repressed look, like she was gripping the desktop a little too tight to keep from slipping away.

"Sorry, needed to dig around behind Ralph, and his leaves are getting everywhere," Jax apologized, as she handed a mask to Saunders to coax her from her perch.

"Who?" Saunders' face went from strain to quizzical confusion.

"Just, a plant. In my berthing. Nevermind," Jax huffed.

"A plant?"

"Yup."

Saunders studied her again. Jax braced herself for prying questions.

"If it is an EMF problem, will this cut back on it?" Saunders asked. It wasn't what Jax had expected, but the concern made sense.

"Maybe, but there is still power in the stators. And if the shielding is down, then it's probably enough to keep the hallucinations coming, at least until the Station runs out of power, and then we are fucked for other reasons," Jax responded, depositing the oxygen indicator in front of Saunders. The clock was ticking. They needed to start their level sweeps.

"All right, so be ready for anything," Saunders replied, gingerly picking up Jax's cobbled indicator so she could find a way to affix it to her security belt.

"Yes, but first..."

It was worth a few precious moments to drag them both by the Level 5 galley. Saunders had to watch in horror as Jax poured whatever leftover coffee she found from the last time she had brewed any (which couldn't have been more than a few days ago) into a half empty jar of dehydrated coffee crystals. Jax swirled the mix once and chugged.

Mid-gulp, Jax noticed the look of terror on Saunders' face. She stopped, examined her source of caffeine intake, and figured she should at least be hospitable in these trying times.

She held the jar out to Saunders in humble offering.

"No, thanks. I'm good." Saunders took a step back, hands raised in defense. Now she really did look nauseous. Jax shrugged.

"Suit yourself, it's going to be another long night."

Chapter Sixteen

They stood on the landing outside Level 4. Jax hesitated. They needed to check the status of the residents, but whatever cacophony she had heard on their ascent earlier had *not* sounded encouraging. And even if they were hallucinating these events, this would be a whole level of people hallucinating. Some of them might be subdued, but others might be violent. The blood they had found had been very real. Someone remained a threat.

"Okay. We go in. We sweep bunks. We account for the residents, secure them in their quarters when safe, I check the level shielding, the oxygen, we move on," Jax ran through the plan out loud.

She had pulled her coverall sleeves off again and retied them around her waist. Her tool belt was slung around her hips, and her precious wrench was gripped tightly across her chest. Jax wore her oxygen mask on top of her head, ready to be pulled down once they stepped inside the doors.

Saunders stood, mask already on, depressingly empty handed save for the oxygen indicator on her belt. She had also maintained that two paranoid and armed Station employees might not be the best idea.

"If things go south, we cut losses and head down a level," Saunders added, the mask muffling her voice. There was no point in sticking around to see how bad of a party it was. Jax gripped her wrench a little tighter and gave a stiff nod, pulling her own mask down over her face. On her belt the gaussmeter light indicator flickered briefly, as if to signal it too, was ready to go. Saunders glanced down at the clunky oxygen indicator on her belt to make sure it was working, then pulled the door latch open.

Inside Berthing, it was dark. The low glow of the emergency lights crept from the wall edges, barely illuminating the corridor. The two of them walked inside and let the door slide closed behind them. In the dim light, the place was abandoned.

Normally this level was never quiet. Residents were always wandering around, flirting with each other, hooking up in dark corners, desperately seeking some human connection, and doing whatever they could to stave off the boredom. Now it was as stiff and still as the sealed off Supply level should have been.

"Where is everyone?" Jax whispered through the vent on her mask. She doubted Saunders could hear her though the face shield. She didn't like how the clear plastic warped her vision. That was exactly the thing they were trying to avoid when trying to stave off possible hallucinations.

Saunders considered which route to take, and, like everyone always seemed to do, turned left to walk counter to Station rotation. Jax followed closely. If Saunders had heard Jax, she didn't reply to her question.

A few degrees down the corridor, Saunders froze. Jax nearly collided with her and hauled the wrench closer to her chest to keep from knocking the Security Officer in the back of the head. Saunders silently crept to a berthing door and placed her ear to it. Jax followed and stood close enough to hear the sounds from inside.

Whoever used this room was in there, quietly muttering in sad muffled distress. They were repeating in panicked whispers. "Must stay safe. Must stay hidden," interjected with soft sobs.

Saunders pulled back from the door to look up at Jax behind her, then ushered them both away from the door entirely.

"You did tell them their quarters were safest," she said, with a faint echo through her mask.

"And if there is some mess leaking in through their air vents?" Jax hissed.

"They have emergency masks in there with them. And at least I know they are contained and not stuck dying alone on some locked-off level." Saunders' voice was barely audible through her mask, but her tone was icy.

Jax winced.

"I would be perfectly fine to know they all self-isolated to weather through this, but I can only hope." Saunders still spoke in a hushed voice.

Jax could hardly hear anything Saunders said through the facial obstruction, but it was best to not announce their presence if the goal was to keep residents isolated.

"Let's just check every closed door. I don't want to drag them out here, just to put them back in."

That was perfectly fine with Jax; the less they had to interact with the populous right now, the better, in her opinion.

They made their way from room to room, door to door. At each stopping point Saunders would stick an ear to the wall or hatch and listen before stepping back to join Jax in the center. Jax stayed away from the walls, her wrench providing a source of comfort. At each stop Saunders would either nod or shake her head. It seemed like one out of every five rooms were occupied by a self-isolated, distressed resident. That didn't bode well for the other eighty percent of the group. Either they were too quiet to identify in their rooms, or they were...elsewhere.

Periodically the gaussmeter on Jax's hip would flash a change in reading, but every time Jax checked, it was no different than any other boring day on the Station.

About thirty degrees around Level 4, they ran into their first resident. Saunders and Jax froze in unison as they saw him shuffling across the corridor, his feet just visible beyond the curve of the Station. As one, they flattened their backs to the wall. The resident was mumbling and pacing in a zig zag that wound closer and closer to them.

"If I look out into the void, it will eat me. There is no salvation from the endless expanse." It sounded like some bullshit scripture, or just madness. He came fully into view. Saunders caught her breath in her throat.

"Dorne," she said.

Once again, Jax was reminded of how much time Saunders had spent getting to know everyone who came through the Station. They waited, pressed hard against the wall, as Dorne wandered into full view. He kept on repeating his lament, and his eyes were glassed over. Jax coiled in anticipation but felt a hand on her arm. Saunders was holding her back.

Dorne passed them, shuffling his feet and zigzagging away to the far wall. He then abruptly changed direction and shuffled directly toward them. He must have seen them; there was no way he hadn't, and Jax was ready to spring, but Saunders' hand held firm. In another moment Dorne switched direction again, now shuffling away and past them. Jax felt Saunders' hand relax. She looked down at the Security Officer who was watching the man's retreating back.

"Best if we don't interrupt that either," she said, and motioned for Jax to follow her.

They continued. A few degrees from where they had frozen in Dorne's path, Jax spotted the primary air vent to the first major arc length of the Berthing level. This time it was Jax's turn to shoot a controlling arm out across Saunders' path. The Security Officer shot her a look of annoyance, but Jax just peered down her nose at the shorter woman, through the warped plastic of her oxygen mask, and gestured for the oxygen indicator on her belt.

Saunders narrowed her brow in confusion and Jax gave out a frustrated huff.

"Oh, come on. I'm taller and I can reach closer to the vent. Just hand it to me," Jax hissed. Saunders pulled the indicator from her hip with the same precise efficiency with which she might have pulled her taser.

"You could have just said so," Saunders whispered, but she didn't expand on her complaint.

Jax took the indicator and held it as close to the vent as she could reach. She still fell several feet short.

The indicator remained dormant.

"Does that thing even work?" Saunders asked, inquisitively, her voice still hushed. Jax gave her a sidelong glance.

"I mean, I'm not an expert in *everything*, still *just* a 'jack-of-all-trades,' but it worked last I checked."

"Maybe since you're taller, and 'closer to the vent,' that's why you were freaking out so much earlier," Saunders offered, voice still low. Jax pulled her arm back down and shoved the oxygen meter back into Saunders' outstretched hand. She glowered at the other woman and shifted the wrench in her grip to settle the awkward weight between them. Saunders turned and carried on down the corridor.

At the Sixty-degree mark of Level 4: Berthing, all of hell opened up to swallow them whole.

They had not seen any more wandering residents. The halls had been clear, dark, and devoid of shuffling, skittering, or any other manner of life. They had only encountered sporadic instances of residents who had chosen to barricade themselves in their quarters.

At some point they both noticed a lighting shift. They had passed the first wedge of the level which was mostly residents' quarters, and they were reaching the first swath of common spaces, including the gym, and a galley. This was the place Jax hated the most, as it was where residents would congregate and flirt and scramble over one another as they called dibs on whatever cute piece of fresh meat came from the most recent transport. It was this area that had earned the place Jax's nickname of "The Meat Market."

As they rounded the curve of the Station, the temperature rose a few degrees, and the lighting became bright and overbearing. Jax had to squint as the commons came into view.

The Meat Market had become a literal meat market. All along the counter tops and surfaces of the midsized galley and common lounge, were great slabs of red, dripping carcasses. Sides of choice cuts were hanging from hooks that had been hung from the ceiling panels. The lighting was a harsh backsplash on the gore covering the counters, the floor, and the chairs. The walls were streaked in blood, as if throats had been slashed, in series, to start the butchering.

All of it was human. Here there was an arm, and over there was a stack of legs, waiting to be turned into chops. On the main counter a full torso waited to be split into smaller cuts of meat. The sides of raw flesh hanging from the meat hooks had the distinct shape and shade of human bodies, the ribs split open down the center for cleaning them out. Against the back wall, there was a gaping, sightlessly staring pile of heads. A single large butcher knife was stuck in a chopping block, its blade and handle still dripping. Mercifully, the butcher seemed to be out of the shop.

A slaughter had happened here and would very well continue. The walls seemed to echo with screams of unbridled terror; screams only cut short by the glinting, swinging chop of a meat cleaver.

A hot panic rose in Jax's chest. Her lungs constricted. She backed away from the mess and slipped on the blood coating the floor, her work boots losing traction all together. She fell hard, her wrench shattering the silence as it clattered into the metal floor panels.

This seemed to alert some entity deep within the Market, as more lights brightened, and noises at the edge of her hearing clarified. Was that the sound of a cleaver being pulled from a block? In her desperate attempt to scramble away, Jax slipped on a mess of entrails that had been discarded on the floor. Her vision swam, and she became dizzy. She thought she could hear footsteps, and her heart told her it was the butcher returning.

Strong arms grabbed her, and she screamed. She flailed in a desire to ward off whoever wanted to take her head; to add her flesh to the surrounding scene.

Saunders hooked herself under Jax's shoulder and hoisted her up. Saunders was a full four inches shorter than Jax, which made for an awkward hoist, but she somehow got a grip on Jax's side and hauled, overpowering Jax's panicked flailing.

Jax was losing it. In the distance the gaussmeter on her hip was beeping off the charts. She was going to be sick to her stomach. Her chest felt tight. The oxygen mask stifled her. She ripped it off to better fill her lungs.

"They're dead! They're all dead! He's coming!" She was gasping through gritted teeth. Through her blurry vision she tripped over someone's head on the floor. It rolled away, eyes staring blankly as it spun from her boot, a grimace of shock and pain frozen on its features. Had they died knowing they were destined for resale on a grisly butcher's block? Jax felt bile rising in her gut.

"I know, I see it too. Time to go." Saunders' voice was a steady beacon in her ear. She was half dragging Jax's weight down the hall now. They rounded the curve, reaching the next stretch of residential rooms. Jax was still slipping from the blood on her boots, scrambling away from the thunderous footfalls of a psychopathic butcher coming for her market value.

Around the curve, Saunders' strength seemed to give out and she dropped Jax to the floor, sliding her down against the wall. The harsh light from behind faded from Jax's vision, but the panic remained. Jax was hyperventilating, trying to suck in enough air to breathe and calm herself, but she couldn't push the sight of the Market from her mind. She cried out against the wall, pushing herself back as if she could disappear into an access panel.

Saunders straddled her hips and grasped Jax's shoulders hard.

"Jax! JAX!" she called. She sounded far away. She sounded like she wasn't real. Maybe she wasn't after all. Maybe Jax was really alone on this Station, and had been for ages, years even. Maybe the day-to-day life she imagined had all been a hallucination from the start and, in reality, she was an empty husk, wandering the halls, wasting away while fabricating her own existence in her head. Saunders had never actually been there, had never exhibited an unnatural, and certainly unearned patience and interest in Jax, had never invited her into her quarters for a drink, had never dragged her into bed with her.

Saunders was shaking Jax again. One hand was on Jax's shoulders, gripping her tight, the other was on her forehead gripping her hair and pushing her head back. There was a rising urgency in Saunders' voice as she said Jax's name over and over again.

The panic started to ebb. Jax got a solid lungful of air. With it came the familiar, the real. Saunders was leaning over her, peeling an eyelid back to check for Jax's responsiveness. She was so close, it sparked a memory in the back of Jax's struggling brain. Jax could smell her sweat, and a lingering hint of soap. It was familiar, it was close, and it drew her back to the present.

Her eyes opened. She hadn't even realized she had closed them. Saunders had dropped back on one heel, still straddling Jax's hips. As Jax regained her senses, Saunders released her grip, letting her arms drop to her sides. Jax leaned her head back against the wall behind her.

It was dark again. She didn't know how far they had moved past the gristly sight they had found, but the harsh lighting was gone, and so was the blood. She noticed Saunders brought the wrench as she had hauled Jax out of there.

"I lost you there for a moment," Saunders said, like she was assessing someone at a crime scene.

"And you thought I was worth finding again?" Jax responded weakly, unsure of the words she was saying.

"Yes?" Saunders replied as if there was no other appropriate answer, but her expression seemed to betray some level of unease. At some point, she too had removed her oxygen mask, leaving just the clean outline of her face, looking back at Jax.

Jax's brain seemed sluggish. Had she been screaming? The halls remained achingly quiet. Jax suddenly found herself yearning for the days when this level was full of life and human connection and not death, carnage, and endless quiet.

"You didn't see that back there?" Jax croaked.

"I did," Saunders confirmed, and her mouth was set in a grim line. Her normally bright eyes were a darker, deeper jade in the dim lighting. She pushed herself off Jax and stood up, looking back down the corridor the way they came.

"Look, we may need to give up on this level," she said. She scanned her surroundings. "If it really is hallucinations, then it can't hurt us, but if everyone else is seeing this too, then the danger is going to be other people, not the visions we keep seeing," she said. Jax was more worried she would soon be unable to distinguish between visions and "other people." She was already having a hard time.

Jax nodded in agreement and pulled her now blood-free boots under her in a valiant attempt to rise. Instead, she vomited to the side, her brain still seared with images of raw flesh, and slaughtered souls. Saunders stepped forward with her hand out, but Jax put her own hand up to keep her away.

Saunders stepped back into the corridor as a heavy blur of a human body emerged from a closed berthing door and rammed a twelve-inch kitchen knife through her shoulder.

Saunders grunted like she had been punched in the gut and arched her back against the assault. The blade protruded out the front of her right shoulder, and her arm curled in agony. The assailant grabbed her left upper arm to hold her fast against the blow he had dealt her and pulled the knife from her back with a horrifying slicing sound. The Butcher, in searing reality, drew back his arm for a second, surely fatal stab, twisting the other arm of the Station Security Officer to immobilize her. Jax had a blood chilling image of Saunders being added to the pile of heads displayed in the Market.

This blood-thirsty entity, clearly more than a hallucination, shifted for a throat cutting motion. His arm swept up in a vicious arc to cross Saunders' torso, but the action was interrupted as Jax hit the Butcher square in the gut.

She managed to plant her feet more firmly, the second time around, to launch herself at the figure. She knocked him to the far wall and the momentum carried her down on top of him. The impact forced him to release his grip on Saunders' arm, sending her sprawling and bleeding to the side. Jax, having found herself on top of Butcher, struggled to right herself. His bulky mass sprawled beneath her, knife skidding to the side with the impact. The Butcher made some feeble motion as she extracted herself, but then fell still.

As Jax pushed herself off the slumped assailant, she saw the tapered end of the spud wrench, which she had grabbed like a bayonet, buried deep in his middle.

The figure was no longer moving, his eyes half open, his chest showing no indication of breathing. He was wearing a faded and torn, scruffy green jacket with a patch logo that looked to be part of a transport company. Though the garment was covered in varying degrees of fresh and drying blood, the name on the chest was still legible: "Paul."

"Oh shit, it's long-haul Paul," said Jax. "What do you bet, he's the one behind the actual attacks and the blood we found—"

"Jax."

Next to her, Saunders lay where she had fallen over, clutching the heavy flow of blood pouring from her stabbed shoulder.

Their time on Level 4 was up. They needed to get down to Medical.

Chapter Seventeen

Jax dragged Saunders down the nearby access route, which was one of the official auxiliary ones only available to Station staff. In a sudden role reversal, it was Jax who now had to shoulder the slumped and barely conscious Saunders onto a med-bay surgery table, the infamous wrench sticky in her other hand.

These waypoint stations were all equipped with a standard medical supply layout. Several separated med-bays were clustered around central locations of support systems. The level also housed overflow berthing quarters for use when the Station was at capacity, if that ever occurred.

Once upon a time, these stations had been staffed by a permanent medical professional, and Jax assumed that was probably still true in more frequented corners of the universe. But on these more remote stations, it was more or less expected that any crew utilizing the Station as part of their holding pattern would also have a medical specialist with them. Anything else would be outsourced to first aid and the Station's extensive guide of automated emergency medical procedures. There was catch-all equipment and supplies for treating injuries like broken bones, cuts, scrapes, and other possible general ailments. There were all the necessary features required for resuscitation, ventilation, and incubation. If the Station database and a handy group of volunteers couldn't fix you, it was probably better for you to just die anyway.

Jax threw open cabinets and slammed keys and touchpads to activate the medical system computers. Saunders was still awake, but she seemed out of it. Jax's panic was rising again, overflowing in the form of a constant stream of bullshit pouring from her mouth.

"Station full of friggen maniacs, they can't even handle some stupid spooks. I should replace every kitchen utensil with sporks, they don't deserve knives, if all they plan to do is carve each other up with them. Try *that* with a shitty half-spoon hybrid fork that sucks at both things at once."

She deposited an armful of supplies she had grabbed on the surgical table, without any clear idea whether they were the right supplies. The screen behind her was sluggish to respond. She needed that computer readout; otherwise, she wouldn't know what to do.

"Come *on* old girl, I give you everything I've got, and you're just in a taking mood right now, aren't you?" The Station seemed to groan around her in response, like it was waking up with them trapped inside.

Jax rambled out more sweet nothings for her ward, as if her words might keep her precious Station from dying around her.

She looked about at the straining walls. Was this also part of the hallucination? Were the walls bending along with her ability to process their fate? Her glance dropped to her other charge, bleeding out on the table in front of her. Jax grabbed a wad of sterile bandage and pressed it front and back to Saunders' wound to try to stop the bleeding. Saunders was not responding and had started to shiver.

"Not you too. Don't leave me alone in this mess, Saunders!" Jax slammed her hands through the pile of medical supplies to see she had not found any thermal blankets in her search. In a moment of desperation, she hauled the slumped form of the Security Officer up against her chest and wrapped Saunders in her arms, pressing a hand firmly to the stab wound and holding her, willing her squeezing embrace to stop the shaking.

Jax felt entirely out of her element. Saunders was not a wayward engine, or broken circuitry. She was monumentally more than that, and not something Jax could fix by swinging a comically large wrench. Stuck, arms ensnared in her effort to quell the Security Officer's shock, Jax could barely turn to look at the blank computer screen. In her arms, Saunders passed out.

"Nooooo," Jax shifted to put her hand on Saunders' face, lifting her head and slapping her cheek.

"Wake up, dammit!" she swore.

Another shake and Saunders opened her eyes again. She knit her brow together and tried to sit up, but Jax tightened her grip across her chest.

"Don't move. I just need you awake," Jax said.

She had a minimal amount of first-aid skill, whatever she could pick up through the years hopping planet to moon to transport to Station, but no real credible medical expertise.

Jax extracted herself from Saunders briefly to jab at the computer screen again, but it remained black.

Realization hit. Tertiary computational systems would fail first, as power drained from the system. That seemed so unfathomably stupid at this moment.

Jax turned slowly back to Saunders, shivering on the table. She drew Saunders back up to her, holding her fast, and pressed her hand back to her bleeding shoulder.

"I want you to know Saunders, I might be a true burning trash heap of an asshole, but I never intended for you to die on this wretched shit can of a Space Station," Jax said quietly, next to Saunders' ear.

Saunders was not responding.

Jax figured there was more she should say before it was too late, but she didn't know how to put anything else into words.

The Security Officer looked incredibly pale. But she was awake, blinking, breathing, and staring into the middle distance. Jax let her breathing calm, in an effort to match Saunders' breath. She pressed her face to the side of Saunders' head and willed her mind to clear.

They sat there, together, quiet for moments stretching outward from them, like the stars that seemed to steadily wink from existence every time they passed a window. Their hours were already ticking by, the Station had a countdown to death, and everyone onboard did as well. It seemed overwhelmingly helpless.

Jax wouldn't be able to find the patch, fix the system, and save the day like she had briefly hoped she might. Her whole purpose on this infernal Station was proving to be worthless.

She went back to glowering. It was always easier when she hated everyone, when all she had to worry about was staying as far away as she could. She was just a shitty engineer, with a pet weed, and a knack for doing the bare minimum until it was time to run away again.

But there was no running from this one. Not this time.

Jax let her mind slow and ease away from her cloak of disdain. She felt the weight of Saunders pressed against her and felt the weak pulse just under the soft skin Jax's face pressed into. How she ever thought this person was her opposition, Jax could not recall. It was as if her memories were turning hazy, like they were also part of the hallucination. In the lengthening void stretching before them, Jax could only remember how badly some part of her wanted their night together, had welcomed the company, and she felt a pang of confusion.

Why had Jax thought she needed to run from Saunders? Saunders, who always checked in on her to make sure things were running well, who went out of her way to make Jax's work easier, who was always there to help, to throw her arm out and pull Jax from her nightmare. And now all Jax could understand was how badly she wanted to see Saunders live.

In her arms, Saunders had stopped shivering. Jax felt panic setting in again, until Saunders stirred. Her breath hitched as she pushed herself apart from Jax.

"I wasn't planning on dying here either," she coughed, wincing as she shifted. She propped herself on her left elbow.

"Help me take this jacket off," she said, fingering the hem of her security jacket faintly. Jax swallowed a feeling of elation and helped her shrug out of the garment that was shredded and covered in blood, just like the items they had found stashed around Station.

This uncovered the stab wound and started a fresh wave of bleeding. Saunders gritted her teeth.

"I don't know what to do Saunders, this is not my area of expertise and the computer—" Jax felt the flood of garbled words break free again.

"I can walk you through this," Saunders managed to squeeze out. Jax looked at the wound, then Saunders' face. She nodded, grabbed an elastic band from the accumulated pile and tied back her hair to keep it out of her face.

"Use the clotting gel—it's the blue tube," Saunders instructed. It was one of the things Jax had found in the storage locker on the wall. "Right. That one. I don't think he got an artery or I would be dead already, but I can't be sure what damage was done and the bleeding needs to stop. Each tube has a sterile wrapped pointed tip that you need to install on the end." Jax was following along mutely, insistent on not missing a step.

"Right, now, this is going to suck for both of us, but you need to stick the tip into the wound opening front and back. Start in the front where the exit is and squeeze half the tube contents into the wound." Jax had stopped, her hand on the tube's plunger, its sterile plastic point in the air. She faltered. At no point had Jax ever wanted to cause Saunders physical pain.

"You need me to..." she eyed the bloody mess that was Saunders' shoulder. She made a feeble jabbing motion to help her finish her sentence.

"Or you could just let me die, I know you don't like me," Saunders offered.

That snapped Jax out of it, and she lowered the pointed tip to the stab wound exit.

"Inside you?" she said, numbly.

"Wouldn't be your first time. Don't flake out on me now," Saunders replied, hoarsely.

Jax blinked, shook her head to clear the image that involuntarily crossed her mind, and gave one last furtive glance at Saunders' face. Saunders gave a nod, and Jax jabbed the plastic tip into the ripped flesh of Saunders' shoulder. Saunders made a cry that sounded like it was mostly rage, and her back arched off the table. Jax quickly plunged half the tube contents, then removed it from Saunders' shoulder. Saunders relaxed to the table surface, panting. A sweat broke out on her forehead, causing her hair to stick to her face in darker brown tendrils.

After a minute of breathing heavily, Saunders attempted to roll to her side. Jax saw her struggle and put a hand on her hip and ribcage to push. Once Saunders' back and shoulder were clear, she exhaled.

"Time for round two."

Jax didn't give Saunders, or herself, a chance to think about it. She jabbed the tube back into the stab wound and plunged the rest of the tube contents in. Saunders cried out and nearly arched off the table, but then fell back down again to lay still, her breathing the only motion Jax could see.

A few minutes passed by.

Jax was torn between nervously watching the clock, knowing they had limited time to solve the Station issues, and watching Saunders, pleading silently that she would be okay. By her estimation, they had already burned through a couple hours, and they hadn't even checked for shielding issues yet. Maybe the problem was on Level 4 still?

Saunders stirred next to her.

"Right, well, I'd like to avoid having to do that ever again," she said.

She reached over the pile of medical supplies Jax had dumped and pulled out some wrapped sterilization wipes. She ripped them open with her teeth and winced as she cleaned up around the ragged edge of her shoulder wound. Jax took the hint and took another wipe to clean the back stab as well.

"I'll need the staple gun. The gel is standard issued field medical equipment, it'll help the internal healing, numb the nerves, and dissolve in a few days. But the skin needs to be held together to prevent infection," Saunders said.

Jax could do nothing more than nod dumbly at this, as she had absolutely no idea what Saunders was saying. She reached for the medical staple gun hooked to the wall and handed it to Saunders. She took it, looked down past her chin to the stab wound and pressed it to her shoulder. She made a brief grunt as the staple punched home, but the wound was closed and did not appear to be bleeding any more. She rolled over again and handed the gun to Jax. Jax set her face and punched one staple home on Saunders' back, who didn't make a noise this time. Instead, Saunders rolled back flat and stared up at the humming blue lights.

"Was it good for you?" Saunders mumbled, low, to the ceiling lights.

"What?" But there was no response from the Security Officer. Jax leaned back against the counter. She let the minutes tick by.

"Tell me about that plant of yours, Jax. I wouldn't have expected you to care for something so…reminiscent of Earth…" Saunders' voice sounded tired, and far away. Jax studied the prone form on the table before her.

"It's from the biofiltration room upstairs," she replied.

"Heh, I was told that place was defunct when I got here. That everything was dead," Saunders replied.

"No, not everything," Jax mumbled.

"And you named it 'Ralph,'" Saunders stated. It was not a question. The silence descended around them again.

After what seemed like ages, Saunders sat up and swung her legs over the side of the table. She hung her head low, then gently tested the range and flexure of her shoulder. She winced, unable to move it effectively, but nothing started bleeding again.

Jax watched Saunders carefully, catching every small movement and shift. She felt a wave of relief that Saunders wouldn't be the next victim of her dying Station. Jax wasn't sure how to break the silence so, instead, she grabbed a prepackaged sling from the pile and tossed it at Saunders, who picked it up, but held it numbly in her hands.

"Well, if that's who has been hurting people on Station, I would say we've dealt with that problem, at least. It's maddening though, I swore I saw him just the other day," Saunders finally said, as if it was a casual conversation.

Jax crossed her arms over her chest. Her hands were still covered in blood; her own, Saunders', and various residents'. It felt like a weird get-out-of-jail card to know her first murder had been just a hallucination, but the blood covering her wrench and coveralls was real. So had been the guy with the knife, but she was certain he was right where she left him, very much solid, and very much dead, after she had hauled several inches of industrial steel through his midsection.

"Maybe you were hallucinating already. I haven't been able to tell who belongs here and who doesn't, more so than usual even. But the real Paul...my guess is he went mad early. Maybe he was more sensitive to it, and his way out was murder," Jax said glumly. It gave her a queasy feeling. If one guy figured bloodshed was the answer to quell the madness, then others might as well. "Do...do we think Paul hurt...uh anyone else?" Jax asked, dreading the idea of finding bodies stuffed around her Station.

Saunders was silent for a minute, and Jax had to glance at her to make sure she was still awake. She was. But her stare had drifted to the middle distance, out of focus.

"I don't know. I thought I accounted for everyone. Clearly, I was wrong," Saunders finally replied. "There may be more victims we haven't found yet."

The sickening visions of the Market came flooding back to the forefront of her mind. Maybe it wasn't a hallucination, but a premonition.

"I'll assume you aren't going to die anytime soon though, right?" Jax asked, instead of emptying her stomach of more abhorrent coffee like she had done upstairs.

"Hopefully not, no," replied Saunders. Jax felt another wave of relief.

"Good. So, let me ask you something. Back up there, how was it that you managed to seem so...*calm*...in all that?" Jax asked. "I mean, you saw the same disgusting freakshow I saw, right?"

"Yes, I saw it," said Saunders evenly, still hanging her head and testing the range of her shoulder. "Your 'Meat Market' in the flesh so to speak."

Jax winced. Saunders tilted her head back and raised her more mobile hand to rake her sweat soaked hair from her face, slicking it back behind her ears. "It's nothing I haven't seen before," she said flatly, finally looking up.

Jax dropped her eyebrows in an incredulous look of disbelief. She leaned her head forward as she made unwavering eye contact with Saunders, whose heavy-lidded eyes were now an inch higher than Jax's from her position on the table.

"I told you I served a military contract," Saunders replied to Jax's silent request for elaboration.

"You told me you were stuck on a rock for five years mopping floors," Jax huffed out in disbelief.

"I was," Saunders said matter-of-factly. "This place might be far off the radar from it, but there's still conflict out there, otherwise they wouldn't have military rear details on random asteroids. My unit was supposed to be reserves, but we got hit with some crossfire." Saunders paused. Jax was not ready to let her leave it at that.

"So, you're telling me you're a damned combat veteran?" Jax implored. Saunders rolled her eyes and squared her jaw at Jax.

"I was stationed as a medic there, feeling like I wasted my whole career just to be stuck sweeping up pebbles. *My whole unit* got obliterated. Looked pretty similar to that scene up there." She narrowed her eyes at Jax, who gulped a mouthful of air. Saunders also took a deep breath and delivered her conclusion.

"I was supposed to save them; that was my job. But when the opportunity finally came, there wasn't much left to save. They offered any of us who survived a new contract with bonus, but I figured my time was up. I wanted to go somewhere I could actually help people." Saunders gripped the edge of the surgical table and leaned her weight forward on her extended arms. Her shoulder seemed to take the stress. Her head was tilted to the side as she stared back at Jax with steady, sharp, green eyes.

Jax's head hurt with a pounding realization.

"You...you lied to me, back...back in the galley the other night. You said your contract was uneventful. You conveniently left out this entirely significant detail, then went and tried to pry my whole life story out of me."

Jax felt incensed, and naked all over again. Her prior confusion over why she felt so wary of Saunders slightly dissipated. Saunders had claimed more of her vulnerability from her than she had been willing to exchange in return, despite the very candid explanation that Saunders had just provided. Saunders exhaled and rolled her eyes up to look at the far wall.

"I hate to break it to you Jax, but as mysterious as your life story seems to be, at least you haven't told me you were responsible for the lives of thirty people who never got to see the light of their own sun again. I'm sorry you had some academic plans go awry in your life. I just didn't think my gritty backstory was good first-date material," Saunders replied dryly. She dropped her gaze back down to Jax.

Nevermind. That made perfect sense, and it also threw so many other things into sharp relief. Priorities, personalities, motivations; Jax was struck with the magnitude of what their interactions might have really meant to the Security Officer. She closed her eyes and put her hand to her brow as if holding back a headache. The med-bay lights were too bright.

"I suppose 'not being able to do my job' is just a character trait of mine," came Saunders' voice over the hum in Jax's head as she processed this wave of new information.

This statement shredded Jax's last clinging vestige of defiance. She had spent the last week berating Saunders for a shit job as Station Security when really, Saunders was probably the most qualified person for the job in all of Jax's term on Station. The regret of her shitty behavior mixed with the dread of what they had witnessed.

Jax sank to the floor, pulling her knees to her chest and covering her face in her hands to shield her from the all-too-mild expression of the fully capable Station Security Officer. She sat like that for several minutes, letting the waves of stinging guilt ripple by, until she could think clearly again. There was a lexicon of things she wanted to say, but she couldn't find the right words, so she stuck to what was in front of her.

"So, who's nightmare was that up there?" Jax said through eyes squeezed shut and fingers squeezing her temples. "I'm the one who refers to it as a 'Meat Market.'"

"Who knows?" responded Saunders, who seemed to consider her last comment as a gracious victory blow that she did not need to exacerbate further. "Maybe we are feeding off each other's memories. As far as I'm concerned, this is uncharted territory." She eased herself off the slab and back to her feet on the floor. She swayed slightly, caught her balance and rotated her shoulders again.

"I think we need to finish the job, though," she said.

Saunders wasn't wrong, and probably had never been wrong. Nearly three hours had passed, and they hadn't even checked the Medical level. Well, beyond the fact that the life-saving computer systems weren't working. They had confirmed that.

Saunders held up her shredded jacket but decided against it. Instead, she wrapped her shoulder in gauze and bandages, and strapped it to her chest with the sling to immobilize it. She then walked to one of the hallway access panels. Jax was surprised when she opened it up and pulled a spare nightstick from inside.

"You're not the only one who has gotten familiar with this Station," she said. "I figured I should better equip myself to match your level of weaponry."

"Excuse you—this is my emotional support wrench. What about 'not threatening the residents'?" Jax asked. Saunders looked down at her bandaged shoulder, then back at Jax.

"I think we are beyond that."

Chapter Eighteen

The prospect of another sweep of Medical weighed heavily on Jax's consciousness. The daunting discovery of blood and carnage in an air vent had launched Jax and Saunders on this twisting, intertwined, grim adventure through the concentric rings of Jax's formerly safe space station stronghold. Jax suppressed a shiver, and she couldn't be sure if it spawned from the memory of someone hiding in the ceiling voids, or the memory of desperately trying to hold the life into Saunders. Or the gravity of Saunders' revelation about her past. For all Jax knew, the feeling was all-encompassing.

They resumed their search of the level with a heavy quiet, that implied neither knew what to say in the deafening silence. The corridor echoed with their footsteps and the shadows of the search they had conducted only a few days ago. But it felt like a millennia, before the Market had exploded in violent carnage, before the Station crawled with phantoms from the deepest nightmares of the universe, and before they had fallen into bed together.

Jax felt the strangest sense of déjà vu as she swept a dark room with the gaussmeter. She flinched at every dark corner, expecting someone to crawl out, boots skittering inhumanly fast, to launch at her, shredding her flesh as much as her emotions had shredded at the thought of losing Saunders. Jax's head throbbed with the weight of it all.

Jax willed herself into as much calm as she could manage and drifted closer to Saunders. The notion of resenting the Security Officer's company suddenly seemed foreign to Jax. She now found herself elated and relieved to have the short, vibrantly alive form of Saunders near her shoulder, as they moved room to room. For what felt like the first time in Jax's life, she was willing to engage further, in conversation, in interaction, but was entirely silenced by her own shock at this realization.

What was Jax supposed to even talk about with Saunders? What sort of conversation was she supposed to have with someone she had worked with already for, what, a year? With someone she had just patched up from being stabbed? Someone she had just discovered had a far more intense background than she ever could have imagined.

Was she just supposed to ask about Saunders' favorite twenty-third century cover bands of twentieth century hair metal? Should Jax let Saunders know how many times she had fixed a blown fuse, or rewired the circuitry to the Security quarters so Saunders could keep playing her music, even though it wasn't efficient? Was it too inappropriate to choose now as the ideal moment to tell Saunders that Jax really didn't hate her music, just hated the fact that she *liked* it? Jax really just hated that Saunders reminded her of a time in her life when she was less bitter, less distrusting of everyone, and more open to the idea of a future. *Was* that an appropriate conversation topic with the only person she had slept with in nearly ten years, *especially* after they had just wandered through a cannibalistic hellscape?

Could Jax ask about why Saunders seduced her? Considering Jax just killed a man in self-defense, that didn't seem appropriate either.

No, Jax hadn't killed a man in *self*-defense. She had killed to defend Saunders. Then she had pleaded with the universe to let her save Saunders' life, as if she had wanted nothing more. Shouldn't they, maybe, *talk* about that?

For some reason "Hey, so now that I have your blood on my hands, and know your traumatic origin story, can you explain why you wanted to get my pants off so badly the other night?" just didn't sit well with her. Something about all the ideas and information Jax had absorbed these last few exhausting hours told her those weren't appropriate conversation starters. Maybe what Jax did need to come clean about was exactly what damaging heartache had sent her running halfway across the universe to hide here. After what Saunders had just told her, it seemed only fair. Horrifying, but fair. Jax wasn't ready for that.

But the awkward silence crept up Jax's spine compelling her to speak: to disturb the dead air around them.

"Is that why you were offered the position here?" Jax attempted, before realizing she had held half a conversation in her head already. She was inherently aware the last amicable conversation they had revolved entirely around Jax and her absurdity, and not nearly enough about who Saunders was as a person. Saunders looked over from the other side of the corridor.

"I'm assuming you mean the medical experience?" Saunders asked, eyebrow raised. Jax looked up tentatively and nodded. "They do try to cover all their bases. The more skills someone employed out here has, the less people they need to employ. Medical experience has been a requirement for Station Security for decades now," Saunders answered.

Jax made a gruff noise in response, more so because that also made too much sense. There probably existed some cosmic record, etched in the stars of some distant universe, of all the things that made too much sense, but Jax had chosen to ignore in favor of some self-constructed bullshit.

"That's probably why they were willing to keep a 'jack-of-all-trades' employed here for so long, even if it would be against others' better judgement," Saunders offered.

Jax felt the conversation die around them. Saunders probably wasn't keen on dredging up her background if it contained even half the horrors they had seen upstairs. And here Jax had been glowering in deep space for eons over her own stupidity. Her breath caught in her throat at the thought, and she hated herself even more.

Saunders must have heard the change in breathing because she came closer and looked down at the gaussmeter probe in Jax's hand.

"What exactly are we hoping to find here?" she asked. Jax snapped out of her grim stupor over the fate of the person standing next to her and followed her line of sight. Her eyes lingered on the Security Officer's finger that still prodded the box on her tool belt, then to the meter's glowing readout.

"It reads magnetic field strength. It's probably useless in this mess, since it's for small electronic components. I assumed that if we saw it spike, we could isolate where the problem is," Jax responded.

"I'm guessing you weren't paying attention upstairs." Saunders spoke as if she were a bit distracted. Her eyes were still down at Jax's hip, or at least, on the meter on her hip.

"No, I was a bit preoccupied," Jax admitted, in an understatement. She was looking sideways at the woman next to her, as if waiting for some new revelation between them. Saunders closed her eyes and shook her head, stepping away.

"What about the oxygen indicator? Did you give up on that?" Jax asked after the retreating woman.

Saunders looked back at Jax in confusion for a moment, then surprise. She made a frantic jolt for her belt with her free hand, grasping at nothing, her nightstick whipping around in the process.

"I think I left it upstairs!" Saunders groaned, after another moment of searching. Jax bit her lip in thought, and not at all to avoid comment on Saunders' uncanny ability to lose her hardware in the field of action. That probably was not a productive conversation starter.

"All right, well, then let's hope there really isn't anything wrong in the air vents for now. I guess we're stuck with electromagnetic fields. I mean, I *do* know there is a power routing problem," Jax replied.

Then another moment of recall struck her.

"Wait, we left the masks up on Level 4 as well," Jax blurted out. So much for either of them keeping their supplies organized.

"I mean, there are extras down here..." Saunders gestured at the medical supply lockers surrounding them.

"No, but we still saw all that mess upstairs. Wouldn't the fact we were wearing them, but still seeing...stuff...mean that it's not the air vents?" Jax had paused in her scan to work through the process of elimination in her head. Saunders had stalled where she had been reaching for a nearby supply locker to look back over at Jax.

"Okay. Valid point," she conceded. Jax felt the tips of her ears burn at the lack of argument, both from Saunders, and from herself. She shook her head to clear it again.

"Sorry, just, you can grab another, but they damn near got in the way upstairs, I'd rather not," Jax offered, quietly.

Saunders closed the medical supply locker, and fidgeted, swinging her unconstrained arm. The extendable nightstick swished around her kneecap, as she bounced slightly in Jax's wake down the corridor.

"I just want to know the source of these visions," she finally said, sounding frustrated. Jax knitted her eyebrows together in confusion.

"Well, I mean we had a few theories. Unfortunately, I'm mostly just an expert in technical systems, not deep space weird fuckery. But you said maybe we were also feeding off each other..." she trailed off. The phrase "feeding off each other" had a more horrifying meaning after their encounter upstairs.

"No, but I mean the content, not the source. Not the EMF or air vents. Who does it start with? Is it Paul? Did one person start tripping and it set off a wave? Like a contagion? Or is it isolated to whomever comes in contact with this field you keep talking about?" Saunders was looking up at the walls. Jax moved over to the far side of the corridor to check the conduit box located there.

"I mean, I feel like it starts with paranoia," Jax postulated. Saunders looked back over at her and squinted. "That's what EMF supposedly does. It elevates feelings of paranoia. So, if it were so astoundingly strong, then it would elevate more than just paranoia maybe?" Jax was reaching. She had a background in magnetics, gravitation and propulsion. This was decidedly *not* part of her failed thesis.

But she was already talking; so why stop now?

"I've been hearing things for days now. Just, little sounds at first...then—"

"Seeing things." Saunders finished. Jax looked over at her. Saunders' face had an expression of resignation.

"Uh, yeah. Like someone in a ceiling void who couldn't be there. For example." Jax offered this, over her shoulder, before returning to scan another length of conduit residing behind a wall panel.

"So, you *did* see someone up there. Maybe they weren't real, but you still *saw* them," Saunders said from behind her. Jax shuddered at the memory. "That probably explains why I..."

Jax looked over at Saunders, who had trailed off. Saunders shot her a fleeting look before, for once, being the first to break eye contact.

She found something in between them to stare at instead.

"Fears," Saunders amended, almost dreamily, from across metal floor panels. Jax narrowed her brow. She had finished scanning the conduit box; no spikes to the normal background field to be found. Jax made her way back over to the Security Officer.

"What?"

"So, it plays off our fears," Saunders elaborated, looking up into Jax's eyes, with something that looked earnest and uncomfortable. But her words still confused Jax. "The things we see, they are echoing our fears, and then we feed off each other, creating full scale nightmares for everyone to enjoy together."

"Okay, first off," Jax threw her hands up and flinched from the direct stare, "why did you have to phrase that like this is something intelligent? This is just a space station. A shitty tin can, spinning out in the middle of nowhere. And second: you have an interesting definition of 'enjoy.'" Jax had felt a spike in adrenaline at the thought of this being anything more than a Station failure.

"I'm just saying, I think there is a pattern to what we are seeing. A reason," Saunders countered, shifting her feet and bobbing her head to regain Jax's eye contact.

"I still don't follow you. There's been some horrific shit going around, but I don't ever remember dreaming about *that.*" Jax punctuated her statement with a hoist of her wrench up to the ceiling above them, and what would be the floor of Level 4.

"Well, think about it. One of my biggest fears is failing my team, my people, and recalling the abrupt conclusion of my term of service. You are afraid of the station residents."

"I am *not* afraid of the Station residents! The fuck?" Jax blurted out.

"You're afraid of their advances. You're skittish around them and offended by their social interactions. You think they are out for your blood half the time, figuratively speaking of course," Saunders stated, wryly, unslung arm now crossed smugly under the one in the sling.

Jax's earlier, warmer, feelings toward her coworker were cooling. Jax wasn't spooked easily, it was one of the few things she had going for herself, even if she had experienced a moment or two, in claustrophobic ceiling voids, with swarms of insectoids, murderous residents, and bloody slaughterhouses. On second thought, it had been a weird week.

"I'm just saying, first the attacks by zombie residents, then the bloody mess we found upstairs; it seems pretty plausible to have been built from things we are harboring as our own personal nightmares brought to life," Saunders concluded with a half-shrug, as if this was a perfectly normal thing to be debating.

"Or it could just be some resident freaking out. Like Paul. Maybe this whole thing is over now he is out of commission upstairs? It's been quiet ever since," Jax proposed. She would circle back to Saunders' earlier jab at a later, more opportune moment.

"Maybe. I'm the type of person who feels better when I have a plan. I figured maybe we can be better prepared if we know our own fears," Saunders offered up.

Jax looked up from scanning the wall with the gaussmeter and caught Saunders still looking over at her. She didn't have time to heed it as a warning.

"So, tell me Jax: what other nightmares do you have brooding in there with you?" Saunders asked, melodically, from the wall opposite Jax.

"What, other than running out of coffee?" Jax quipped, promptly *not* offering up her real fears.

"I'm serious. You clearly have encountered enough terrifying experiences to eject you across the stars, what else might we expect out here?" Saunders pressed.

Jax suddenly wasn't in the mood. This didn't need to be a close examination of her psyche in a haunted space station.

"Look, I have a damned good reason for my escape, I told you that," Jax lied. Saunders rolled her eyes.

"Oh, of course Jax. I have the *most* sympathy for you, really," she replied.

"I'm touched," Jax growled, eyebrows narrowed.

"I know; I was there for that too."

"*Fine!*" Jax gritted her teeth and exhaled. She busied herself with the probe in her hands, trying desperately to not give Saunders the satisfaction of getting a rise out of her. "So, then tell *me*. What else are *you* afraid of?" she shot back at the Security Officer.

"Me? Most likely further rejection and never getting the chance to explain myself. Don't dodge the question. What else, Jax? Aside from your fear of being a cheap date?" Saunders' shoulders were squared up to Jax where she stood in the corridor, her eyebrows raised in a challenge, feet planted evenly under her hips.

"HEY! Now that is a *low* fucking blow—" Jax had roared to life. She had been hoping this would stay a benign dialog to keep both their nerves at bay. But apparently Saunders liked it rough. Jax whirled around, finger raised, wrench gripped tight to her side, fully intending to express how little she appreciated getting charmed into bed by attractive coworkers with cheap alcohol; but she froze in place.

Jax caught the satisfied look on Saunders' face out of the corner of her vision, but then her expression shifted. Jax's sudden halt and the drift in her line of sight put her focus just over Saunders' shoulder.

"Don't tell me," sighed the Station Security Officer, and her face fell. "There's something behind me."

A chitinous skittering sound replied for both of them. Jax was cemented to the spot watching the hideous form of the deep space insectoid crawl up the wall, not a few inches from the back of Saunders' shoulder.

"Arachnophobia," Jax managed to mutter. "There weren't supposed to be bugs in space. Seemed like a good deal to me at the time."

Why was she not moving yet? Her vision had zeroed in on the lengthy, twitching feelers that were emerging from behind Saunders. The Security Officer was also not moving, having gone stone-cold still, save for a slight nod in resignation. Seconds drained past as they both considered their predicament.

Then, something like the result of a grand-daddy longlegs having aggressive sex with a common field cricket in the crater of a nuclear detonation descended between them on a thick, sticky, sinuous, butt rope and that launched them both into motion.

"Oh, FUCK no!" roared Jax, swiping with her wrench and knocking the monstrosity from its abdominal lunge line. Saunders pivoted and hefted her only defensive weapon against the thing targeting her spine for its next egg sack injection.

The proprietor of the ceiling assault impacted with the floor panels in a muster call for their many legged comrades. The swarm poured out into the hallway. Saunders maneuvered closer to Jax, chest perpendicular to Jax's shoulder, and fixed her glance behind them.

"They aren't real, right? So, they can't really hurt us," she stated, almost directly in Jax's ear. Jax was backing up, trusting Saunders had her blind spot covered and there was not another swarm cornering them.

"I thought upstairs was fake until twelve inches of kitchen knife got intimate with your shoulder," Jax said, under her breath, staring down the horde as it closed in on them.

"Well, now, don't be jealous—"

"And I *felt* the last one of these skittery fuckers crawling up my leg. I'm not taking any chances," Jax replied through clenched teeth, taking a step back to put more space between them and the swarm. She was relying on her sense of touch to tell where Saunders was positioning herself.

"Fair enough." Saunders pivoted her feet to cross her left arm over, her chest now flush with Jax's side. Her hand shot out and Jax felt the nightstick at her back. Behind her, Jax heard skittering. So, they were surrounded.

"Looks like we'll go down swinging then," Saunders said. Jax felt the warm, solid press of Saunders' muscular back against her own as the Security Officer shifted to take a position at her back facing the opposite direction. Jax gripped her wrench tight, hefting its weight up to her shoulder.

"I don't plan on going down at all," Jax stated.

"Shame, you're good at it."

Jax didn't get a chance to reply, as the first creature, with legs in too many places to count, flung itself at her. Behind her she felt Saunders also shift her weight under threat.

Jax jabbed at the incoming interstellar insectoid, aiming to spear it on the end of her wrench. The creature's exoskeleton protected it from being impaled, and instead it made a horrific screeching sound as it was knocked aside and scuttled away. Another lunged from the floor to her kneecaps, and Jax shifted her momentum downward to jab the whole of the wrench into the abdomen of this creature. A cringe inducing crunch sound accompanied a spray of space bug viscera that absolutely coated Jax's hands.

"Why do they have to crunch? I HATE the crunch!" she bellowed, this time kicking another away with her boots. To her back, she heard Saunders grunting and took the chance to check over her shoulder, just in time to see the Station Security Officer land a solid swing of her nightstick in the middle (thorax? These were not normally constructed looking bugs) of something with razor sharp looking mandibles, crushing it and getting her own sticky spray of guts as a reward.

"Ha, that's three!" Saunders roared, with what, absurdly, sounded like enjoyment.

"What the *fuck* do you think you're doing, keeping score?!" Jax shouted, before she had to pivot again and baseball swing the wrench head into an oncoming wasp-looking creature. The spray of dismembered legs and wings rained over her.

"Five!" grunted Saunders, in response. "Well? Keep up Jax!"

Unfortunately, Jax was rewarded for her momentary distraction at the Security Officer's off-hand bug killing skills by being enveloped in sticky ropes of webbing. She swore, flailed in retaliation, and knocked the sticky matter aside with her wrench, which was now coated in it. The fibrous residue entangled itself in her arms and hair and sent shudders of revulsion down her spine. She kicked out again, knocking several bug manifestations aside in a sweeping motion, feeling the webbing rip as she strained to fight against its tangled snare.

"This is *not* a competition!" Jax roared. But Saunders was busy with her own distractions. She seemed to be slowing down.

"How do we stop them?" called Saunders, and Jax could tell that the exertion so soon following her injury was probably not helping matters.

"We need to get out of here!" Jax replied, pulling off thick webbing from her face, and backing up to the side of the corridor to prevent them from becoming entirely surrounded and overwhelmed.

"Well, if you're not too busy getting tied up over there, I'm open to ideas," called Saunders.

Jax *was* too busy plowing through a swarm of grasping feelers and segmented legs to think clearly. She glanced up at the swarm direction. They were pouring from the air vents. Jax counted they were seventy-five degrees from the Common Access point, which meant they were back under where the Market had come alive. They needed to shift down corridor; change this from an ambush to a chase.

Jax aimed one work boot at the nearest set of gnashing mandibles and kicked, sweeping a path for her to back up toward Saunders.

"Seventy-five degrees to Common Access!" she shouted over her shoulder, ramming her wrench through another nightmare bug like a lance.

"Unfortunately, that's where they seem to be coming from!" called Saunders, who took aim at something with a few too many nasty looking stingers like she was nailing a field goal. Her boot connected solidly with her target, and sent it smashing into the wall, where it burst into a slimy mess. But her follow through on her kick had put her off balance and another creature, like a mutated centipede with lopsided wings, latched on to her extended foot. "Shit!"

Jax swung her wrench at the floor to create room around her as she backed to where Saunders was trying to shake off whatever was clinging to her foot. Jax swung into place and smashed the poor head of her beloved wrench into the coils of the creature still piled on the floor, bisecting the segmented body and leaving it in two writhing halves curling in on each other. The twitching end latched to Saunders' foot fell off to die with its other half.

"I hear you have a bug problem ma'am," Jax said, though mostly she said it to the poor smashed end of her wrench. It would be useless for cracking open the sewage system again, though that might be a blessing in disguise.

"Shut up and get us out of here, Jax!" barked Saunders.

Jax paid for her moment of wrench remorse as some*thing* with razor sharp mandibles landed a vicious bite below her left knee. Jax roared again, this time in searing pain, and hauled her leg out of reach from the gaping maw of the revolting creature. Saunders swung her nightstick, busting a gooey crater in the insectoid's main body segment. The creature fell back in a death curl and Jax and Saunders shifted back against the wall, grasping for each other in the sea of roiling insect legs. Jax swept wide with the wrench, and an opening emerged in the swarm.

"Move!" shouted Jax, ignoring the burning sensation in her leg. It was all in her head, but they needed to get the hell out of there before anything else could pretend to hurt them.

They made a break for it down the corridor. The swarm followed, on the floor, from the vents in the walls, and across the ceiling. More space-age spider crickets dropped from sticky lines and Jax had to dodge and weave as they pushed around the curve of the Level back to Common Access.

"Get the door!" Jax called as the exit came into view.

Saunders already had her access card out to get them off the Level. The doors opened and Saunders scrambled through. Jax took two steps out the door, planted a foot and turned to address the assault bearing down on them. She gritted her teeth against the sting of the deep scratch on her calf, solidified her grip on her dearly beloved steel companion, and swung her whole form into a glorious slap shot at the lead skittery antagonists. The wrench head collided with exoskeleton bodies, smashing them to pieces and driving the remains into the swarming crowd behind it. Saunders slammed her hand down on the door latch, arresting the remaining swarm.

"Okay they might not be real, but that at least *felt* satisfying." Jax reveled in her follow-through as she stared at the glittering, many-segmented bodies now covering the glass windows of the level.

Saunders had bolted away from the doors after sealing them. Now the strong hand of the Security Officer grabbed Jax by the tool belt and hauled her out into Common Access.

They hit the back wall, watching the shadows of the swarm on the door. The Station groaned around them, and it drew Jax's attention to the stairs ascending and descending dimly in either direction from them. She half expected the swarm to pour up into the stairwell from some hidden point below them. Saunders still had a hand on Jax's tool belt and some instinct had compelled her to pull Jax back from the stairs leading downward. Jax scrambled back to the wall, bumping into Saunders and looked back up.

The bugs were gone. Jax looked down at her hands, boots, and coveralls. Her forearms had been entangled in the sticky webbing and she had been covered in the squashed guts of insects from the depths of hell. Now she was clean and clear of any gore. The only soiling on her clothes was the dust of her aging Space Station and her own sweat. And the dried blood of the man she had killed. And blood from Saunders who had not died in her arms only an hour earlier. Okay, Jax was filthy. But they were both still alive.

Jax's attention went to the hand still gripping her toolbelt, attached to the one mobile arm of the injured Security Officer. Her shoulder bandages were showing some blood soaking through. Clearly, fending off a chittering swarm of ravenous cosmic locust mutants was not the best recovery plan for shoulder stab wounds.

Jax absentmindedly reached out to check the bandages on Saunders' arm, got as far as brushing the end of Saunders' shoulder, then withdrew her hands. Saunders wasn't even paying attention.

"I want to know what makes them disappear," the Security Officer huffed. Jax snapped her attention away from Saunders' shoulder, and by extension the rest of her, currently gripping Jax by the waist and glistening with sweat from exertion.

"Maybe it was that hole-in-one I just scored," Jax offered.

"While I certainly have faith in your ability to score a hole in anything, I'd still like to understand what we are up against," Saunders replied.

"Do you just...have these saved up somewhere?" Jax coughed.

"It's a defense mechanism," Saunders replied. "Besides, you might have a 'hole-in-one,' but I had a higher score!"

"Oh yeah, you won the game. Congratulations Saunders. If that's how you plan to deflect swarms of hallucinations no wonder you're still gripping me as a human shield," Jax scoffed, indicating the white-knuckle grip on her screw driver pouch, still very much attached to her belt. Saunders quickly let go.

"Sorry; just wanted a prize, I guess," Saunders replied hastily.

Jax had to take a moment to stare pointedly at the woman. It was hard to comprehend exactly how to register half the shit coming out of Saunders' mouth.

But Saunders was already shifting.

"Jax, please tell me your escape across the stars didn't have anything to do with monstruous arachnids following you? Or your research opened some sort of portal to hell? Because that is just a bit too Lovecraftian for me right now," Saunders groaned, putting her face in her hands. It was now or never to come clean.

"No, nothing like that," Jax grunted, hefting her poor wrench. Saunders peeked up over the edge of her hands to glance at her wearily.

"No, nothing like *that*?" Saunders pressed.

Jax fidgeted under the sharp stare. Then, like the torrent of skittery bugs they had just fought off, the truth rushed, vicious and twitching, out of Jax before she could swallow it back down again,

"I slept with my boss."

The tips of Jax's ears burned. Saunders pulled her hands slowly from her face, her side-eye glance holding Jax just out of reach.

"What?" the Security Officer asked, slowly.

"That's what I was running from," Jax grumbled. "On Earth. I got seduced by a rival research group, quit my original team for the hot boss, slept my way onto the project, then got kicked to the curb once her next conquest came along. I didn't even know it was happening. I thought I could trust them, but she kept my research, and I got blacklisted to every university within the solar system." Jax rushed the words out, trying to get this over as fast as possible.

Saunders had turned to face her now, head tilted sideways and a bit forward, brow narrowed, her eyes greener and more piercing than ever. Jax shrank under the scrutiny.

"That's *it?*" Saunders hissed. She looked shocked and annoyed at the same time. Jax winced.

"All this...secrecy, this bullshit, this self-righteous, asshole attitude, it's all because you slept around to get ahead, and then ran away when it caught up with you? Because you...fucked around...and found out?"

Jax felt her neck flush at the accusation.

"I *told* you I was a mess!" she objected. "And I had nothing left for me back on Earth, not even family. No one wanted a damned thing to do with me. I *loved* her. I thought she loved me. Turns out I'm just an easy target. I had no *choice* but to run, if I wanted to salvage even a scrap of my dignity. At least it doesn't have anything to do with all the horrendous bullshit going on right now!"

"Oh, you are a piece of fucking work, Jax. All this time I've been even remotely sympathetic," Saunders growled. She looked as pissed as Jax had always expected her to be. "Well that all makes sense. Especially your bullshit piety regarding the residents, fucking hypocrite. All right, fine." Saunders jutted her chin out at Jax, who flinched.

"Fine what?" Jax asked hesitantly. She wasn't sure she could handle any more revelations under her current state of duress. But instead, Saunders smirked.

"Fine, we're even. You know my backstory, and now I know yours." (Jax would hardly call that even.) "Though I'll admit it is a bit disappointing. Whatever. No more accusing the other of hiding things. Aren't we coming along *fantastically,*" Saunders said, her voice dripping in sarcasm.

Jax wanted to argue, but her energy was waning. There was also a wash of relief from finally admitting her real reasons for her isolation so far from humanity, no matter how bullshit they might be. At least Saunders hadn't rubbed in her more valid reason for wanting an escape. Jax shook her head and turned to the stairwell. A sting of pain radiated up her left leg and she sucked in her breath.

"What?" The tonal shift was shocking. Saunders was immediately next to her, voice shifting from the previous accusatory tone to one full of concern. Jax stared in bewilderment at the Security Officer, instead of looking down at her calf, which radiated pain. But Saunders was already attending to her, so Jax looked beyond the deft hands of the other woman.

Her boots and clothes were completely clear of leftover bug viscera, but there was a very distinct rip in the leg of Jax's coveralls. She reached down, past where Saunders was inspecting, and gingerly pulled the length of the leg up, showing the skin underneath, and a long, red gash.

"But I thought they were hallucinations?!" Saunders exclaimed, kneeling to examine the injury. Jax was leaning over too, attempting to get a better look, and nearly toppled over on top of the shorter woman.

"Don't ask me. I'm making this shit up as I go!" Jax hissed again through her teeth as Saunders prodded the wound.

"Does it hurt?" Saunders asked, inquisitively.

"No, it feels amazing—OF COURSE it fucking hurts, Saunders!" Jax growled, as the Security Officer prodded it again.

"Maybe you scratched yourself while fighting?" Saunders looked up. Jax glared down at her. She stepped back from where Saunders crouched and dropped the leg of her coveralls.

"Maybe it's not worth it for me to stand here showing a little leg in Common Access. We'll take care of that later. Let's just assume, from now on, everything is fair game as far as danger goes," Jax stated. Saunders hoisted herself up wearily from her crouch, to meet Jax's stare. The enormity of their mission still weighed heavy on them, and it clearly washed away whatever accusations Saunders might have about Jax hiding her past.

Jax hefted the wrench, now looking a little more battle weary, having cleared their path through the nightmares, fended off a real assault, and made her way to the top of the stairs. Her leg didn't even hurt *that* much. Maybe she *had* just scratched it in the fray. Jax looked back to make sure the Security Officer was following her. Saunders was looking back at Jax with an unreadable expression.

"Not such a bad idea to carry a Murder Wrench, now, is it?" Jax said and turned to head down to Level 2.

Chapter Nineteen

The Common Access landing outside Level 2 was refreshingly free from any swarm of nightmares. Jax dug out the two flashlights she had found in her bunk before leaving Level 5, neither more than a small maintenance light. She handed one to Saunders. The doors to the level looked ominous. No light shone from the small porthole.

Around them the Station groaned again, loudly protesting some massive external load to its structure. It ached with the sound of a thousand straining bolts and steel beams. It was the loudest sound yet, and Jax backed up against the railing, looking up through the bowels of her keep.

"Is that also part of the failing core? Are we out of time?" Saunders asked, looking around as if she could see the sound waves reverberating.

"No, it couldn't be," Jax replied, but it was mostly to herself. "I know what it sounds like when the rotationals are off, this isn't it."

The Station structural integrity was an entirely different beast, but Jax couldn't be certain there wasn't a connection between a dying core and what sounded like the pressure of a thousand fathoms of water straining at the joints, waiting to crush them. In fact, she was keen on solving the core issues to remove it as a potential culprit, perhaps making the next fix easier to conquer.

"Keeping the station alive is your whole personality Jax, maybe this is your fear and we're hallucinating these sounds?" Saunders interjected. Jax scowled but couldn't disagree.

"There is something actually affecting the structure. I half suspect it's throwing us off course. The star trackers were struggling to pick up our navigation points earlier. The sounds are real, I just don't know how to fix them, or what exactly is causing them. Not yet. I had some theories, but I can't handle that on top of everything else we have going on. She's just going to have to wait. I'll have to deal with it eventually, but right now, that sounds like a tomorrow problem."

"Well, I'll pencil you in for structural repairs on Tuesday then? Or does Tuesday not exist out here?" Saunders replied. The Station groaned again around them, as if commiserating with Jax.

"Any deep space denizen knows we measure time out here in cycles of existential dread, or did I get saddled with a Security Officer who still goes by days of the week?" Jax replied, gently reaching her fingers out to feel the low-level aftershock vibrations in the metal.

"So, we're right on schedule."

"The way you manage to keep track of my work schedule is infuriating, no offense," Jax admitted, candidly.

"How do you think I feel? Apparently, I'm stuck in deep space with someone whose longest and most successful intimate relationship is with a space station. No offense."

At this, Jax pulled her fingers back from the tender touch she bestowed on her precious Station. That was a low blow, but she figured she deserved it. Jax doubled down on her caress, just for emphasis, and languidly stroked her hand up the wall of the stairwell.

"Yeah, well she's been a bit of a bitch lately, I'm not sure it's working out." Jax looked back up the length of Common Access to her nest on Level 5. Then she dropped her eyes to meet the piercing green of the Security Officer's stare, this time returning a challenge.

"You both have so much in common. It wasn't my intention to be a homewrecker." Saunders in pain from stab wounds and battles waged with nightmares, was apparently Saunders on fire.

"Sounds like she's wrecking herself. So, were we going to finish this sweep job, or should I strap on my rivet belt?" Jax said hitching a single eyebrow. She scrutinized Saunders standing at the door frame.

Saunders paused without a counter response, her mouth open, a look on her face that left Jax feeling self-satisfied.

A temporary standoff loomed between them, and they came to rest at an impasse, the brevity of the moment fading. Saunders gave a long exhale, saving her snappy retort for later, turned, and reached out her access card. She hesitated one last time, looking over her shoulder at Jax. They made eye contact again, and Saunders swiped. The doors opened with a small, pressurized hiss. The air inside was cold.

Pitiful lights on, wrench and nightstick raised, they entered the level. It was oppressively dark. Jax had routed some moderate auxiliary power back to the level from the core, but the lights were still all burnt out. She popped open a storage panel in the wall and pulled out a larger flashlight. It had a better beam, though nothing like Saunders' security light, which remained useless on Level 1.

"I'm thrilled at the idea of repeating that little adventure in the dark," Saunders mumbled, training her beam around.

"I'd prefer it with the lights on too," Jax replied, closing the locker.

"As I've discovered recently," came Saunders' voice from behind her.

The looming mystery beyond them stifled any answer Jax might give. She was less afraid of fighting off another skittering horde and more afraid of finding she had indeed sentenced someone to a slow and agonizing death on a locked off Station level. Ahead of them lay the various bay doors leading off to the multitudes of storage compartments for Station supplies. Jax turned back to Saunders where she stood haloed in a ring of weak light from the flashlight in her hand, darkness pressing in around her.

"We're going to have to check every one of these, aren't we?" said Jax. Saunders nodded next to her. This was going to take forever, but this was a search and recovery operation, and they had an obligation to their posts.

They started on their route. One by one, they opened each storage bay and walked the rows of supplies. Nothing seemed out of place, and the gaussmeter barely blinked. It was so incredibly dark.

By around the third bay Jax started hearing it again: the scuttling shuffle of feet in the darkness. The air tensed and she could see Saunders stiffen. She was hearing it, too. Jax shone a light on the gaussmeter. This storage unit was reading a high level of magnetic field. She looked up to make eye contact with Saunders.

"The bugs again?" asked the Security Officer.

Jax stilled her movement and trained her ear to the silence around them.

Nothing.

Then a shuffle from the corridor.

"This sounds like footsteps. Human footsteps. It could be the missing residents?" Jax offered feebly, her voice lower than a whisper.

"But how could they access a locked level?"

"I think some of them found my back access routes," Jax replied.

Saunders stepped closer so they shared a halo of light, and Jax dug the scrap of green fabric from her pocket.

"I think this came from Paul's jacket."

"Jax," Saunders said, picking up the small shred, "That means we need to check all your hideaways too!"

Jax's heart sank. There wouldn't be enough time.

"Let's just...finish the levels first. I have several of my routes locked off anyway. I riveted a few others shut as well. We only have so much time left to finish this search," Jax suggested.

They cautiously backed out of the storage locker and into the corridor. Nothing swarmed from the oppressively inky darkness of the curving walls around them. The next locker was the one from short-term stores still awaiting its next transport. This was the one that Saunders had read off the manifest.

Jax gave the corridor one last sweep with her light while Saunders swiped her card for container access.

The locker housed one single, large, deep space transport crate. It was the type that could latch to the outside of a transport and freefly through space. The meteoroid-resistant panels were made of high-impact carbon composite, lightweight, and sturdy. This load had needed to be hauled in from Docking though the freight airlock connecting directly to the large cargo lift-shaft to Supply. It was certainly large enough to hold a swarm of cosmic critters.

A sweep around its exterior revealed no breach in its seals, and no evidence of ravenous escape. Nothing else occupied the space. Saunders popped the latches with her one free hand, her nightstick tucked under her restrained arm. Jax slipped her wrench into her tool belt and helped pry off the storage container's lid.

Inside were hundreds of drill bits, used for resource mining. They were probably slated for one of the exoplanets several months' journey away that were being ground up for their materials.

Jax grabbed one of the parts, but it was stuck fast. She put her flashlight in her teeth and pulled with both hands, but it still wouldn't budge. She tried to step down from the opening but found she was now also stuck. Her wrench was held firmly against the storage case, and, since it was looped in her belt, the wrench held her firmly in place as well.

"Well, fuck" she said. Saunders walked around to shine the light on Jax's predicament.

"What's wrong?" Saunders asked. Jax had swiveled around in her belt and put her boot against the storage bin in an effort to dislodge herself.

"Magnetized," she huffed, in her effort to pry herself loose. "There's a massive alternating current running through this section of the Station, and it's magnetized the cargo. And it means I'm stuck."

"But these cargo containers aren't made of metal."

"The drill bits are," Jax grunted, her frustration mounting. She leveraged her hips to push the wrench, but it merely scraped against the container panel.

"I'm assuming this might be an important clue for us?" Saunders mused, watching Jax struggle. Jax caught the bemused expression on Saunders face and scowled further.

"I checked the corridor before we entered," Jax wheezed. "And it's right at the seventy-degree mark, same degree as the Market, and where we had to be exterminators upstairs." She switched positions again and resumed her yanking. "My guess is this conduit is sourcing the EMF. It should be shielded, but instead it's bleeding over—*huff*—into each Level at this point around the curve. *Hnnnnnnngh*," Jax strained. She shot a venomous look at the clearly entertained Security Officer.

"This spot is strongest, so my guess is there's an added electrical short." Jax was still stuck solid, the length of her wrench refusing to divorce the strong magnetic pull of the container. Everyone wanted to grab her by the tool belt these days. She panted with the exertion of trying to free herself. Then she gave another fruitless heave.

"It sounds like your EMF theory is shaping up to be a pretty good guess," Saunders stated.

"It might—*nrrrrrrng*—also be why the lights were acting up. Is this fun for you, Saunders?"

"Oh no, this is amazing. Please continue," Saunders replied, gesturing to all of Jax.

"*Saunders*, are you going to fucking help me?" Jax asked, boiling over with frustration.

"I never thought I would hear you ask," Saunders replied. She, too, wrapped her one unconstrained hand around the bottom of the wrench, and placed a boot against the cargo wall. Jax wrapped her hands around the top and lifted both feet up against the side of the container. They pulled, Jax putting the entirety of her leg strength into her effort, and the wrench pried free.

The sudden release, and the fact that Jax's feet were not on the floor sent them both toppling over into the space behind them. By luck or mercy, the wrench avoided knocking anyone unconscious, but in a crueler turn of fate, Jax found herself sprawled on top of Saunders, arms spread to either side of her face to brace against a worse impact. Saunders' hands, even the one in the sling, had flown up to protect her but had wound up on either side of Jax's ribcage. The familiarity of it was jarring.

"Funny running into you like this. You come here often?" Saunders said innocently.

"Shut up," mumbled Jax, as she hustled back to her feet, gripping the wrench tightly and holding it away from the heavy pull of the magnetized crate. She wasn't in the mood for more of Saunders' teasing at the moment.

Saunders didn't say anything more. The shuffling sounds of feet were coming once again from out in the corridor.

At the storage locker door, they both waited, breathlessly. There were certainly shuffling steps out there now. They could both hear it clearly. Jax raised her wrench protectively and Saunders gripped her flashlight and nightstick until her knuckles turned white and shone in the dark. They shared a three count before throwing open the door onto the corridor.

No one walked the halls. But they were not alone. All along the floor in crumpled piles were dead bodies. All of them suffered from the slow freezing decompression of a locked off space station level, as if Jax had condemned an entire population to die in her effort to secure her nightmares.

They walked, gingerly, down the narrow isle between corpses. At first Jax ached with the thought these had been the remainder of the residents, the ones who had not self-isolated on Level 4. But there were far too many of them. It looked like over a hundred. And the level had been locked off before she had seen the Station residents and told them to isolate. Who were these people?

With every step, Jax felt a growing sense of dread, mixed with swelling guilt. She had failed them. They were blood on her hands, even if they weren't really here in the first place.

The complete lack of light, save for their flashlights shining over the prone figures, made for an eerie, unsettling feeling. Jax couldn't tell if they were dead or sleeping. Did one just move? Would they swarm them like the horde had a level up? Or were these real people, true undead, capable of inflicting legitimate damage? The scratch on her leg throbbed in response, as if reminding her they might not be able to tell the difference between reality and imagination anymore.

They were passing storage rooms now, not bothering to check. The adrenaline from their fight one level up against the inhuman horrors of the swarm of interstellar insects was replaced, slowly, with the sticky terror of the haunting sight around them.

The deeper they wandered into the level, the more bodies they found until they had to step over them instead of around them. Hundreds now; more than Station capacity could hold. Jax aimed her flashlight up to the ceiling, illuminating the degree indicators to determine how far they had traversed on the level.

One hundred and seventy-five degrees.

There was her cart full of lights, looming out of the dark like a shipwreck sunk in a sea of bodies.

A few paces more and a soft sound filled the space. Thus far they had not heard the shuffling footsteps since entering the corridor. The only sounds Jax had heard were their own echoing footsteps, and the tense breathing of Saunders next to her. Now more shuffling sounded from behind them. It was quiet, like the settling of air in the surrounding void, but they both whirled around and shone their lights.

The bodies lay prone and still.

Jax scanned the gradual curving slope of floor up to where it disappeared past the ceiling. Saunders followed her gaze.

Nothing was there.

Jax and Saunders turned back around to face a wall of standing, staring dead. Their eyes were glassy and vacant, they stood shoulder to shoulder, packed tight and surrounding them. In the moment they had turned around the bodies behind them had also stood up. They were closing in on them. Packing tighter and tighter. Jax and Saunders tried to shove their way through; but the more they moved, the closer the undead crowd encroached upon them.

The faces in that crowd were familiar. Here was a resident that Jax had actually bothered to talk to once, and there was a face that she was certain she had left on Earth eons ago. It was too much. The hallucinations were drawing from deep memory now; she wouldn't be able to tell what was real and what wasn't any more. The edges were closing in again, and Jax actually missed the thrill of their earlier space bug battle, as if preferring her fate to be full of action than despair.

From somewhere adrift in the sea of pressing dead Jax heard Saunders' voice, getting carried away from her in the crowd.

"Shit. It's my rear detail squad." Saunders' voice sounded resigned, lost to her own sinking feelings of failure.

Jax knew whose faces Saunders was seeing in the crowd. They were going to be stuck here, unable to escape the throng of dead they had left behind throughout their lives, sinking to unreachable depths in the darkest part of deep space. The Station would die, and they would too, along with it. What did that matter, out here so deep in space? To anyone they had left behind, they were so far away, so impossible to reach; for all it mattered, they might as well already be dead. Her path to this Station had inevitably been a one-way ticket. At one point in Jax's life that was probably exactly what she had been hoping for. A sudden pinch in her chest told her that wasn't the case anymore.

Across the battering sea of dead bodies Jax heard Saunders cry out again.

"I'm sorry!" It served to pinpoint her location.

In a sudden spark of clarity Jax recalled a moment, and a feeling, and a grasping truth. In this mob of hallucinations there was one thing she knew to be real and solid. It was something she had sensory proof of, to know it existed, alive and well.

"Saunders!" Jax called with a desperate shout.

She swung her shoulders around to break room for movement, using the wrench like an oar in a frothing, foaming sea of ghosts, and pushed her arms out toward the sound of Saunders' voice. She mercilessly elbowed some corpse in the face and barreled her way through. Her light shone on Saunders briefly and she threw her hand out to blindly grasp, finally feeling her fingers brush the warmth of Saunders' living, breathing chest.

Jax grabbed Saunders by the tank top and pulled, yanking Saunders through the crowd of lost souls and hauling her hard against Jax's body. Wrench discarded, flashlight dropped, Jax wrapped a hand in Saunders' hair and pulled her lips to hers to kiss the Station Security Officer.

Eyes pressed shut, arms wrapped hard around the shorter woman, Jax held tight. Saunders stood rigid before relaxing into Jax's unyielding hold. Her hands snaked up to grip Jax's back like a lifeline as her lips parted to kiss her back.

Jax poured every emotion she could recall into that contact. She drew on her real feelings for Saunders, forgiving her for their rush to intimacy, for every teasing joke at the expense of her insecurity between them. She relented to herself, giving in to how badly she wanted more from Saunders, how much she had been yearning to feel her close again, and how much she found herself fallen for the Security Officer.

Jax allowed herself to admit her own denial to herself of human contact. She rejected the absurd reasoning for her self-isolation and surrounded herself with the memories of their one night together, drunkenly discovering each other. She used it to fuel the knowledge that this person, out of all the others, was real, and not a manifestation of her imagination.

Jax willed herself to trust, despite years of suspicion and self-defense, and gave in to whatever the outcome might be.

It felt like a cyclone of wind in the form of impacting vengeful dead battered them from all sides. Jax hoped that it was only the dead, and not the very real threat of the living succumbing to madness. Then she forced herself to drive it from her mind and focus only on the warmth of Saunders pressed into her arms. The cyclone reached a crescendo, then stopped abruptly.

Jax opened her eyes and broke away from Saunders. The Security Officer hesitated a moment, her eyes half lidded, lips still parted, then seemed to return to her senses;

awakening from whatever hallucinatory spell had been cast on them. She pushed herself out from Jax's embrace to look around. They had both dropped their lights to the floor, which was now clear of bodies, dead or alive, save for them, and one other.

Saunders didn't say anything. She stepped out of Jax's reach, and silently made a direct path toward the figure on the floor against the wall. Feeling like there might be something left hanging in the air between them, Jax scooped up her discarded flashlight and followed.

It was the woman from the CC footage. Saunders knelt to check her pulse as Jax provided the light. As Saunders pushed the body her face came into the pale circle of light. What was left of it showed a gaping eye socket, surrounded by vicious lacerations.

"Yeah, she's dead. And I recognize her too." Saunders confirmed.

"How?" Jax asked thickly, through gritted teeth.

"T-shirt. She was part of the drop squad awaiting deployment. They'll need to know as soon as we get this wrapped up," Saunder replied. Jax felt a sinking feeling in her gut.

"So, I killed her then," she said flatly.

"Looks more like blood loss to me. My guess is she suffered a similar early sensitivity like Long-Haul-Paul. Probably seeing things, like the rest of us. Most likely she was self-inflicting as her mind started to go. Or maybe it was Paul. The tapes might show us some better angles if we comb through them, but she has a lot of tissue damage that looks to have been in decay before the deep freeze set in," Saunders wrapped up.

"The idea that hallucinations might drive someone to rip their own face off does not make me feel better about the state of things," Jax replied, swallowing hard. This might be worse than what they had seen up on Level 4. At least that scene had been their imagination.

"Based on how real those things up in medical felt while scuttling up my back, I think I could be driven mad enough to do some serious damage. Especially since we still don't know if you actually got bit by one. Maybe these *aren't* self-inflicted..." Saunders trailed off. Jax gulped at the implication.

Saunders ran a last check over the victim, as if this care, even in death, might somehow alleviate the suffering she had experienced. Jax looked away, shuddering at the thought of how maddening it might have been to claw her own face off to escape an assaulting deep space insectoid, real or not.

"We can leave her here for now. We probably need to sweep Level 1, then get you back to the core before this place starts to float," Saunders said, standing up. Her jokes were done.

She was determinedly ignoring what had just passed between them, standing amongst the dead, and Jax was fine with that. She hadn't had a chance to examine her actions thoroughly enough to be ready to address it just yet.

"I'm all for getting out of here," Jax said. "I think I know what power conduit is causing the EMF spike, but we should finish the full sweep just to be sure."

She looked up and down the corridor. It was faster to sprint the length and get back to Common Access. It might not even matter though. She had a hunch about where the problem was, but Jax still had no idea how to save them.

Chapter Twenty

They didn't run into any other hallucinations on Supply, opting to make a straight shot for the exit. Back in Common Access, Saunders re-sealed the doors. She turned to Jax with a look betraying a different kind of pain than from her shoulder, now out of its sling.

"What was that? Back there?" she said, quietly. Jax let a panicked roulette wheel spin in her head for a moment. It wasn't like she didn't know what Saunders was asking, but she had kissed her back. There had been this profound moment of connection between them before they had broken apart. But the look on Saunders' face didn't instill confidence that worst was now behind them. Jax wanted to protest, but instead the ball landed on "truth."

"You are the only person I actually know on this Station. The only person I have *truly* known, in *years* even. Everything here is transient and shifting and my only rock has been the Station itself, and now she is failing too. I'm failing her. It's all falling apart. But *you*. You are tangible, and you are real. I know what you smell like, I know the sound of your breathing, I know how warm you feel. I hoped that surrounding myself with you would ground me, and hopefully you too," Jax said. It wasn't poetry, and it probably didn't even make sense.

Saunders was standing, arms tightly crossed over her chest in defense, eyeing Jax with scrutiny. If Jax had hoped for a warm, embracing smile and a happy ending, she wasn't going to get it.

"You have spent a week treating me like absolute shit, Jax," she said. Saunders had swept aside her bravado of jokes and innuendo in this moment. She looked raw. Jax felt the cold sludge of discomfort and regret slither around her and wished for them to be anywhere else in this moment. Didn't they still have a space station to save? She looked away.

"I *liked* you. I thought we could maybe team up a bit, maybe you would realize I was genuinely into you, and then you turned into the most insufferable shithead I could have imagined. And that is just not okay!"

"I know," Jax said quietly. There wasn't really an excuse for that. She absent-mindedly rubbed at the scratch on her leg as an outlet for the awkward feeling crashing down on her.

"Do you?" Saunders said. Her voice was cracking a bit. "That hurt Jax, all of it! It's tortuously lonely out here and I saw you and felt maybe it was going to be okay. I have spent years getting over the last person I cared about dying bloody in stupid crossfire. I have taken my time admitting to myself there's a reason for me to like someone again. Then I saw this person who clearly cared so deeply for her work, whose sense of loyalty kept us alive on a daily basis, who didn't take shit from anyone but was still reliable at the end of the day. I saw someone who I thought I could connect with.

"And for a brief moment we did connect, and I saw how great it was, and then I felt how absolutely terrible it could really be. I wanted to go back to that asteroid to escape it. That's probably why Level 4 warped reality like that.

"I only wanted more of you, Jax. But you push everyone away, without even looking over your shoulder. Like hell if anyone ever really cared for you, you were going to burn that bridge before you ever even came to it!"

Jax hurt, and not just the burning radiating from the phantom bug-bite. Her whole chest ached with an uncomfortable pain. She hazarded a look up at Saunders who had hot, frustrated tears in her eyes that accompanied the waiver in her voice. It betrayed the confident swagger Saunders had in this very stairwell not an hour earlier, besting Jax in a duel of backhanded comments. Jax yearned for a return to that moment, or a return to a week ago before she let her own insecurity abolish the world around her.

"I—" Jax started, but there wasn't much to say. She deserved all of it. She had wrapped herself in layers of treacherous space station and piled herself under resentment and bitterness that hid her well from the prying eyes of humanity, protecting her from the pain it could cause her. In her wake, she had caused nearly the same damage that had driven her this deep into space in the first place.

"It probably doesn't matter, since I can't see us surviving this mess so easily, but I put a call in yesterday to cut my contract short," Saunders said. "I figured you would be happy knowing I was gone, and you would be left alone. Clearly, I was never very good at this job anyway. I asked to leave with the research crew in three weeks."

And just like that, Jax knew she had achieved a terrible goal, one that she now hated and despised: she had run Saunders off Station.

She let the weight of this realization sink over her. She felt a sharp, angry rip somewhere deep in her chest. It made breathing hard. Suddenly she hated this Station. She hated its confined walls, and its unforgiving mistress of deep space beyond. She hated the dark, the cold, and the unyielding that it represented. She yearned for open spaces and sunlight, for fresh, uncirculated air.

She understood, with a sick and deafening realization, that these were all things she might never experience again. And the only small piece she could have held onto, of all those warm and brighter opportunities, was leaving on a transport with the once sunny disposition of the Station Security Officer. She felt like she needed to say something, even if it wouldn't change how incurably terrible she was as a person.

"I don't have a good excuse." Jax felt her brain seek out anything she could assemble into a thought, to try to tell this stubborn, perfect example of what she found to be right in the universe exactly what she felt.

"I've let my own bitterness and stupidity poison everything around me, and you are right about that. But you aren't right about everything." Jax took a deep, shuttering breath, and squeezed her eyes shut to say what came next. "I do like you. In fact, I have been maddeningly *into* you, have been from the moment I saw you, and that *scared* me," Jax said. It wasn't going to help. She could see Saunders' expression closing off, but she was already talking, and couldn't stop.

Pouring everything she knew into kissing Saunders to stay grounded in a sea of death had opened the gates to a different kind of hell. Jax was reeling from giving in to everything she had held back for so long. Now it was almost an argument she was having with herself.

"I have been atrocious, because I have spent my life building a fortress around myself and you showed up and knocked it down, without even saying 'please.' And you came here, with your beautifully infectious positivity, that I can still barely understand, and your ability to see the best in everyone, myself included, and I wasn't ready for you. But I could have been." Jax realized she was talking to herself still and redirected her voice back to the Station Security Officer, who was wearing a mask of pain.

"If I was given the time, I wanted it. But it was too fast. I wasn't ready. So instead of seeing how much I wanted this, I let myself get pissed off about it. I couldn't let myself trust you the way you needed me to. Hurting you was never something I wanted to do," Jax said, defeated. Heartbreak was a feeling she thought she could outrun. Here at the edge of the universe, it still caught up with her. "When it comes down to it, I only know how to be the worst version of me, no matter who gets caught in the collateral damage. You don't deserve that."

A few silent moments ticked by. Jax felt that if she looked at Saunders, she would fall to pieces like she had back on Level 4, so instead she stared though the wall of the stairwell, leading to whatever awaited them below. The silence stretched achingly between them in the abandoned stairwell of Common Access.

"We need to finish our sweep of Level 1. Can I trust you to get through this?" came Saunders' voice finally. It was sharp, and efficient. Jax's heart sunk, though she did not know what hope she had been holding out for.

But there was still a job to do. Her Station still needed her, and if she couldn't prove herself worthy of Saunders then she could still prove herself worthy of the only other relationship she had ever trusted, no matter how much she wanted to be free of the bond. Jax steeled herself enough to look up at Saunders and nod.

The gravity had already dropped notably in Common Access, indicating the drain of power trickling away. They were short on time. They headed down to Level 1.

* * *

Level 1 was gloriously better lit than the previous levels. It seemed almost like daylight. The windows even seemed to let in some other-worldly light source, as if the stars were screaming out in space. And it was quiet, in a calmer, un-haunted sort of way.

There were no transports docked at this time, which left the view ports entirely clear. With the airlocks vacant, there were few places to hide, save for the security office and quarters, the supply lift shaft, a few docking conference room spaces, and the measly transport repair shop Jax had slimmed down to the bare necessities. Saunders retrieved her busted and broken taser from the hallway outside of Security. Jax wondered if they should bother checking the office, even though they had only been there a few hours ago. Saunders seemed to share her apprehension. A sweep of the area with the gaussmeter revealed nothing foreboding about the rooms that had thrown them together in the first place.

They passed the empty ports in silence for several degrees, finding nothing unusual. Jax kept her thoughts to herself, under the assumption she could only do more harm if she bothered to open her mouth again. She scanned the power conduit running along the base of the wall, routing to each and every outboard rotational. The gaussmeter indicator remained deceptively dormant, even as they neared the engine at two-hundred and fifty degrees: the first engine to fail just a few days ago.

Jax lingered here, running her hands over the panel readout on the back wall. It was blank now, as useless as the medical computers that had failed them up on Level 3. But she spent added time around the routed conduit she knew existed behind the wall panels, leading to her precious engines. She crouched to examine the breaker switch embedded at the apex of the wall and the floor. Jax realized she had not taken note of where the major engine failure cascade had started. She had been too overwhelmed with trying to halt the failure. In fact, Jax had been overwhelmed by too many things in such a short period of time. What else had she missed?

"Jax."

The soft sound of her name made Jax jump. How many times had Saunders snuck up on her, quiet and unassuming, to make Jax leap with a jolt, nearly flinging herself into deep space? Why did Jax now react with relief instead of aggravation? She looked up at the Security Officer who had said her name quietly, and evenly, given their last exchange.

"Yes?"

"Do you really think it's your station core causing all of this? The hallucinations? The things we are seeing. Hearing. Feeling?" Saunders seemed to be earnest in her questioning. Jax felt a small knot of unease settle in her stomach.

"You think it's the air vents still?" she asked, trying to keep her voice calm and even.

"No, not that; but it feels like this could be so much more than just the station," Saunders mused. She was trailing Jax again, following like a shadow as she went panel to panel.

"I don't know. I'm an expert in engines, and Station's systems, not the mysteries of deep space. I can only come up with explanations within the scope of what I know. Occam's Razor and all that..." Jax trailed off. Saunders was silent. Jax kept scanning, but she was struck by the urge to keep talking.

"I know I really thought I was losing it for a moment there," Jax stated. Saunders had wandered to the next airlock over to look in the port space. Jax took a deep breath and turned toward her in time to see Saunders turn to look back. Their eyes met, and Jax held the contact.

"I wasn't sure *what* was going on. I thought I was going insane. But it would come and go, you know?" Jax couldn't remember a time when she felt this conversational. She wasn't sure what she was hoping for. At the bare minimum, she was hoping *not* to hear some absurd quip from the other woman. Saunders seemed to register this, as her reply surprised Jax instead.

"I do know," Saunders agreed. "I knew you were an awkward introvert, with atrocious social skills. But you were suddenly, so...awful. And then, a *far* shiftier weirdo than normal. I thought *I* was going insane."

Jax felt the color drain from her face, down to her feet. She quickly broke eye contact and continued her scans down the corridor. She was vaguely aware of Saunders' shadow in her wake, but she wasn't ready to keep hearing about how much she had screwed up. That shame still burned the back of her neck.

"I figured you had to be going nuts if you thought sealing off an entire level without telling me was the right course of action. Only someone having a full meltdown would think that's the right thing to do. And your competence is probably your best feature, Jax," Saunders seemed to be musing now.

"Maybe it would have been better for you to have stayed away from me," Jax heard herself mumble. The flush on her face faded enough that Jax felt comfortable stealing a glance back at Saunders. She found herself being assessed by an appraising green stare. "I told you, I'm a mess."

"Jax, I'm sure you *think* you're an abomination of a person. In fact, you've told me as much. Recently *tried* to show me as much. I'm sure you're even proud of the fact. But for the rest of us, it just seems like you don't get out much," Saunders hummed off to the side. Jax stalled where she scanned. A single cog in her mind was crunching to a halt with the overload of revelations she had processed in the past several hours. Saunders didn't seem to notice though.

"But yeah, I thought I was losing it too," Saunders continued, as she meandered away, leaving Jax rooted to the spot. "I was freaking out that I had gotten the manifests wrong, missed a resident, lost someone…In fact, I'm still not sure I know *exactly* how many residents there are, if I'm being honest." Saunders shot a guilty glance over her shoulder at Jax.

"I knew it didn't make sense," Jax replied, almost quietly to herself. But Saunders continued onward.

"Then, you *really* seemed to snap. I was worried about you, even if you told me not to be, and I was worried about me. It all only calmed down once you and I started working on this." Saunders kept walking down the corridor, now leading their search by a few steps. Jax could only glance after her until she eventually uprooted herself, scanning as she went, her mind fuzzy, like static.

It was Saunders who broke the silence again.

"Jax, tell me more about yourself? The real you. No more secrets?" Saunders asked, meandering away. It surprised Jax, and turned the static in her head to a blank slate.

"I already did—"

"You take things apart and put them back together again. Sometimes making them better," Saunders filled the gap. Jax followed after mutely, barely paying attention to the gaussmeter. "You apparently have a plant in your room you care for, despite your massive disdain for other living things or reminders of a terrestrial origin. You harbor a past of mysterious academia. Who could fault anyone for taking interest in you?"

Jax swallowed hard, unable to find a response that adequately countered Saunders's point.

"I like puzzles," she managed to mumble. Saunders looked over her shoulder at her.

"I just like figuring out how things work. Mechanisms, the one weed that didn't die, gravity. I used to do the crossword when I still bothered to read the data dumps from Station Management. It's how I keep myself going out here," Jax elaborated.

Saunders didn't reply, but she gave Jax a smile. It wasn't the playful curl to her lips that had gotten Jax in trouble before, nor was it the tired resignation from their toils in the bowels of her Station. It was a calm flash of relief that split Saunders's face briefly. The Security Officer turned away as they meandered.

They continued in silence for the next several degrees of the outermost Station level. But now the silence was warmer, comfortable even. The gaussmeter remained unresponsive, showing only a steady baseline. Jax had hoped it would confirm her suspicions about the power surge location, but it betrayed nothing. The only sign of activity was the abandoned lab equipment erected by the research team. Jax strolled up to it, wrench casually slung over her shoulder.

"What were you doing letting them set this up here?" Jax asked, as casually and inquisitively as she could, and she squatted down near one of the instruments to better examine it.

"Collins said there were some gravitational signatures they noticed on approach last week and they asked if they could run some scans. I figured nothing else interesting happened around here, so why not?" Saunders replied from over her shoulder, without even a hint of irony. She, too, seemed intent to find other topics of conversation. Jax snorted, and peered at the equipment.

"It's calibrated wrong," Jax stated, absentmindedly reaching out to adjust a knob before realizing it was not her experiment to touch. She pulled her hand back and stood up. Saunders had her head cocked to the side, looking at where Jax had been pointing.

"It's some standard lab equipment. I had something similar once. It measures gravity readings by converting them to magnetic signatures.

"There are a lot of similarities between magnetic charge attraction and the gravitational force equation. It's what led to many of the deep space transport systems." Jax was wandering off in her own world, the thoughts bringing her back to a different life, filled with research, success, and less loneliness. Next to her, Saunders was quiet. Jax snapped out of her reverie.

"Then again, if the Station has been saturated with massive electromagnetic fields, I suppose that would affect their calibration." She looked at Saunders who raised her eyebrows.

"You really are...good...at this stuff, Jax," she said. Jax looked back at the equipment. She didn't know what else to say. She turned her body first, her stare lingering, then shifting to Saunders.

"All just part of the past," she sighed. They moved onwards.

When they made it back to Common Access they paused to reassess, their previous stairwell conversation long in the past.

"I think we are clear on this level," said Saunders, she turned to look at Jax, who was shouldering the wrench.

Jax allowed herself to make eye contact. She suddenly wanted nothing more than to reach between them and close the space again, to feel how warm and soft Saunders felt pressed against her. But that time had long since been left behind. Saunders looked past her out of the nearest windows. Jax also turned, hesitantly. She had, at one point, been enthralled by the look of deep space, now it just coiled around her, smothering. She wasn't ready to see more nightmares beyond the walls of her Station.

"It *is* empty out there..." Saunders trailed off, which encouraged Jax to hazard a glance of her own. "And it seems like every time I look outside, if I'm not hallucinating something horrible, I just see fewer and fewer stars," Saunders stated, stepping towards the wall of the Station. Jax knew the feeling. She let herself step up behind Saunders, avoiding getting too close.

"We really are alone out here, aren't we?" Saunders asked, rhetorically. Jax wasn't sure how someone should reply to a question like that.

"Tell me, Jax. Is that why you came out here? To be dead to the world, and anyone you left behind on it? The further you go, the less likely you are to come back. We're far enough out here that there really isn't any return, is there? We just fade quietly into the stars, like a memory?" Saunders asked this as if she, too, were very far away.

"The only person I left behind on Earth was who I used to be. I think I came out here to find out who I could be," Jax responded softly. She stepped closer to the Security Officer, as if Saunders had her own gravitational field pulling her in. "Is that why you came out here?"

"I think I came out here to forget," Saunders replied, still gazing out into the oppressive swell of deep space. Jax sank into those depths again for a moment. She let the insatiable indifference of the infinite void beyond the safety of the Station walls consume her a heartbeat longer before she felt gravity drop further, and urgency return.

"I need to get to the core and restart things, otherwise this is going to throw us into Zero G and a dead spin," she said, because staying on mission was the only thing that could ease the discomfort.

"I'll come with you," Saunders added, breaking her trance with the arcing stars outside the Station windows and turning to look at Jax.

Jax felt a familiar, instinctual response welling up: a *'you don't have to'* but she swallowed it back. Saunders's company was all she wanted right now. If she had only three weeks left to convince Saunders not to leave, she would need to take every moment possible. It might be too late, but she might still have a chance. Maybe Jax needed to leave on that transport, too.

They turned towards the entrance to Common Access. Jax thoughtlessly reached down to rub her calf again.

"Don't scratch!" Saunders interjected. Jax looked up, surprised that she was even scratching in the first place.

"Does it hurt still?" Saunders asked. Jax pulled the leg of her coverall up again. The injury just looked red. It wasn't festering, or swelling or bubbling over with the larval forms of whatever had attacked them on Level 3.

"I dunno. I didn't even realize I still had it. It *had* to be just from the fight; it doesn't *look* like a bug bite..."

"Still, we should get that cleaned up when this is over. Maybe not on Medical though..." Saunders amended, almost as an afterthought.

"All right—" Jax started to say. A loud *BANG!* Like metal on metal echoed around the curve of the Station. An ultraviolet flash snapped at the windows. They both turned towards the sound and heard it again, this time with the clear crunch of damage.

The flickering lights outside pierced the edge of Jax's vision. The words "Core Arc" echoed in her head. Another smash, now with a cracking sound. Something else was destroying their Station. They looked at each other, then they crept towards the sound, Jax hefting the wrench and Saunders extending her nightstick.

The lighting shifted again, dimming with the lack of power. As Jax advanced, she caught a sight of her reflection, once again being shown back to her in the glass of the portholes. As the reflection passed an airlock on the opposite side of the main windows, the light overhead flickered green, indicating it was in use.

"What the fuck?" Jax snapped her head around to look at the actual airlock indicator, but it was still red.

"What is it?" Saunders asked, having back tread a few feet to return to where Jax stood now, confused. Another aggressive clang echoed in the corridor.

Jax swung around to look at her reflection again. The airlock light was still green. But only in the reflection.

"Saunders...what do you see...over the airlock right there?" Jax asked hesitantly.

The Security Officer gave Jax a quizzical look.

"It looks like an air lock. And it sounds like there are problems somewhere else?" Saunders replied.

Jax swung around to study the reflection again. The reflected airlock indicator now shown red, matching the actual airlock indicator across from it. Saunders was scrutinizing Jax's hesitation.

"I think we're about to see some more shit..." Jax warned. Saunders set her face in grim determination and nodded.

"Right, this isn't over."

It was just a single resident.

Never had Jax expected a single resident to pose a threat to her Station and all that surrounded them, but it had been a week of firsts. Now they came face to face with a new, horrifying concept. Where Jax had been thinking it would be another crazed lunatic playing with ill-deserved galley cutlery, another swarm of bugs and corpses, or maybe even a manifestation of the Station herself as a jealous, possessive lover, they were instead faced with something far milder, yet far more threatening.

It was one of the military contingency: a squad-mate of the ill-fated woman on Level 2. He was busy ripping a side panel off the Station wall. He was red in the face and muttered to himself. His hands were bloody with the task of disemboweling metal Station paneling.

With sinking horror, Jax realized the panel being assaulted housed the primary override controls of one of the major docking ports. As no transports were currently docked at the Station, all the docking ports were nothing but empty airlock gateways to the hungry vacuum of deep space. And some psycho space marine was intent on smashing his way out of the Station, in an act that, if successful, would rupture the entire side of Level 1, depressurizing the whole structure and killing everyone inside.

This was an absurd concept, as a single person should be entirely unable to destroy the Station on their own. The docking hatches had failsafes: the airlocks were not supposed to just unlatch without proper engagement, and this airlock's indicator mercifully still shown red and locked. But the Station was dropping closer and closer to power failure, and if someone was just crazy enough, and just motivated enough, they could inflict enough impact to send the Station into emergency evacuations.

As they crept closer, he caught sight of them and scrambled up, brandishing a crowbar (that's *mine,* Jax thought).

"Don't come any closer! This is the way out, and I won't let anyone keep me from it," he said. That checked the box for "crazy." He went back down on his knees and continued smashing the airlock override panel. Every blow made Jax increasingly uneasy. The resident seemed to get more frustrated.

"Hey, buddy, let's maybe not decompress everyone, okay?" Jax called out to him. A firm hand on her hip drew Jax's attention to Saunders at her side, who shook her head minutely to silence her.

The resident popped back up again.

"I need to let them in! They wait in the darkness!" he pleaded, blood dripping from his hand where it gripped the crowbar with inhuman looking strength.

Jax felt a cold tendril snake up her spine. It had to be coincidence she had been hearing scratching at the airlock. It had to be hallucinations. Or maybe this guy scratching all along. Anything was better than whatever he was currently insinuating. And *anything* was better than letting something else on this Station.

He took a step closer, brandishing his fist, and Jax gripped her wrench tighter in response.

"Why does the way need to be shut? It should be open for anyone who needs passage!" he cried and raised the crowbar to the glass window. Station windows were even thicker than the outside armor, but every material had its breaking point and Jax saw glass shards chipping off with the crowbar's assault.

"Hallucination or not, if he is real, and if he succeeds, we're all fucked," said Jax, landing on "nutso resident" and not "horrors of the deep prying at our threshold." This whole night had been full of crazy, but she was certain she knew the real reason behind it.

The space marine chose that moment to draw on his apparent inhuman reserves of strength and swung a mighty round of crowbar at the window. A clear spider crack appeared. Jax hoped that was a hallucination, as there was no way the glass could shatter that easily, but it was hair-raising, nonetheless. She felt a hand on her arm and looked down. Saunders was staring at the resident, her feet planted in a wide defensive stance and one hand on Jax's forearm. She squeezed, almost reassuringly.

"Right, well you're real, so let's get him under control, then get back to the core."

Jax gripped her bloodthirsty murder wrench as Saunders took a step forward. The Station-assaulting resident looked up to see Jax's precious defense weapon of choice and must have figured it was a better tool for Station window smashing.

"You bring the harbinger of fate, to pierce these walls and let forth the reckoning!" He rose and tossed the crowbar at them. Jax ducked, Saunders dodged.

"Funny; I just call her 'Lady Torques-a-lot.' What fucked up scripture has he been reading?" Jax swore over to Saunders.

The resident crouched as if readying himself to spring toward them. Saunders had already adjusted her approach, but he managed to get his bulk in the way. This caused Saunders to shift her weight and sidestep his trajectory.

Jax was suddenly in the crosshairs of someone intent on divesting her of her trusted wrench and using it to murder the whole Station. She reacted by gripping the wrench like a driver and making a full swing to deflect the incoming resident. This mostly just threw her off balance. She lifted a foot to offset the momentum of the swing and follow Saunders in her path. But then, a new sound groaned up from the center point of the Station; a sound that Jax *was* familiar with this time. A grinding, crunching noise that no amount of regular maintenance and lubrication could alleviate. The corridor lurched around them, then, the gravity was gone. Their time was up.

Chapter Twenty-One

The Station was equipped with handholds along the walls and floor in the event of gravity loss, but if you happened to be in the exact wrong place, at the exact wrong time, you could find yourself royally screwed.

Jax was entirely without traction and enacting a study on the basic laws of rotational dynamics as she spun toward the center of the corridor. The Station saboteur had managed to lock a foot on ripped wires that Jax *knew* would take weeks to repair and replace if she wasn't doomed to die in the next half hour. He was reaching aimlessly for her and Saunders as they both floated awkwardly out of his reach.

The level lighting dimmed to the red alert lighting, causing the entire floor to appear as if it were bleeding. Jax took the briefest moment to consider how fitting that seemed. Her Station was in its death throws, and she was floating about like a seed on a breeze, useless. Saunders was flailing next to her, also out of reach of the nearest handholds, but tumbling far less than Jax.

"Jax, you need to get to the core," Saunders shouted. The windows outside flashed the odd ultraviolet lighting again, as if to emphasize the absolute state of screwed they were in.

"Clearly," Jax shouted back. Her spinning was making her feel nauseous. "But we can't leave this guy here. He's got a head start on us, and that airlock won't hold forever. He seems to think rapid depressurization is a good life choice for us all. Besides—"

To really knock this statement home, Jax's momentum spun her so she was upside down with respect to Saunders' orientation. The Station groaned around them as if it knew its time was short.

"I'm a bit inconvenienced at the moment." She flailed gracelessly, swinging the wrench out in an offhand attempt to snag the far side of the corridor. Saunders seemed to be faring better, as she had not been in motion when things went Zero G, so she was not currently rotating.

"I'll take care of this. Get back to the core and get this reset!" she shouted.

"I'd love to, really I would, but you and I seem to have a real problem with making a connection right now, at least with the Station floor," Jax replied.

"Jax," called Saunders. She grabbed at Jax's passing boot. Jax's flailing with her wrench at least had nudged her closer while attempting to snag a hand hold. Saunders' fingers grasped her prize of Jax's foot, and this momentum change spun Jax again.

Now closer to right side up, Jax crashed into Saunders, sending them both drifting further from the floor. Below, the resident, who had abandoned his desperate reach for Jax's armaments, rained a hail of weak blows on the Station, resorting to the bloody remains of his fists to force a Station airlock breach. At least he had less leverage in the missing gravity.

Saunders clawed her way up Jax's body, managing to grab her shirt, and pulled Jax to her. They spun in the middle of the corridor, their combined mass slowing the rotations. Now, chest to chest, face to face, Jax could almost breathe Saunders in.

"I hate to break it to you, but this might be worse," Jax said looking into sharp, green eyes. Saunders broke the stare and looked over her shoulder at the Station floor swinging up behind her as they spun, weightless. Then she looked back at Jax, taking a moment to study her face.

"Jax, I need to tell you. I never meant to rush you," Saunders revealed. Her eyes searched Jax's face for a moment. Jax's ability to form thoughts dissipated in the space between them as they spun. Saunders' grip on Jax's shirt tightened, and she pulled, crashing her lips to Jax's as if it might be the last action she could willingly take. Then she extended her arms away putting space between them, without letting go. Jax was frozen in shock, slave only to their rotation.

"Try not to take this too personally," Saunders said, her eyes now on fire as she hoisted her hips up, planted both her tactical security boots squarely in Jax's chest, and kicked.

It knocked the wind out of Jax's gut and launched her backward. Her back hit the wall hard enough for her to see stars inside the Station. Despite the impact, Jax managed to throw a hand out and snag a hand hold. Her trusty wrench was tossed away and she looked over her shoulder to see it revolving slowly down the corridor, carried by its own momentum. She shuddered at the sound it made as it connected with a wall panel ten degrees down the corridor.

Jax looked down to see Saunders had knocked herself in the opposite direction, colliding with the irate resident. She had managed to line herself up enough to hit him with a solid tackle, wrapping her arms around his profusely bleeding and smashed hands as he attempted to further destroy the airlock. They were now locked in a wrestling match, and Jax was horrified to see that someone, though she did not know who, had retrieved the crowbar, as it was now swinging madly in their contest. Jax was struck by an urge to rocket herself from the wall back down to assist, but Saunders broke free for a moment and screamed up at her.

"What are you waiting for? Get back to the core!"

That was her signal. Jax gritted her teeth, took one last look at the Station Security Officer pummeling an irate madman, and turned around the pivot point of the hand hold. Leaving Saunders to her battle, she soared back down toward Common Access.

If only gravity could be off more often without the threat of a dead Station, Jax's tiresome scramble up and down electrical conduits would be replaced with the rapid and graceful flight of her body flying through zero gravity. She entered the Common Access shaft and saw it was clear of any nightmares.

It was still a stairwell, and not a straight shot, but she could grab the railings to launch herself from one level to the next. She passed the dark void of Level 2, with its singular dead victim curled far along the curve of the Station above her head. She passed the sterile looking glow of Medical, where Saunders' bloody jacket floated in a forgotten corner of a medical bay. She passed Berthing, and saw, briefly, the panicked floating bodies of the very much alive and un-slaughtered residents. And she arrived at Level 5: Power and Life Support.

With the gravity off she only had one last option to keep the Station from dropping into total failure. She needed to restart the core, which might very well reboot the EMF field that had started this madness. But it was madness or death, and she felt certain she didn't want to die just yet.

In through the core access strut, the climb was effortless. Then Jax was there, in the core, floating, wrapped in the layers of her deep space fortress, in the love of her life who had finally, after all these years, decided that she too, would reject her.

"Talk to me, baby. Tell me how to save you," Jax called out to the Station around her. It was no longer rotating. There was no risk of electrical shock, or momentum impact. It was a dead stick. She dropped herself into the pressure suit and made her way down to the reactor. She needed to get it restarted.

There was a manual restart process, and she broke open the emergency access panel covering the switches. The Station's real heart was a nuclear reactor which supplied the exceptional amount of power required to rotate the whole Station fast enough to induce gravity.

Jax keyed through the steps, geared up the start-up sequence and flipped the main breaker switch to send power through the Station, kickstarting the outboard rotational engines again. It would burn pure power first as it got back up to momentum, then the stator would recharge and the system would reach equilibrium. The switch circuit closed and a massive arc bloomed across her head.

Until this moment, the hallucinations, paranoia and dread brought on by a mutating EMF field had been slow growing; smoldering to life around her without her even being aware until it was too late. Then she had found a way to ground herself, to let the building EMF charge flow down and away, leaving her free of her prison of mental horrors. That lightning grounding rod had been Saunders who she had left, fighting to preserve the Station's integrity down on Level 1.

Now, a massive arc of shorting electrical charge hissed over her head. It hit her suit, nearly frying its ground connection and drained through the stator leading down to Level 2: Supply.

The hallucinations roared to life all at once, hitting Jax like a sledgehammer of violent assailant fists, chitinous insectoid bodies, and the rising tide in a sea of the undead. They swarmed around her, crowding her vision and deafening her ears. Something squirming with maggoty, larval tentacles burst from the bug scratch on her leg within the suit, and coiled itself, clammy and unyielding, around her limbs, strangling her, pulling her taut in the core, taking over her body, ripping it from reality.

The electric blue arc of pure power shorting from the reactor to the massive collection of magnetic coils created an electromagnetic field so powerful she felt the very fabric of deep space ripping around her. She had prostrated herself on her knees to save her mistress Space Station, but instead it decided it wanted one last drop of blood before winking out into the night. Far below, she hoped that Saunders wouldn't have a chance to notice when the core failed entirely, blasting them all out into the void.

Her vision was fading, either from passing out, electrical shock, or the swarm of bugs desperate to claw off her face. The monstrosity coiling from her leg wound wrapped tight around her, cutting off feeling to her extremities.

In her ear, ever so softly, she heard a voice.

"Jax, do you read me?" It was her helmet communicator. Saunders' voice echoed through the hazy field of electricity and nightmares. Was it real?

"I'm in Life Support. What's going on up there?" came her voice again.

"Resident?" Jax asked, strangled. It didn't seem important, but it was all she could manage.

"Under control. The screen readouts are freaking out. What's happening?"

"Reactor." Jax was out of energy.

She needed to break the switch: the restart sequence had failed. She tried waving her hands to brush imaginary monstruous bugs from her vision, felt the slimy horror that emerged from her leg coil tighter to restrict her movement, but she saw the open switch right in front of her.

Jax gave a strangled cry, forcing her arms against whatever abomination writhed within her suit, reached out and grabbed the switch, bracing herself against the far wall, and slammed it closed.

The electrical arc overhead cut off. The hallucinations fell from view. She lay there, suspended weightless, suit steaming from where the arc had passed through its ground connection. Her body ached, but it was her body. Her leg tingled, but nothing sprang in threatening tendrils from her wound. Something clanged above her. She tried looking up but the suit restricted her. She leaned back in the small space to better angle her vision upward.

Saunders looked back down at her from the access strut.

"What happened?" she called through the comms panel on the wall near the access hatch. Jax heard her voice in her ear. She suddenly felt less alone.

"I tried the restart, and instead it backfired. Massive electrical arc. I had a hunch the core was arcing this whole time, and I didn't know how to stop it. It's entirely unstable, and it's routing straight down through Supply. It's going to build the largest EMF yet, this place will be a whole new dimension of chaos. I don't know how to save it." Jax's body ached from the convulsions of the assaulting hallucinations and the arcing electrical current.

"I tried, Saunders. I tried to save her," Jax cried out.

"I know, Jax."

"If only I could have," Jax felt out of breath, as if she had been running in dense gravity. "It would have been worth it."

"What would have?" Saunders called from above. Her voice sounded small.

"Me. I would have been worth it," Jax whispered.

"Jax...I don't know why I have to tell you this, but you are worth more than this station," Saunders said softly.

Jax exhaled carefully, willing her heartrate to slow, seeking the calm of the core she knew and loved. The moments dragged past, until Saunders called down to her again.

"So, this is it?" Saunders asked, hanging on the comms button and sounding defeated.

Jax exhaled again and opened her eyes. She was ready to say, "Yes" when it hit her.

"No."

"No?"

"I have one last trick up my sleeve. I can shut off the power routed through the strut passing under the storage locker on Level 2. That's where the main EMF is emanating from. Then I need to bring the core back online, but slowly, one stator coil at a time, to reach stability. It's how I used to get my experiments running back in school. The last coil can be the outboard engines. It should keep the Station running while we call for the support repairs we need, and it will keep the EMF low. We can brief the residents, but it shouldn't be as bad as it's been." Jax was out of breath, and she hoped some of her explanation made sense to Saunders who was clinging to the access spoke ladder.

"What do you need from me?" Saunders asked.

"See those isolation switches up by your head? I need you to throw them. All of them. A pair for each stator. Black before red," Jax added the last part hastily. Saunders had hoisted herself halfway through to grab the first set of switches. She threw them all, then turned back to Jax. Jax gave a weak smile, then realized it wasn't visible through the helmet visor, so she also gave a pitiful thumbs up.

Jax rotated to face the offending reactor switch.

"Saunders! Get the hell back!" she called and wished she had stayed in position to watch and make sure the Security

Officer had followed the order. Next to her she busted open another panel. This one had a hand crank, used for calibration of current values during Station repairs. Jax needed to use it to manually apply current where current was needed, one stator at a time.

"All right, bitch! Let's try this dance again!" and Jax grabbed the switch, and wedged her pressure suit boots against the narrow core walls.

This time there was no arc. The core hummed as power leaked back into the core from the reactor. Jax felt way more in control. She turned to the hand crank and dropped it to the lowest current value, then tilted her body back up to call to Saunders.

"Saunders, flip the first set of switches, red before black!" Saunders emerged from the access hatch and reached for the first switches. Jax saw them flip. She reoriented herself to the hand crank and turned it up to thirty percent current. She tilted her body back up and called "Great! Skip the next set! I repeat: skip the next set, unless you want to eat space bugs for eternity!"

Saunders skipped the second set and flipped the next pair. Back to the crank. The fourth and fifth sets followed. No arc bloomed, and no phantoms closed in. With the four stators in operation, the last step in the process of getting the outboard engines operational again was to get the second stator online.

"Okay, Saunders, I need you to flip those last ones, and I'm going to throw them on low current. And then I need you out of here in case it arcs again. Seal the core behind you in case of a pressure breach!" Jax angled herself up to look. Saunders was still staring down at her from the hatch above.

"Don't go doing something stupid and heroic, Engineering," she said, and she reached up for the last set of switches. She flipped them, then withdrew into the hatch, closing the bulkhead behind her.

Down in the core Jax had cranked the manual current control down to zero. Now she slowly turned the crank to increase the percentage.

No electrical arc occurred.

She pushed a few percentage points further.

No hallucinations.

A little more.

The Station groaned and she saw the outer core shell start to rotate, slowly. It was working.

A few more percentage points and the rotation sped up.

There. Locked in at fifty percent current and the outboard engines kicked over.

She would need to make sure both outboard rotational strings survived the shutdown, but the Station gravity was returning. She waited. Five minutes, ten minutes, twenty minutes, and the stators showed a charge. She grabbed the hand crank and lowered the current for Level 2 down to ten percent.

There would still be an electromagnetic field, but it would be low. They could survive that.

The heart of the Station was beating again.

Jax sealed the access to the reactor and the hand calibration crank. Then she let herself drift in peace for a moment, her eyes closed, her ears tuned to the body that surrounded her. The Station made no ominous noises, or structural groans. There was no crackle of over-arcing electricity. It hummed with the same peaceful deep throbbing sound that had given Jax so much comfort over the years.

"Atta girl! Just keep us going a little longer. I swear, I'll get us help." Around her the Station's normal quiet hum had resumed, comforting, and familiar.

Then, she heard a different noise from the shaft overhead. Jax grabbed the walls and pulled herself up the weightless core to the hatch opening. Crouched there, braced against the ladder in the spilled over weightlessness of core proximity, was Saunders. She peered apprehensively at Jax in the scorched core repair suit.

Jax felt herself smile, though it would be mostly obscured by the burnt visor. She scrabbled with the helmet to remove it. Saunders shifted forward, her head now peeking into the core from her perch, reaching an arm in to help pull it off. They managed, and Jax shook her head out, releasing the helmet to let it float above both their heads. Saunders pulled her arm back to once again steady herself on the ladder.

"Did that work?" Saunders asked. Jax looked down past the bulk of her suit. Nothing was arcing, or shorting or crawling from the corners of her periphery.

"I think so?" Jax took a moment to glance around the poor, abused core to her Station. It was going to need a whole lot more work than she could do on her own. She looked up, shifting her body in the bulk of the pressure suit so she could refocus on Saunders who was following her gaze down into the Station's damaged heart.

"We need to call a repair team here," Jax stated. "I can't fix her all on my own after this," she said, resigned.

"You took such good care of her Jax," Saunders said softly. Jax exhaled. Her home, her solace for a decade, needed real care and salvation. She had reached the end of her service.

"The Station will probably have to be decommissioned," Jax said, letting that truth settle around her. She reached out to the walls near her.

"Are you going to be okay with that?" Saunders asked, sincerely. Jax looked up at her, into the face of the first person she had trusted in the entire duration of her exile.

"I suppose it's time to run off to something else," Jax said. Saunders' face was impassive. "I hear there's a research transport leaving in a few weeks," she followed up with.

Jax locked eyes with the Station Security Officer, and the corners of her mouth twitched, slightly. Saunders threw her arms into the core and around Jax's neck to kiss her, under zero threat of death, destruction or alcoholic influence.

Chapter Twenty-Two

Saunders helped Jax painstakingly peel off the steaming, scorched pressure suit, limbs stiff from the arc and the grip of the thing that curled itself around Jax from the inside. Jax winced at the ache in her muscles, most likely the result of bracing herself against the core walls than anything else. Saunders supported her down the access strut to the corridor of Level 5.

Once in the dim light of the main level, Jax sank to the floor, exhaling heavily. The cool metal panels of the corridor walls felt like the perfect eternal resting place for her exhausted frame. She dragged her coverall leg back up. Jax squinted her eyes shut, not wanting to see the true state her of leg, but soft, familiar fingertips on her skin caught her by surprise. She looked down to see Saunders inspecting the injury on her leg.

"It's still just a scratch," Saunders muttered gently, her face close enough that Jax could feel her breath on the skin of her calf. It made Jax shiver. Saunders looked up.

"It was alive," Jax stuttered in response, *mostly* from the horrific memory. "I felt it moving. It wrapped around me, kept me from turning off the core." The memory was already fading, and sounded ridiculous even to Jax as she said it.

Saunders squinted at Jax then looked back down, brushing her fingers over the surrounding area. Jax flinched.

"I mean, you also had full core voltage arcing through your suit. Even I know that would restrict your motion." Saunders pulled her hand back.

"If I didn't know any better, I would say it looks like it's already healing. At least, it looks better than it did downstairs. Does it hurt?"

Jax looked down at the thin, red line on her skin. It really did just look like she had brushed against some wayward rivet in need of fixing. But she could still imagine the snaking coils of wrath emerging from it, if anything, by feel alone. She looked back up at Saunders, holding the green eyes longer in her stare than she had ever let herself do before.

"No. But I can't say the same for the rest of me though. That arc was a bitch." Jax dropped her coveralls down to hide her leg and groaned from the ache in her limbs.

"Well, I'd be shocked too, if she found out I got the girl."

Jax looked up meekly at Saunders in confusion.

"Okay, okay, sorry. You'll probably have to take it easy for a bit. Your muscles probably clenched when the arc passed through the suit. You'll need some time to unwind, maybe let me take care of you," Saunders winked.

Jax snorted, but also let her face relax. The tension in her body was already releasing. In fact, Jax felt years of tension dissipating under the comforting weight of the woman who now sat astride her. She took a moment to study Saunders where she knelt.

"What about yours?" Jax said quietly, reaching out to brush the edge of the bandages on Saunders' shoulder. She let her fingertips drift lower to brush the outside of Saunders' arm, and Jax reveled in the contact. The other woman looked down like she had forgotten her shoulder even existed.

"Oh, it hurts like hell, but I'm also still pretty sure I was stabbed by a real person, not a hallucinatory maniac," Saunders replied. Jax shook her head to remove any more terrifying implications of that comment. She looked back at Saunders, now face to face with her. A moment passed. Saunders leaned in and kissed Jax briefly, carefully. She lingered, forehead pressed to Jax's, arms snaked around Jax's back to hold them in an embrace. The moment enveloped them in a comforting escape from their surroundings before Saunders pulled back to rise from the flooring.

"We probably need to make sure everyone else is also okay," Saunders suggested, looking at the walls around them.

"I want to check the CC footage before we go anywhere," Jax sighed, already missing the comforting weight of the other woman in her lap. Saunders nodded and, for at least the second time in the day-cycle, hooked a strong hand under Jax's arm to hoist her up to standing. This time, Saunders continued holding on, pulling Jax's body close to her. Jax leaned on the warm figure beside her and allowed Saunders to help her walk gingerly down the corridor to the Power and Life Support control room.

Each level's footage loop scanned a complete circle of corridor. The cameras were off in Supply, but the readout indicated the doors were locked. Medical was clear, Jax could make out the bay they had used to repair Saunders' shoulder in. Not a single skittering bug in sight.

Level 4 was certainly livelier. Residents had spilled from their quarters, but instead of chaos, they were tending to each other. Paul the long-haul transport pilot, who had lost his battle with sanity early, was having his body tended to by his teammate and other residents. A few had spilled out into the Common Access stairwell and were making their way down to Level 1. It looked like they were calming down, gathering as if to watch a sunset on a beach after a long day.

"Let's go join them. They'll want answers," Saunders said.

"Wait. I want to check the navigation readout," Jax stalled. She called up the star tracker status again. This much power malfunction could have really drawn them off course. And the Station's structural issues might have further exacerbated the issue. Jax wanted to make sure they at least had their location in space pinpointed. If she needed to call the repair teams out, she would need to at least send them updated coordinates so a team could find the Station.

Jax shook her arms out as she waited for the trackers to load on screen, letting her tightly constricted muscles continue to release. The ache from the core electrical arc was already fading. As she waited for the trackers to load, her fingertips fell on the discarded leaf clipping from Ralph. She gingerly picked it up and twirled it in her fingers. Jax snorted.

"What is it?" Saunders asked quietly beside her.

"Oh, nothing. Just, all these problems we needed to fix, and I still need to figure out what's bugging my plant," Jax huffed, absentmindedly tracing a finger along the snaking hole pattern on the dead leaf's surface. Her head felt like TV static: fuzzy and unfocused. Saunders gently pulled the leaf from Jax's fingertips.

"Pests? There aren't any pests on a station like this..."

The screen blipped to life and the tracker scans finally came online. Usually, the star trackers cycled a few moments, pinpointing their anchors and waypoints, then presented the results. This time the screen kept scrolling. Various waypoint searches cycled and recycled, failing to target any anchor points or guiding stars. Jax stared at the endlessly scrolling readout, growing nervous the longer it took.

"Come on..." Jax mumbled under her breath.

"What's wrong?" Saunders asked, her arms snaking around Jax's shoulders, her body pressed behind Jax where she sat in the chair. Saunders' voice was filled with exhaustion. Jax didn't want to add to it. She sighed.

"It's just taking its time to pinpoint our location from the star trackers. We probably shifted location in space without the core functioning," Jax replied. "I didn't account for the fact that shutting down the core would affect the stabilizing engines. It's going to probably take a while to call up the new coordinates. I'll send a ping out to the comms relay beacon to let Station Management know we shifted, but I'll need to send the coordinate updates to the repair team when we call them out here," she concluded.

"Can we just let it run while we go and check on everyone?" Saunders asked. Some distant memory of herself told Jax she could tell Saunders to go on without her, but she didn't want that. She turned from the scrolling screens to look up at Saunders and nod.

Saunders held out a hand to Jax, who looked at it, searching for the last time someone had made her such an offer. She decided she didn't care how long in the past that had been. She grasped Saunders' hand, lacing her fingers between those of the Security Officer. They made their way down to Level 1: Docking.

On the landing for Level 1, they expected to find anxious residents full of questions, but instead they were met with people who seemed to be preoccupied with walking the level in wonder.

Jax and Saunders emerged to the main corridor. One of the residents, a member of one of the research teams, sprinted past them, knocking their shoulders. The woman turned around and hastily apologized before continuing her sprint. Jax realized most of the residents were rushing to congregate by the windows across from Common Access. She looked over at Saunders who glanced up briefly in concern, then back at the group.

"You didn't do anything stupid with that guy who was breaking the airlock did you?" Jax asked.

"If by stupid you mean knocked him out cold and tied him to the back wall, then yes, but he's thirty degrees around the bend still," Saunders replied. They walked over to the group of people, who by now were standing so close together Jax couldn't see out of the windows.

"Did he manage to break enough of the glass? We should probably get everyone back from the windows..." Jax started.

"What's going on here?" asked Saunders, in what Jax assumed was her most authoritative, Security-Officer-type voice. It sounded absurd coming from her compact frame. The crowd parted, some looking back at them and others shifting to the side. One woman stepped toward them.

"Officer Saunders, is the station okay?"

Saunders glanced back at Jax as if looking for the official answer. Jax cleared her throat, winced at the lingering pain in her sore muscles, and spoke up.

"It's stable, I know there's been a few weird things going on, but they should be under control now—"

"With all due respect Engineering, I think you need to look outside," the woman interrupted. Jax didn't have the energy to be annoyed at being interrupted, so she went silent and scanned over the tops of the crowd blocking the main portal windows.

"What's outside?" Saunders asked beside her, voice sounding small.

The crowd parted slightly. Jax got a view of the bank of large porthole windows opposite Common Access. On any other station, in a more picturesque section of the galaxy, these windows would have framed some breathtaking expanses of deep space. On this Station, it had only ever been dark.

Now, the dim lights of the interior seemed to emphasize the reflection of the knot of residents as they stood crowded together. Jax saw herself, standing in the center, flanked by people she hardly knew, and clutching at Saunders, who she desperately wanted to know better. The windows reflected this scene, then they shifted.

First, an ultraviolet blue light flickered at the edges of the windows.

Then, what looked like a swarm of grasping shadows enveloped the group. Jax flinched and swung her head around in a panic to see where the hallucinations were coming from, as shouts and screams erupted from the panicked group. But nothing attacked them in the corridor. Jax looked back at the windows as they reflected the airlock lights cycling green and red, even though she was certain they were showing locked behind her.

She stepped forward, toward the windows, through the throng of distraught residents. Saunders followed her.

"Jax, I don't think we solved the issue with the hallucinations..." Saunders said hoarsely at her shoulder, gripping her hand tight. Jax didn't respond. Some force was drawing her forward again, toward the inches-thick glass and the endlessly deep and unfathomable void of space beyond.

If Jax relaxed her vision, and let the reflected images register in her brain, she could see ghastly specters and heinous acts showing back at her. But something told her it was just a reflection. Like the reflection she had seen of Saunders running after her, days ago, when it was all Jax had really wanted.

The weight pulling her forward was real now. Despite the spinning rings of the Station, some gravity vector dragged Jax, Saunders and the residents toward the windows.

"Jax! Jax, what is going on with the gravity?" Saunders shouted, bracing herself against the window as she held off against getting crushed by another toppling resident.

"There *is* something out there," Jax whispered, a feeling of thrill and horror gripping her.

Saunders had managed to help the falling resident gain their footing beside her and had re-braced against the wall where Jax was letting herself get pulled closer to the glass.

"What are you talking about? You always said nothing is ever out there?" Saunders responded. She sounded terrified. And the implications of what Jax had said *were* terrifying.

But something *was* outside the Station.

As the windows reflected all manner of potential nightmares inside the Station walls, Jax stared outward. And whatever was beyond them finally opened its eye and stared back.

"I think that is what my laboratory equipment was picking up out there," said the woman from earlier. She had also managed to find herself wedged against the glass near Jax, who recognized her now as the researcher Saunders had tried introducing her to ages ago.

"Jax, Rose, what is that?" Saunder said, shakily from Jax's other shoulder.

A large rift has torn open across the dark void of space, opening like a massive eye to some cosmic behemoth that had been sleeping just beyond their Station walls. It yawned from one end of their scope of vision to the other, forming an incomprehensibly large tear across the fabric of space-time.

"You saw gravity signatures that indicated this was out there?" Jax asked in what she could almost call rapturous awe, not sure if the researcher was still by her side or not.

"Nothing like this exists yet in our known universe, but we knew *something* might be going on," the diminutive academic replied, sounding studious and inquisitive.

The stars beyond the rift seemed to wink out of existence as it spread wider. Where the rift interior began to open before them, the ultraviolet light Jax had attributed to a failing core arced outward toward the Station.

Jax relinquished her grip on the window ledge to slap the glass in amusement. A spider vein of a crack spiraled out from where her hand made contact, then immediately faded.

"Those star trackers...they're never going to find us..." she stated. There were no stars to track in that rift. The trackers were five levels up, cycling uselessly, endlessly.

The horrible reflections began to overlap behind her, and Jax hazarded a glance over her shoulder. The residents were in chaos, but there was nothing otherworldly *inside* the Station. Just the potential of infinite nightmares, infinite possibilities, reflected back at them in the depths of a cosmic anomaly that had never before been witnessed.

Jax looked back at herself, reflected in the glass. Saunders clutched at her side, holding her close. A slithery looking tendril of a shadow snaked its way up behind Jax, blocking out part of the scene reflected behind her. It pulled from somewhere deep within Jax and threatened to coil back around her limbs where it had surely tried to claim her up in the Station core. But Jax put her lanky arm around Saunders' shoulders and squeezed. Saunders hugged her in return and the tendrils dissipated to join the other reflected chaos.

Around them, the Station groaned loudly, protesting the abnormal force, and lurched forward.

"IT'S PULLING US IN!" someone screamed from the chaotic corridor behind them.

They were on a sinking ship. The yawing rift was pulling the Station closer, enveloping it. The horizon was almost beyond the frame of the portholes now, swallowing the Station whole.

Jax barked a laugh, which garnered looks of further alarm on either side of her.

"Heh, there's no way the Station core could have been the culprit," Jax explained, elated, almost giddy. She was trying to keep the hysterics down, but it was damn near comical.

Maybe she was finally losing it out here on the edge of darkness. Or maybe they were about to get dragged into an abyss with no idea of what might greet them on the other side. Now she was laughing.

"We really thought it was some kind of power surge! Fucking stupid!" Jax chuckled, as the Station lurched forward again, passing the lip of the rift. The windows reflected a thousand possible outcomes back at them.

"You think *this* is what was causing the trouble recently, Engineering?" Rose, the researcher asked tentatively through Jax's snickering. Jax took a deep breath to try to collect herself. Saunders looked alarmed and terrified next to her, and the Station had devolved into absolute bedlam. Jax broke her trance as she watched them descend and looked down where her hand gripped the window ledge white-knuckled, then over at Saunders who looked plaintively back up at her.

"Some old space station nuclear reactor isn't going to be strong enough to create mass hallucinations and station structural damage. Ha! I was practically making it all up as we went, for lack of better options. There's no way we could have known it was this though. But, it wasn't the Station's fault. It wasn't *my* fault!" Jax whispered, enamored.

"So, what is this, a black hole?" Saunders asked.

"No, Security, I don't know *what* this is," the researcher replied. The three of them had become abandoned at the windows now, as the rest of the residents fled for whatever corners made them feel safest. Jax was grateful that Saunders held fast.

"But you *saw* it Saunders! *We* saw it. You said something was out there. I should have listened to you. But"—and Jax had to stifle another hail of hysterical giggles—"it's not like we could have done anything about *this!*" *This* was every impossibility happening at once. The Station had tried to warn them, but it was just a fate they needed to accept now.

Pain radiated sharply from Jax's leg injury. The coiling shadows returned all around her. Something aggressively scraped away at the exterior of the Station, as if begging to be let inside. Jax ignored it all now. There wasn't much else left to do.

It was ironic. Years ago, decades ago, when Jax felt like she had to run from her stupidest dalliances, she would have embraced this end. This was what she had wanted: something to take her further away from everything she had ever fucked up. And now, when she finally realized she might actually have something to stick around for, the rift was taking her anyway.

But this time, Jax wasn't alone.

"Jax, what's in there?" Saunders whispered, back pressed tight against Jax's chest.

"Alternative realities, dimensions, new worlds—" Rose attempted.

"Everything. Nothing. There's no way we could ever know," Jax replied. "But we're about to find out."

There was a flashing light, beyond the spectrum of human vision. Jax felt a pressure in her temples, like being forced to wake from a dream, or surface through water from deep below. A feeling, like a thousand shards of glass scattered within her body, sliced, pricked, and splintered. Jax felt like the shards of herself could each catch some strange light from the void and break it into its components, like a hundred thousand possibilities. It was a light that spread out, from one shard to the next, bending away then back again. The surroundings sparkled, fizzled, then darkened, like the endless void of space.

Somewhere in the darkness Jax heard a voice.

"Well," said Saunders, quietly, for Jax alone to hear. She felt Saunders reach for and take her hand, intertwining their fingers. "Wherever this takes us, at least I'll be with you."

She squeezed.

The Station fell through, to whatever might await it on the other side.

ACKNOWLEDGEMENTS

I wrote this book over a Thanksgiving weekend in the middle of the pandemic. I was fired up about something, doesn't matter what, and I wrote this exactly like you might expect an engineer to write a novel. Structure, scope, planning, execution, delivery, review, revise, repeat. It also read exactly like an engineer wrote a novel. Which is why I need to give special acknowledgement to a few people.

More than anything, my wife deserves the biggest shoutout. She read this raw, un-formatted document, written by someone who forgot how to punctuate dialogue, and responded by saying, "This is good! Needs a little work, but you should do something with it!" Much like a toddler showing off her first ever mudpie, I was immensely proud of my work, but also affronted that my mudpie could even remotely be improved upon. But my wife knew how to appeal to my engineering thought process of test, review, redesign, retest. And so, I found the motivation to embark on the seemingly endless amount of revisions ahead of me.

I want to thank Melyssa. In a moment where I felt like I didn't have enough "queer friends who liked sci-fi," she gave the early draft a read and gave me the right feedback to help me feel confident in this book's potential. Not only that, but she spent roughly two weeks printing it all out in installments so she could send me notes on the draft, which, by that point I had already revised twice. I feel like she needs extra recognition for that.

I want to thank Fletcher for also giving me one of the first thumbs up of approval before this book really started to take form. These people are the ones who took this from a fevered weekend project to what would eventually become what you have before you.

Along the way I had excellent beta readers who provided priceless feedback, either via numerous email exchanges, or by just ghosting me entirely after the first thirty pages. All of it was valuable. Extra shoutouts to my sister (for arguing with me), Steph (for telling me it was a fun read), Elizabeth (for helping me work in some extra chemistry), and critically I want to thank Jenn for essentially giving me a free edit which gave this manuscript a fighting chance at being published.

But nothing will ever surpass my wife's ability to be the perfect rubber duck. She let me bounce ideas off her ad nauseum, served as a sounding board and always knew just how to respond to get me back on track. She got to know these characters almost as well as I do, and I don't think this would exist, even in its mudpie form, without her. Don't worry babe, I can't wait to stay up late talking potential sequels with you. Thank you, and thank you to everyone else.

ABOUT THE AUTHOR

A.Z. builds spaceships in her day job. She teaches about spaceships on the side. And now she apparently writes about spaceships in her spare time. Where she finds the spare time is still a mystery. Having been raised on a steady diet of classic science fiction and horror—consumed mostly through the staircase railing after bedtime while her father was asleep on the couch—A.Z. has always maintained a love for space travel and the unknown. This has largely fueled her career in aerospace engineering but originally fueled a passion for writing science fiction stories when she was very young. After a long quantity of months cooped up inside, A.Z. finally returned to her storytelling origins. A.Z. lives in the Mid-Atlantic region of the US with her wife and son, their dogs, several thousand honeybees, and way too many Legos.

Please take a moment to review this book at your favorite retailer's website, Goodreads, or simply tell your friends!